image comics presents

THE WALKING DEAD™

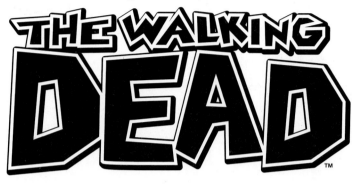

ROBERT KIRKMAN
CREATOR, WRITER

CHARLIE ADLARD
PENCILER

STEFANO GAUDIANO
INKER

CLIFF RATHBURN
GRAY TONES

RUS WOOTON
LETTERER

CHARLIE ADLARD
& DAVE STEWART
COVER

SEAN MACKIEWICZ
EDITOR

For SKYBOUND ENTERTAINMENT

Robert Kirkman - Chairman
David Alpert - CEO
Sean Mackiewicz - SVP Editor-in-Chief
Shawn Kirkham - SVP Business Development
Brian Huntington - VP, Online Content
Shauna Wynne - Publicity Director
Andres Juarez - Art Director
Jon Moisan - Editor
Arielle Basich - Associate Editor
Carina Taylor - Production Artist
Paul Shin - Business Development Coordinator
Johnny O'Dell - Social Media Manager
Sally Jacka - Skybound Retailer Relations
Dan Petersen - Sr. Director of Operations & Events

International inquiries: ag@sequentialrights.com
Licensing inquiries: contact@skybound.com

WWW.SKYBOUND.COM

IMAGE COMICS, INC.
Robert Kirkman—Chief Operating Officer
Erik Larsen—Chief Financial Officer
Todd McFarlane—President
Marc Silvestri—Chief Executive Officer
Jim Valentino—Vice President

Eric Stephenson—Publisher / Chief Creative Officer
Corey Hart—Director of Sales
Jeff Boison—Director of Publishing Planning & Book Trade Sales
Chris Ross—Director of Digital Sales
Jeff Stang—Director of Specialty Sales
Kat Salazar—Director of PR & Marketing
Drew Gill—Art Director
Heather Doornink—Production Director
Nicole Lapalme—Controller
IMAGECOMICS.COM

THE WALKING DEAD, VOL. 31: THE ROTTEN CORE. First Printing. ISBN: 978-1-5343-1052-0 Published by Image Comics, Inc. Office of publication: 2701 NW Vaughn St., Ste. 780, Portland, OR 97210.

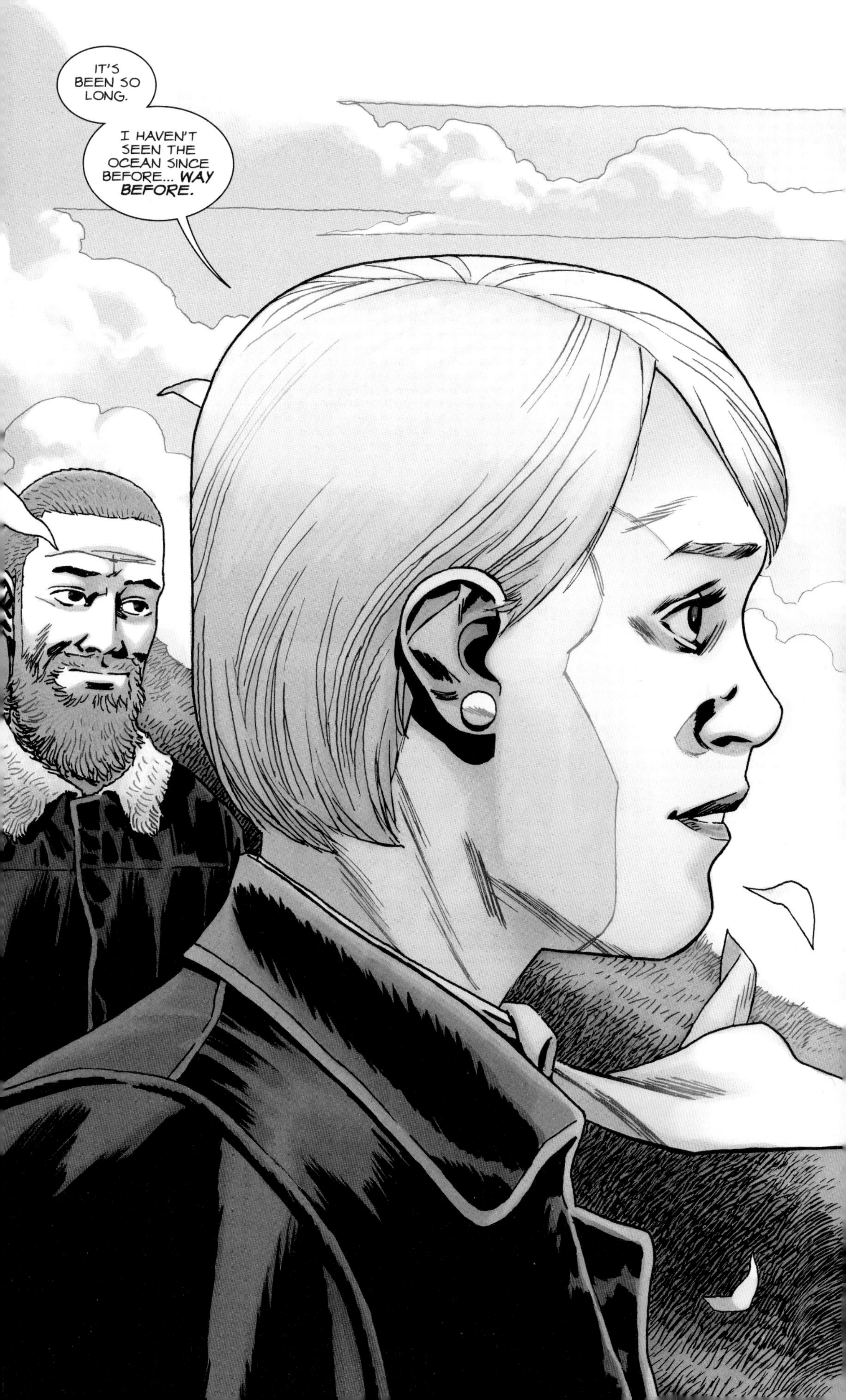
IT'S BEEN SO LONG.
I HAVEN'T SEEN THE OCEAN SINCE BEFORE... **WAY BEFORE.**

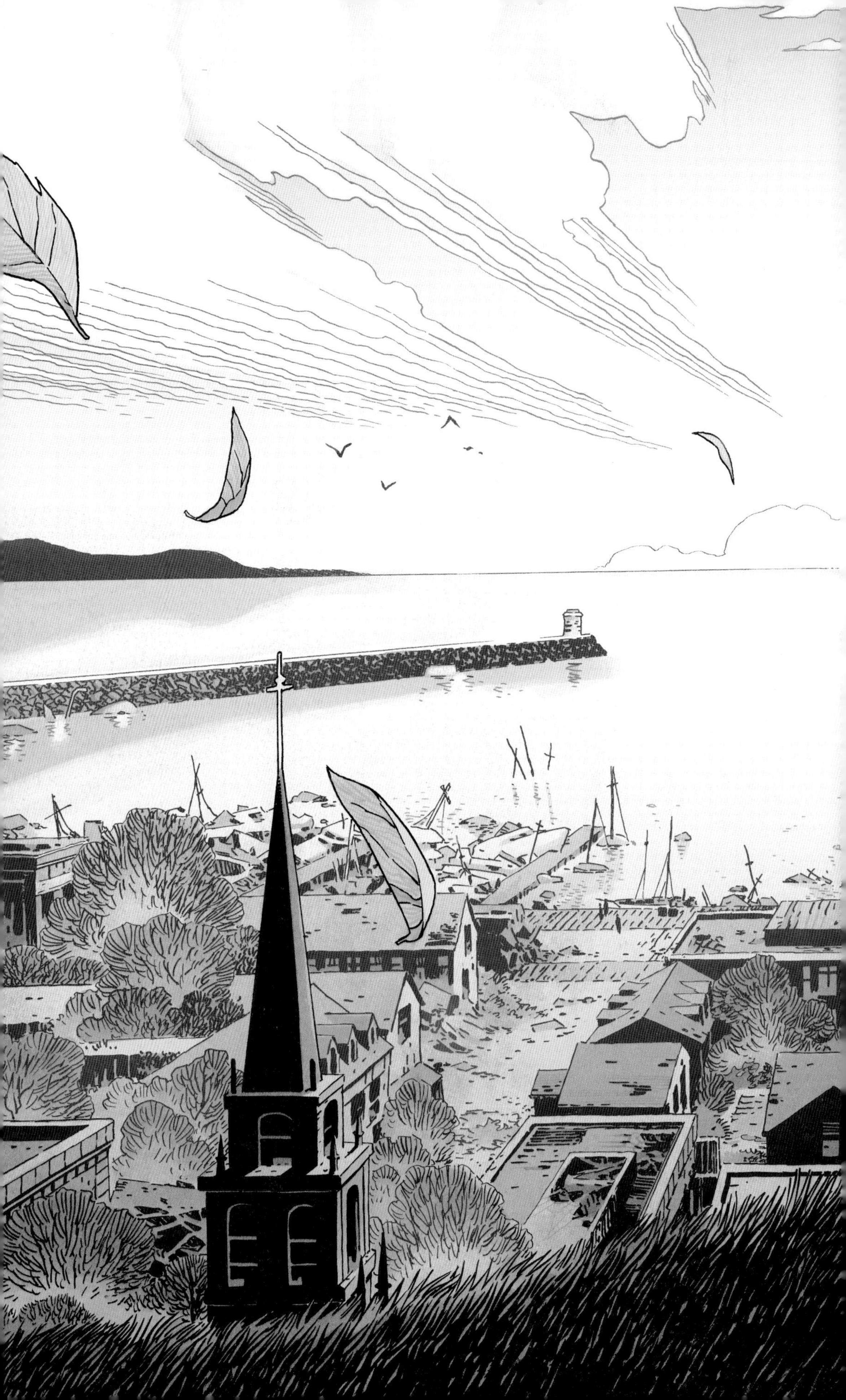

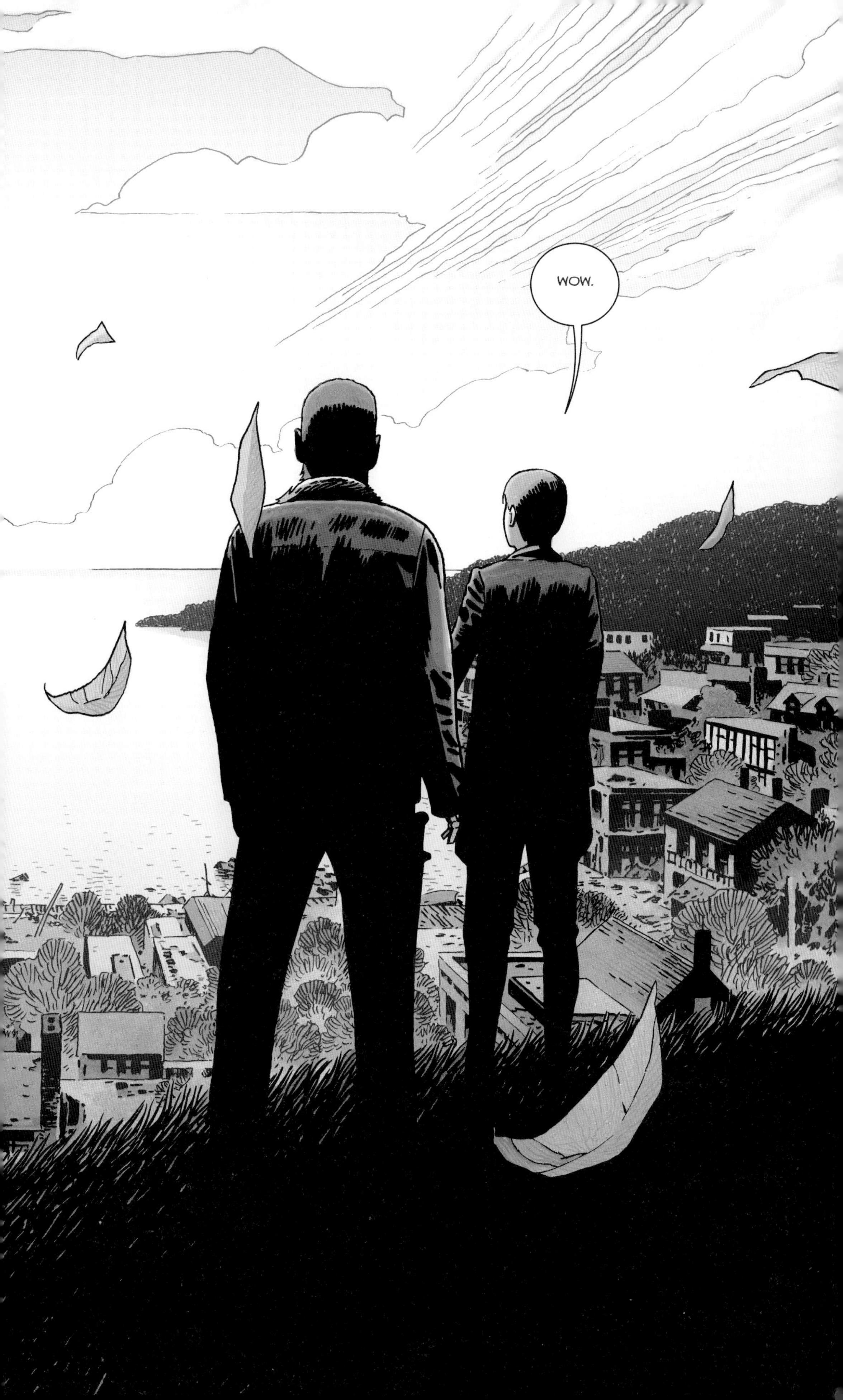
WOW.

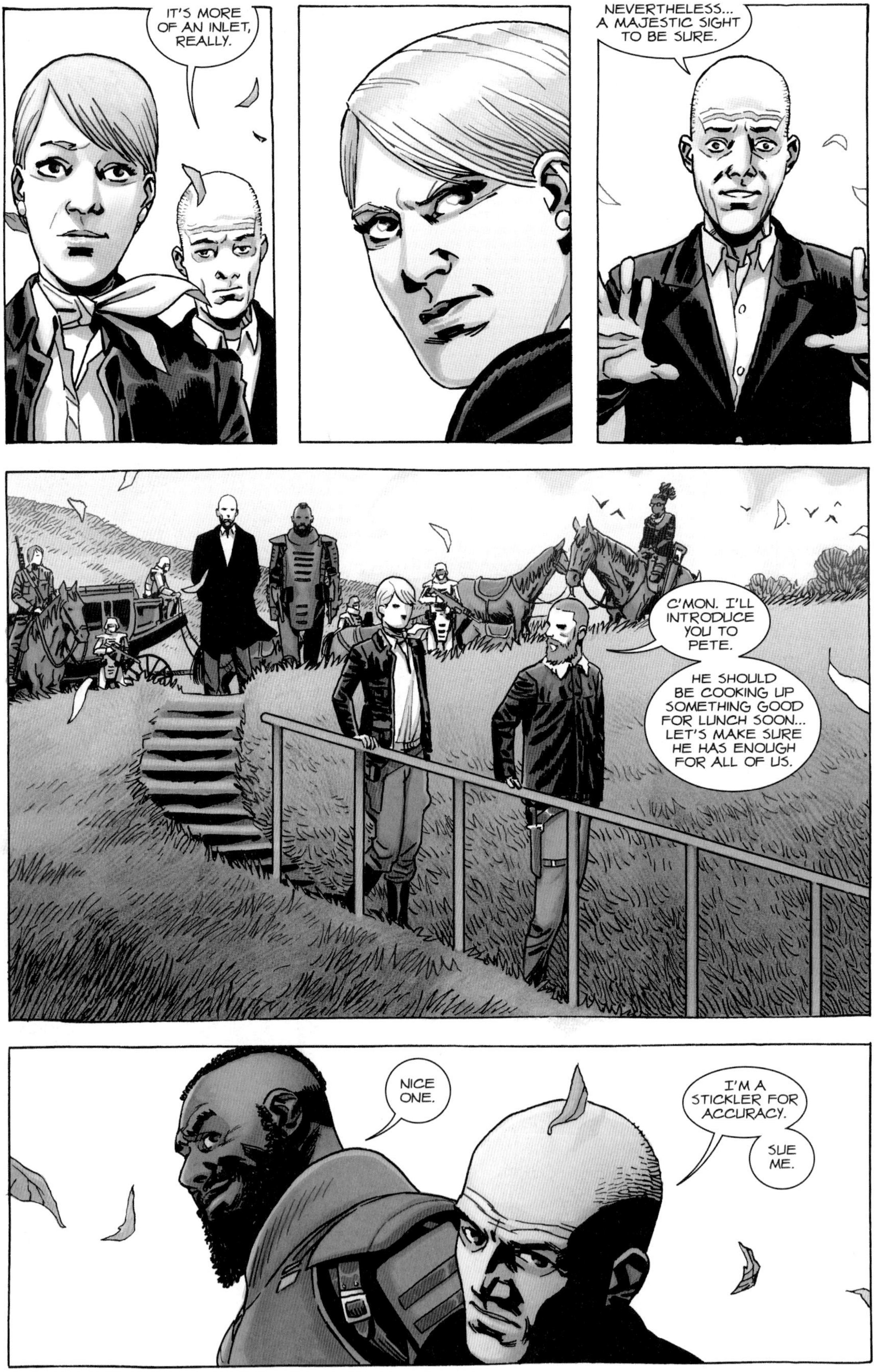
IT'S MORE OF AN INLET, REALLY.
NEVERTHELESS... A MAJESTIC SIGHT TO BE SURE.
C'MON. I'LL INTRODUCE YOU TO PETE.
HE SHOULD BE COOKING UP SOMETHING GOOD FOR LUNCH SOON... LET'S MAKE SURE HE HAS ENOUGH FOR ALL OF US.
NICE ONE.
I'M A STICKLER FOR ACCURACY.
SUE ME.

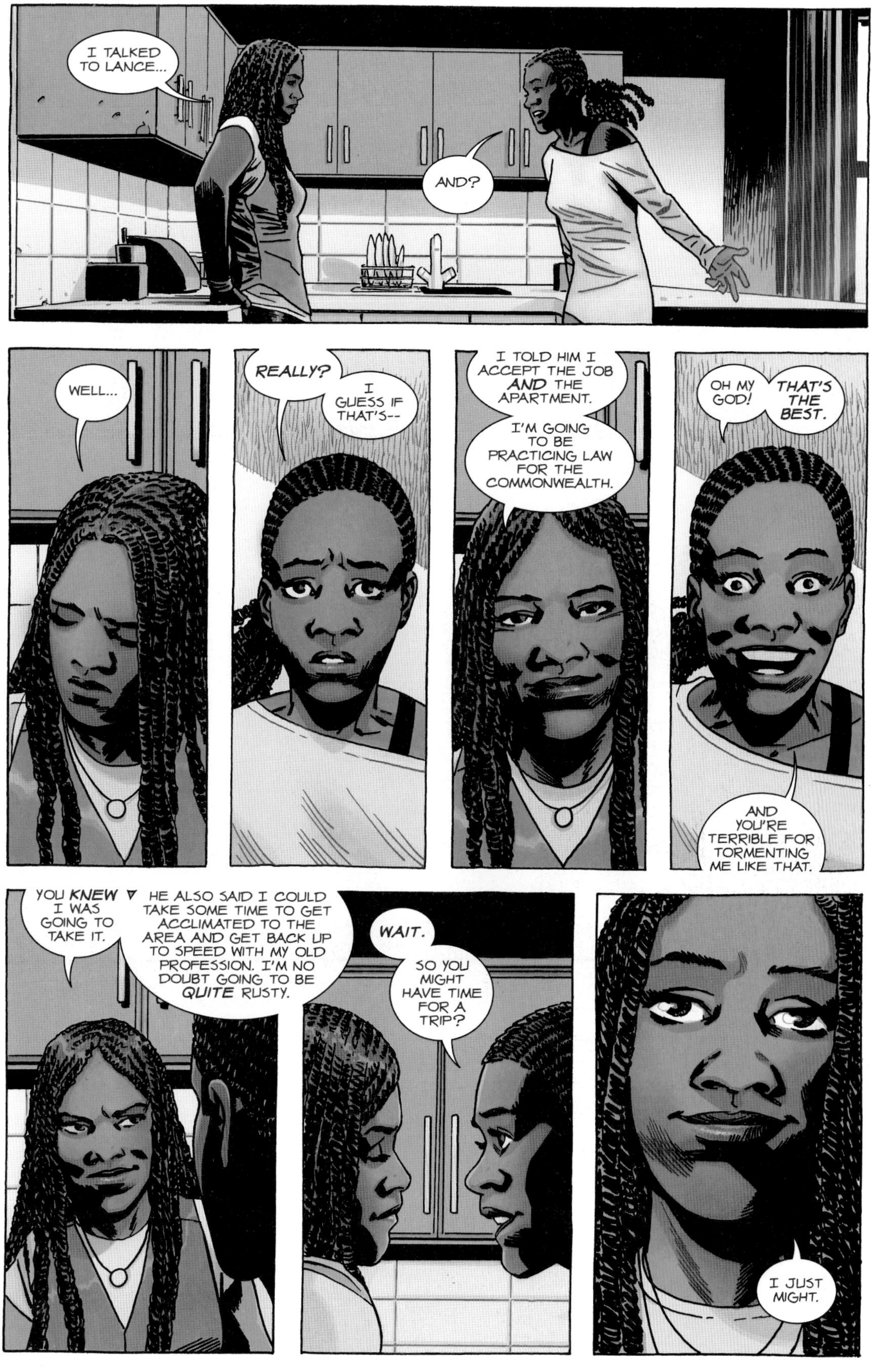
I TALKED TO LANCE...
AND?
WELL...
REALLY?
I GUESS IF THAT'S--
I TOLD HIM I ACCEPT THE JOB **AND** THE APARTMENT.
I'M GOING TO BE PRACTICING LAW FOR THE COMMONWEALTH.
OH MY GOD!
THAT'S THE BEST.
AND YOU'RE TERRIBLE FOR TORMENTING ME LIKE THAT.
YOU ***KNEW*** I WAS GOING TO TAKE IT.
HE ALSO SAID I COULD TAKE SOME TIME TO GET ACCLIMATED TO THE AREA AND GET BACK UP TO SPEED WITH MY OLD PROFESSION. I'M NO DOUBT GOING TO BE ***QUITE*** RUSTY.
WAIT.
SO YOU MIGHT HAVE TIME FOR A TRIP?
I JUST MIGHT.

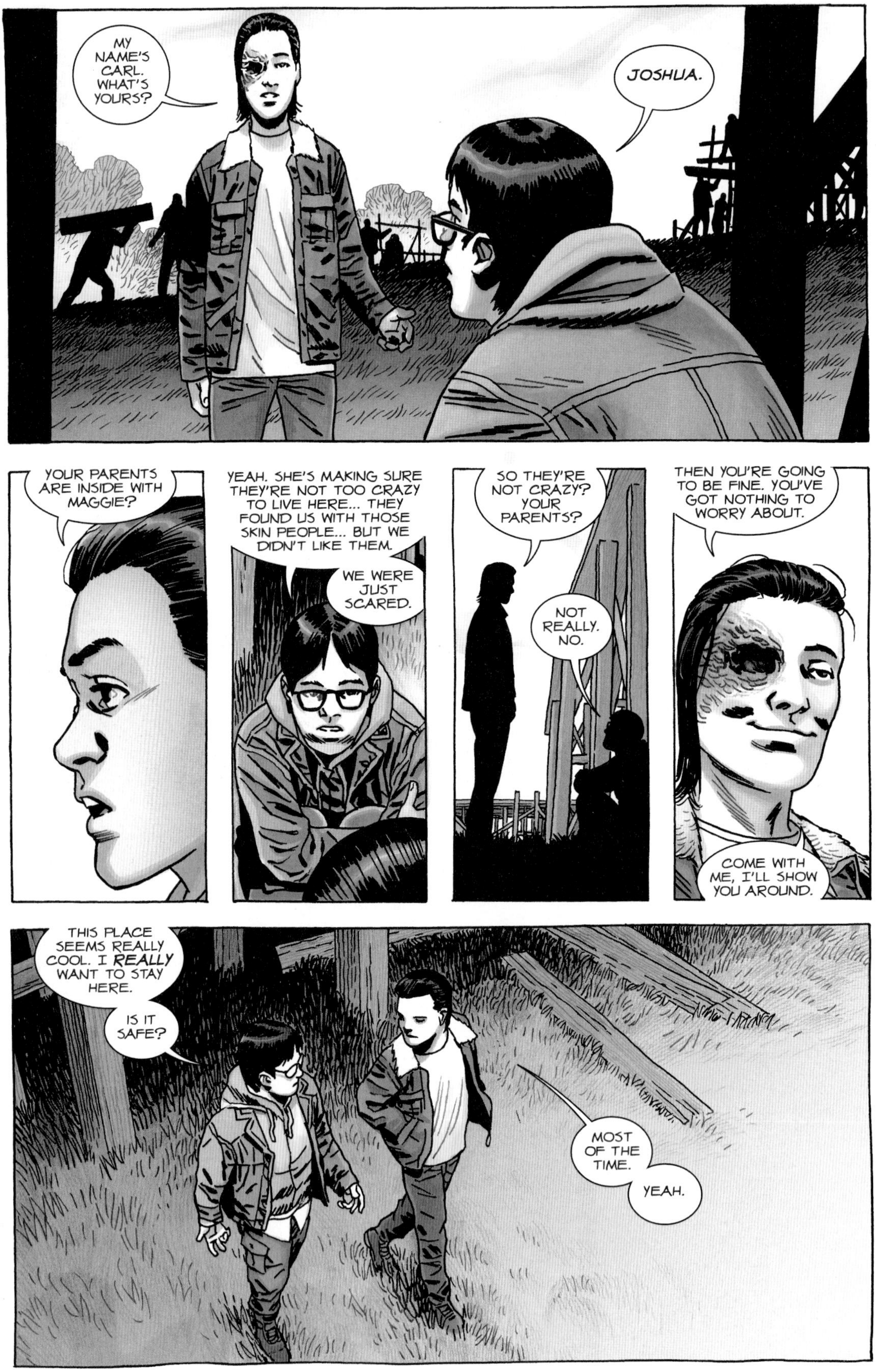
MY NAME'S CARL. WHAT'S YOURS?
JOSHUA.
YOUR PARENTS ARE INSIDE WITH MAGGIE?
YEAH. SHE'S MAKING SURE THEY'RE NOT TOO CRAZY TO LIVE HERE... THEY FOUND US WITH THOSE SKIN PEOPLE... BUT WE DIDN'T LIKE THEM.
WE WERE JUST SCARED.
SO THEY'RE NOT CRAZY? YOUR PARENTS?
NOT REALLY. NO.
THEN YOU'RE GOING TO BE FINE. YOU'VE GOT NOTHING TO WORRY ABOUT.
COME WITH ME, I'LL SHOW YOU AROUND.
THIS PLACE SEEMS REALLY COOL. I REALLY WANT TO STAY HERE.
IS IT SAFE?
MOST OF THE TIME.
YEAH.

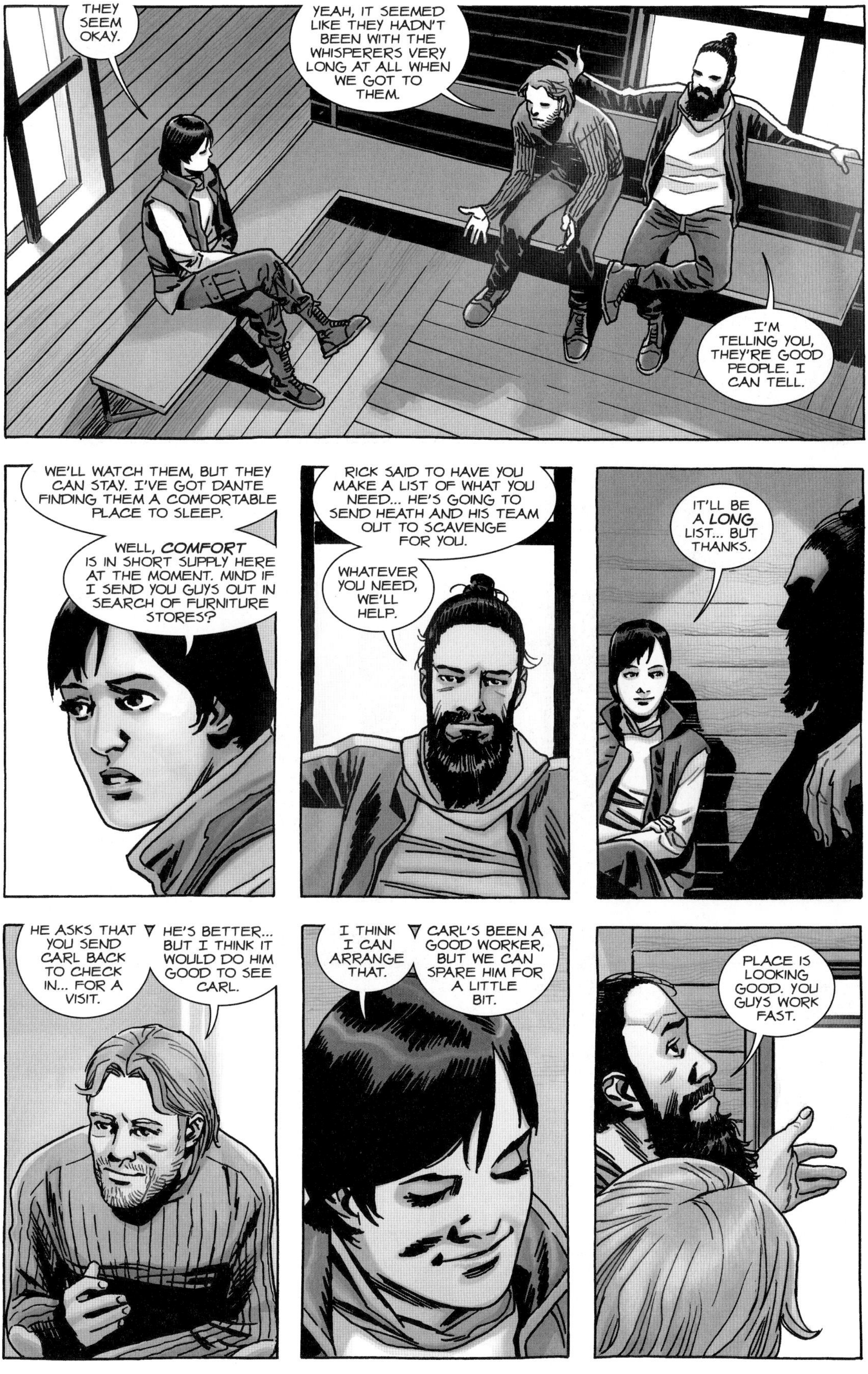

THEY SEEM OKAY.
YEAH, IT SEEMED LIKE THEY HADN'T BEEN WITH THE WHISPERERS VERY LONG AT ALL WHEN WE GOT TO THEM.
I'M TELLING YOU, THEY'RE GOOD PEOPLE. I CAN TELL.
WE'LL WATCH THEM, BUT THEY CAN STAY. I'VE GOT DANTE FINDING THEM A COMFORTABLE PLACE TO SLEEP.
WELL, COMFORT IS IN SHORT SUPPLY HERE AT THE MOMENT. MIND IF I SEND YOU GUYS OUT IN SEARCH OF FURNITURE STORES?
RICK SAID TO HAVE YOU MAKE A LIST OF WHAT YOU NEED... HE'S GOING TO SEND HEATH AND HIS TEAM OUT TO SCAVENGE FOR YOU.
WHATEVER YOU NEED, WE'LL HELP.
IT'LL BE A LONG LIST... BUT THANKS.
HE ASKS THAT YOU SEND CARL BACK TO CHECK IN... FOR A VISIT.
HE'S BETTER... BUT I THINK IT WOULD DO HIM GOOD TO SEE CARL.
I THINK I CAN ARRANGE THAT.
CARL'S BEEN A GOOD WORKER, BUT WE CAN SPARE HIM FOR A LITTLE BIT.
PLACE IS LOOKING GOOD. YOU GUYS WORK FAST.

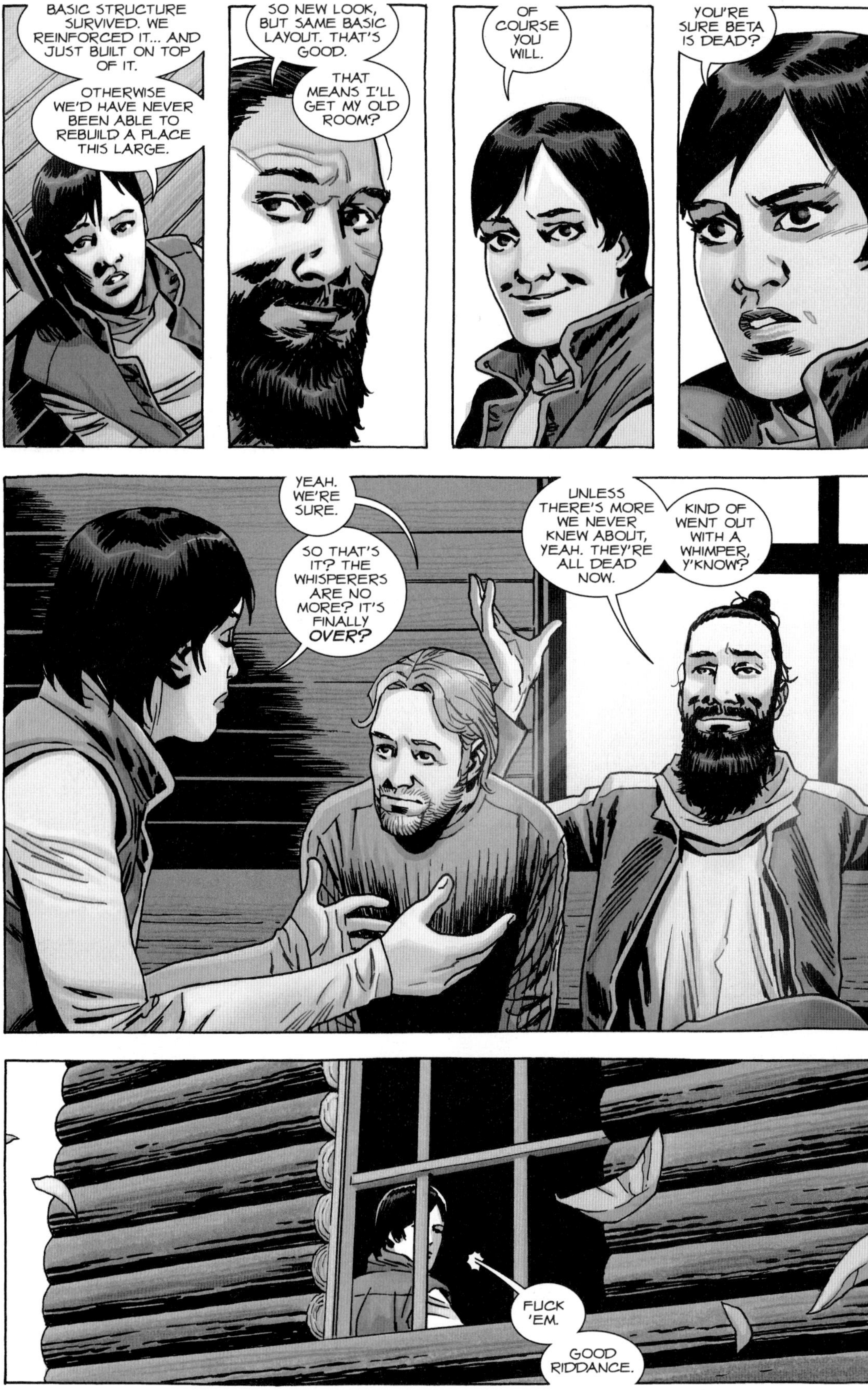
BASIC STRUCTURE SURVIVED. WE REINFORCED IT... AND JUST BUILT ON TOP OF IT.
OTHERWISE WE'D HAVE NEVER BEEN ABLE TO REBUILD A PLACE THIS LARGE.
SO NEW LOOK, BUT SAME BASIC LAYOUT. THAT'S GOOD.
THAT MEANS I'LL GET MY OLD ROOM?
OF COURSE YOU WILL.
YOU'RE SURE BETA IS DEAD?
YEAH. WE'RE SURE.
SO THAT'S IT? THE WHISPERERS ARE NO MORE? IT'S FINALLY *OVER?*
UNLESS THERE'S MORE WE NEVER KNEW ABOUT, YEAH. THEY'RE ALL DEAD NOW.
KIND OF WENT OUT WITH A WHIMPER, Y'KNOW?
FUCK 'EM.
GOOD RIDDANCE.

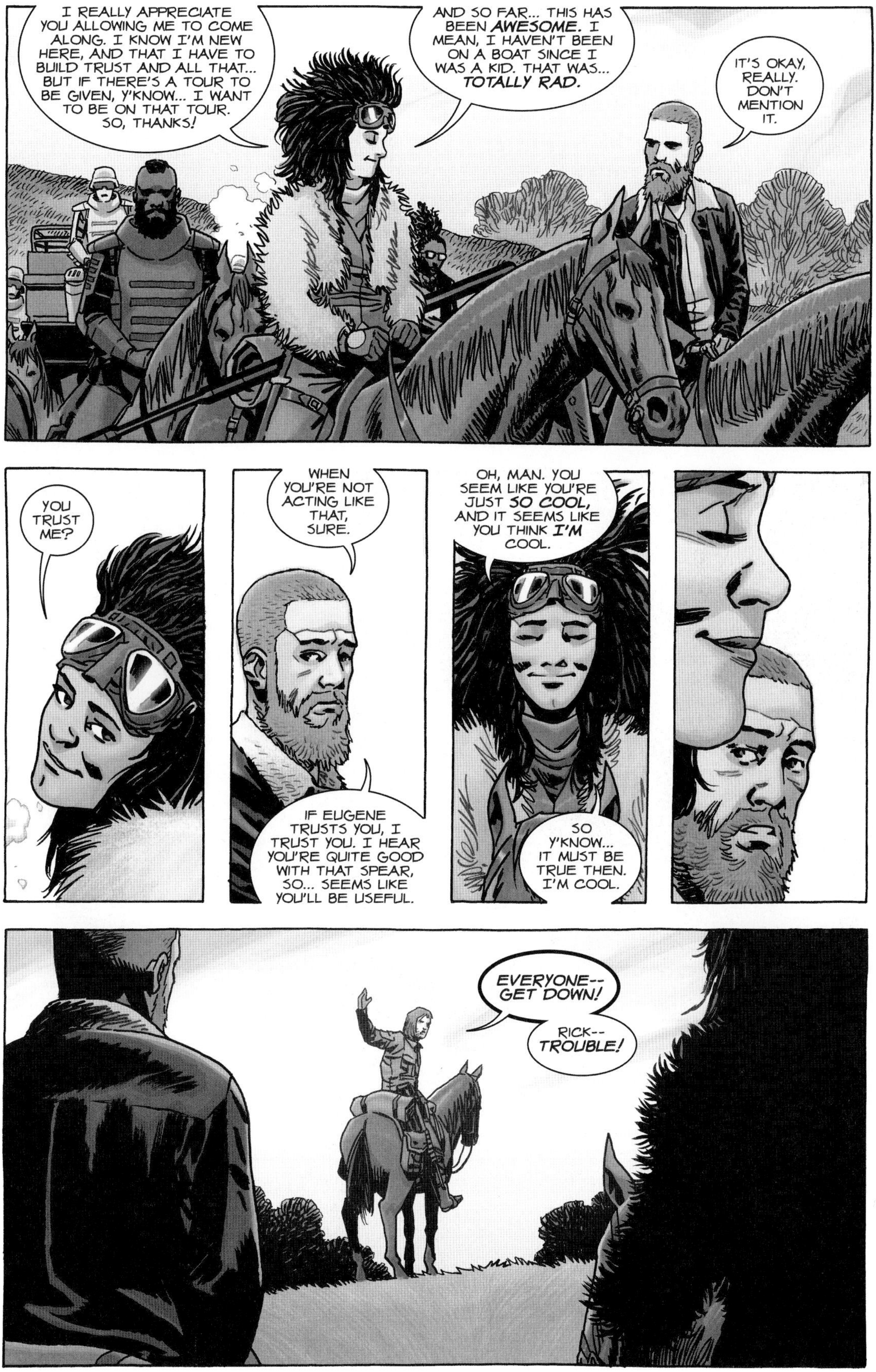

I REALLY APPRECIATE YOU ALLOWING ME TO COME ALONG. I KNOW I'M NEW HERE, AND THAT I HAVE TO BUILD TRUST AND ALL THAT... BUT IF THERE'S A TOUR TO BE GIVEN, Y'KNOW... I WANT TO BE ON THAT TOUR. SO, THANKS!
AND SO FAR... THIS HAS BEEN AWESOME. I MEAN, I HAVEN'T BEEN ON A BOAT SINCE I WAS A KID. THAT WAS... TOTALLY RAD.
IT'S OKAY, REALLY. DON'T MENTION IT.
YOU TRUST ME?
WHEN YOU'RE NOT ACTING LIKE THAT, SURE.
IF EUGENE TRUSTS YOU, I TRUST YOU. I HEAR YOU'RE QUITE GOOD WITH THAT SPEAR, SO... SEEMS LIKE YOU'LL BE USEFUL.
OH, MAN. YOU SEEM LIKE YOU'RE JUST SO COOL, AND IT SEEMS LIKE YOU THINK I'M COOL.
SO Y'KNOW... IT MUST BE TRUE THEN. I'M COOL.
EVERYONE-- GET DOWN!
RICK-- TROUBLE!

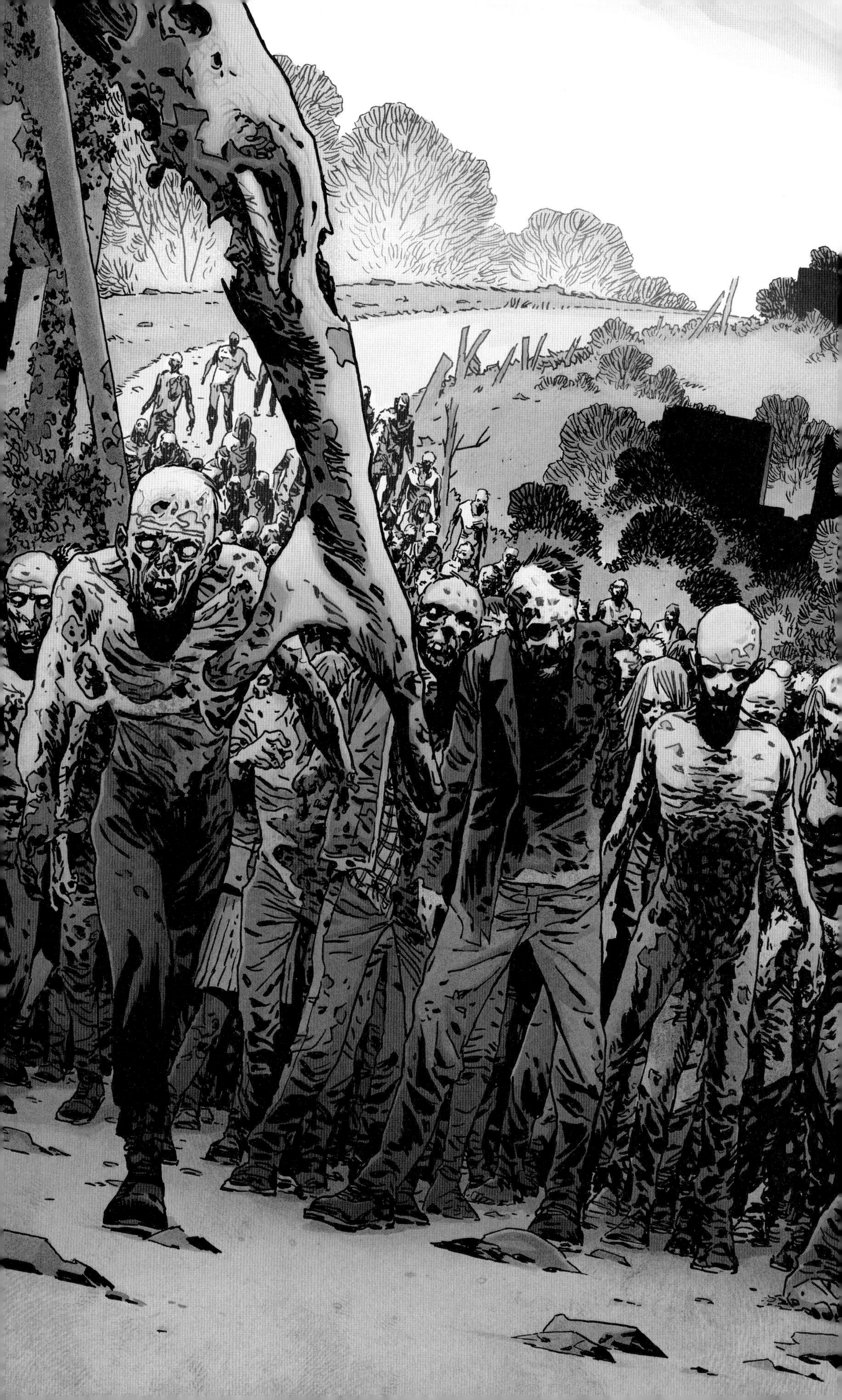

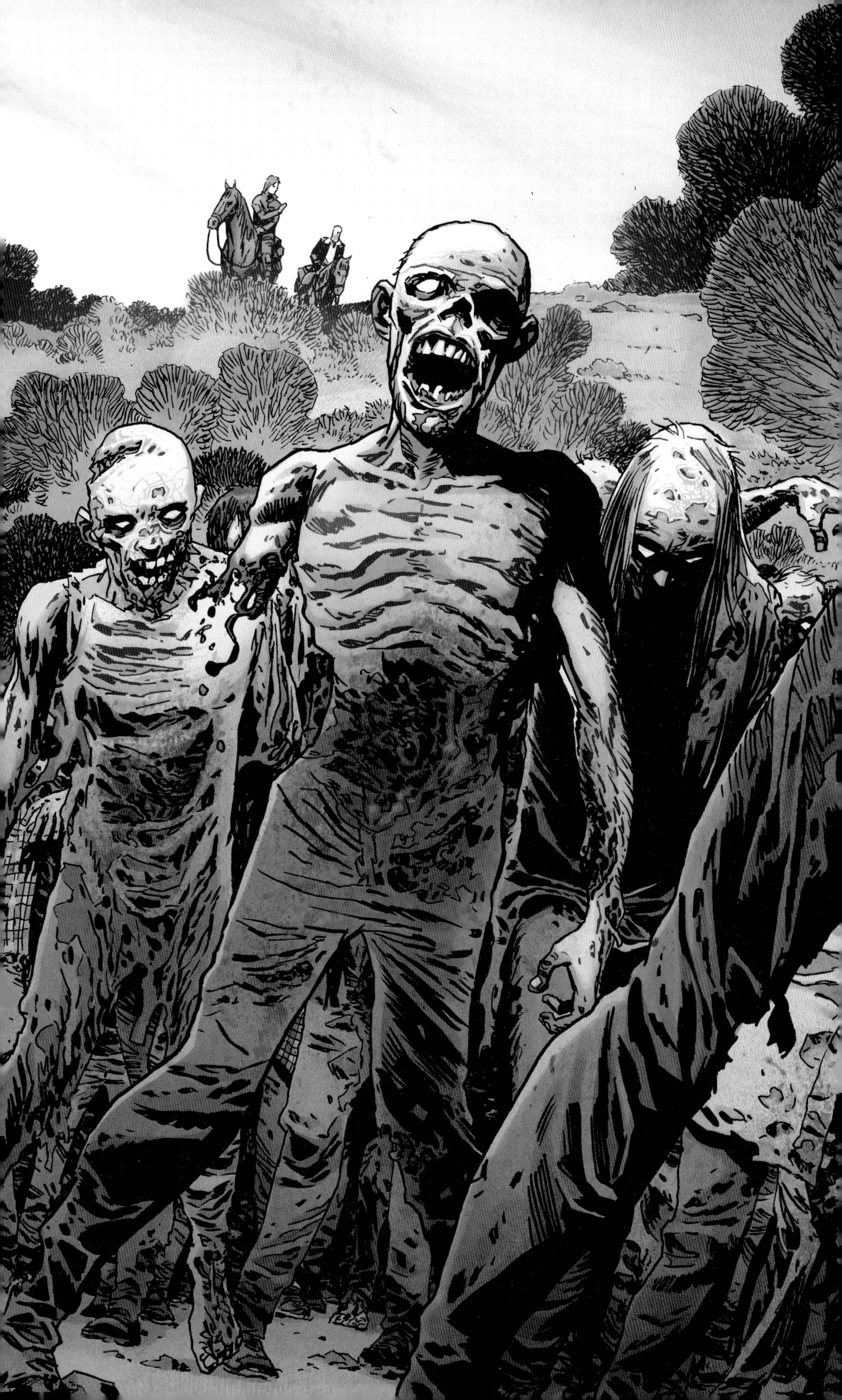

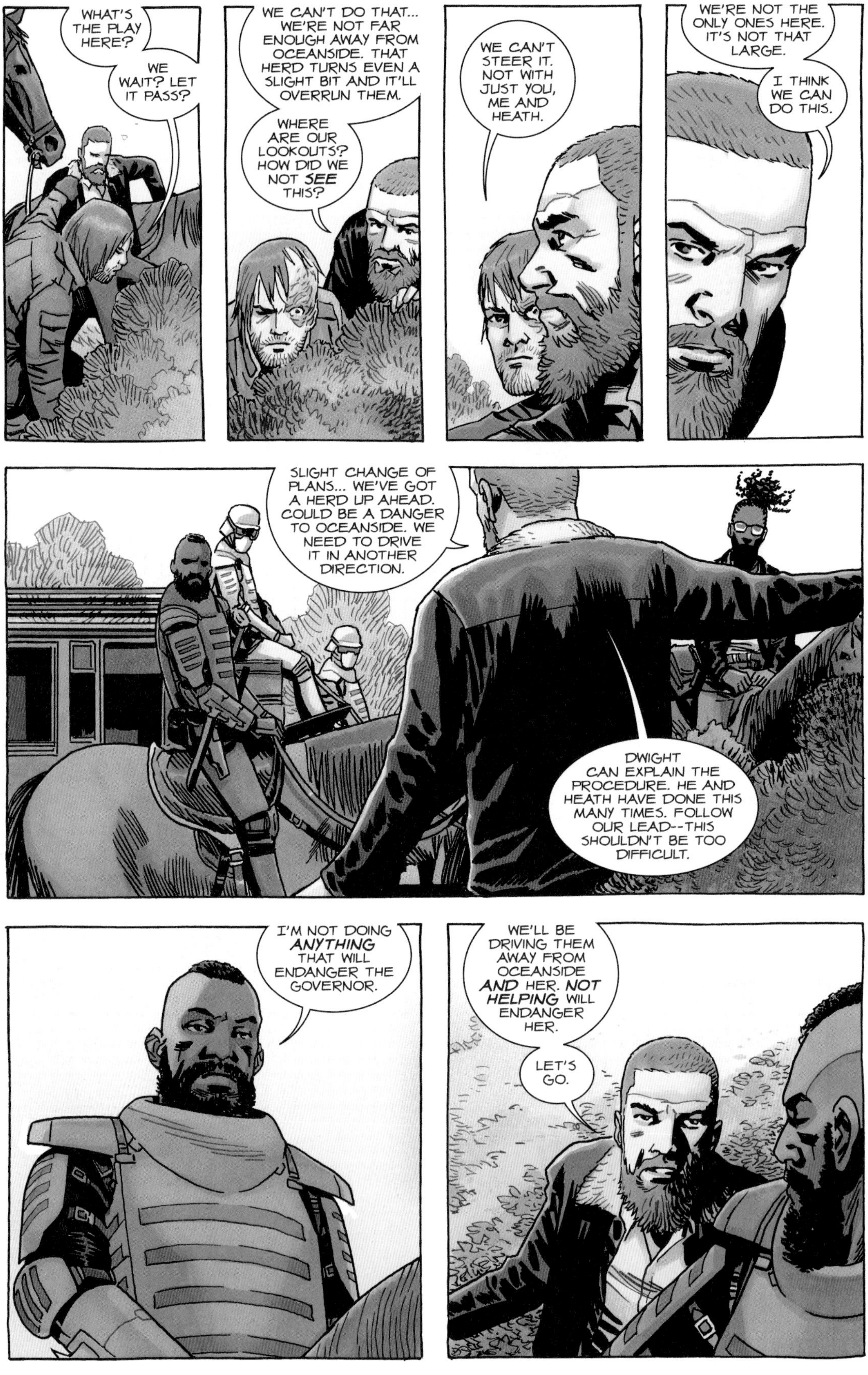
WHAT'S THE PLAY HERE?
WE WAIT? LET IT PASS?
WE CAN'T DO THAT... WE'RE NOT FAR ENOUGH AWAY FROM OCEANSIDE. THAT HERD TURNS EVEN A SLIGHT BIT AND IT'LL OVERRUN THEM.
WHERE ARE OUR LOOKOUTS? HOW DID WE NOT SEE THIS?
WE CAN'T STEER IT. NOT WITH JUST YOU, ME AND HEATH.
WE'RE NOT THE ONLY ONES HERE. IT'S NOT THAT LARGE.
I THINK WE CAN DO THIS.
SLIGHT CHANGE OF PLANS... WE'VE GOT A HERD UP AHEAD. COULD BE A DANGER TO OCEANSIDE. WE NEED TO DRIVE IT IN ANOTHER DIRECTION.
DWIGHT CAN EXPLAIN THE PROCEDURE. HE AND HEATH HAVE DONE THIS MANY TIMES. FOLLOW OUR LEAD--THIS SHOULDN'T BE TOO DIFFICULT.
I'M NOT DOING ANYTHING THAT WILL ENDANGER THE GOVERNOR.
WE'LL BE DRIVING THEM AWAY FROM OCEANSIDE AND HER. NOT HELPING WILL ENDANGER HER.
LET'S GO.

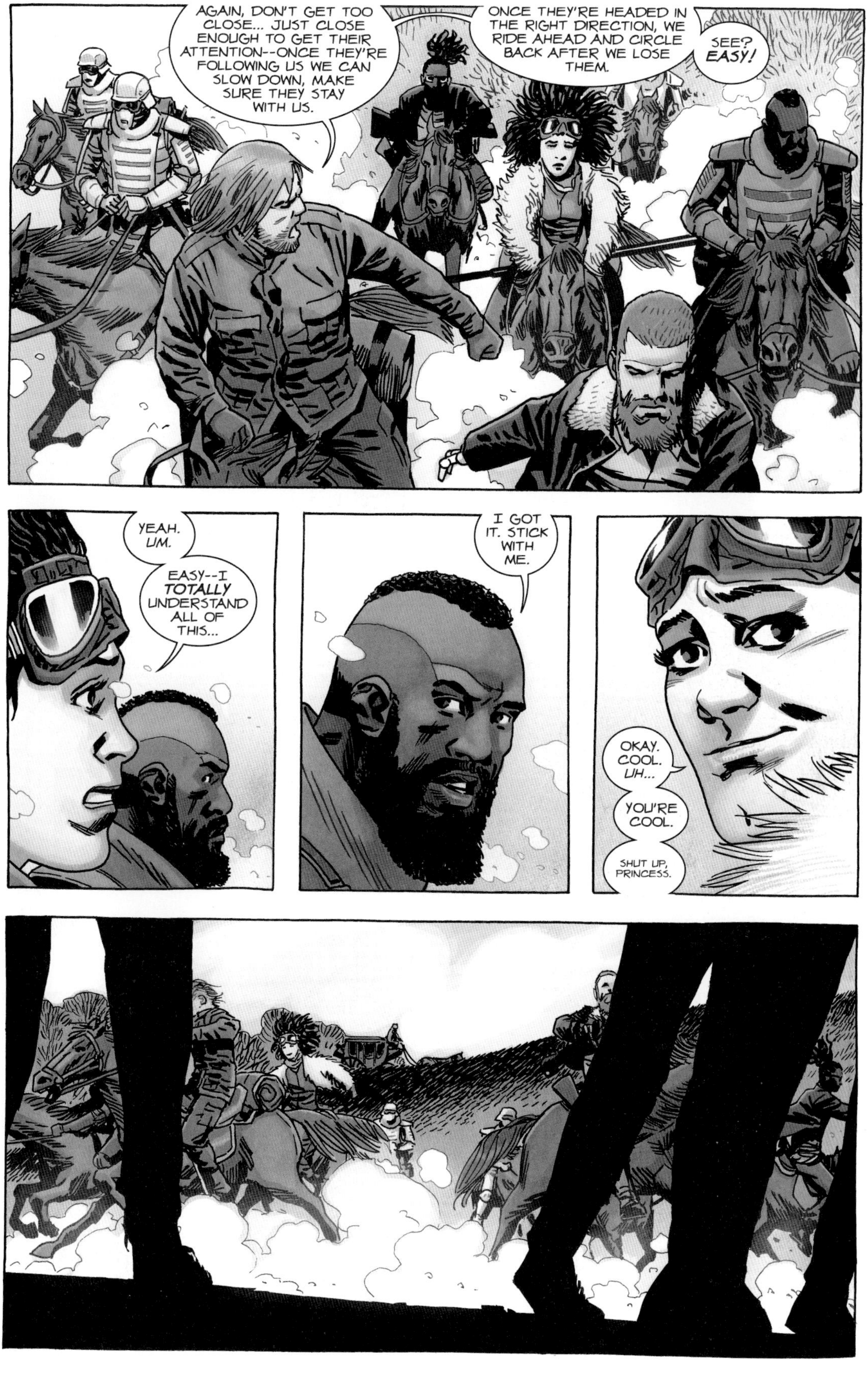
AGAIN, DON'T GET TOO CLOSE... JUST CLOSE ENOUGH TO GET THEIR ATTENTION--ONCE THEY'RE FOLLOWING US WE CAN SLOW DOWN, MAKE SURE THEY STAY WITH US.
ONCE THEY'RE HEADED IN THE RIGHT DIRECTION, WE RIDE AHEAD AND CIRCLE BACK AFTER WE LOSE THEM.
SEE? EASY!
YEAH. UM.
EASY--I TOTALLY UNDERSTAND ALL OF THIS...
I GOT IT. STICK WITH ME.
OKAY. COOL. UH...
YOU'RE COOL.
SHUT UP, PRINCESS.

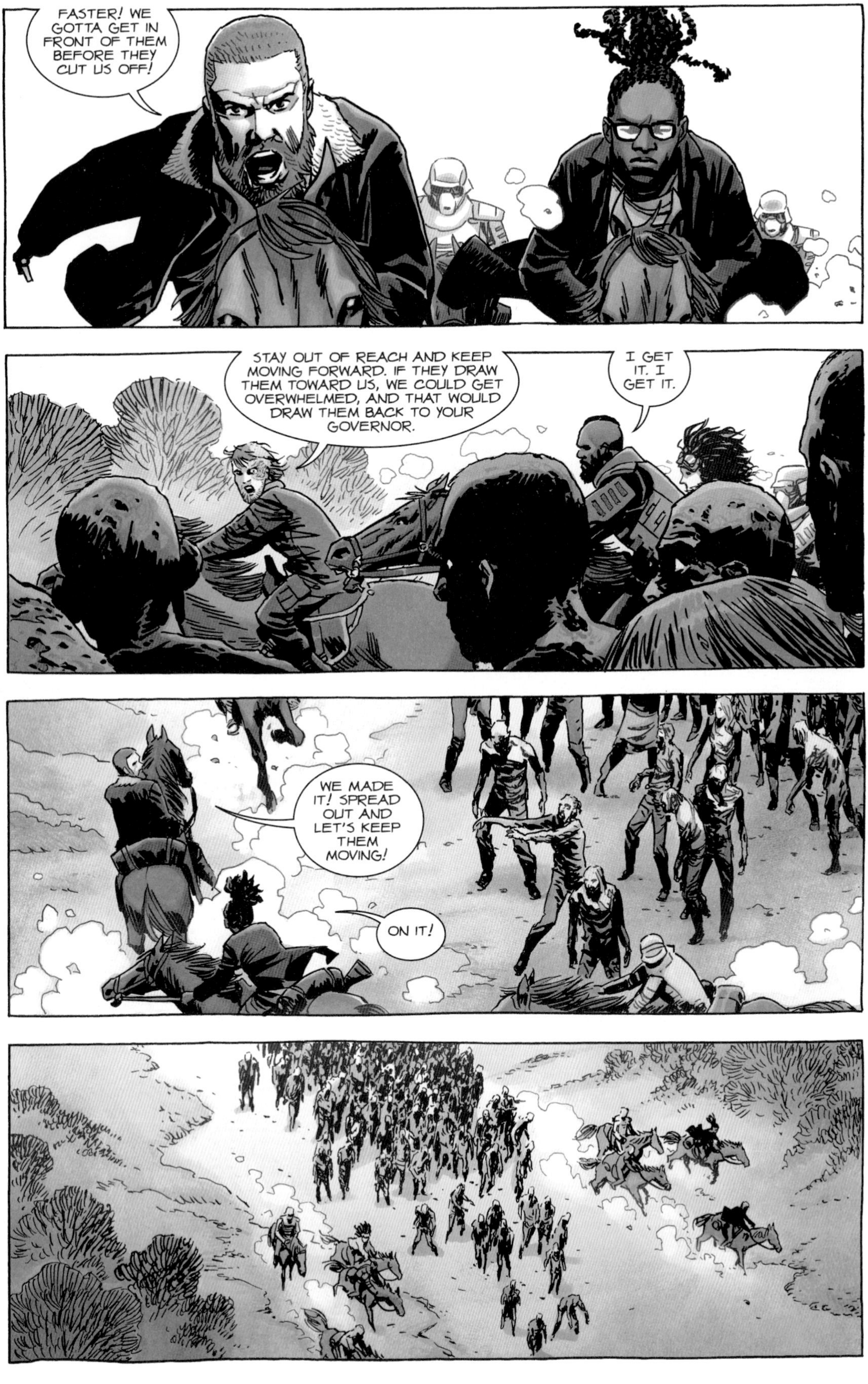
FASTER! WE GOTTA GET IN FRONT OF THEM BEFORE THEY CUT US OFF!
STAY OUT OF REACH AND KEEP MOVING FORWARD. IF THEY DRAW THEM TOWARD US, WE COULD GET OVERWHELMED, AND THAT WOULD DRAW THEM BACK TO YOUR GOVERNOR.
I GET IT. I GET IT.
WE MADE IT! SPREAD OUT AND LET'S KEEP THEM MOVING!
ON IT!

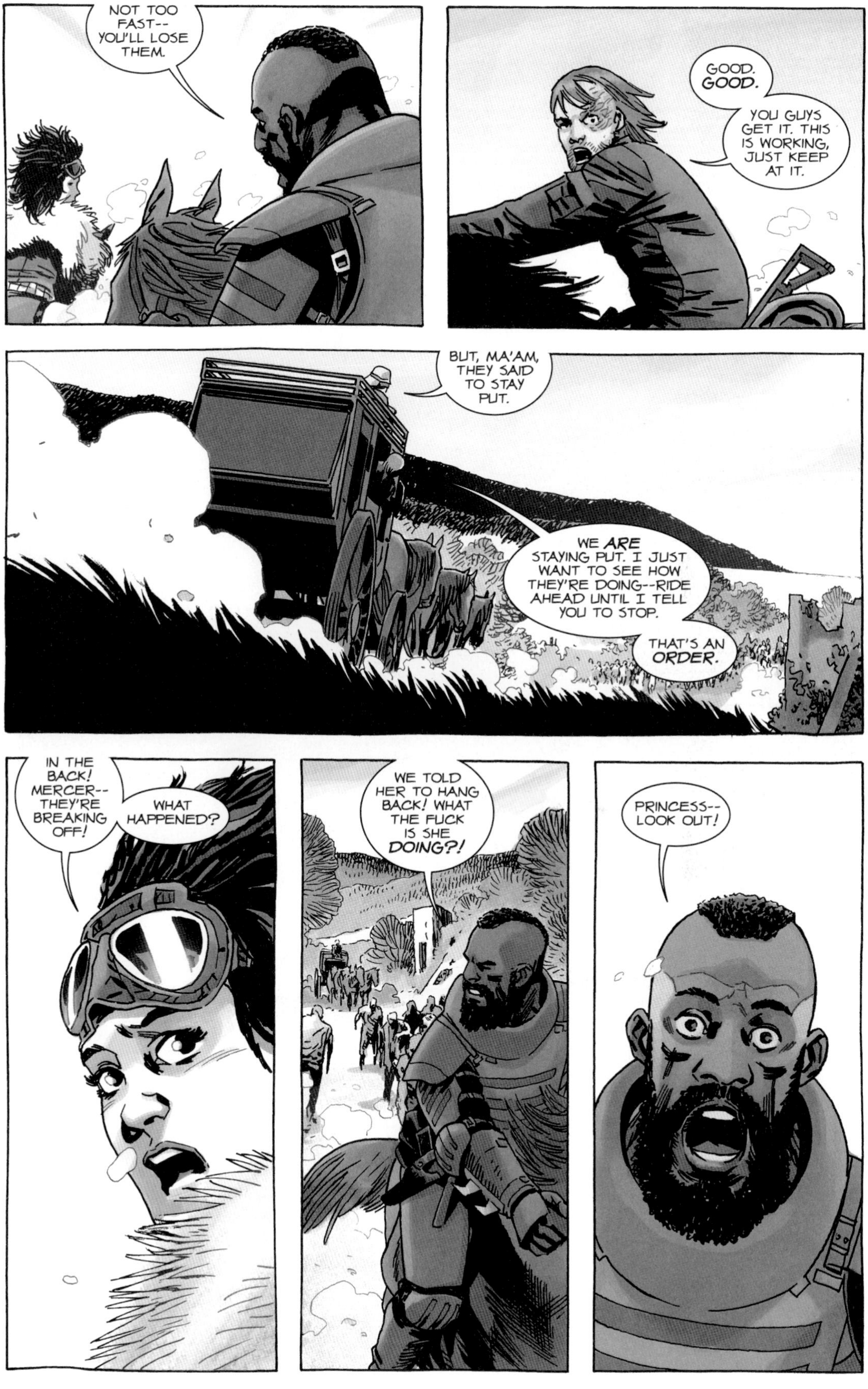
NOT TOO FAST-- YOU'LL LOSE THEM.
GOOD. GOOD.
YOU GUYS GET IT. THIS IS WORKING, JUST KEEP AT IT.
BUT, MA'AM, THEY SAID TO STAY PUT.
WE ARE STAYING PUT. I JUST WANT TO SEE HOW THEY'RE DOING--RIDE AHEAD UNTIL I TELL YOU TO STOP.
THAT'S AN ORDER.
IN THE BACK! MERCER-- THEY'RE BREAKING OFF!
WHAT HAPPENED?
WE TOLD HER TO HANG BACK! WHAT THE FUCK IS SHE DOING?!
PRINCESS-- LOOK OUT!

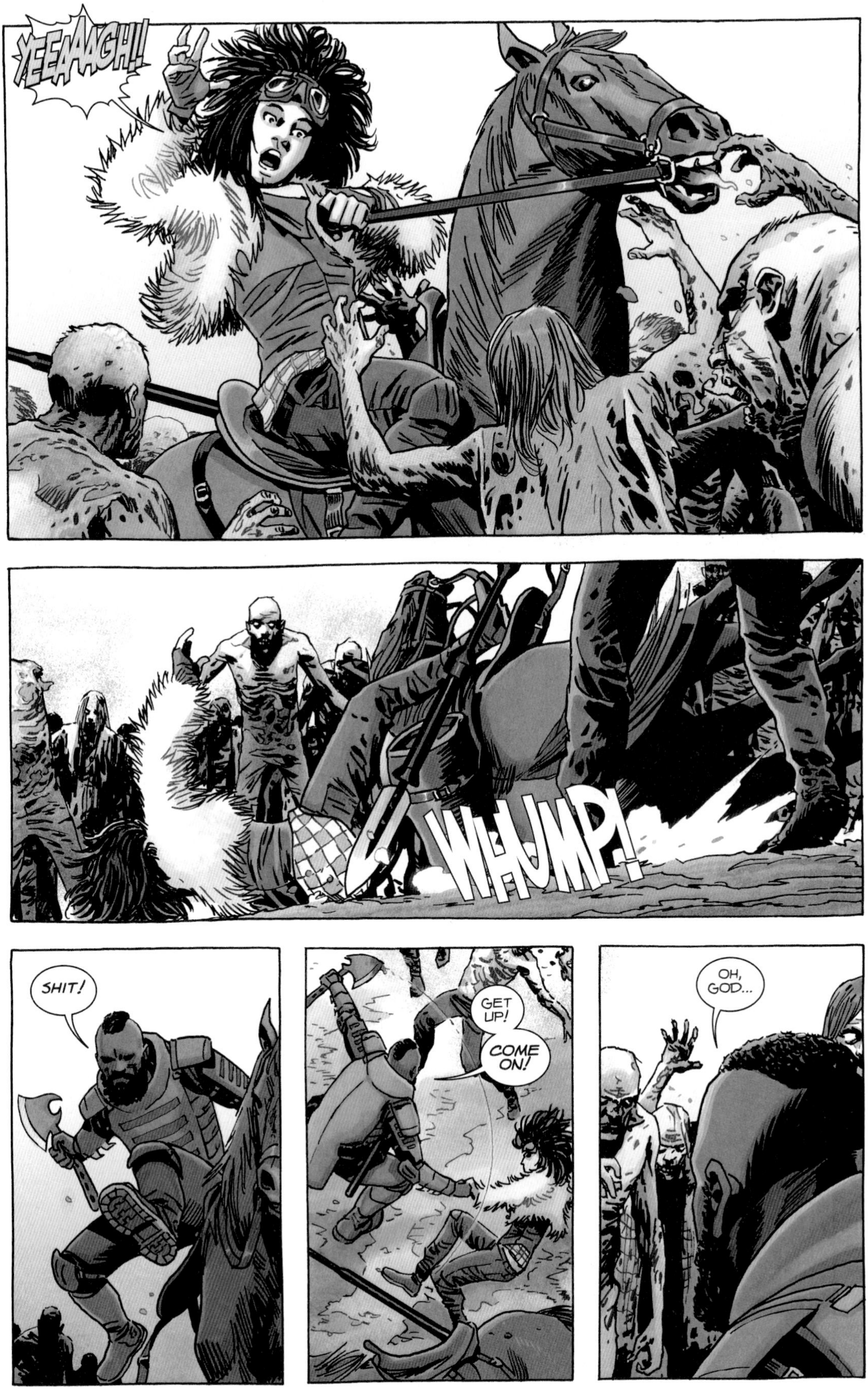
YEEAAAGH!!
WHUMP!
SHIT!
GET UP!
COME ON!
OH, GOD...

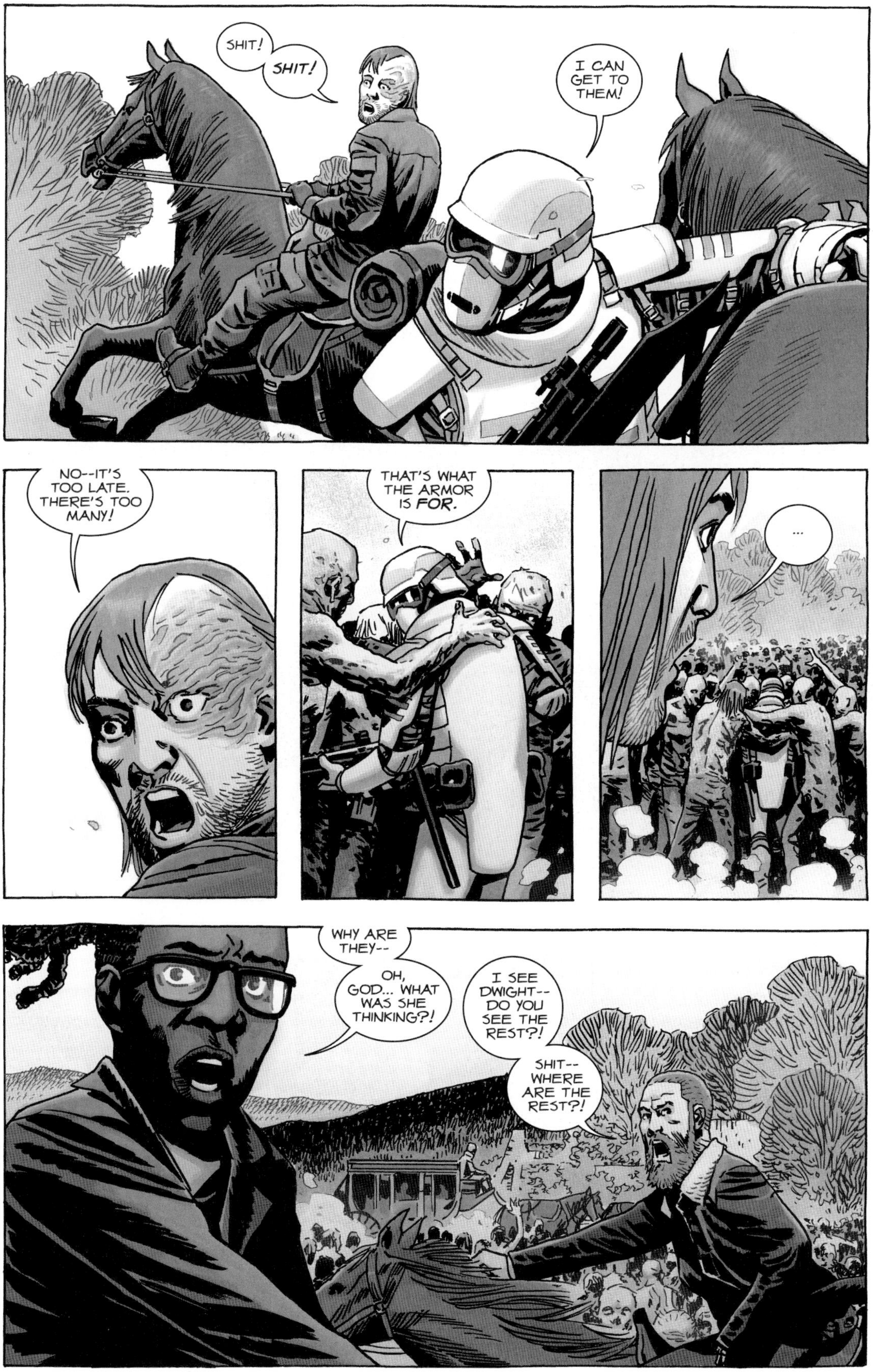
SHIT!
SHIT!
I CAN GET TO THEM!
NO--IT'S TOO LATE. THERE'S TOO MANY!
THAT'S WHAT THE ARMOR IS FOR.
...
WHY ARE THEY--
OH, GOD... WHAT WAS SHE THINKING?!
I SEE DWIGHT-- DO YOU SEE THE REST?!
SHIT-- WHERE ARE THE REST?!

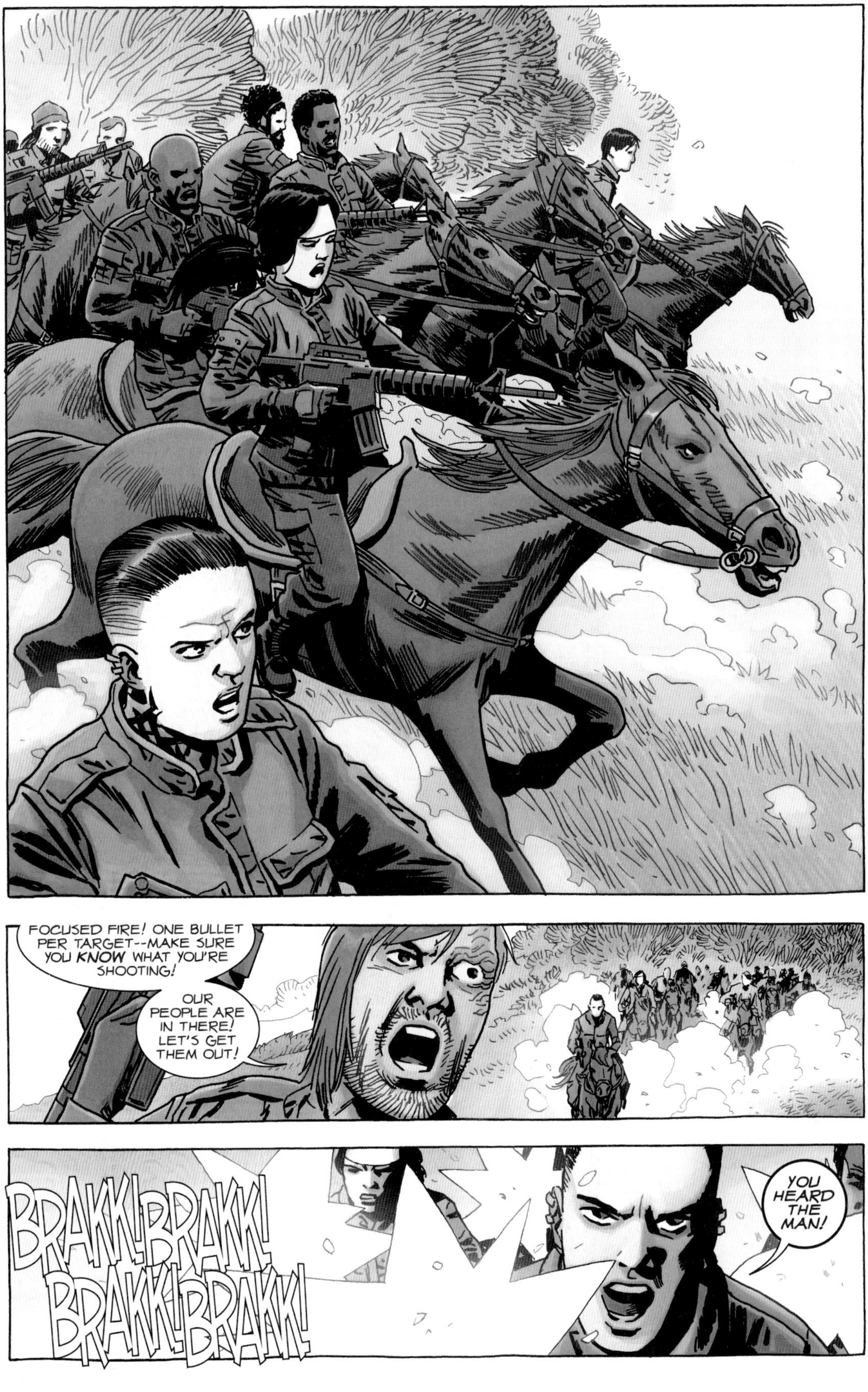

FOCUSED FIRE! ONE BULLET PER TARGET--MAKE SURE YOU KNOW WHAT YOU'RE SHOOTING!
OUR PEOPLE ARE IN THERE! LET'S GET THEM OUT!
BRAKK! BRAKK! BRAKK! BRAKK!
YOU HEARD THE MAN!

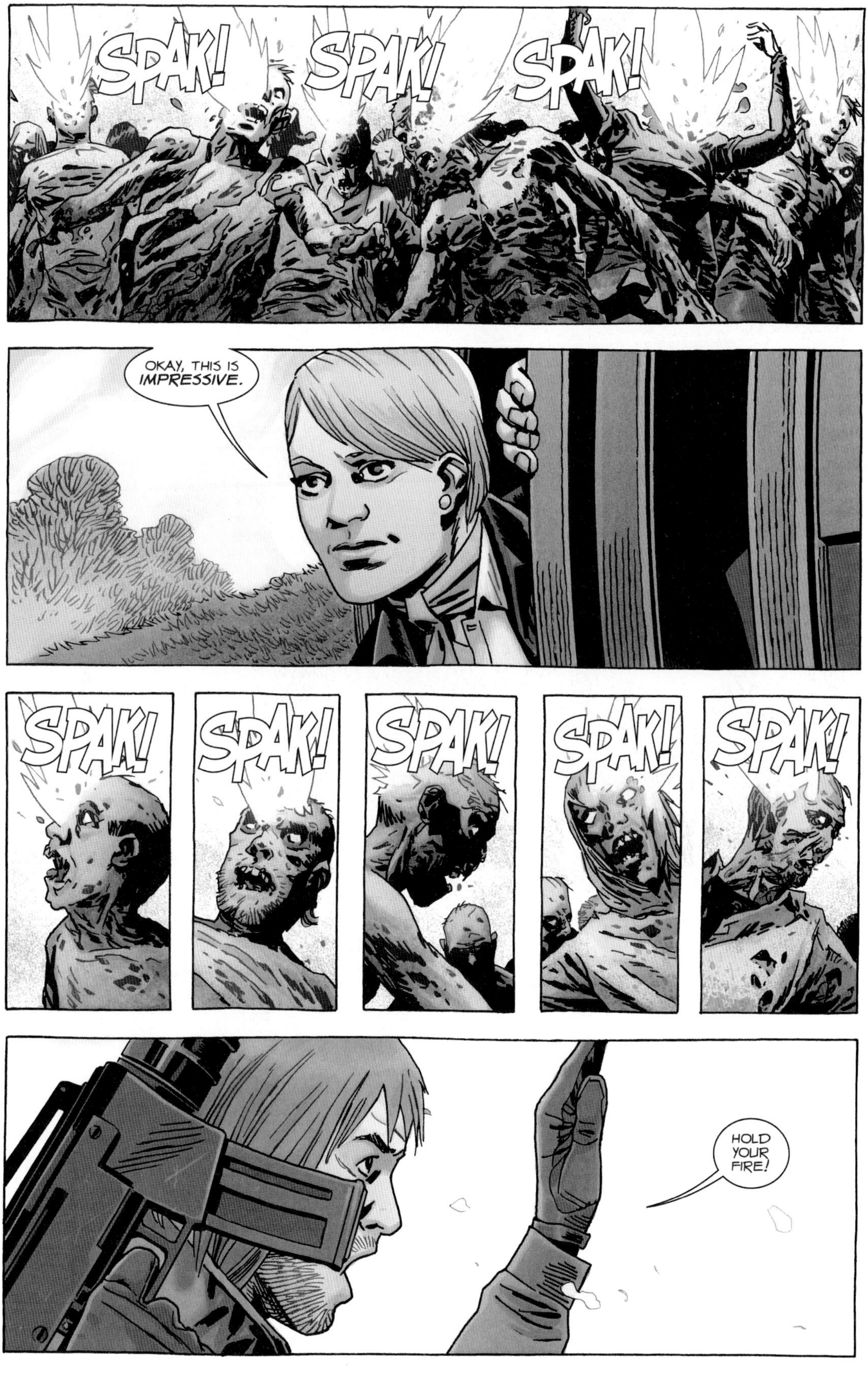
SPAK!
SPAK!
SPAK!
OKAY, THIS IS IMPRESSIVE.
SPAK!
SPAK!
SPAK!
SPAK!
SPAK!
HOLD YOUR FIRE!

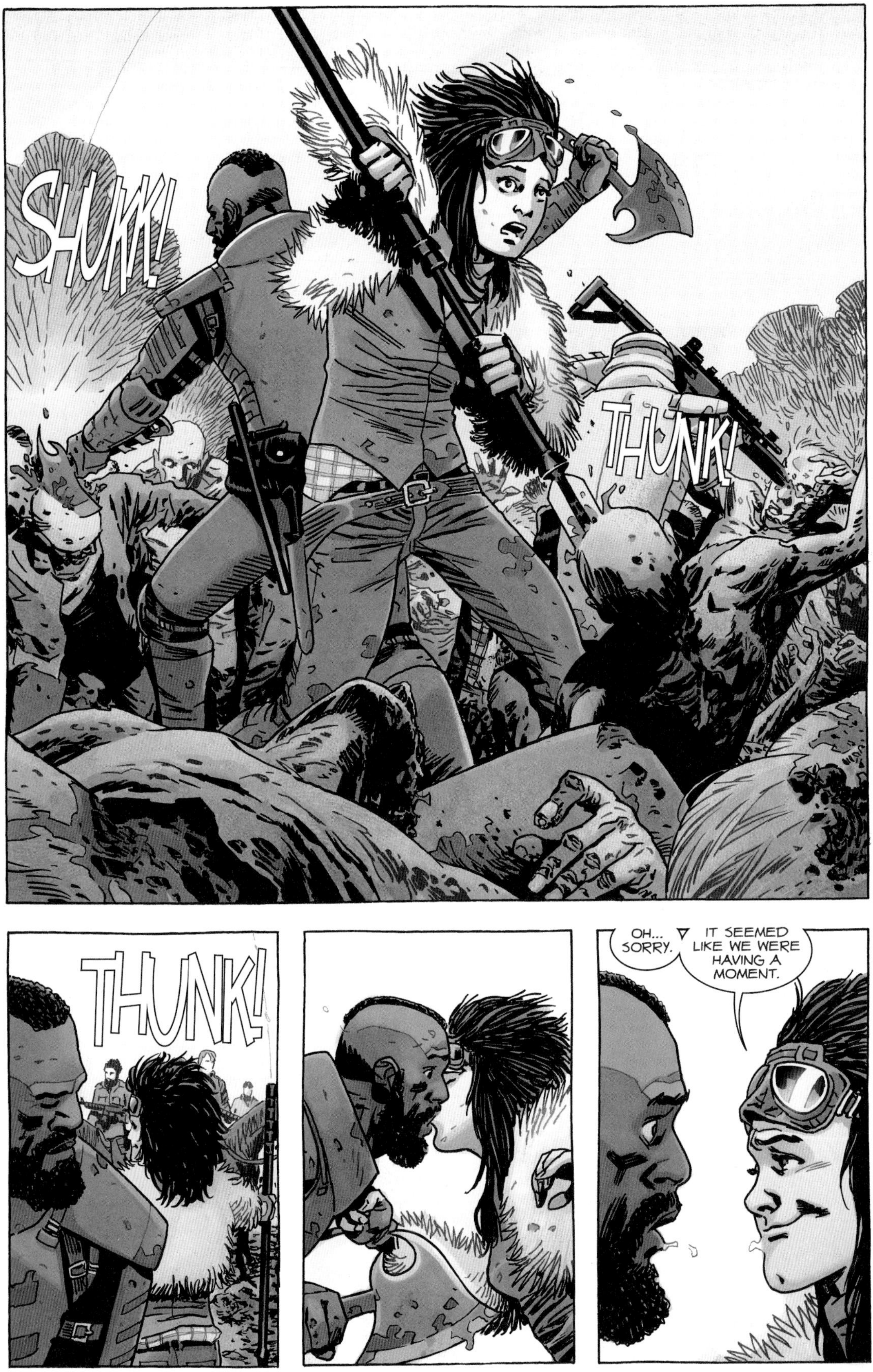
SHUKK!
THUNK!
THUNK!
OH... SORRY.
IT SEEMED LIKE WE WERE HAVING A MOMENT.

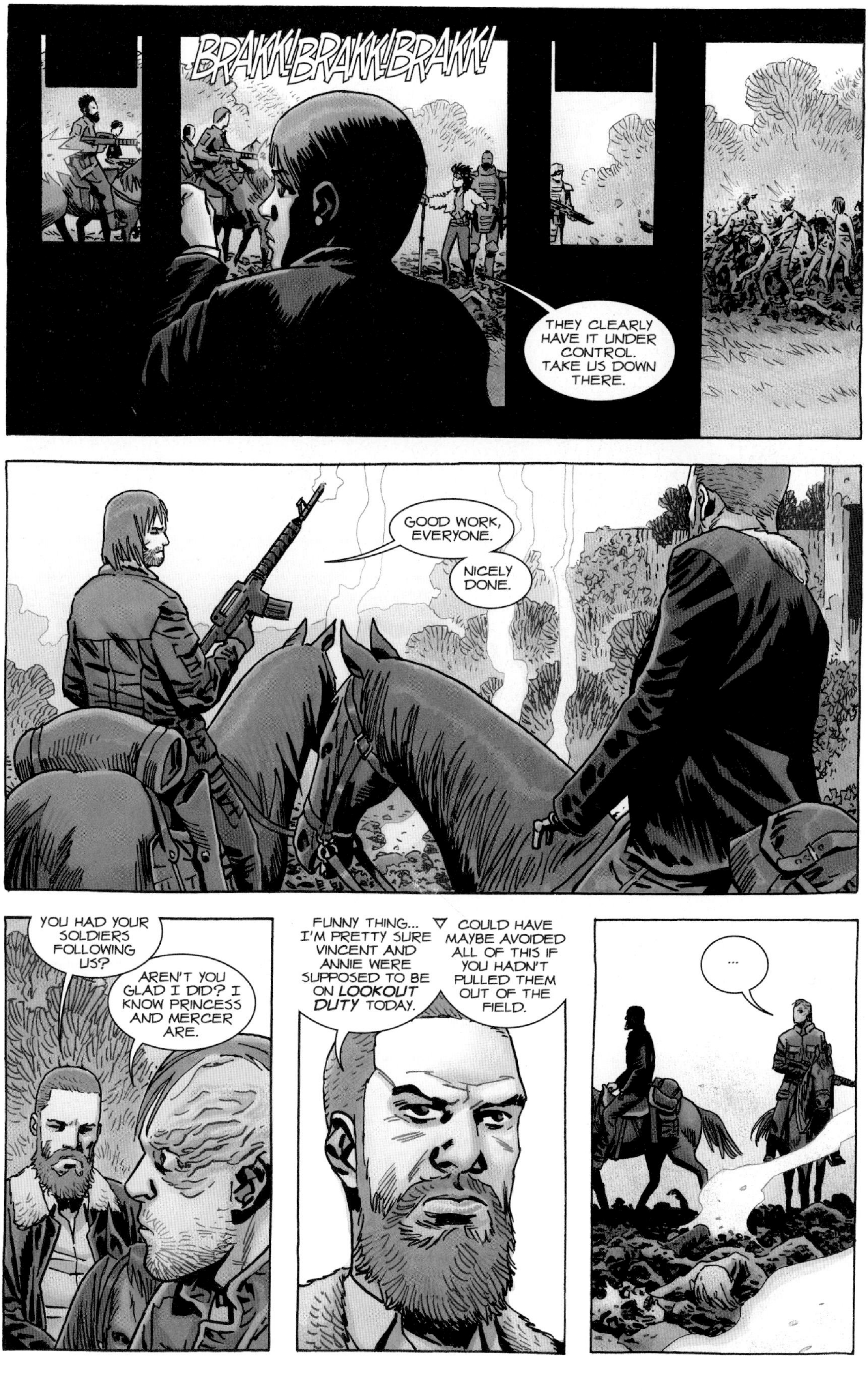
BRAKK! BRAKK! BRAKK!
THEY CLEARLY HAVE IT UNDER CONTROL. TAKE US DOWN THERE.
GOOD WORK, EVERYONE.
NICELY DONE.
YOU HAD YOUR SOLDIERS FOLLOWING US?
AREN'T YOU GLAD I DID? I KNOW PRINCESS AND MERCER ARE.
FUNNY THING... I'M PRETTY SURE VINCENT AND ANNIE WERE SUPPOSED TO BE ON LOOKOUT DUTY TODAY.
COULD HAVE MAYBE AVOIDED ALL OF THIS IF YOU HADN'T PULLED THEM OUT OF THE FIELD.
...

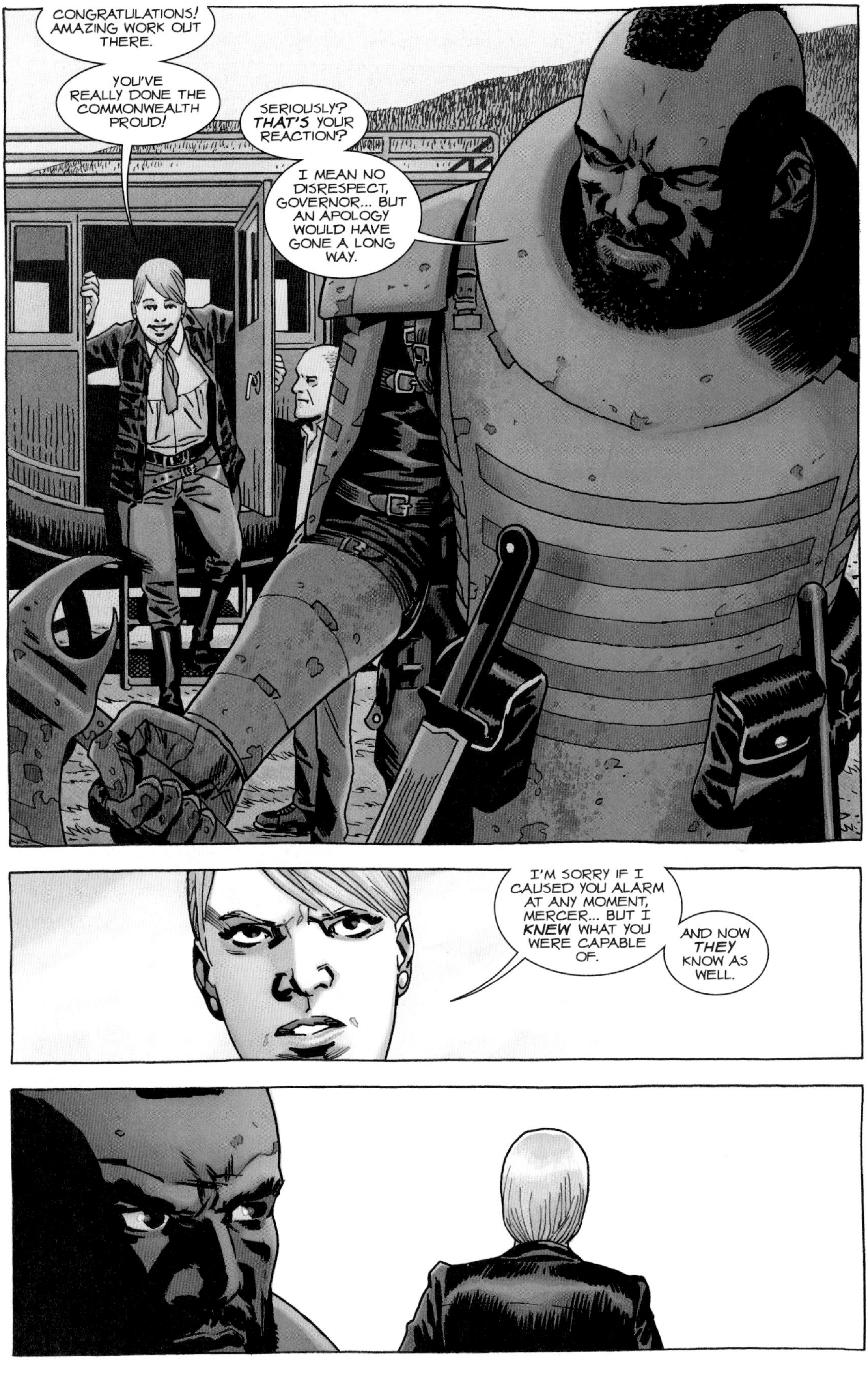
CONGRATULATIONS! AMAZING WORK OUT THERE.
YOU'VE REALLY DONE THE COMMONWEALTH PROUD!
SERIOUSLY? THAT'S YOUR REACTION?
I MEAN NO DISRESPECT, GOVERNOR... BUT AN APOLOGY WOULD HAVE GONE A LONG WAY.
I'M SORRY IF I CAUSED YOU ALARM AT ANY MOMENT, MERCER... BUT I KNEW WHAT YOU WERE CAPABLE OF.
AND NOW THEY KNOW AS WELL.

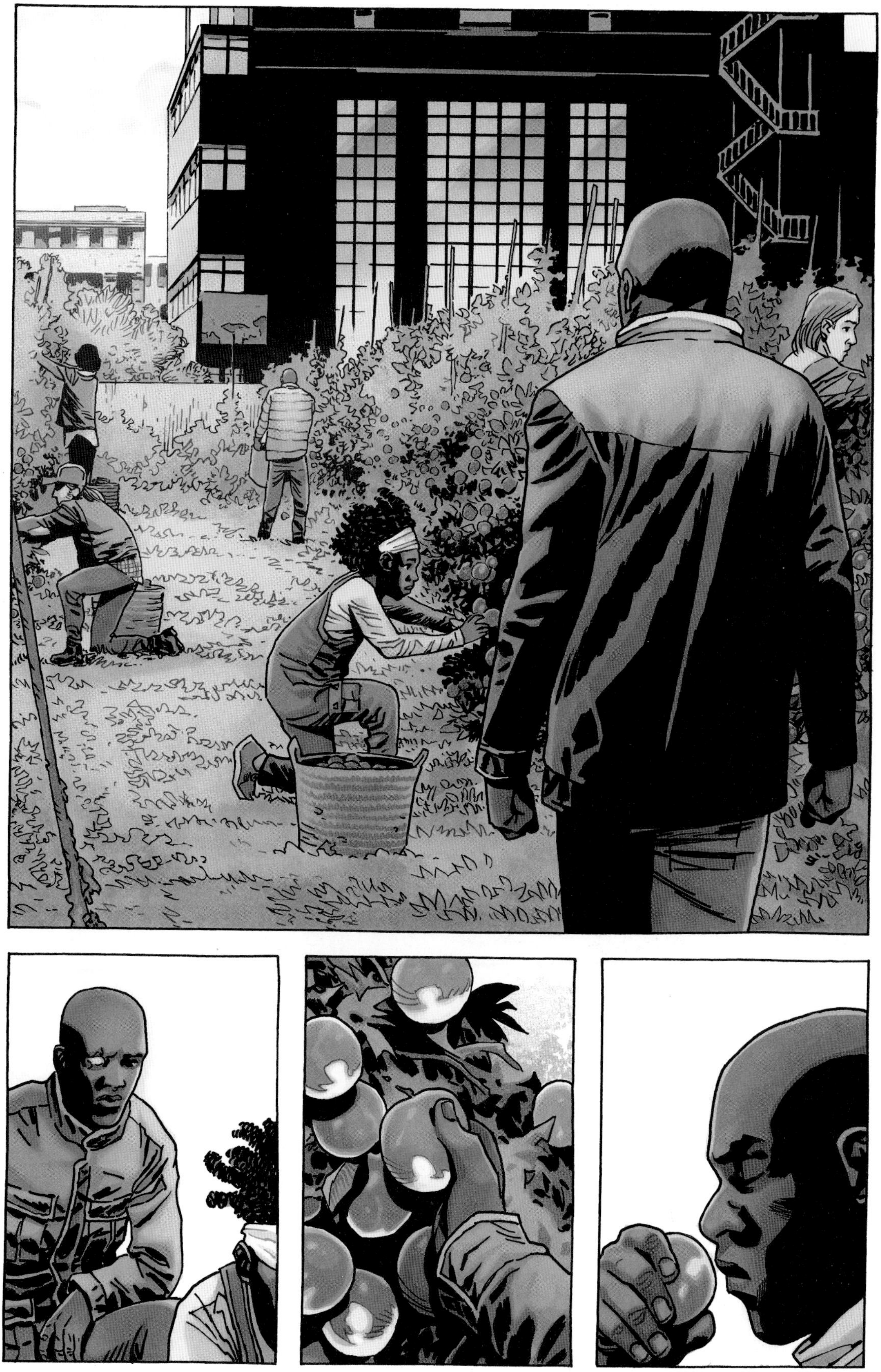

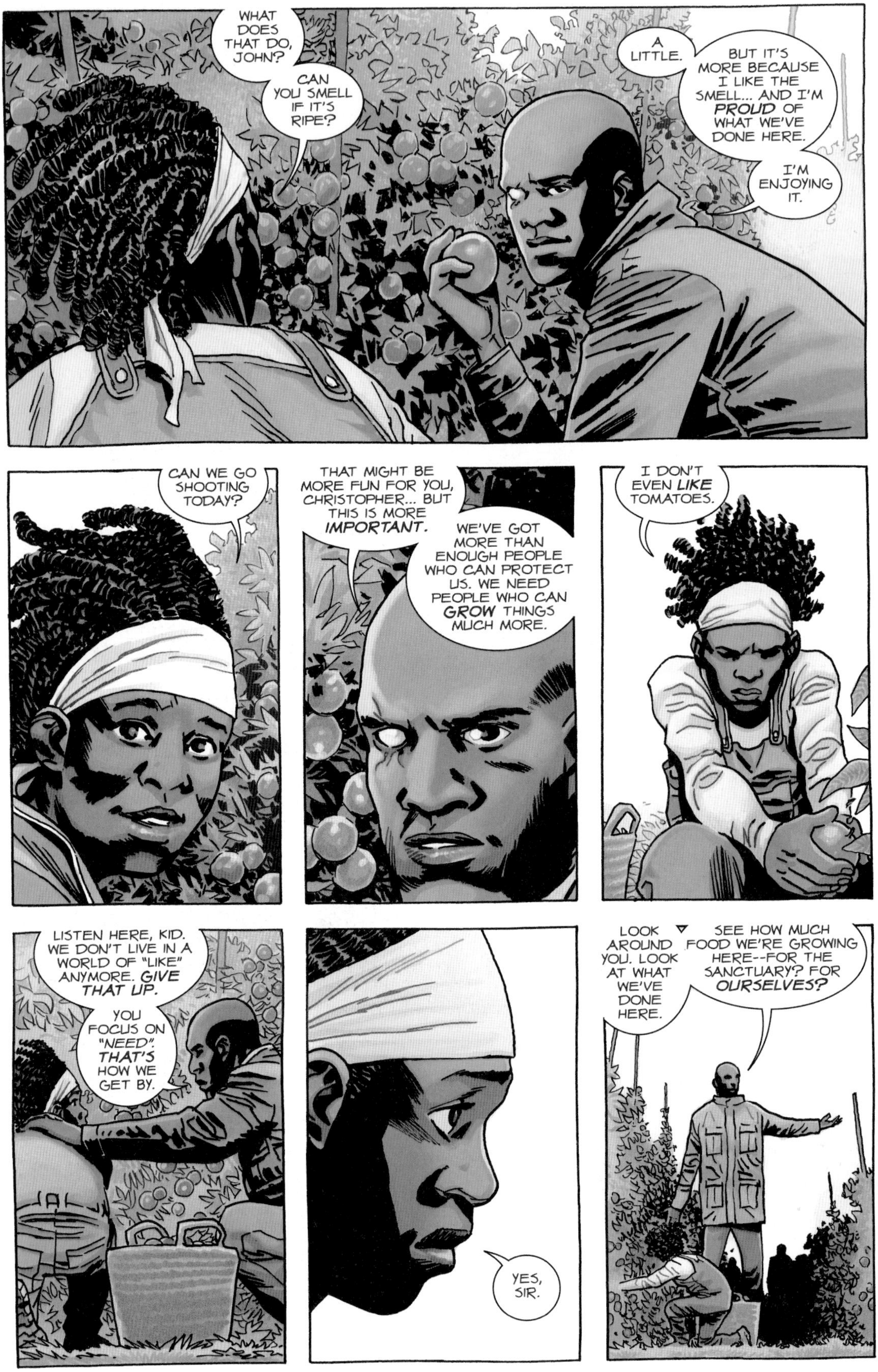
WHAT DOES THAT DO, JOHN?
CAN YOU SMELL IF IT'S RIPE?
A LITTLE.
BUT IT'S MORE BECAUSE I LIKE THE SMELL... AND I'M PROUD OF WHAT WE'VE DONE HERE.
I'M ENJOYING IT.
CAN WE GO SHOOTING TODAY?
THAT MIGHT BE MORE FUN FOR YOU, CHRISTOPHER... BUT THIS IS MORE IMPORTANT.
WE'VE GOT MORE THAN ENOUGH PEOPLE WHO CAN PROTECT US. WE NEED PEOPLE WHO CAN GROW THINGS MUCH MORE.
I DON'T EVEN LIKE TOMATOES.
LISTEN HERE, KID. WE DON'T LIVE IN A WORLD OF "LIKE" ANYMORE. GIVE THAT UP.
YOU FOCUS ON "NEED". THAT'S HOW WE GET BY.
YES, SIR.
LOOK AROUND YOU. LOOK AT WHAT WE'VE DONE HERE.
SEE HOW MUCH FOOD WE'RE GROWING HERE--FOR THE SANCTUARY? FOR OURSELVES?

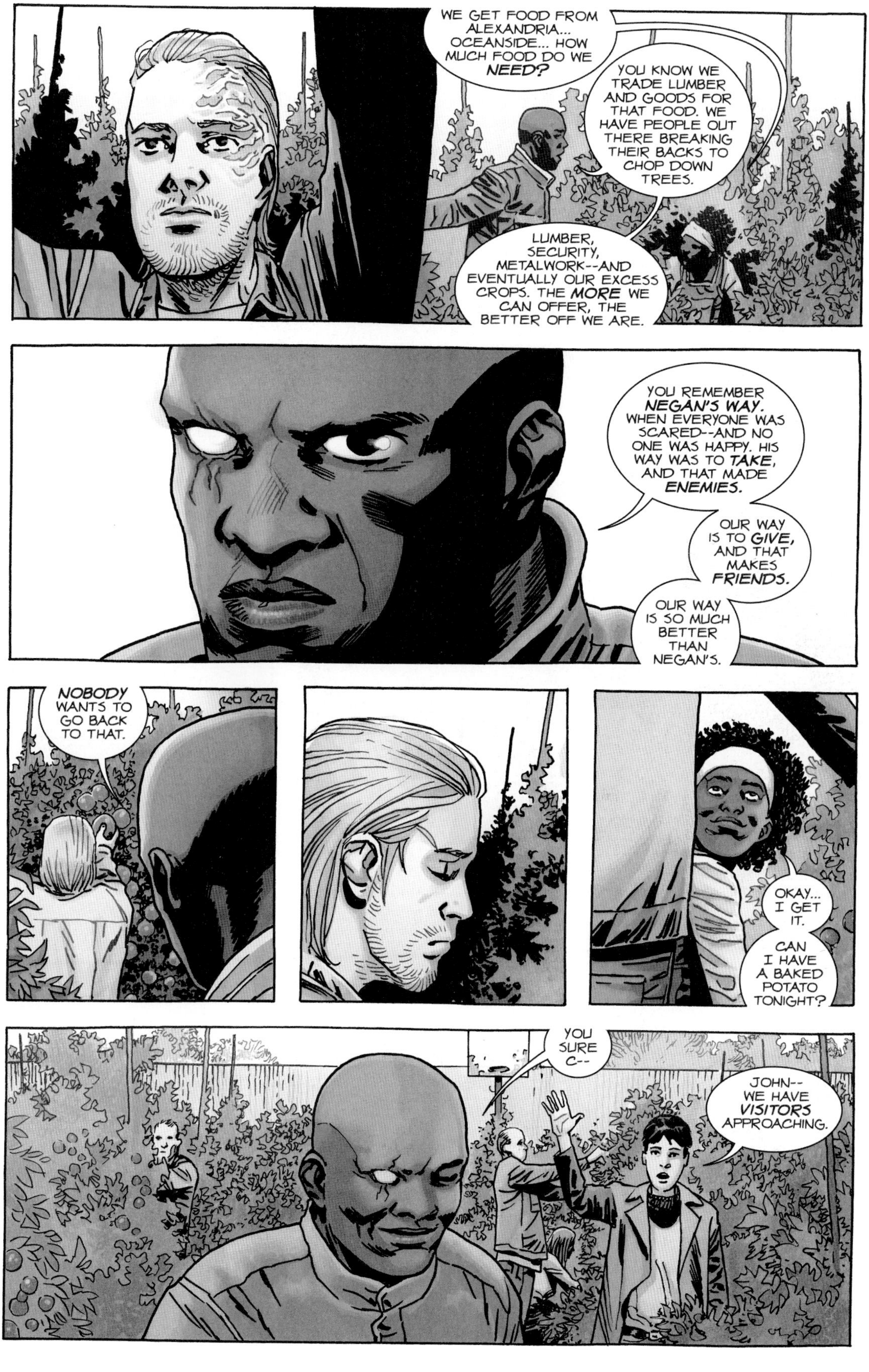

WE GET FOOD FROM ALEXANDRIA... OCEANSIDE... HOW MUCH FOOD DO WE NEED?
YOU KNOW WE TRADE LUMBER AND GOODS FOR THAT FOOD. WE HAVE PEOPLE OUT THERE BREAKING THEIR BACKS TO CHOP DOWN TREES.
LUMBER, SECURITY, METALWORK--AND EVENTUALLY OUR EXCESS CROPS. THE MORE WE CAN OFFER, THE BETTER OFF WE ARE.
YOU REMEMBER NEGAN'S WAY. WHEN EVERYONE WAS SCARED--AND NO ONE WAS HAPPY. HIS WAY WAS TO TAKE, AND THAT MADE ENEMIES.
OUR WAY IS TO GIVE, AND THAT MAKES FRIENDS.
OUR WAY IS SO MUCH BETTER THAN NEGAN'S.
NOBODY WANTS TO GO BACK TO THAT.
OKAY... I GET IT.
CAN I HAVE A BAKED POTATO TONIGHT?
YOU SURE C--
JOHN-- WE HAVE VISITORS APPROACHING.

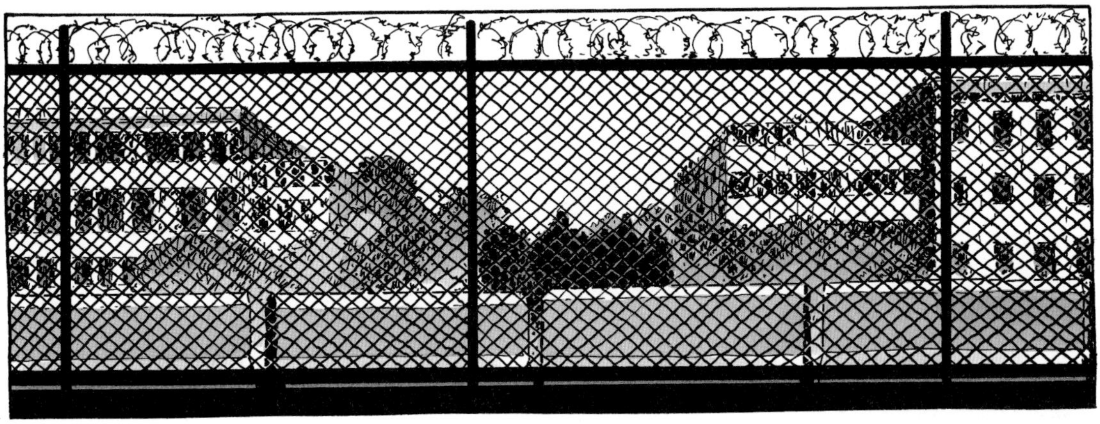

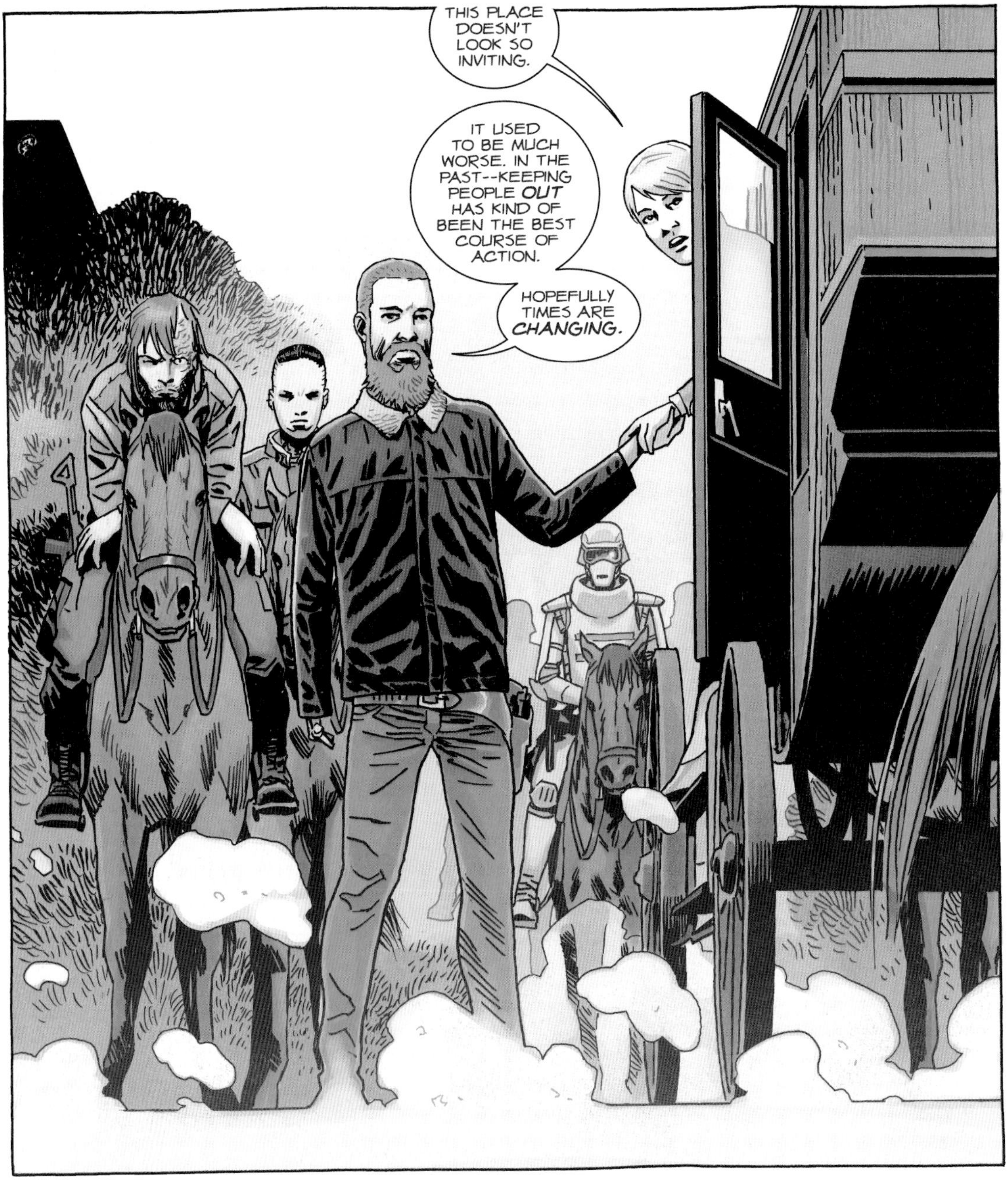
THIS PLACE DOESN'T LOOK SO INVITING.
IT USED TO BE MUCH WORSE. IN THE PAST--KEEPING PEOPLE *OUT* HAS KIND OF BEEN THE BEST COURSE OF ACTION.
HOPEFULLY TIMES ARE *CHANGING.*

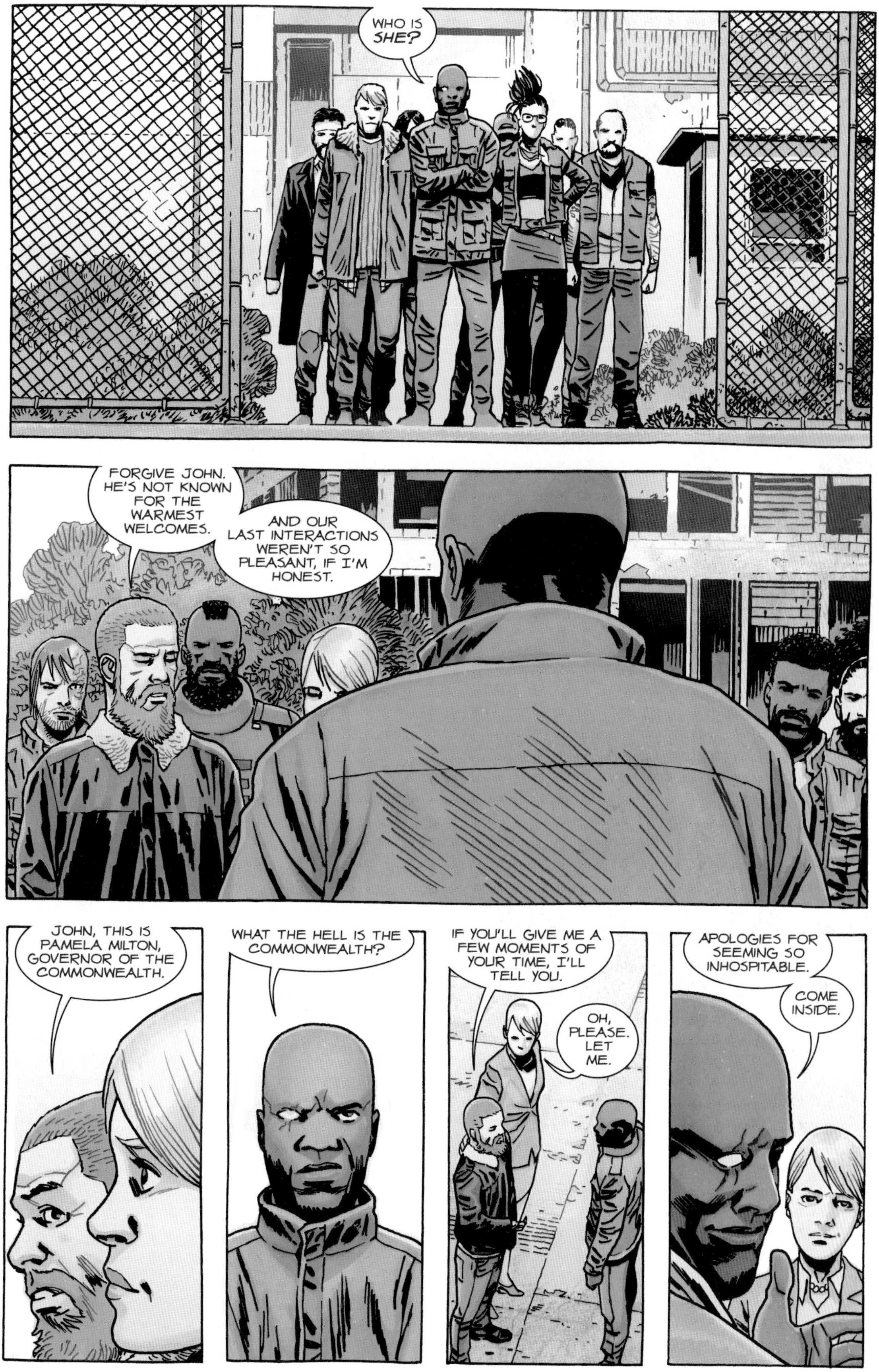
WHO IS SHE?
FORGIVE JOHN. HE'S NOT KNOWN FOR THE WARMEST WELCOMES.
AND OUR LAST INTERACTIONS WEREN'T SO PLEASANT, IF I'M HONEST.
JOHN, THIS IS PAMELA MILTON, GOVERNOR OF THE COMMONWEALTH.
WHAT THE HELL IS THE COMMONWEALTH?
IF YOU'LL GIVE ME A FEW MOMENTS OF YOUR TIME, I'LL TELL YOU.
OH, PLEASE. LET ME.
APOLOGIES FOR SEEMING SO INHOSPITABLE.
COME INSIDE.

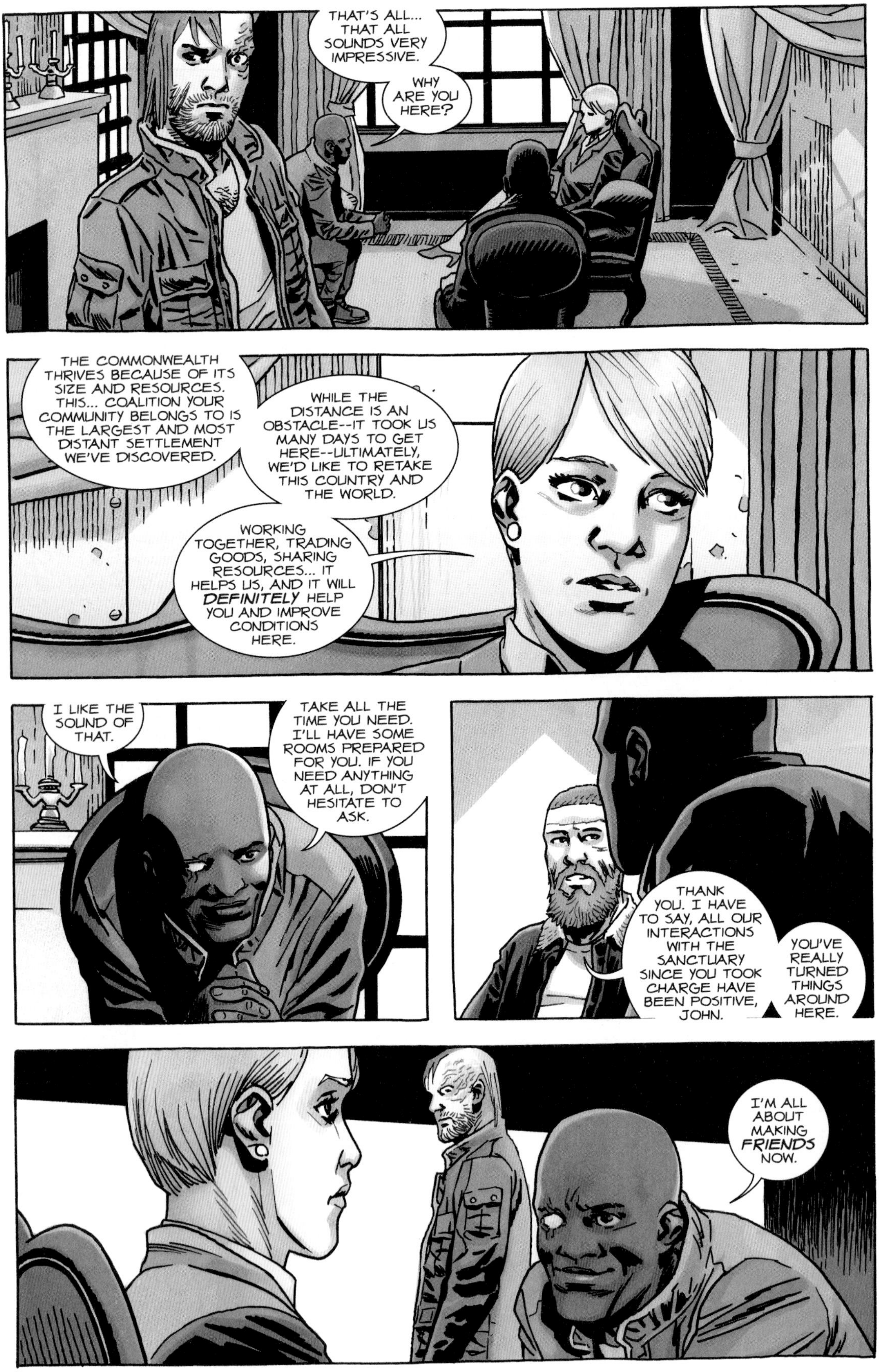
THAT'S ALL... THAT ALL SOUNDS VERY IMPRESSIVE.
WHY ARE YOU HERE?
THE COMMONWEALTH THRIVES BECAUSE OF ITS SIZE AND RESOURCES. THIS... COALITION YOUR COMMUNITY BELONGS TO IS THE LARGEST AND MOST DISTANT SETTLEMENT WE'VE DISCOVERED.
WHILE THE DISTANCE IS AN OBSTACLE--IT TOOK US MANY DAYS TO GET HERE--ULTIMATELY, WE'D LIKE TO RETAKE THIS COUNTRY AND THE WORLD.
WORKING TOGETHER, TRADING GOODS, SHARING RESOURCES... IT HELPS US, AND IT WILL DEFINITELY HELP YOU AND IMPROVE CONDITIONS HERE.
I LIKE THE SOUND OF THAT.
TAKE ALL THE TIME YOU NEED. I'LL HAVE SOME ROOMS PREPARED FOR YOU. IF YOU NEED ANYTHING AT ALL, DON'T HESITATE TO ASK.
THANK YOU. I HAVE TO SAY, ALL OUR INTERACTIONS WITH THE SANCTUARY SINCE YOU TOOK CHARGE HAVE BEEN POSITIVE, JOHN.
YOU'VE REALLY TURNED THINGS AROUND HERE.
I'M ALL ABOUT MAKING FRIENDS NOW.

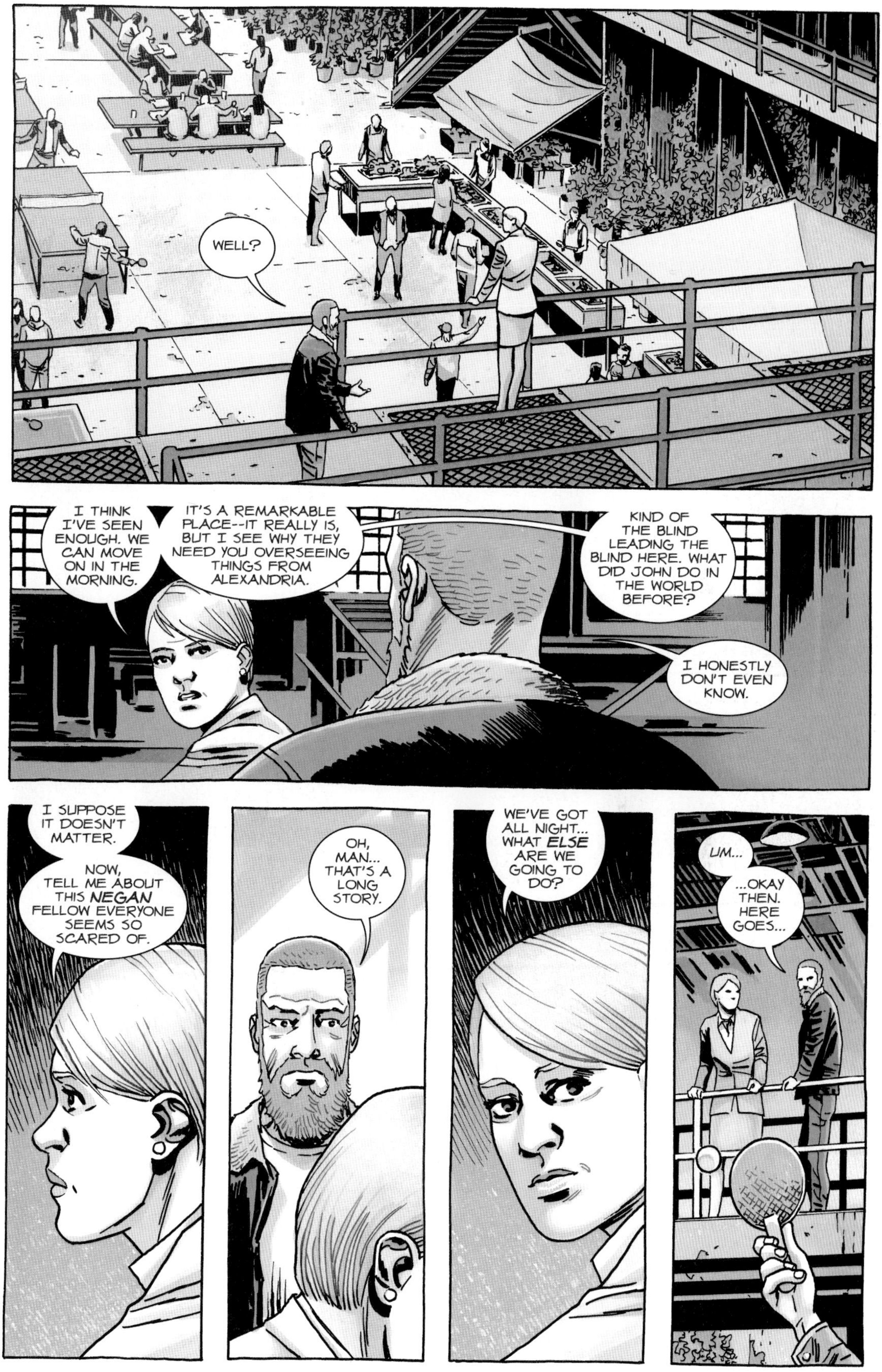
WELL?
I THINK I'VE SEEN ENOUGH. WE CAN MOVE ON IN THE MORNING.
IT'S A REMARKABLE PLACE--IT REALLY IS, BUT I SEE WHY THEY NEED YOU OVERSEEING THINGS FROM ALEXANDRIA.
KIND OF THE BLIND LEADING THE BLIND HERE. WHAT DID JOHN DO IN THE WORLD BEFORE?
I HONESTLY DON'T EVEN KNOW.
I SUPPOSE IT DOESN'T MATTER.
NOW, TELL ME ABOUT THIS NEGAN FELLOW EVERYONE SEEMS SO SCARED OF.
OH, MAN... THAT'S A LONG STORY.
WE'VE GOT ALL NIGHT... WHAT ELSE ARE WE GOING TO DO?
UM...
...OKAY THEN. HERE GOES...

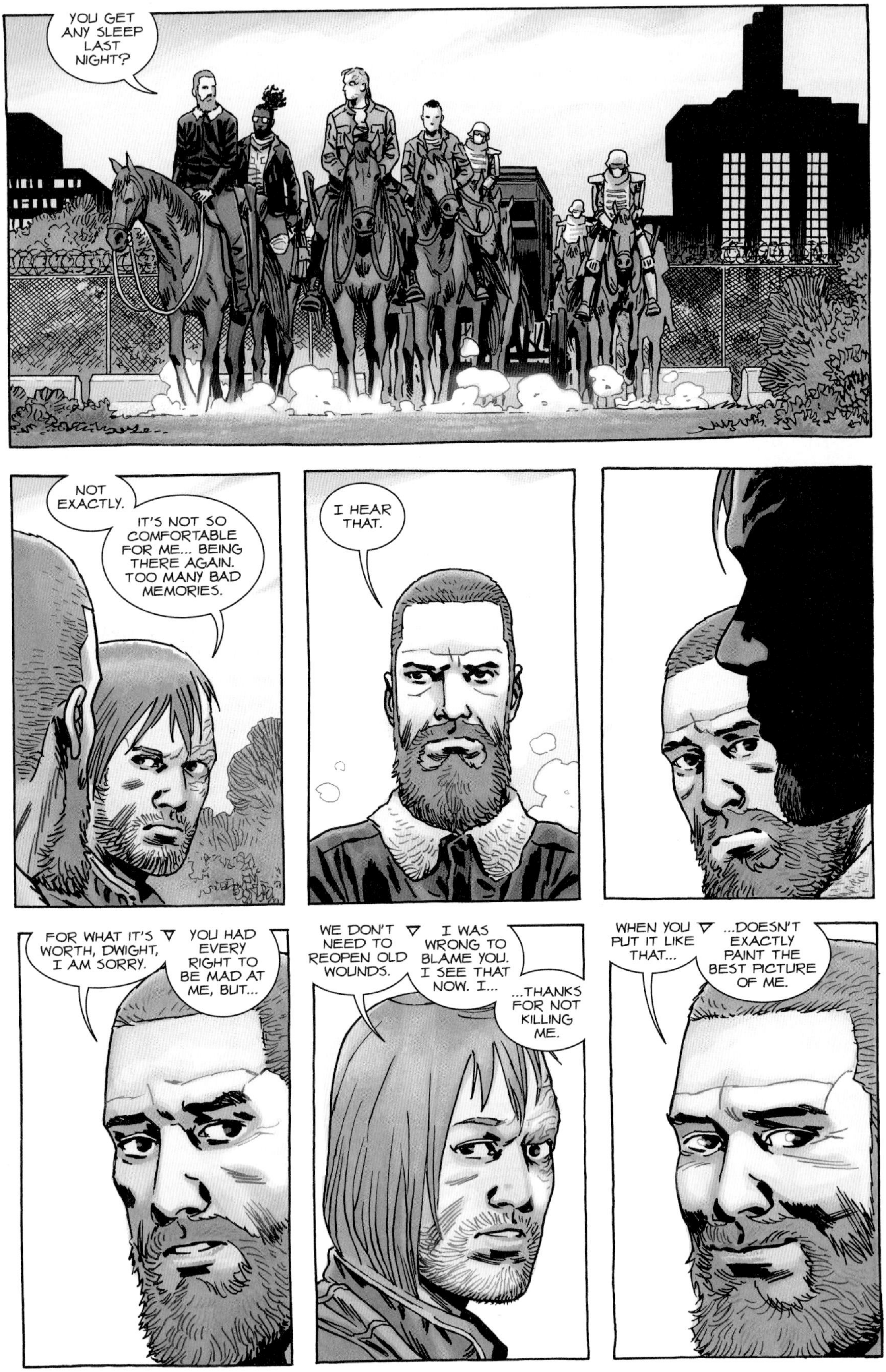

YOU GET ANY SLEEP LAST NIGHT?
NOT EXACTLY.
IT'S NOT SO COMFORTABLE FOR ME... BEING THERE AGAIN. TOO MANY BAD MEMORIES.
I HEAR THAT.
FOR WHAT IT'S WORTH, DWIGHT, I AM SORRY.
YOU HAD EVERY RIGHT TO BE MAD AT ME, BUT...
WE DON'T NEED TO REOPEN OLD WOUNDS.
I WAS WRONG TO BLAME YOU. I SEE THAT NOW. I...
...THANKS FOR NOT KILLING ME.
WHEN YOU PUT IT LIKE THAT...
...DOESN'T EXACTLY PAINT THE BEST PICTURE OF ME.

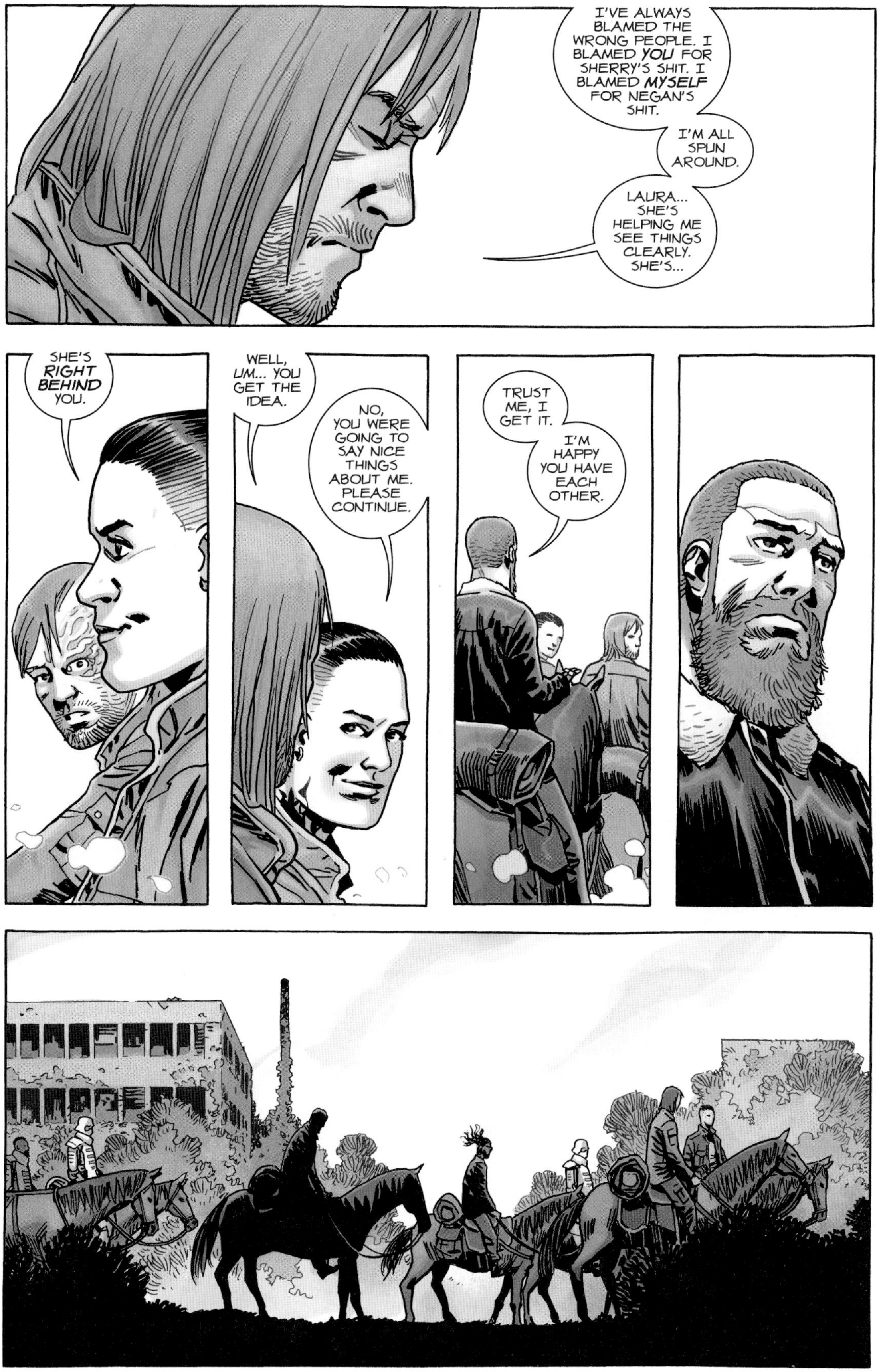
I'VE ALWAYS BLAMED THE WRONG PEOPLE. I BLAMED *YOU* FOR SHERRY'S SHIT. I BLAMED *MYSELF* FOR NEGAN'S SHIT.
I'M ALL SPUN AROUND.
LAURA... SHE'S HELPING ME SEE THINGS CLEARLY. SHE'S...
SHE'S *RIGHT BEHIND* YOU.
WELL, UM... YOU GET THE IDEA.
NO, YOU WERE GOING TO SAY NICE THINGS ABOUT ME. PLEASE CONTINUE.
TRUST ME, I GET IT.
I'M HAPPY YOU HAVE EACH OTHER.

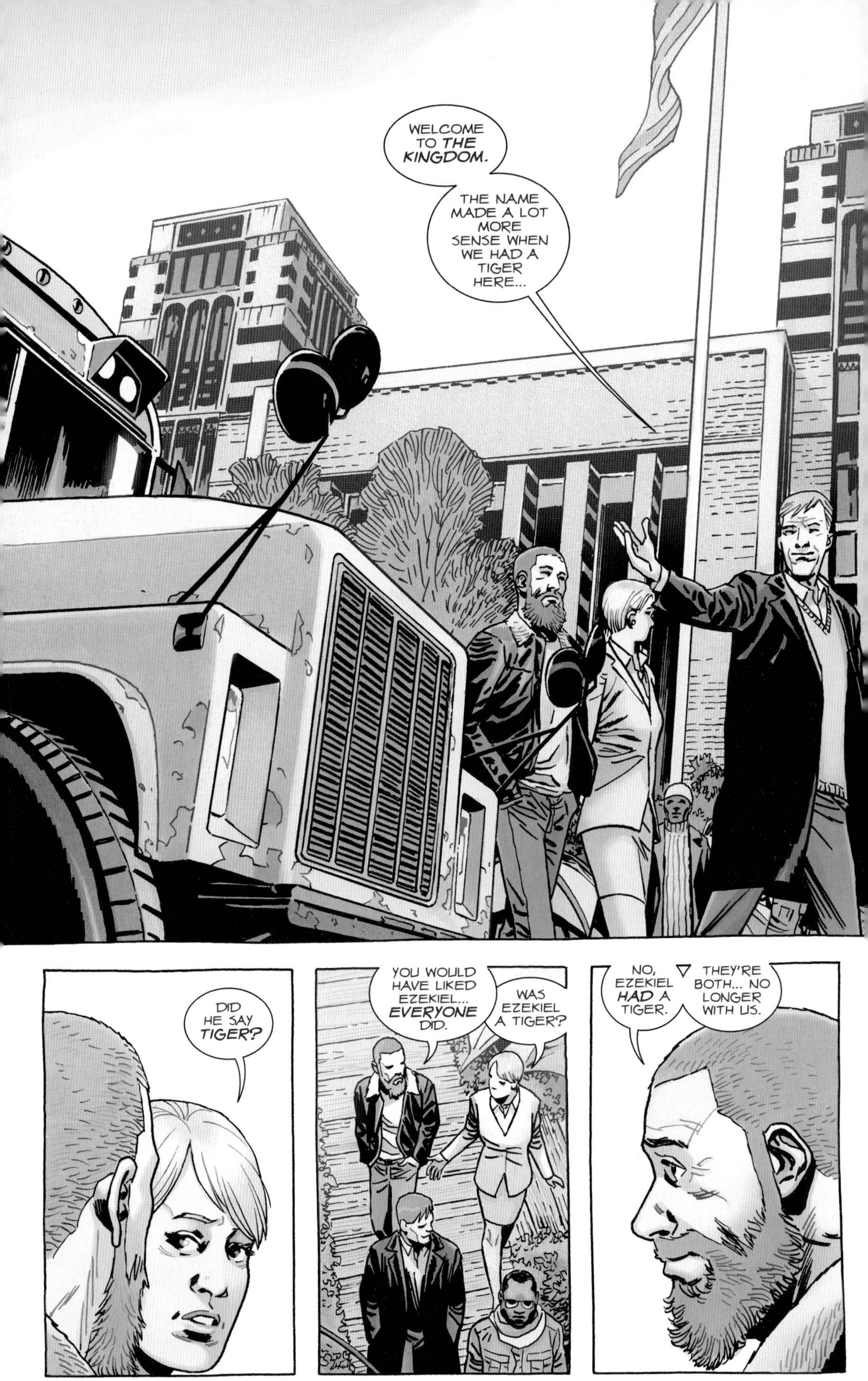
WELCOME TO THE KINGDOM.
THE NAME MADE A LOT MORE SENSE WHEN WE HAD A TIGER HERE...
DID HE SAY TIGER?
YOU WOULD HAVE LIKED EZEKIEL... EVERYONE DID.
WAS EZEKIEL A TIGER?
NO, EZEKIEL HAD A TIGER.
THEY'RE BOTH... NO LONGER WITH US.

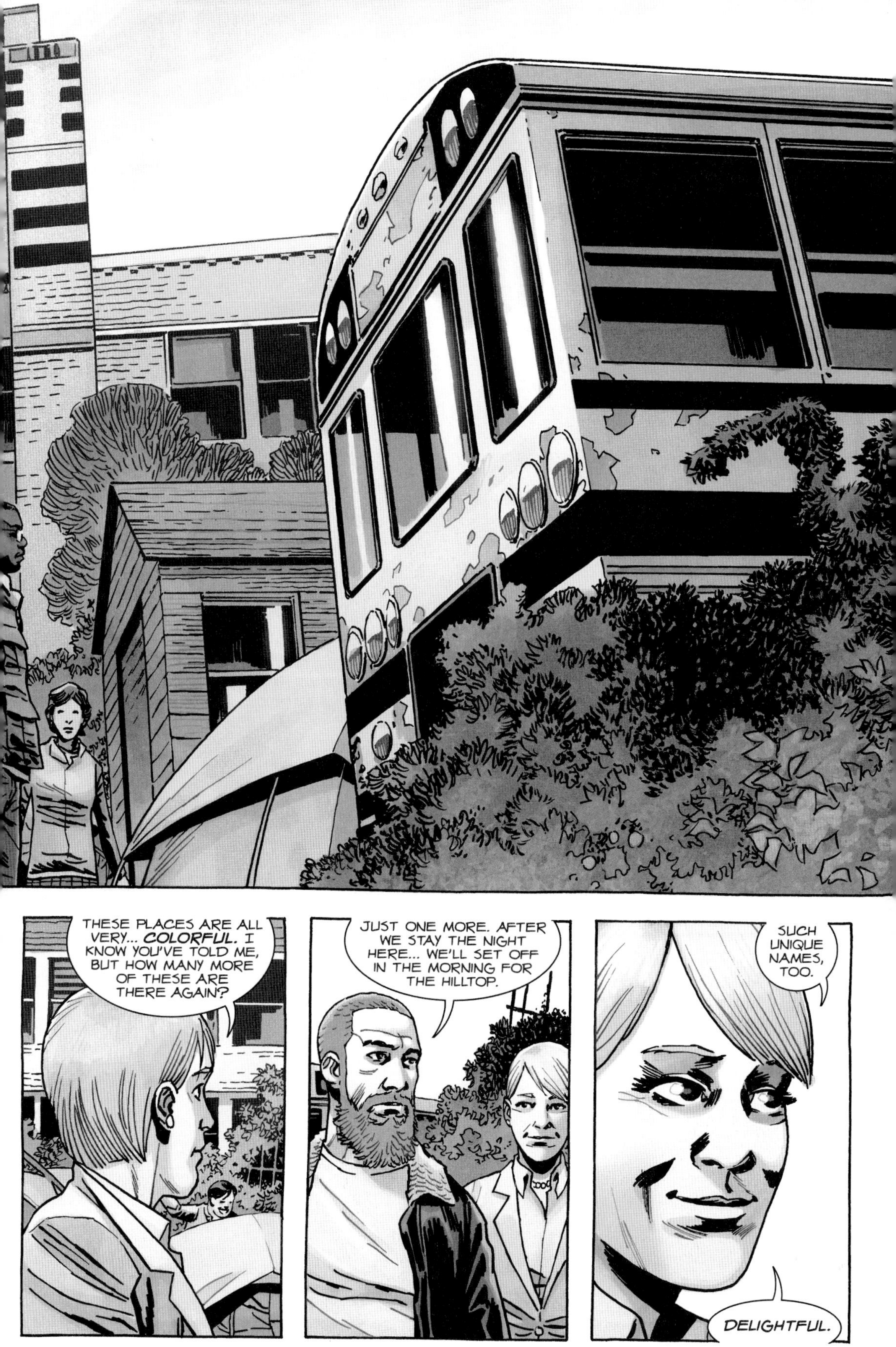
THESE PLACES ARE ALL VERY... COLORFUL. I KNOW YOU'VE TOLD ME, BUT HOW MANY MORE OF THESE ARE THERE AGAIN?
JUST ONE MORE. AFTER WE STAY THE NIGHT HERE... WE'LL SET OFF IN THE MORNING FOR THE HILLTOP.
SUCH UNIQUE NAMES, TOO.
DELIGHTFUL.

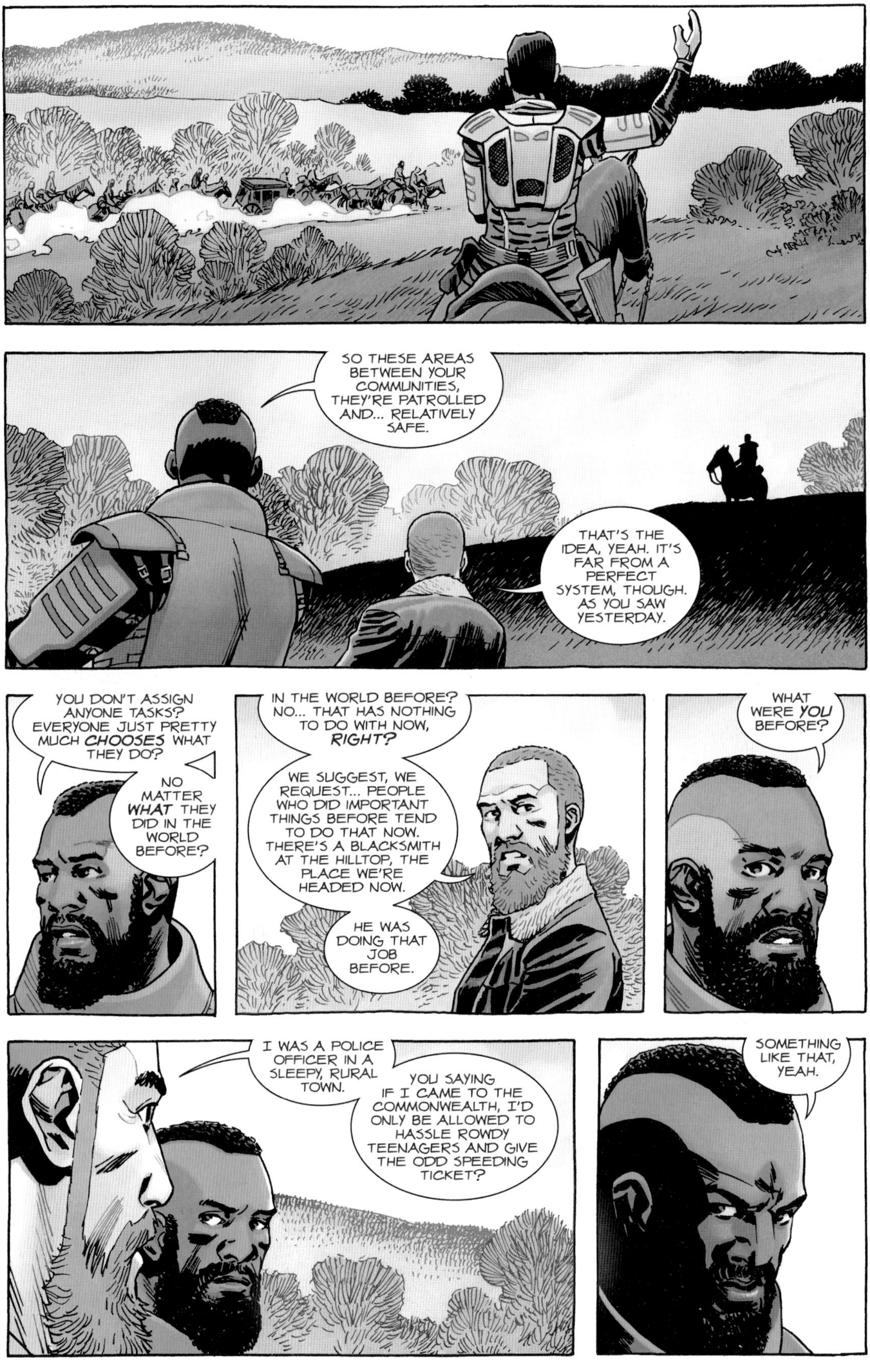
SO THESE AREAS BETWEEN YOUR COMMUNITIES, THEY'RE PATROLLED AND... RELATIVELY SAFE.
THAT'S THE IDEA, YEAH. IT'S FAR FROM A PERFECT SYSTEM, THOUGH. AS YOU SAW YESTERDAY.
YOU DON'T ASSIGN ANYONE TASKS? EVERYONE JUST PRETTY MUCH CHOOSES WHAT THEY DO?
NO MATTER WHAT THEY DID IN THE WORLD BEFORE?
IN THE WORLD BEFORE? NO... THAT HAS NOTHING TO DO WITH NOW, RIGHT?
WE SUGGEST, WE REQUEST... PEOPLE WHO DID IMPORTANT THINGS BEFORE TEND TO DO THAT NOW. THERE'S A BLACKSMITH AT THE HILLTOP, THE PLACE WE'RE HEADED NOW.
HE WAS DOING THAT JOB BEFORE.
WHAT WERE YOU BEFORE?
I WAS A POLICE OFFICER IN A SLEEPY, RURAL TOWN.
YOU SAYING IF I CAME TO THE COMMONWEALTH, I'D ONLY BE ALLOWED TO HASSLE ROWDY TEENAGERS AND GIVE THE ODD SPEEDING TICKET?
SOMETHING LIKE THAT, YEAH.

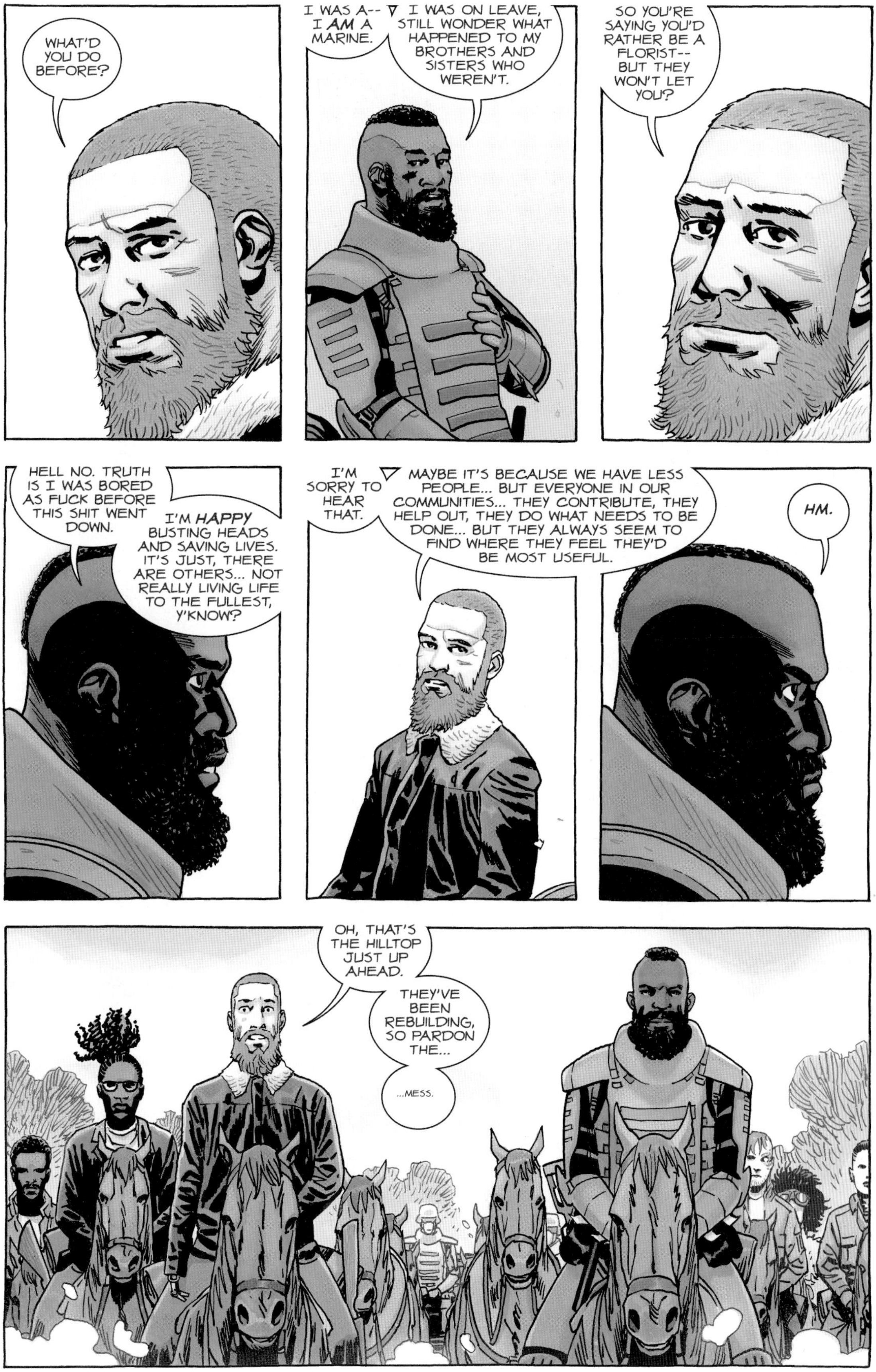
WHAT'D YOU DO BEFORE?
I WAS A-- I AM A MARINE.
I WAS ON LEAVE, STILL WONDER WHAT HAPPENED TO MY BROTHERS AND SISTERS WHO WEREN'T.
SO YOU'RE SAYING YOU'D RATHER BE A FLORIST-- BUT THEY WON'T LET YOU?
HELL NO. TRUTH IS I WAS BORED AS FUCK BEFORE THIS SHIT WENT DOWN.
I'M HAPPY BUSTING HEADS AND SAVING LIVES. IT'S JUST, THERE ARE OTHERS... NOT REALLY LIVING LIFE TO THE FULLEST, Y'KNOW?
I'M SORRY TO HEAR THAT.
MAYBE IT'S BECAUSE WE HAVE LESS PEOPLE... BUT EVERYONE IN OUR COMMUNITIES... THEY CONTRIBUTE, THEY HELP OUT, THEY DO WHAT NEEDS TO BE DONE... BUT THEY ALWAYS SEEM TO FIND WHERE THEY FEEL THEY'D BE MOST USEFUL.
HM.
OH, THAT'S THE HILLTOP JUST UP AHEAD.
THEY'VE BEEN REBUILDING, SO PARDON THE...
...MESS.

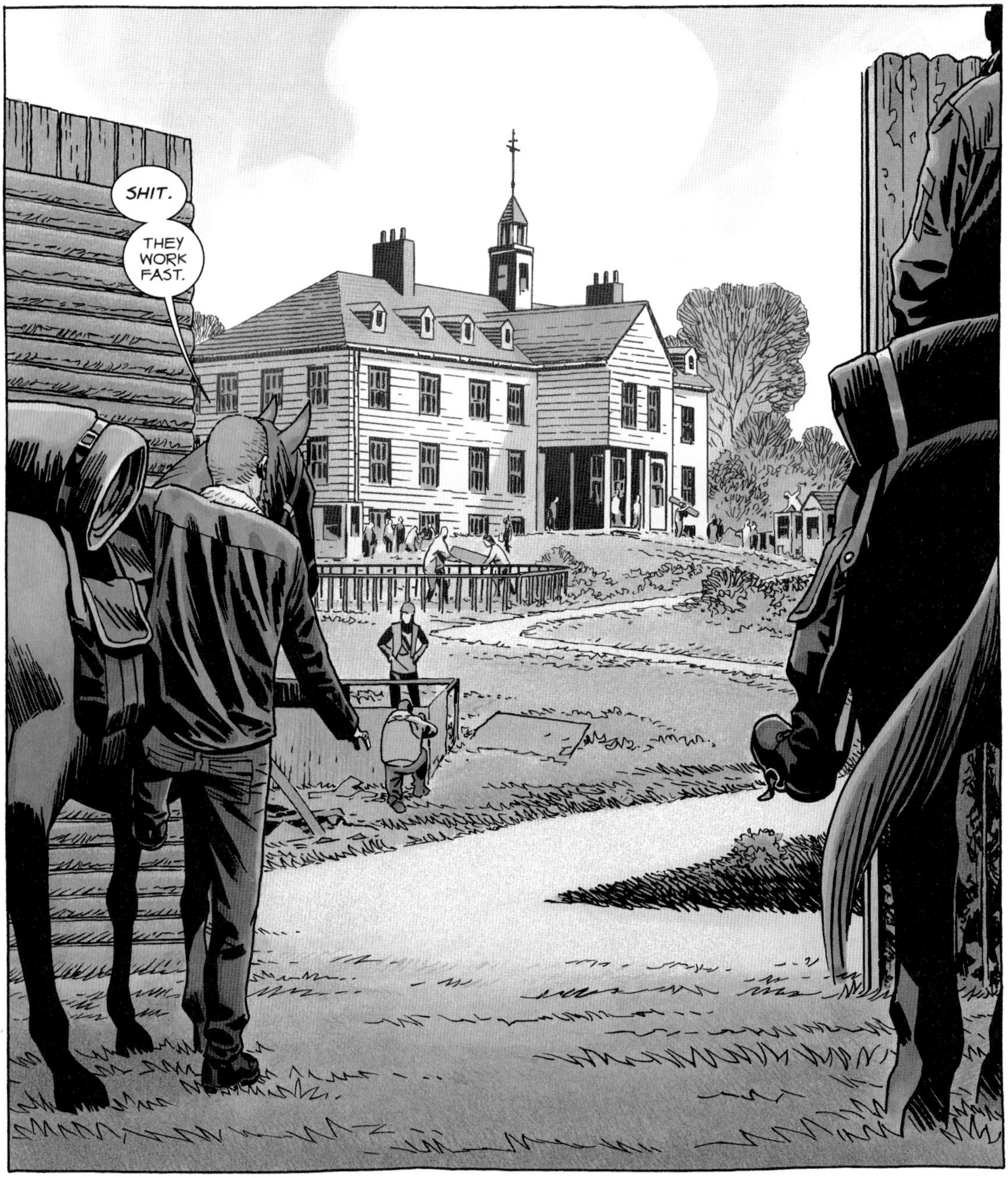
SHIT.
THEY WORK FAST.

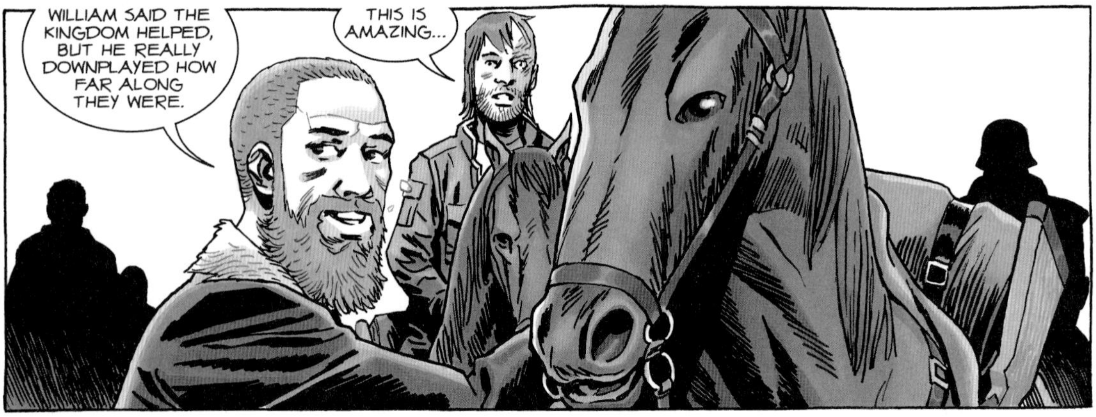
WILLIAM SAID THE KINGDOM HELPED, BUT HE REALLY DOWNPLAYED HOW FAR ALONG THEY WERE.
THIS IS AMAZING...

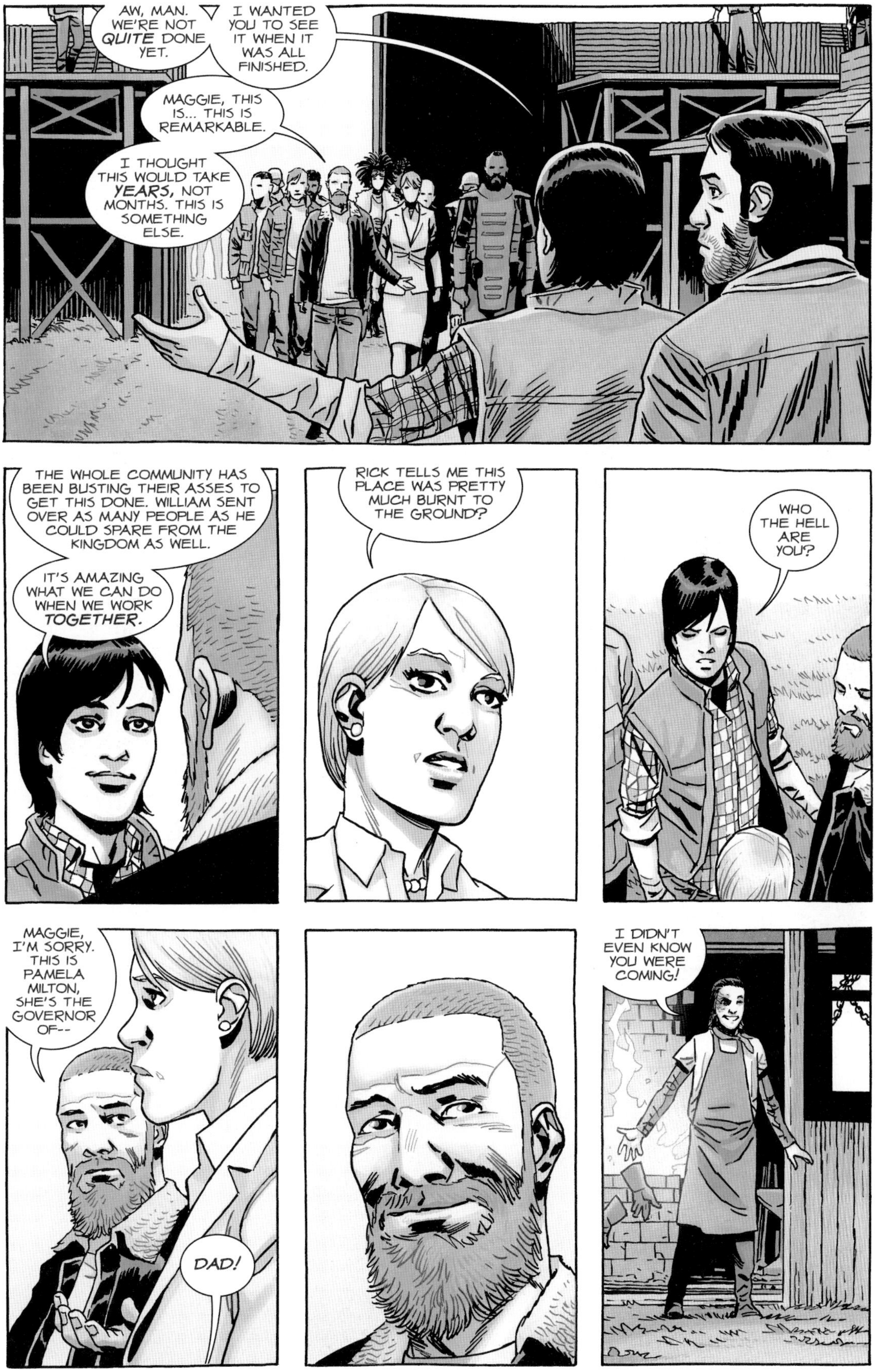
AW, MAN. WE'RE NOT QUITE DONE YET.
I WANTED YOU TO SEE IT WHEN IT WAS ALL FINISHED.
MAGGIE, THIS IS... THIS IS REMARKABLE.
I THOUGHT THIS WOULD TAKE YEARS, NOT MONTHS. THIS IS SOMETHING ELSE.
THE WHOLE COMMUNITY HAS BEEN BUSTING THEIR ASSES TO GET THIS DONE. WILLIAM SENT OVER AS MANY PEOPLE AS HE COULD SPARE FROM THE KINGDOM AS WELL.
IT'S AMAZING WHAT WE CAN DO WHEN WE WORK TOGETHER.
RICK TELLS ME THIS PLACE WAS PRETTY MUCH BURNT TO THE GROUND?
WHO THE HELL ARE YOU?
MAGGIE, I'M SORRY. THIS IS PAMELA MILTON, SHE'S THE GOVERNOR OF--
DAD!
I DIDN'T EVEN KNOW YOU WERE COMING!

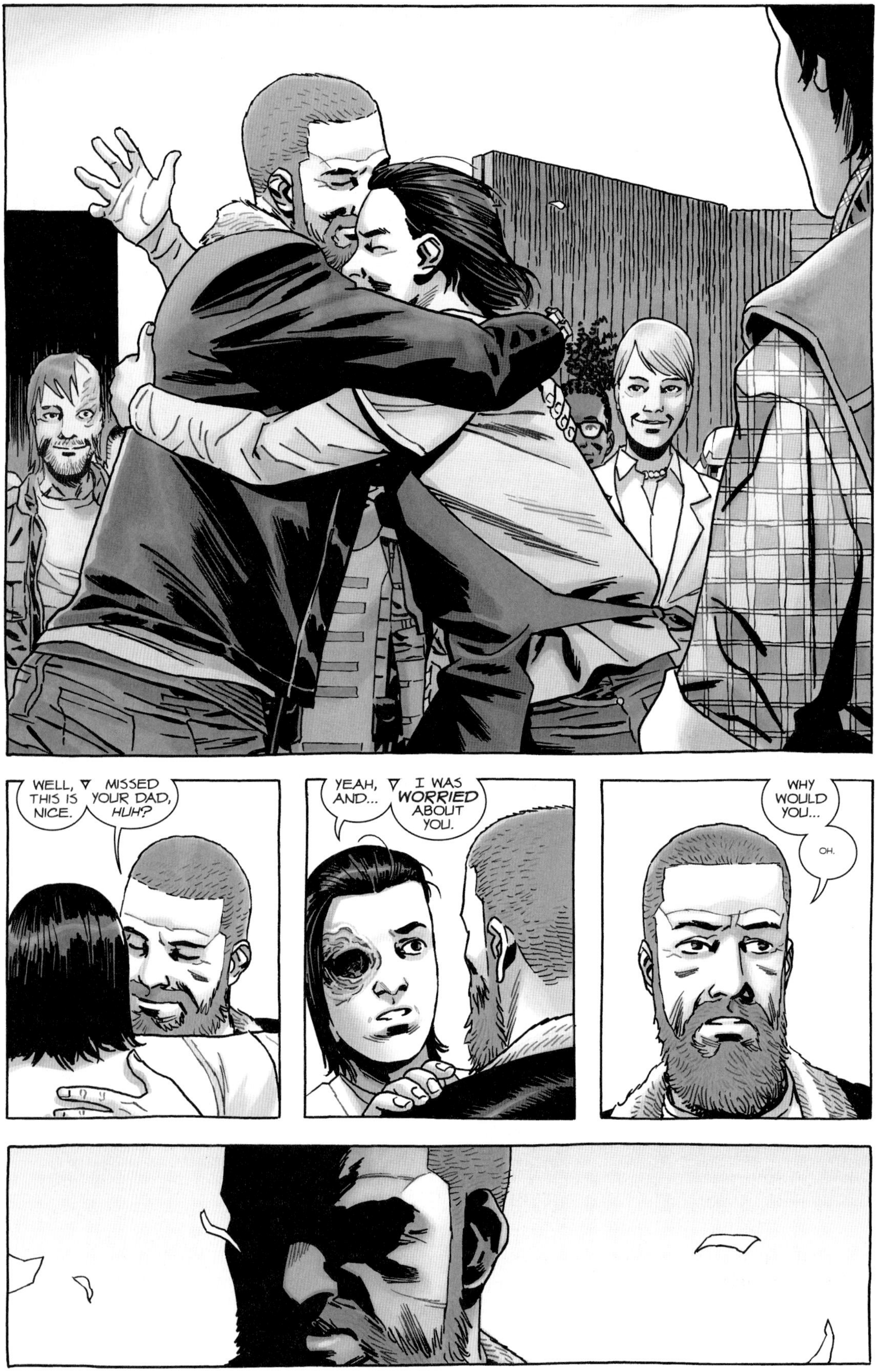
WELL, THIS IS NICE.
MISSED YOUR DAD, *HUH?*
YEAH, AND...
I WAS *WORRIED* ABOUT YOU.
WHY WOULD YOU...
OH.

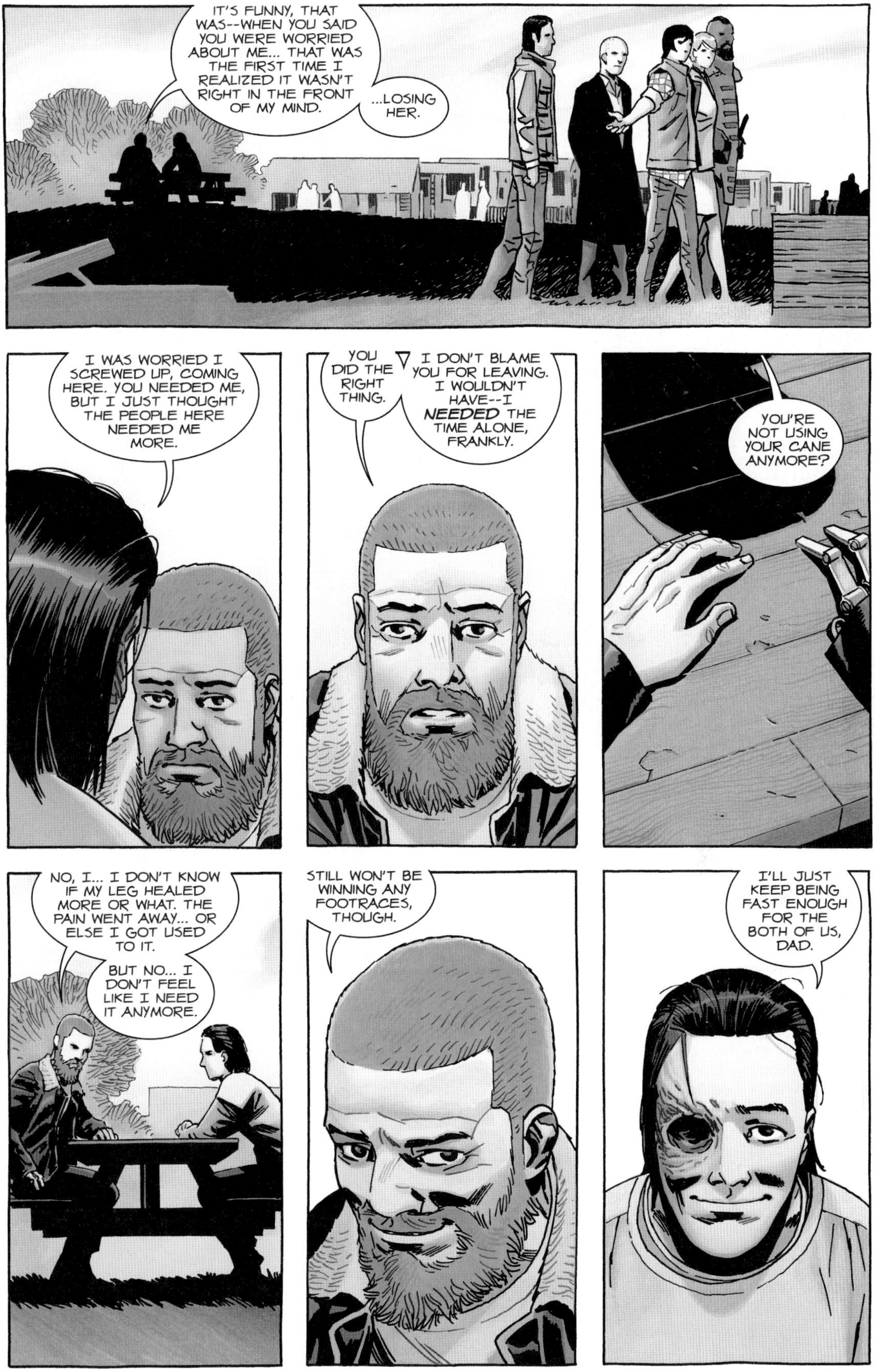

IT'S FUNNY, THAT WAS--WHEN YOU SAID YOU WERE WORRIED ABOUT ME... THAT WAS THE FIRST TIME I REALIZED IT WASN'T RIGHT IN THE FRONT OF MY MIND.
...LOSING HER.
I WAS WORRIED I SCREWED UP, COMING HERE. YOU NEEDED ME, BUT I JUST THOUGHT THE PEOPLE HERE NEEDED ME MORE.
YOU DID THE RIGHT THING.
I DON'T BLAME YOU FOR LEAVING. I WOULDN'T HAVE--I *NEEDED* THE TIME ALONE, FRANKLY.
YOU'RE NOT USING YOUR CANE ANYMORE?
NO, I... I DON'T KNOW IF MY LEG HEALED MORE OR WHAT. THE PAIN WENT AWAY... OR ELSE I GOT USED TO IT.
BUT NO... I DON'T FEEL LIKE I NEED IT ANYMORE.
STILL WON'T BE WINNING ANY FOOTRACES, THOUGH.
I'LL JUST KEEP BEING FAST ENOUGH FOR THE BOTH OF US, DAD.

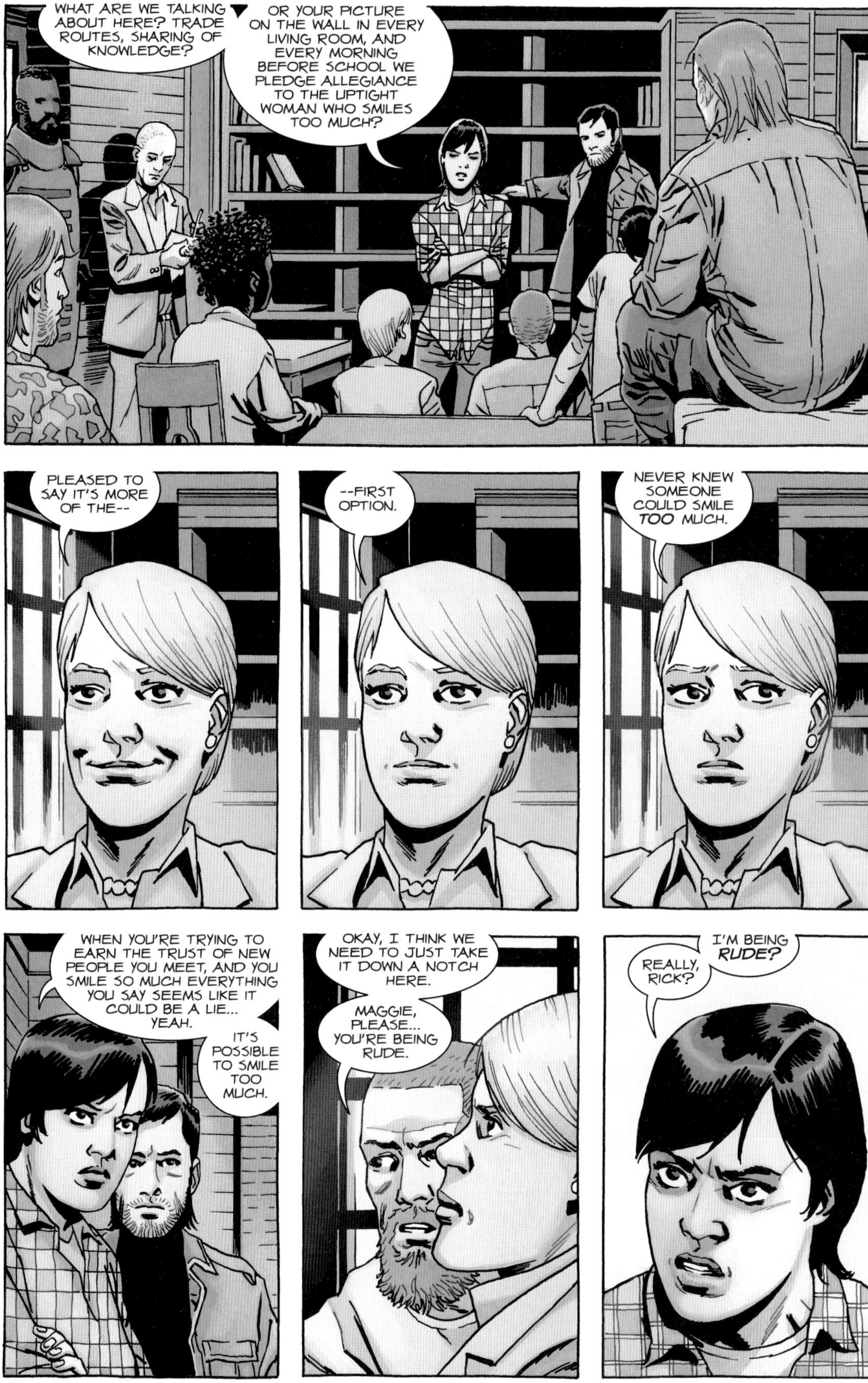
WHAT ARE WE TALKING ABOUT HERE? TRADE ROUTES, SHARING OF KNOWLEDGE?
OR YOUR PICTURE ON THE WALL IN EVERY LIVING ROOM, AND EVERY MORNING BEFORE SCHOOL WE PLEDGE ALLEGIANCE TO THE UPTIGHT WOMAN WHO SMILES TOO MUCH?
PLEASED TO SAY IT'S MORE OF THE--
--FIRST OPTION.
NEVER KNEW SOMEONE COULD SMILE *TOO* MUCH.
WHEN YOU'RE TRYING TO EARN THE TRUST OF NEW PEOPLE YOU MEET, AND YOU SMILE SO MUCH EVERYTHING YOU SAY SEEMS LIKE IT COULD BE A LIE... YEAH.
IT'S POSSIBLE TO SMILE TOO MUCH.
OKAY, I THINK WE NEED TO JUST TAKE IT DOWN A NOTCH HERE.
MAGGIE, PLEASE... YOU'RE BEING RUDE.
I'M BEING ***RUDE?***
REALLY, RICK?

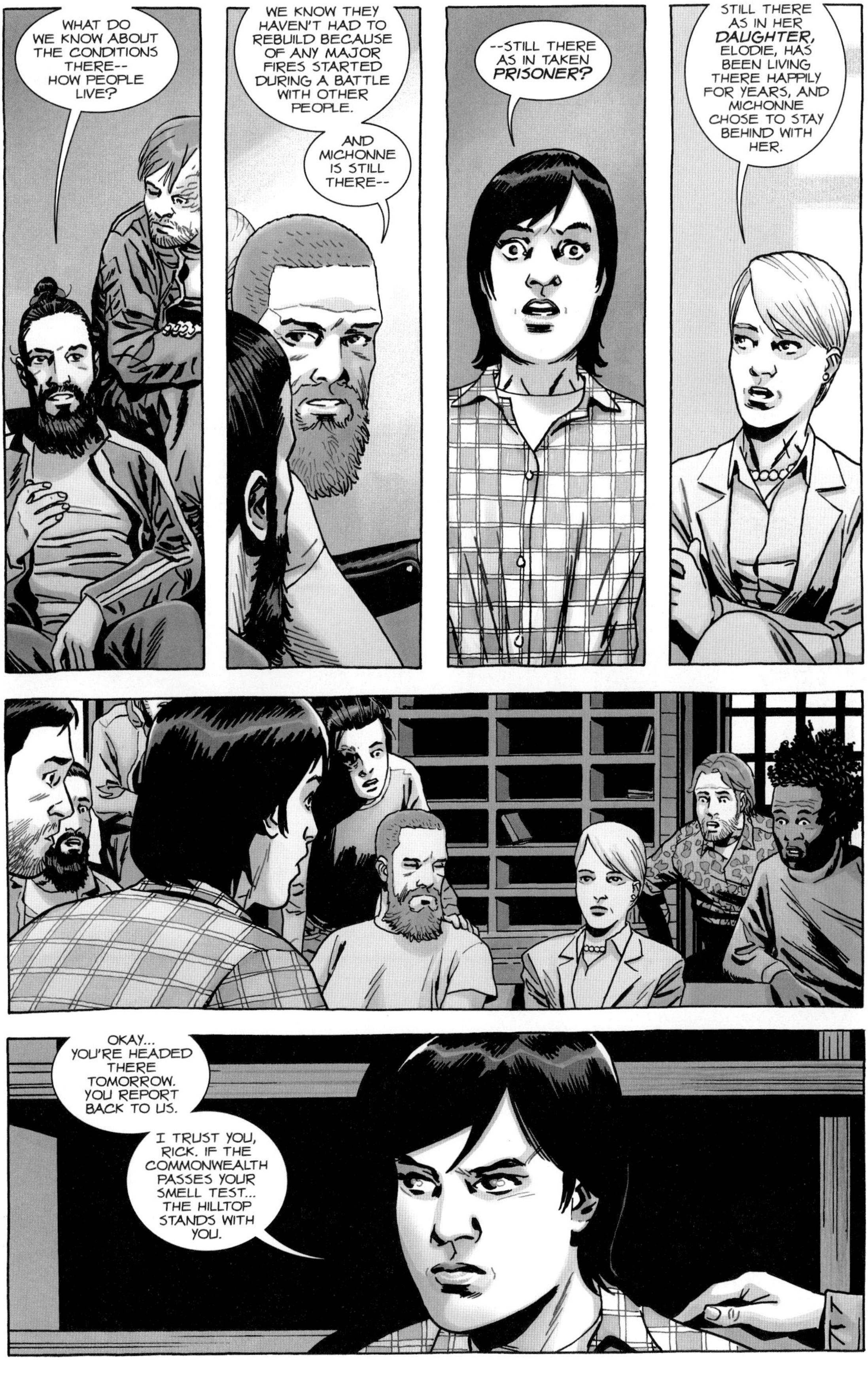
WHAT DO WE KNOW ABOUT THE CONDITIONS THERE-- HOW PEOPLE LIVE?
WE KNOW THEY HAVEN'T HAD TO REBUILD BECAUSE OF ANY MAJOR FIRES STARTED DURING A BATTLE WITH OTHER PEOPLE.
AND MICHONNE IS STILL THERE--
--STILL THERE AS IN TAKEN PRISONER?
STILL THERE AS IN HER DAUGHTER, ELODIE, HAS BEEN LIVING THERE HAPPILY FOR YEARS, AND MICHONNE CHOSE TO STAY BEHIND WITH HER.
OKAY... YOU'RE HEADED THERE TOMORROW. YOU REPORT BACK TO US.
I TRUST YOU, RICK. IF THE COMMONWEALTH PASSES YOUR SMELL TEST... THE HILLTOP STANDS WITH YOU.

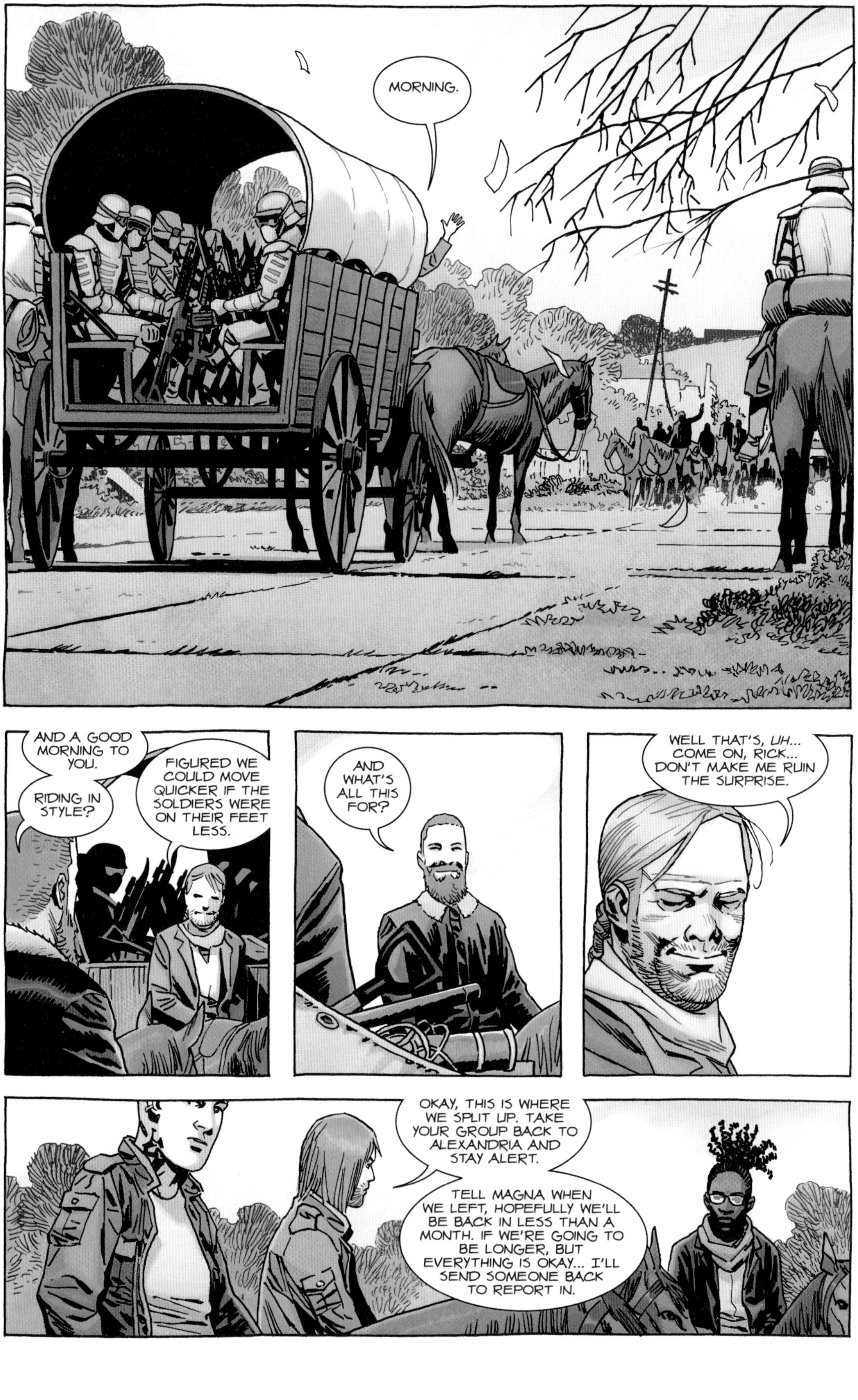
MORNING.
AND A GOOD MORNING TO YOU.
RIDING IN STYLE?
FIGURED WE COULD MOVE QUICKER IF THE SOLDIERS WERE ON THEIR FEET LESS.
AND WHAT'S ALL THIS FOR?
WELL THAT'S, *UH*... COME ON, RICK... DON'T MAKE ME RUIN THE SURPRISE.
OKAY, THIS IS WHERE WE SPLIT UP. TAKE YOUR GROUP BACK TO ALEXANDRIA AND STAY ALERT.
TELL MAGNA WHEN WE LEFT, HOPEFULLY WE'LL BE BACK IN LESS THAN A MONTH. IF WE'RE GOING TO BE LONGER, BUT EVERYTHING IS OKAY... I'LL SEND SOMEONE BACK TO REPORT IN.

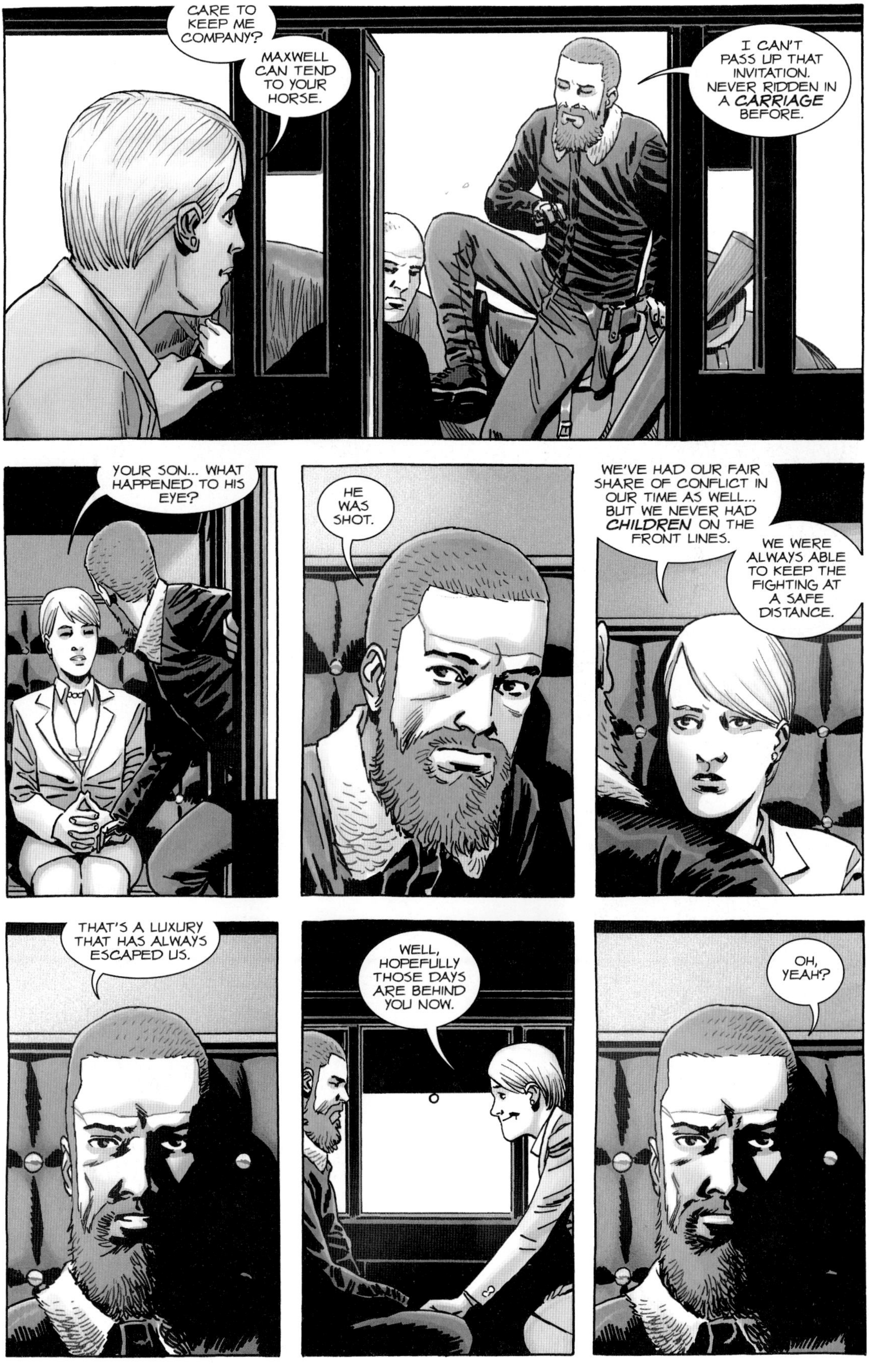
CARE TO KEEP ME COMPANY?
MAXWELL CAN TEND TO YOUR HORSE.
I CAN'T PASS UP THAT INVITATION. NEVER RIDDEN IN A *CARRIAGE* BEFORE.
YOUR SON... WHAT HAPPENED TO HIS EYE?
HE WAS SHOT.
WE'VE HAD OUR FAIR SHARE OF CONFLICT IN OUR TIME AS WELL... BUT WE NEVER HAD ***CHILDREN*** ON THE FRONT LINES.
WE WERE ALWAYS ABLE TO KEEP THE FIGHTING AT A SAFE DISTANCE.
THAT'S A LUXURY THAT HAS ALWAYS ESCAPED US.
WELL, HOPEFULLY THOSE DAYS ARE BEHIND YOU NOW.
OH, YEAH?

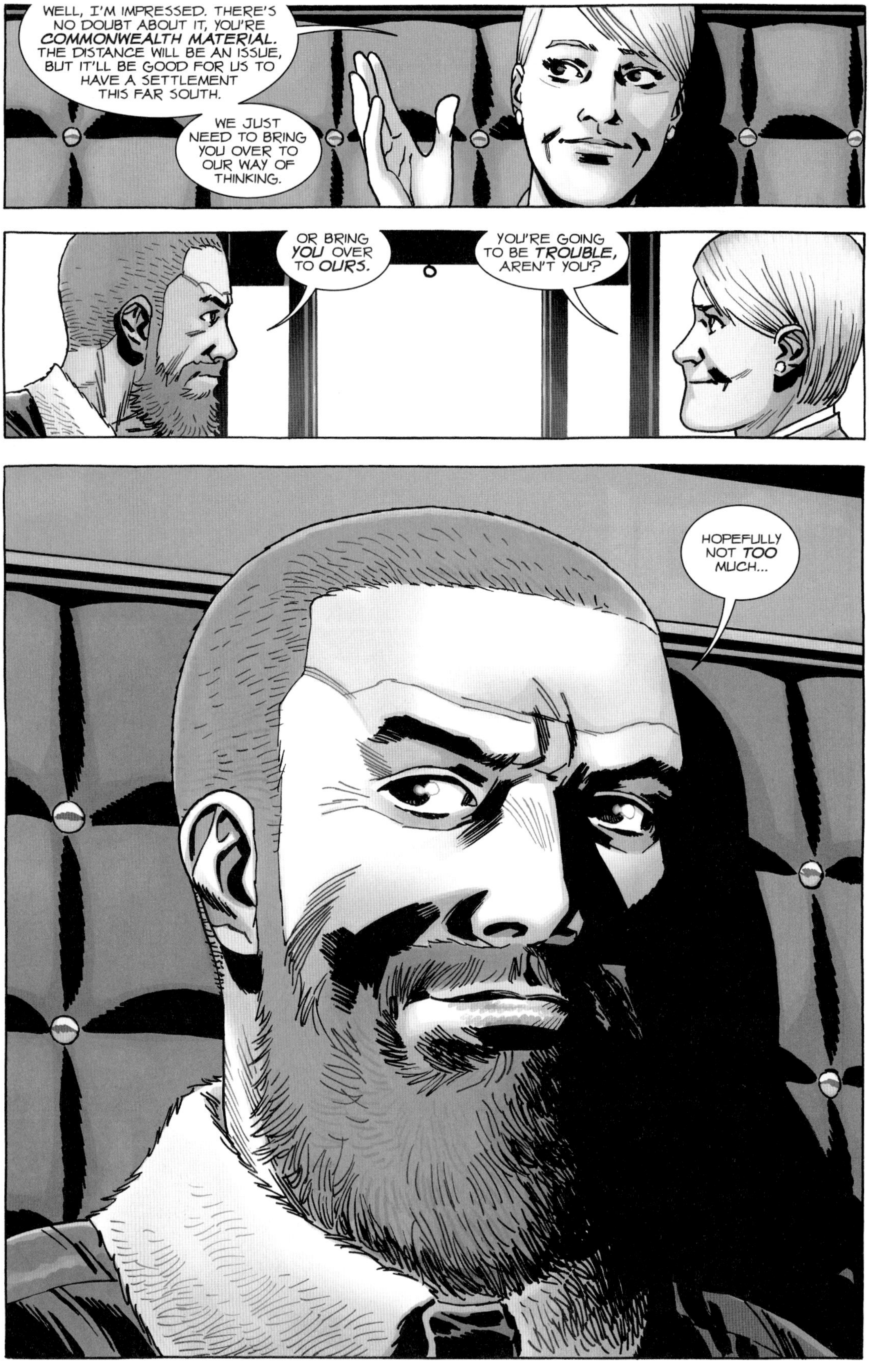
WELL, I'M IMPRESSED. THERE'S NO DOUBT ABOUT IT, YOU'RE COMMONWEALTH MATERIAL. THE DISTANCE WILL BE AN ISSUE, BUT IT'LL BE GOOD FOR US TO HAVE A SETTLEMENT THIS FAR SOUTH.
WE JUST NEED TO BRING YOU OVER TO OUR WAY OF THINKING.
OR BRING YOU OVER TO OURS.
YOU'RE GOING TO BE TROUBLE, AREN'T YOU?
HOPEFULLY NOT TOO MUCH...

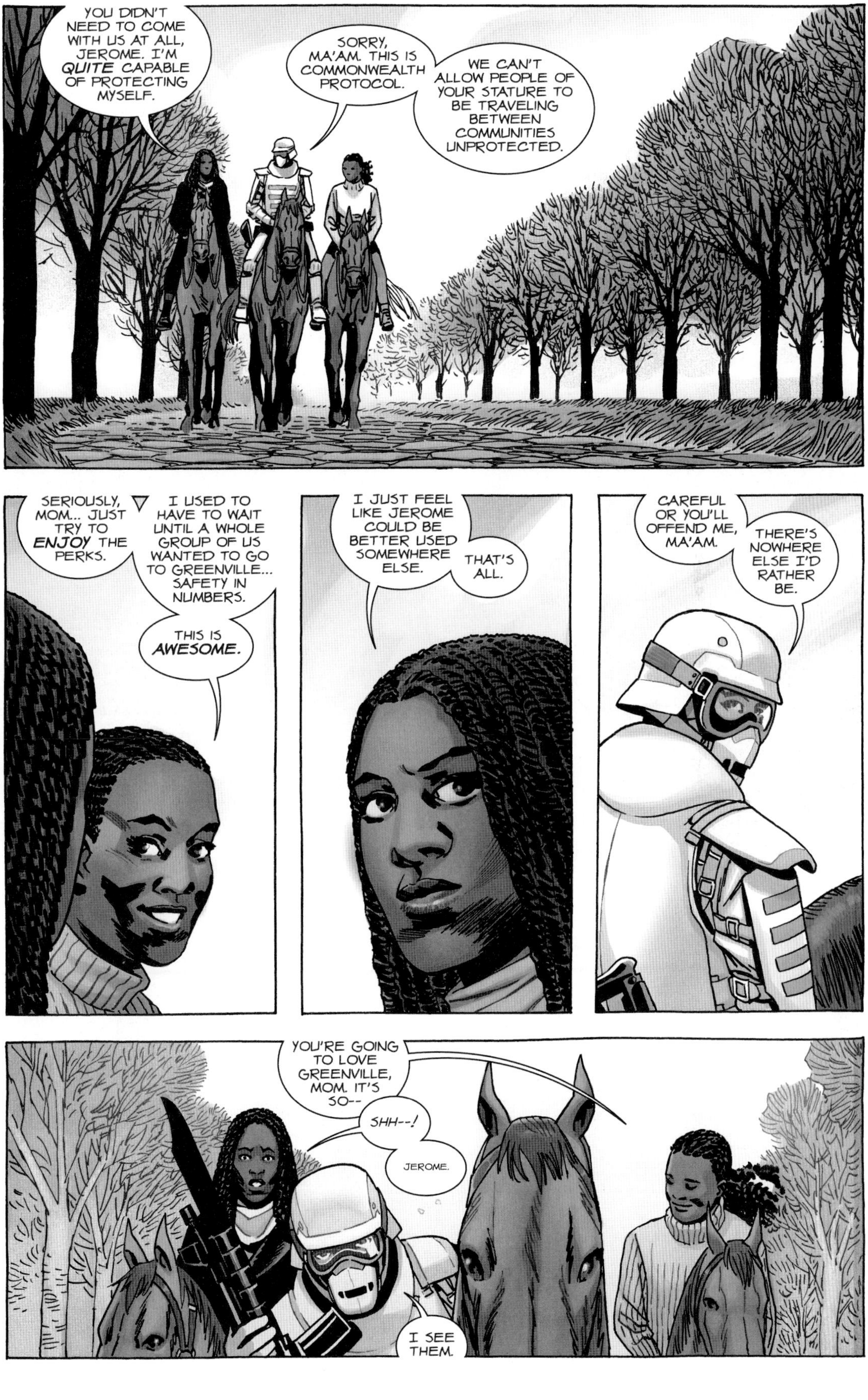
YOU DIDN'T NEED TO COME WITH US AT ALL, JEROME. I'M QUITE CAPABLE OF PROTECTING MYSELF.
SORRY, MA'AM. THIS IS COMMONWEALTH PROTOCOL.
WE CAN'T ALLOW PEOPLE OF YOUR STATURE TO BE TRAVELING BETWEEN COMMUNITIES UNPROTECTED.
SERIOUSLY, MOM... JUST TRY TO ENJOY THE PERKS.
I USED TO HAVE TO WAIT UNTIL A WHOLE GROUP OF US WANTED TO GO TO GREENVILLE... SAFETY IN NUMBERS.
THIS IS AWESOME.
I JUST FEEL LIKE JEROME COULD BE BETTER USED SOMEWHERE ELSE.
THAT'S ALL.
CAREFUL OR YOU'LL OFFEND ME, MA'AM.
THERE'S NOWHERE ELSE I'D RATHER BE.
YOU'RE GOING TO LOVE GREENVILLE, MOM. IT'S SO--
SHH--!
JEROME.
I SEE THEM.

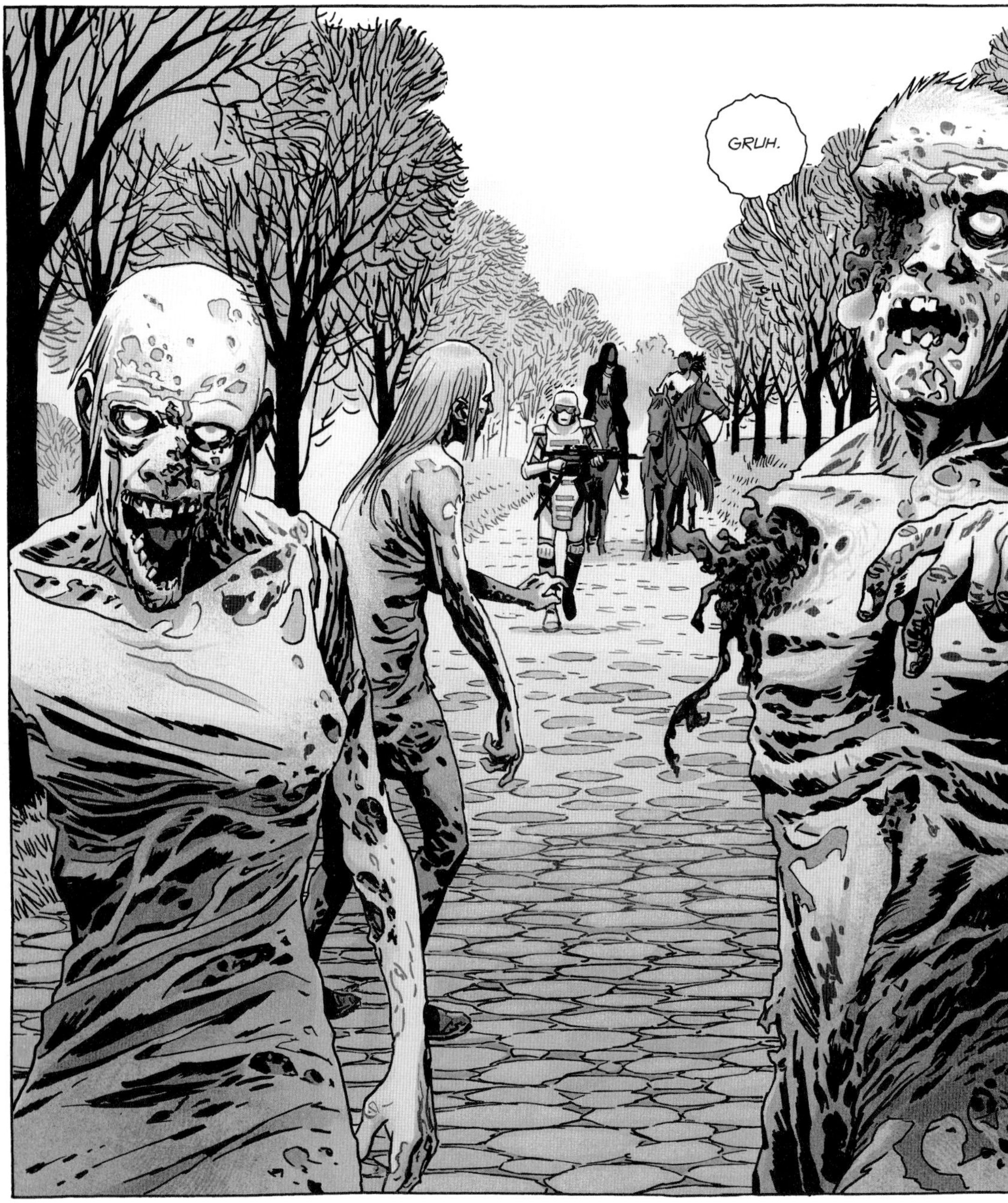
GRUH.

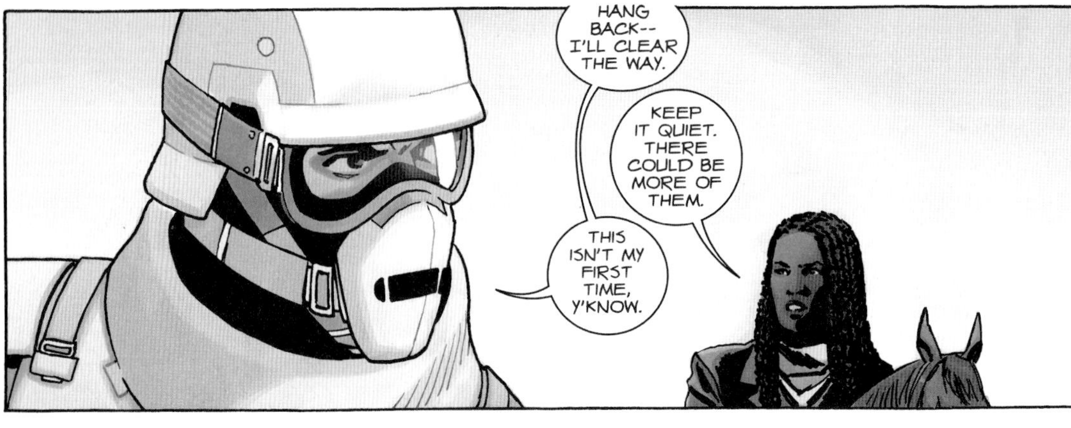
HANG BACK-- I'LL CLEAR THE WAY.
KEEP IT QUIET. THERE COULD BE MORE OF THEM.
THIS ISN'T MY FIRST TIME, Y'KNOW.

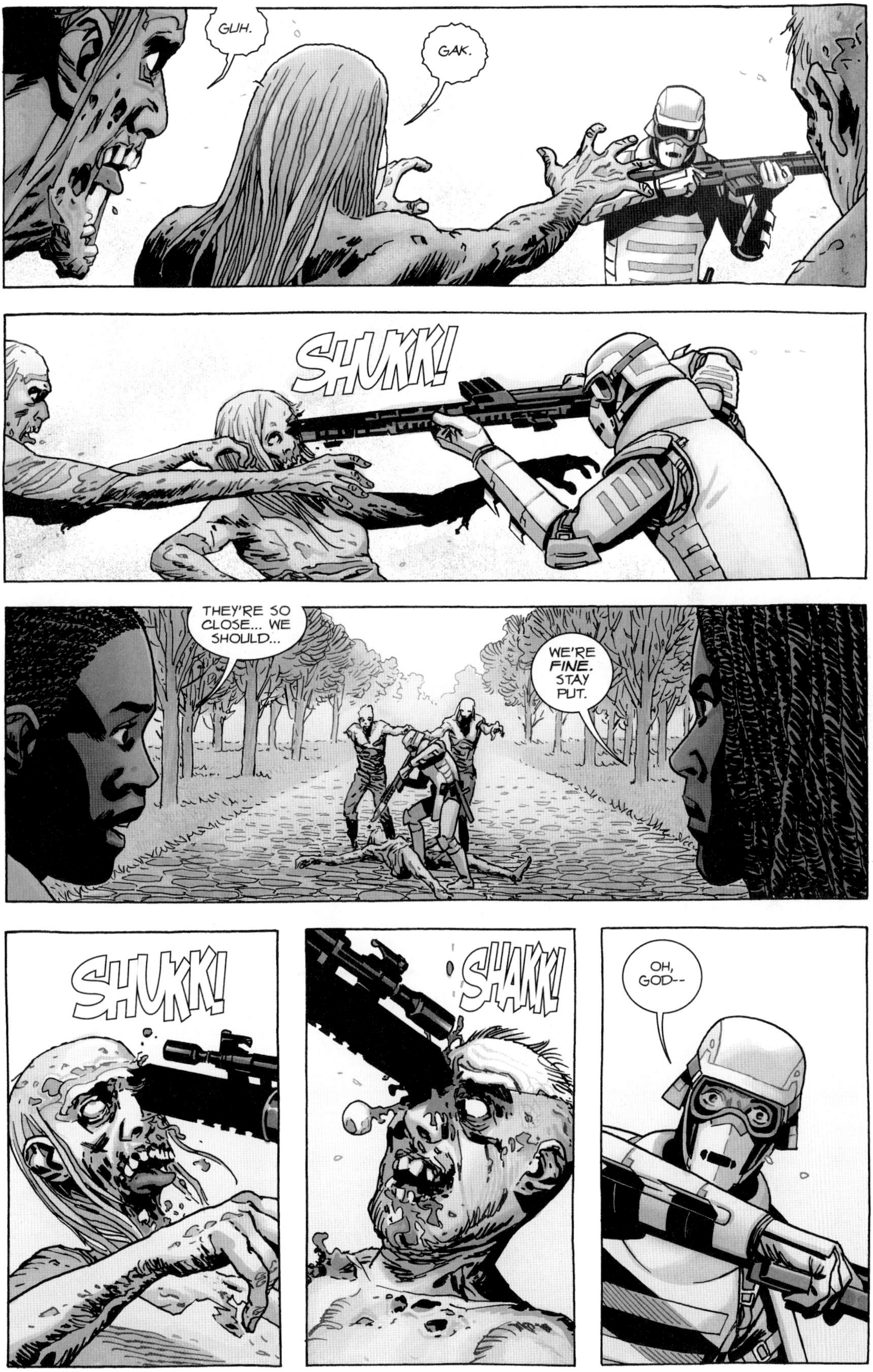
GUH.
GAK.
SHUKK!
THEY'RE SO CLOSE... WE SHOULD...
WE'RE *FINE.* STAY PUT.
SHUKK!
SHAKK!
OH, GOD--

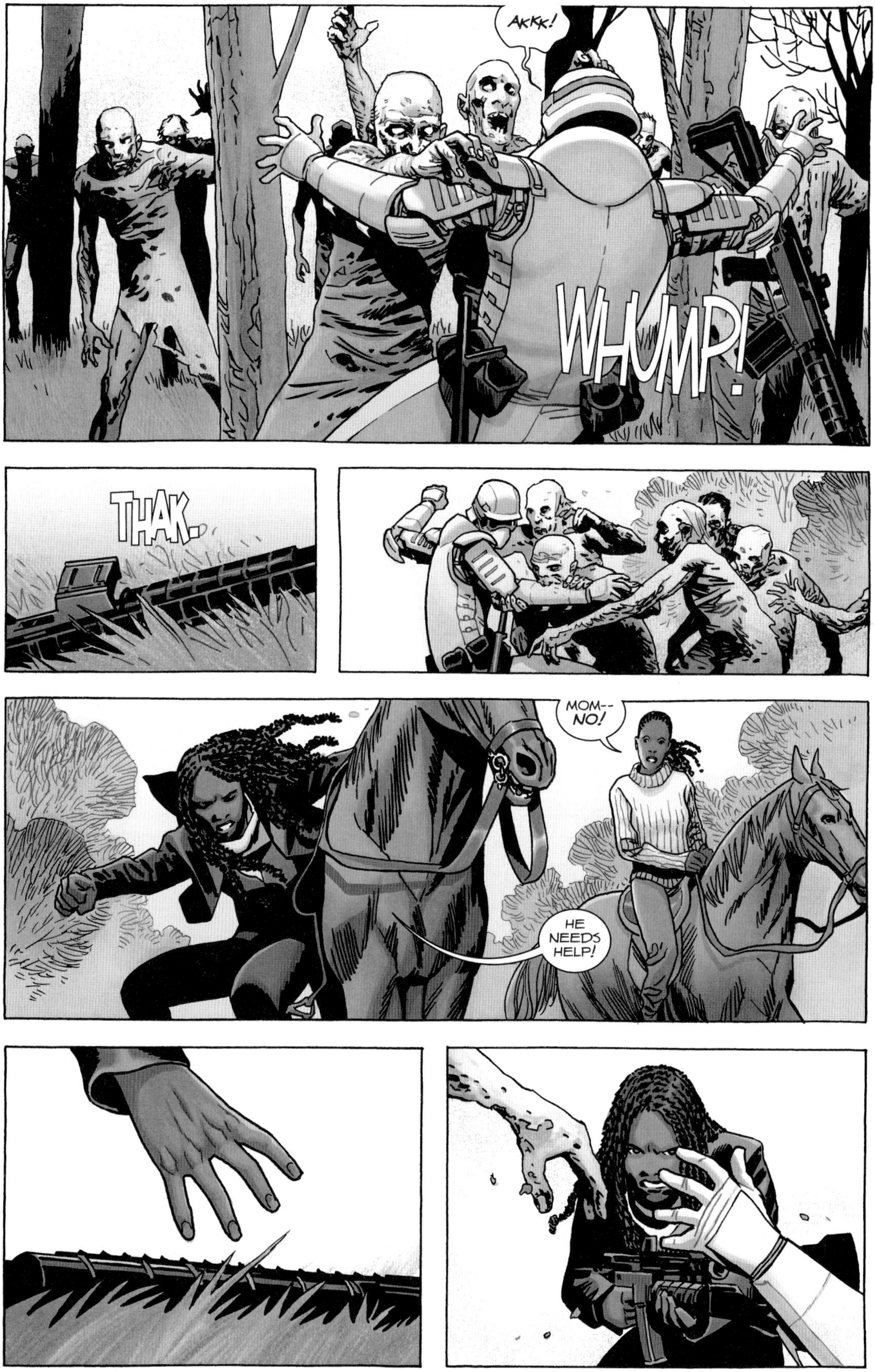
AKKK!
WHUMP!
THAK.
MOM--
NO!
HE NEEDS HELP!

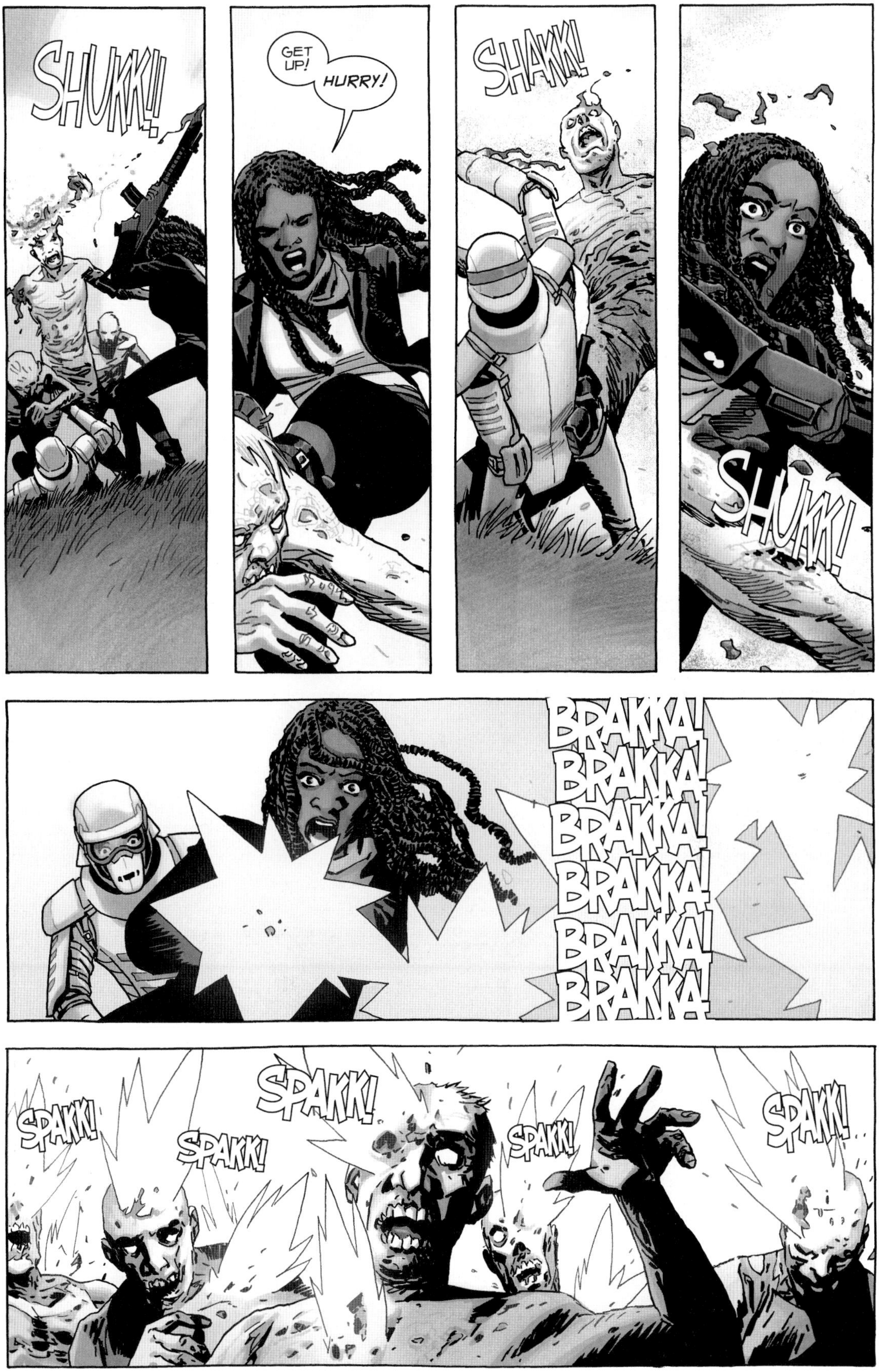
SHUKK!!
GET UP!
HURRY!
SHAKK!
SHUKK!
BRAKKA!
BRAKKA!
BRAKKA!
BRAKKA!
BRAKKA!
BRAKKA!
SPAKK!
SPAKK!
SPAKK!
SPAKK!
SPAKK!

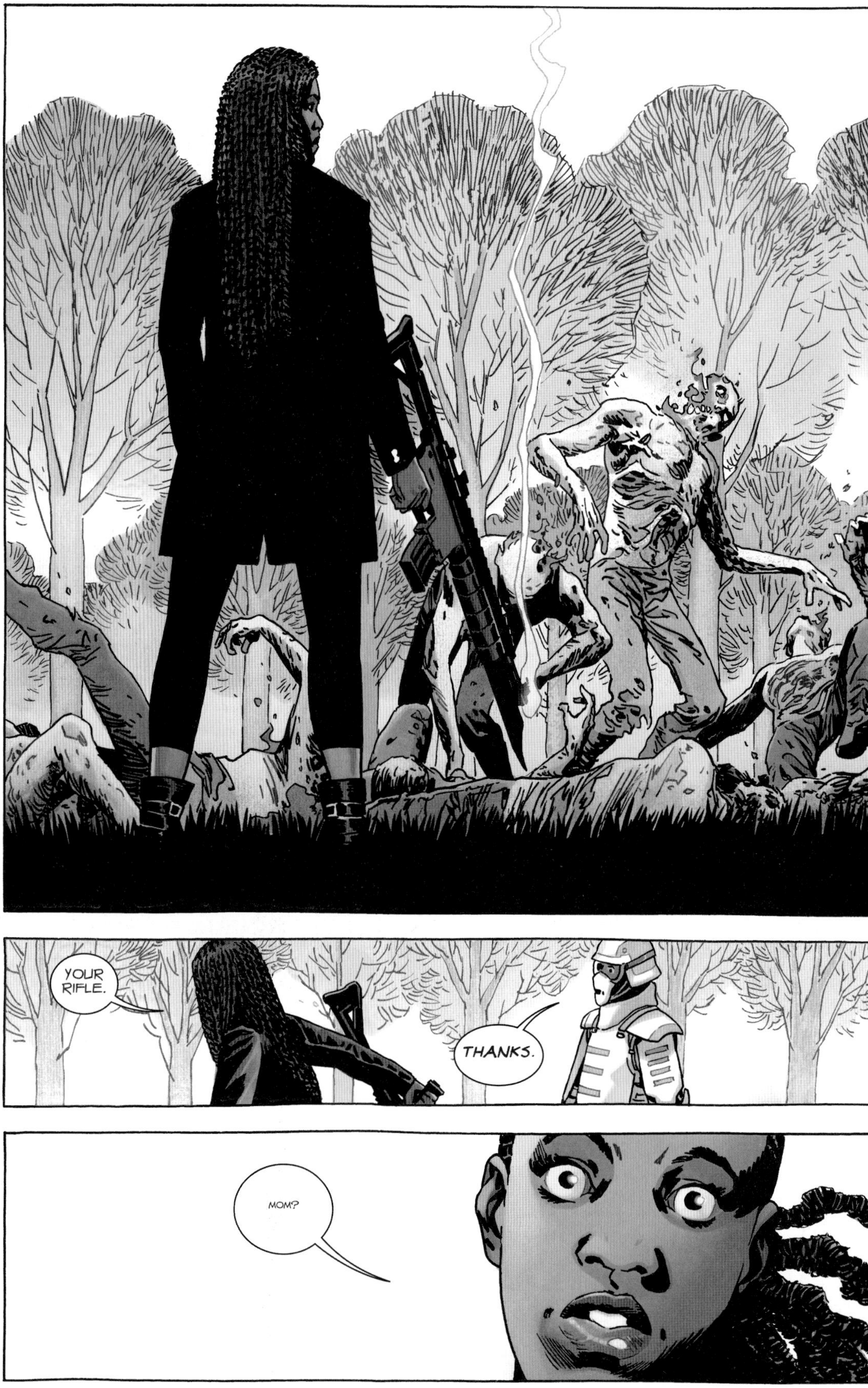
YOUR RIFLE.
THANKS.
MOM?

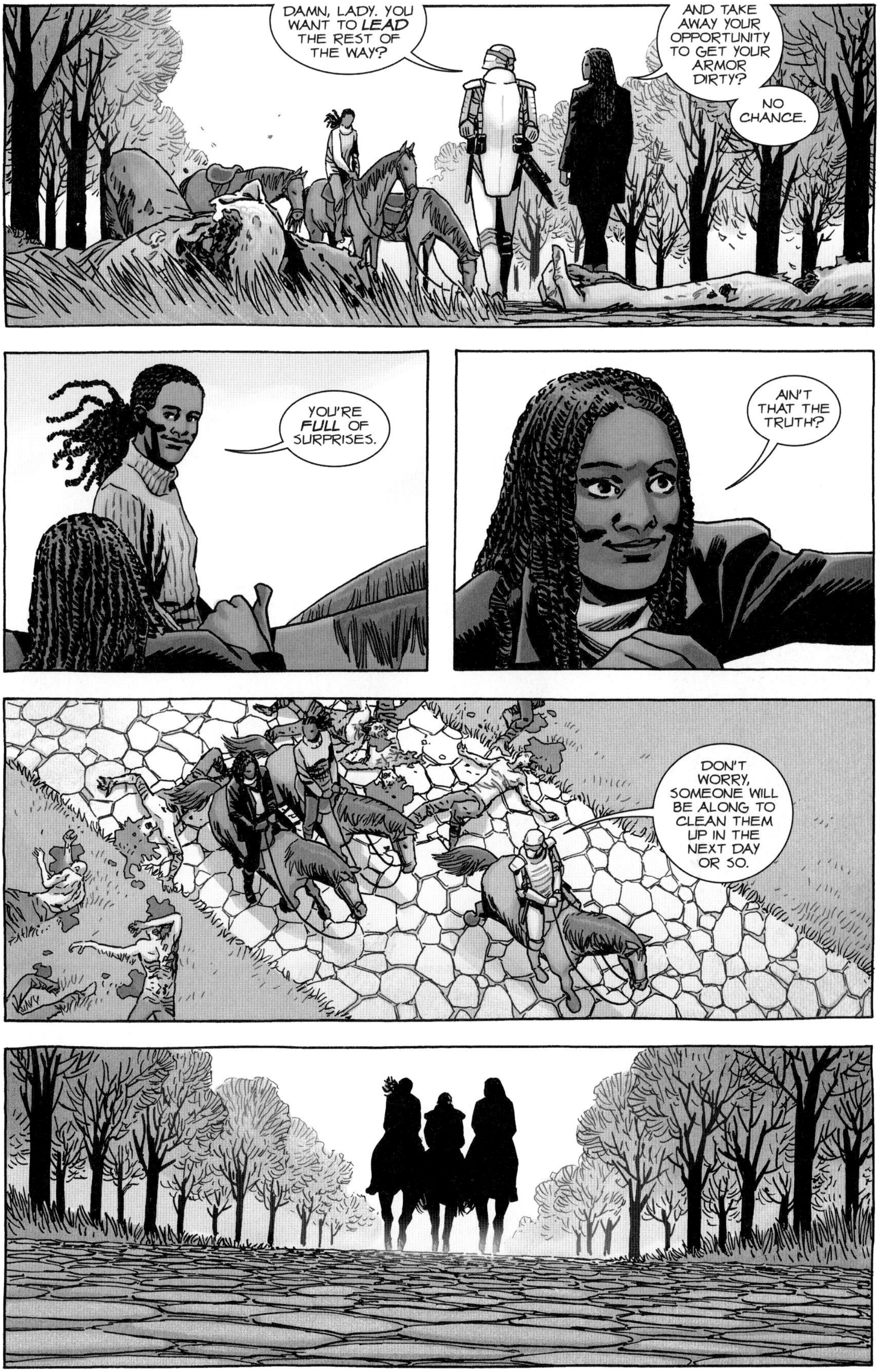
DAMN, LADY. YOU WANT TO LEAD THE REST OF THE WAY?
AND TAKE AWAY YOUR OPPORTUNITY TO GET YOUR ARMOR DIRTY?
NO CHANCE.
YOU'RE FULL OF SURPRISES.
AIN'T THAT THE TRUTH?
DON'T WORRY, SOMEONE WILL BE ALONG TO CLEAN THEM UP IN THE NEXT DAY OR SO.

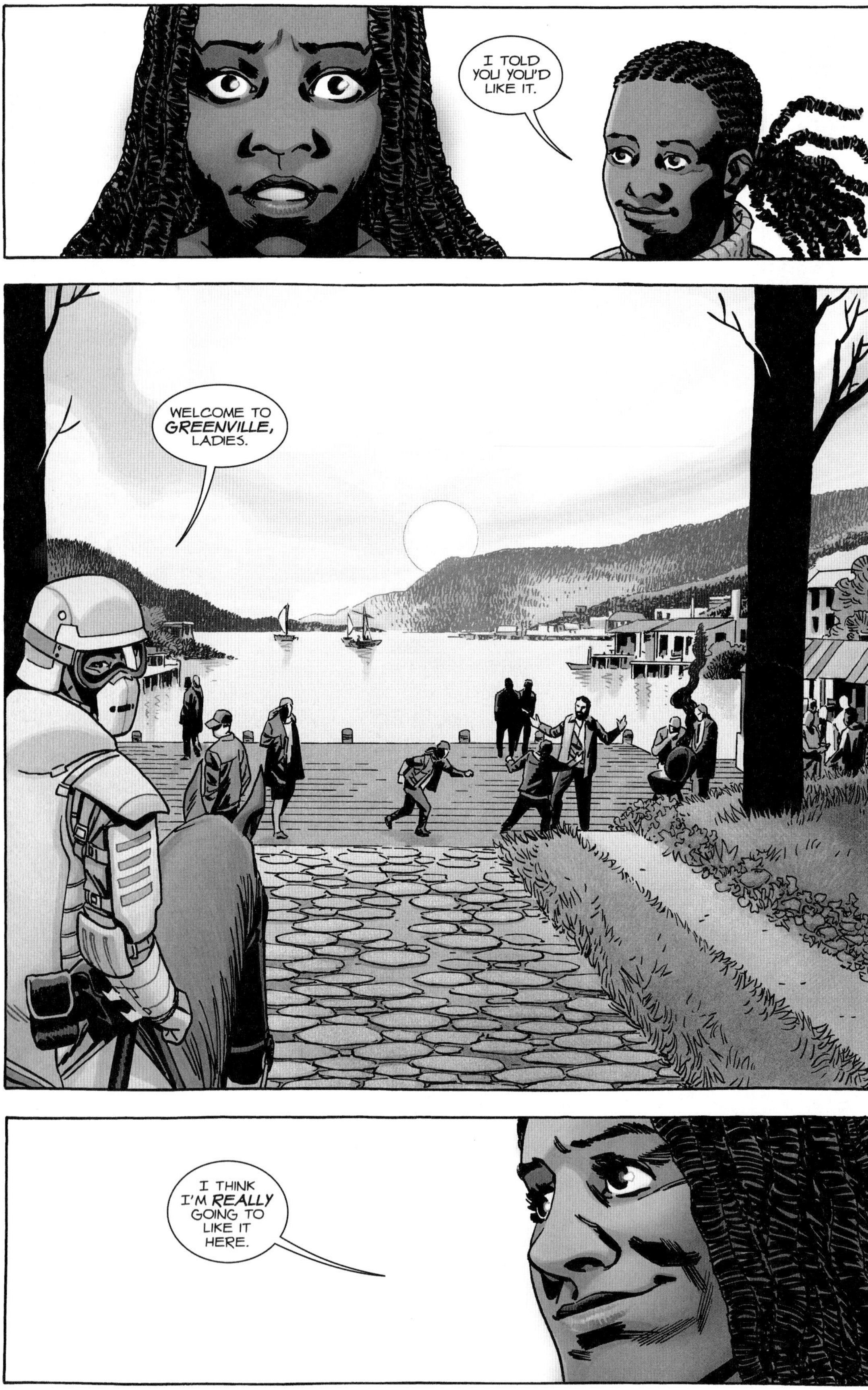
I TOLD YOU YOU'D LIKE IT.
WELCOME TO GREENVILLE, LADIES.
I THINK I'M REALLY GOING TO LIKE IT HERE.

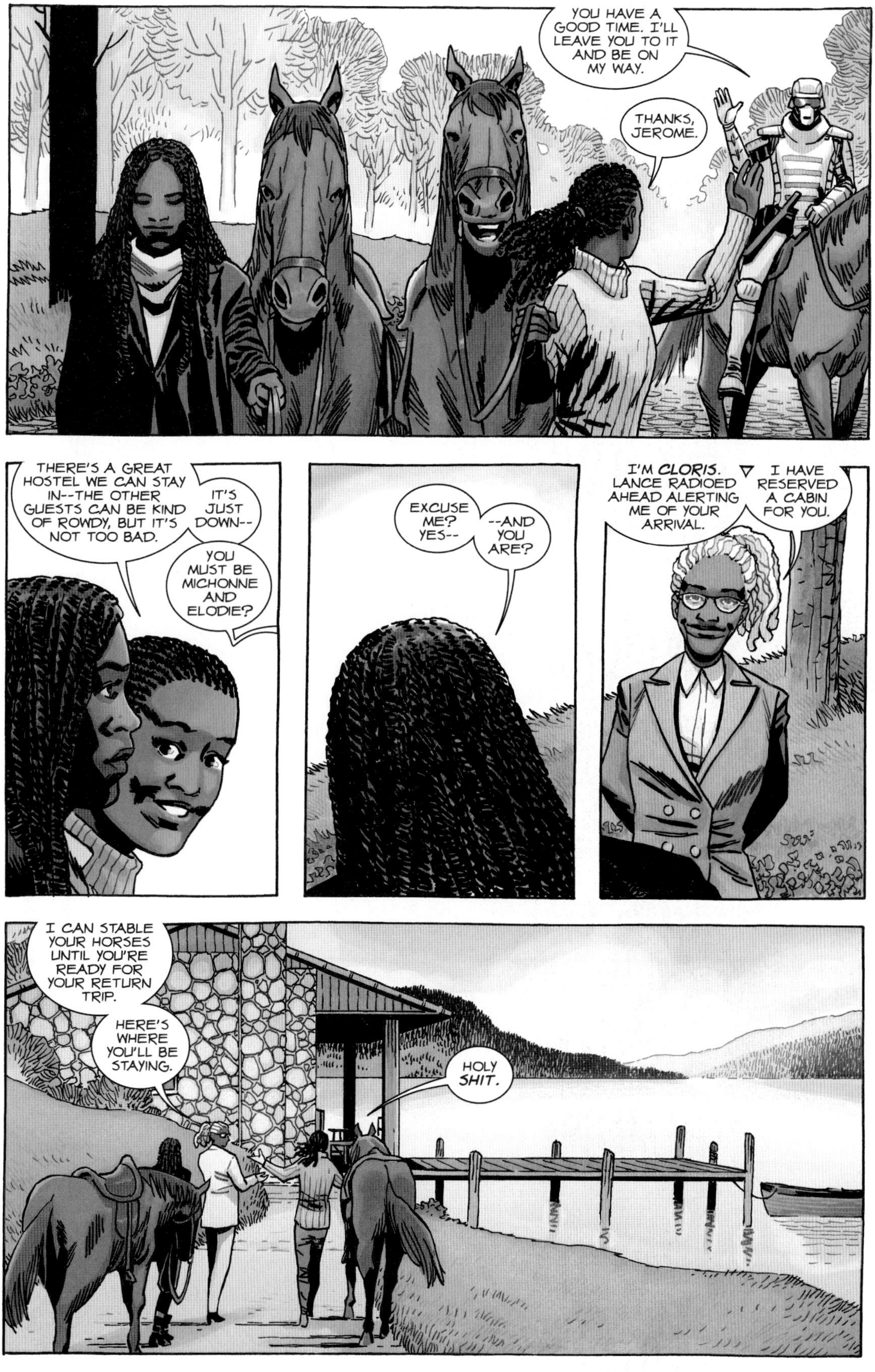
YOU HAVE A GOOD TIME. I'LL LEAVE YOU TO IT AND BE ON MY WAY.
THANKS, JEROME.
THERE'S A GREAT HOSTEL WE CAN STAY IN--THE OTHER GUESTS CAN BE KIND OF ROWDY, BUT IT'S NOT TOO BAD.
IT'S JUST DOWN--
YOU MUST BE MICHONNE AND ELODIE?
EXCUSE ME? YES--
--AND YOU ARE?
I'M CLORIS. LANCE RADIOED AHEAD ALERTING ME OF YOUR ARRIVAL.
I HAVE RESERVED A CABIN FOR YOU.
I CAN STABLE YOUR HORSES UNTIL YOU'RE READY FOR YOUR RETURN TRIP.
HERE'S WHERE YOU'LL BE STAYING.
HOLY SHIT.

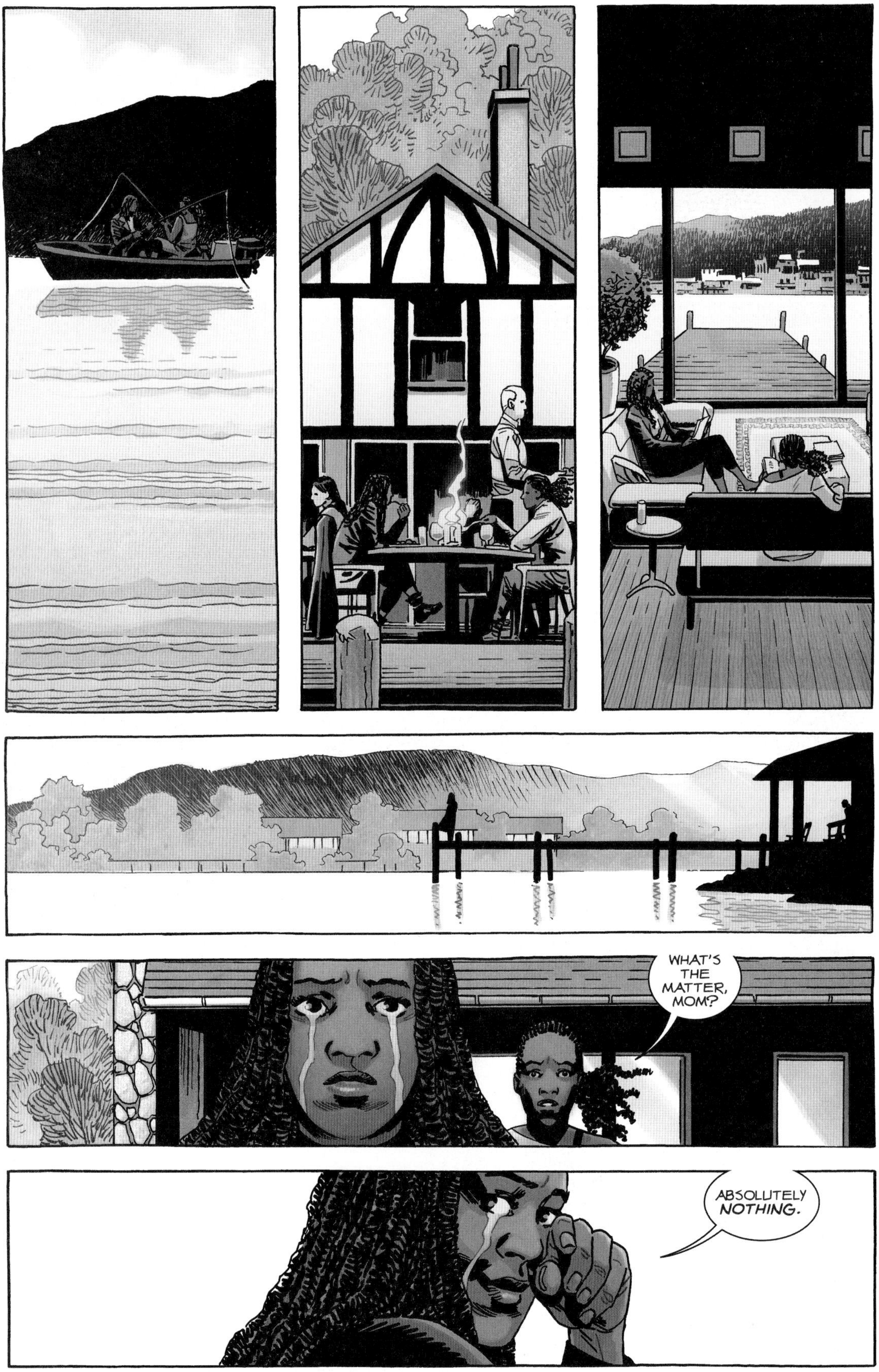
WHAT'S THE MATTER, MOM?
ABSOLUTELY NOTHING.

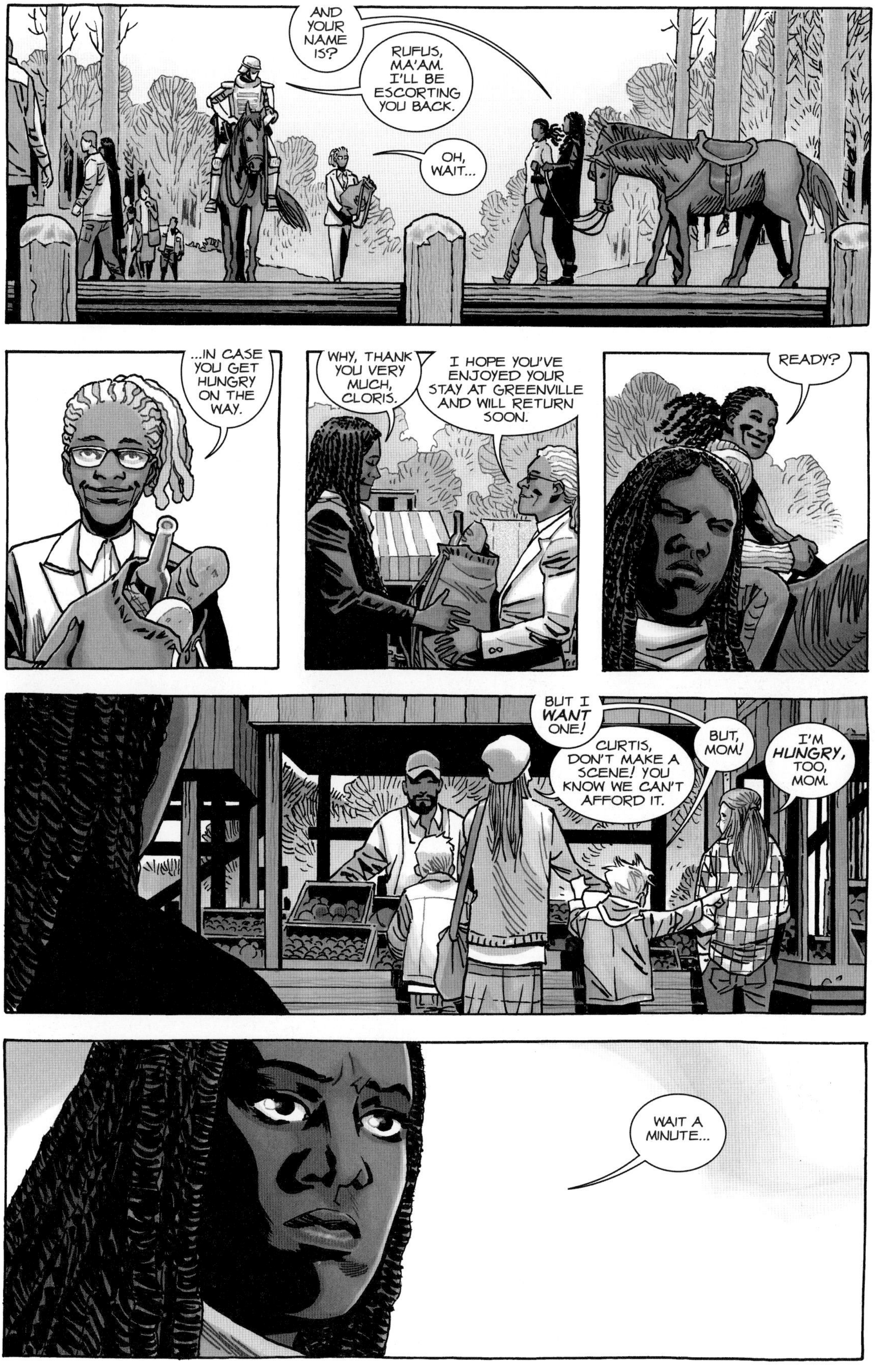
AND YOUR NAME IS?
RUFUS, MA'AM. I'LL BE ESCORTING YOU BACK.
OH, WAIT...
...IN CASE YOU GET HUNGRY ON THE WAY.
WHY, THANK YOU VERY MUCH, CLORIS.
I HOPE YOU'VE ENJOYED YOUR STAY AT GREENVILLE AND WILL RETURN SOON.
READY?
BUT I WANT ONE!
CURTIS, DON'T MAKE A SCENE! YOU KNOW WE CAN'T AFFORD IT.
BUT, MOM!
I'M HUNGRY, TOO, MOM.
WAIT A MINUTE...

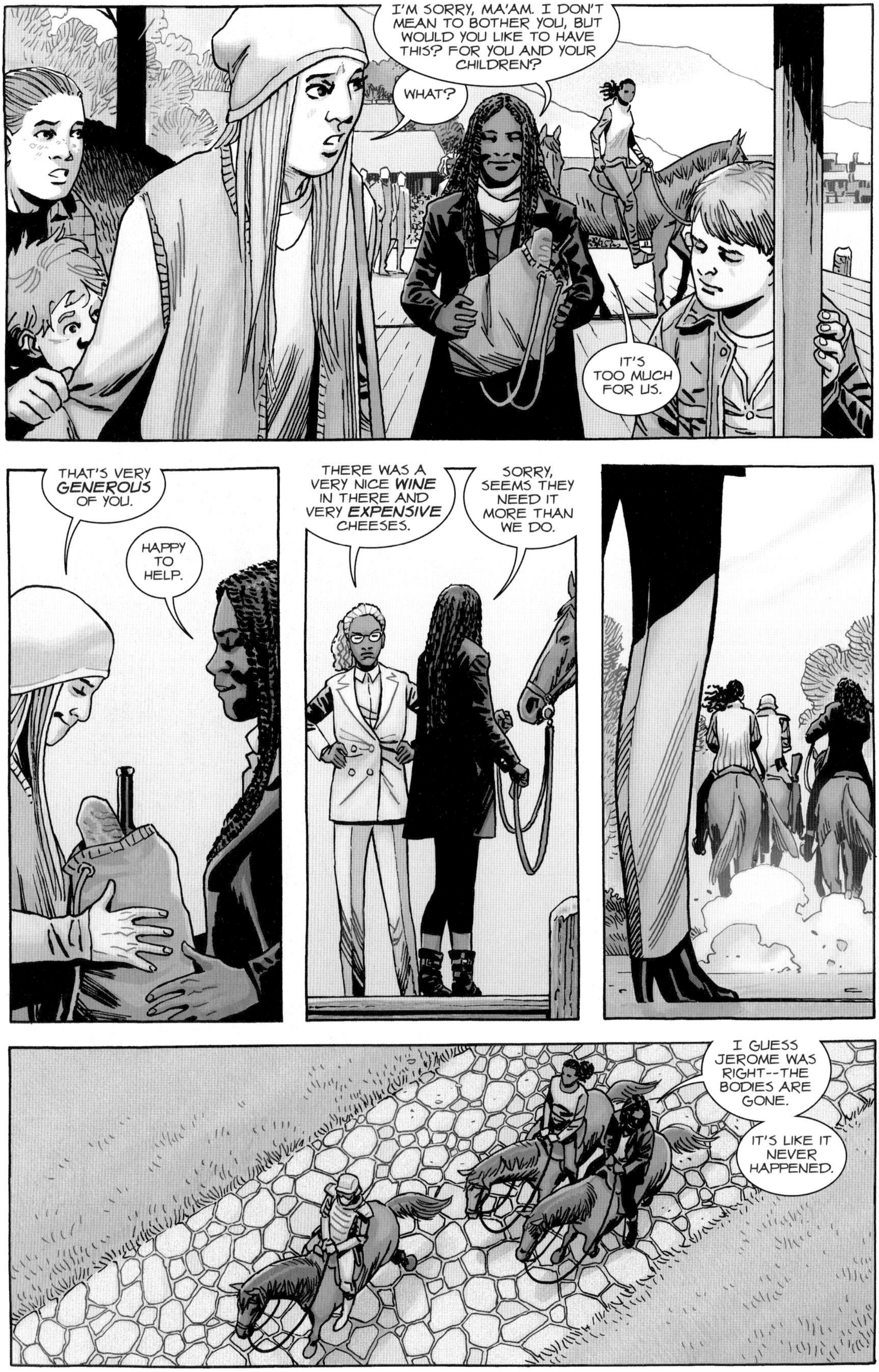
I'M SORRY, MA'AM. I DON'T MEAN TO BOTHER YOU, BUT WOULD YOU LIKE TO HAVE THIS? FOR YOU AND YOUR CHILDREN?
WHAT?
IT'S TOO MUCH FOR US.
THAT'S VERY GENEROUS OF YOU.
HAPPY TO HELP.
THERE WAS A VERY NICE WINE IN THERE AND VERY EXPENSIVE CHEESES.
SORRY, SEEMS THEY NEED IT MORE THAN WE DO.
I GUESS JEROME WAS RIGHT--THE BODIES ARE GONE.
IT'S LIKE IT NEVER HAPPENED.

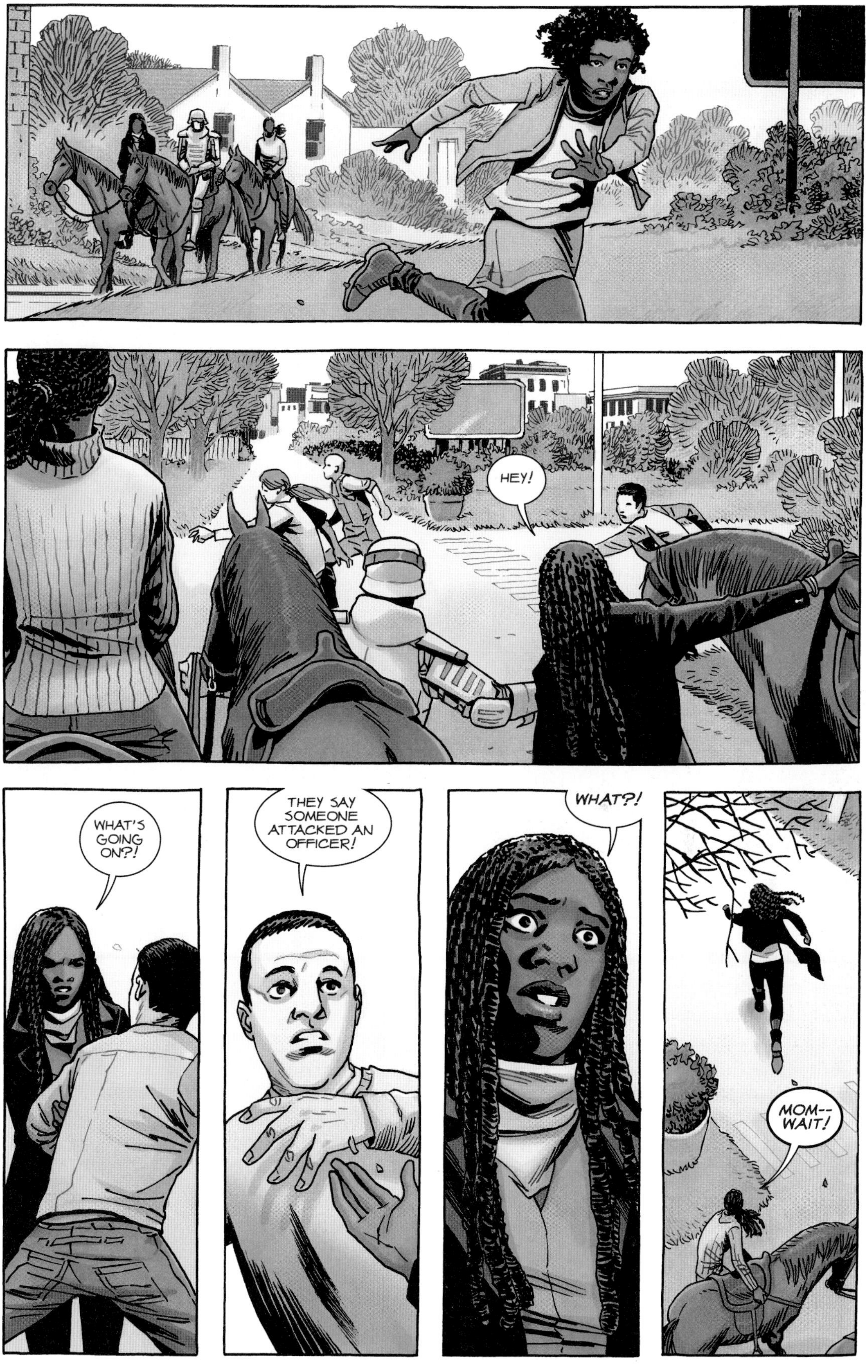
HEY!
WHAT'S GOING ON?!
THEY SAY SOMEONE ATTACKED AN OFFICER!
WHAT?!
MOM-- WAIT!

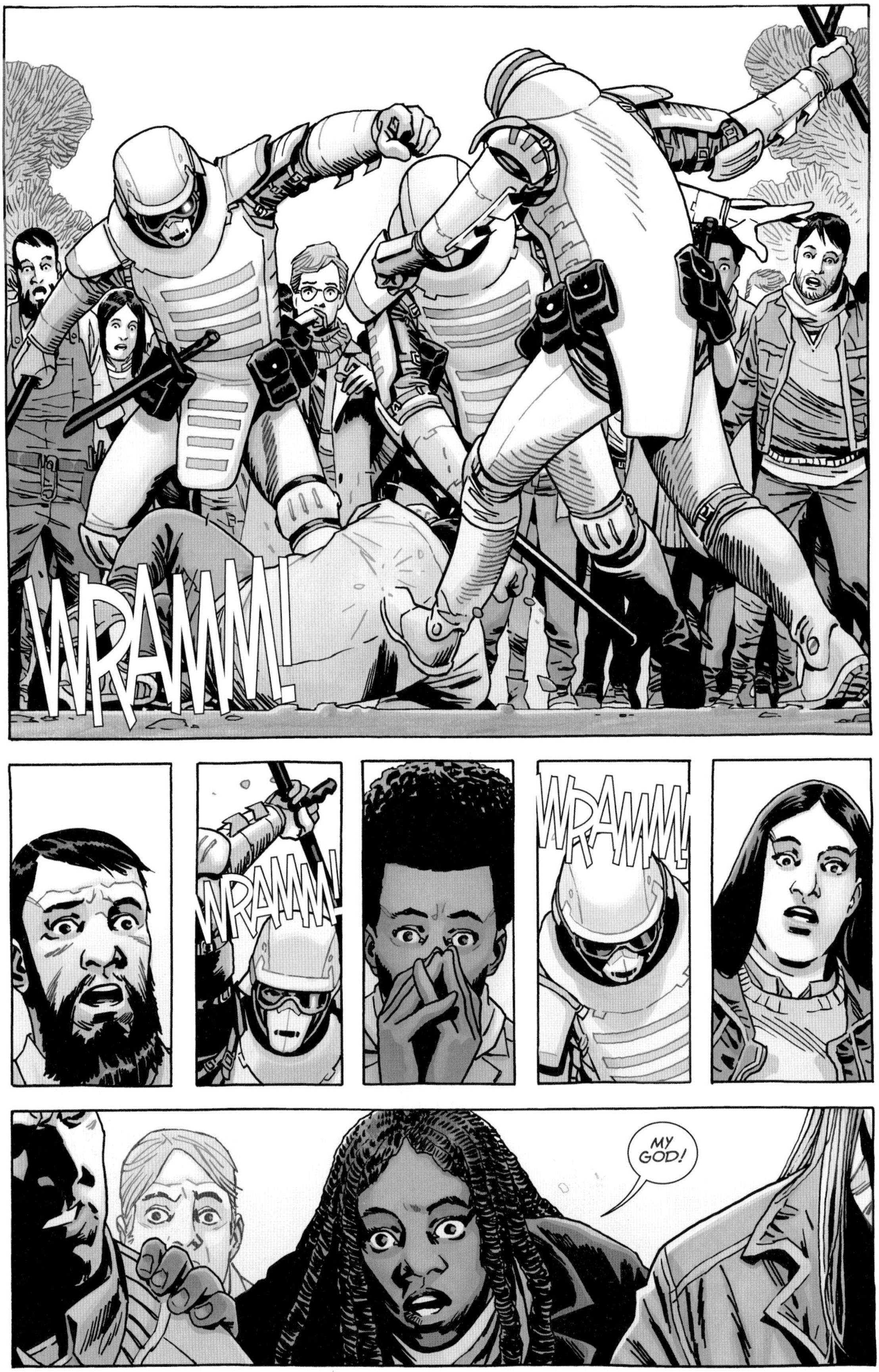
WRAMM!
WRAMM!
WRAMM!
MY GOD!

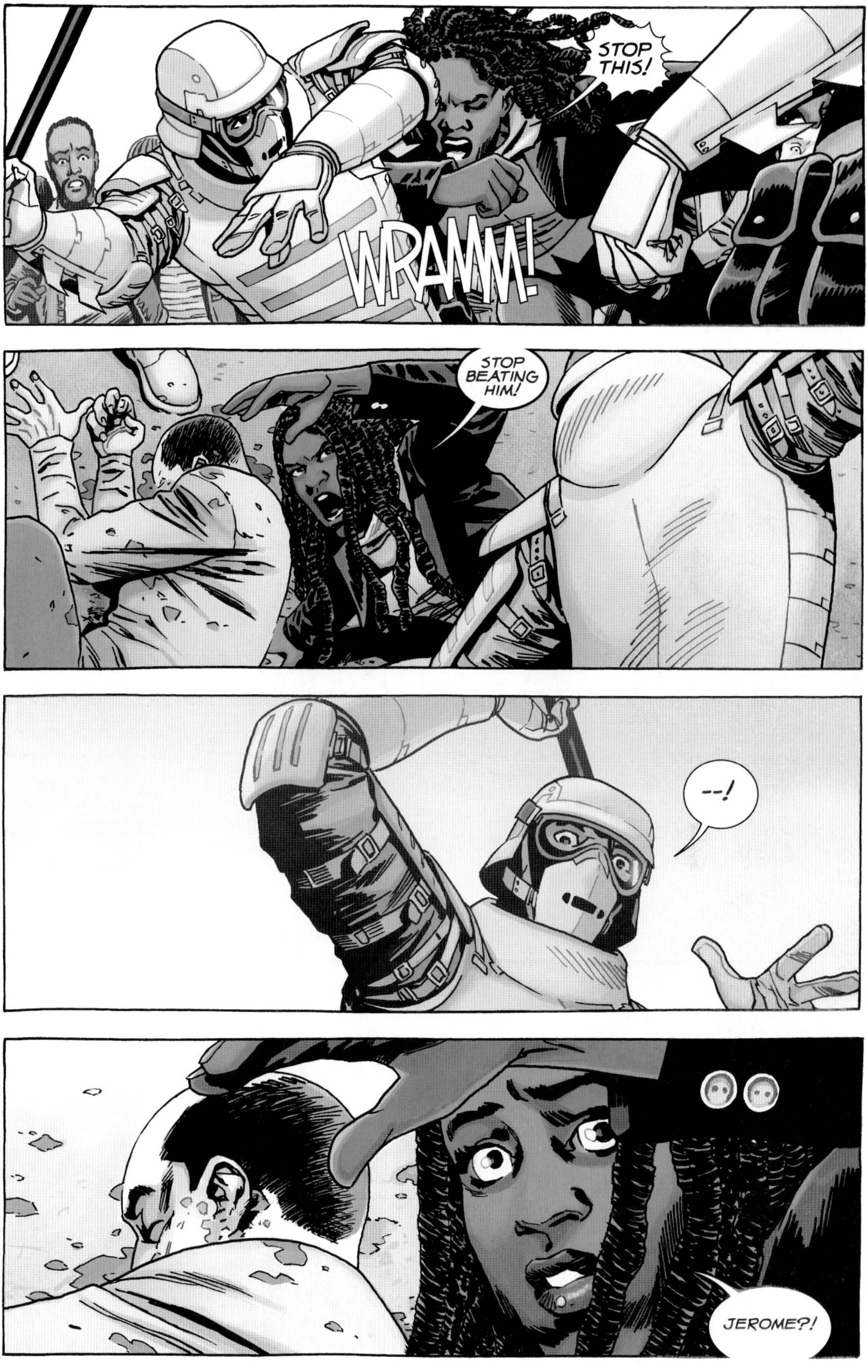
STOP THIS!
WRAMM!
STOP BEATING HIM!
--!
JEROME?!

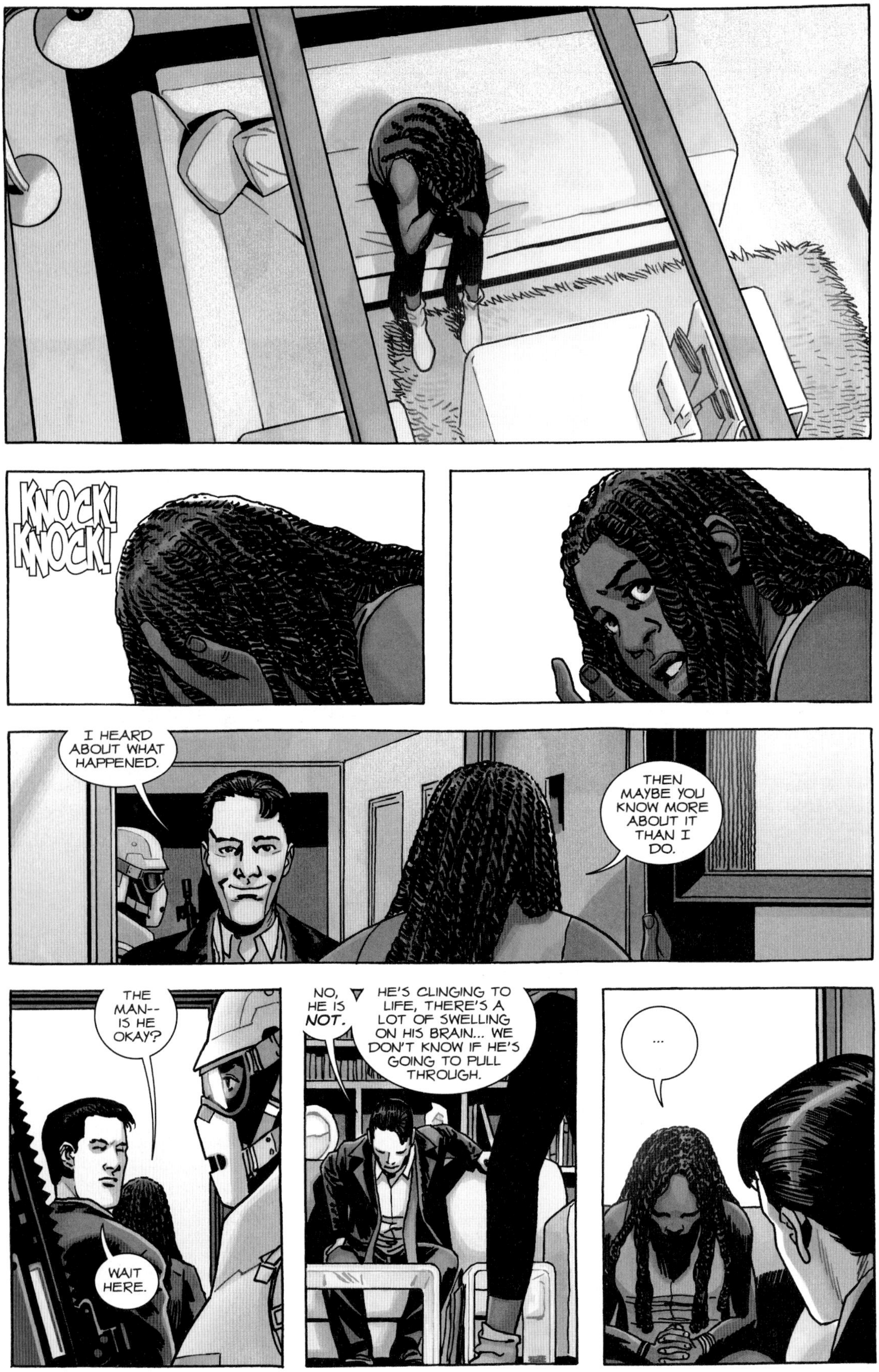
KNOCK! KNOCK!
I HEARD ABOUT WHAT HAPPENED.
THEN MAYBE YOU KNOW MORE ABOUT IT THAN I DO.
THE MAN-- IS HE OKAY?
WAIT HERE.
NO, HE IS NOT.
HE'S CLINGING TO LIFE, THERE'S A LOT OF SWELLING ON HIS BRAIN... WE DON'T KNOW IF HE'S GOING TO PULL THROUGH.
...

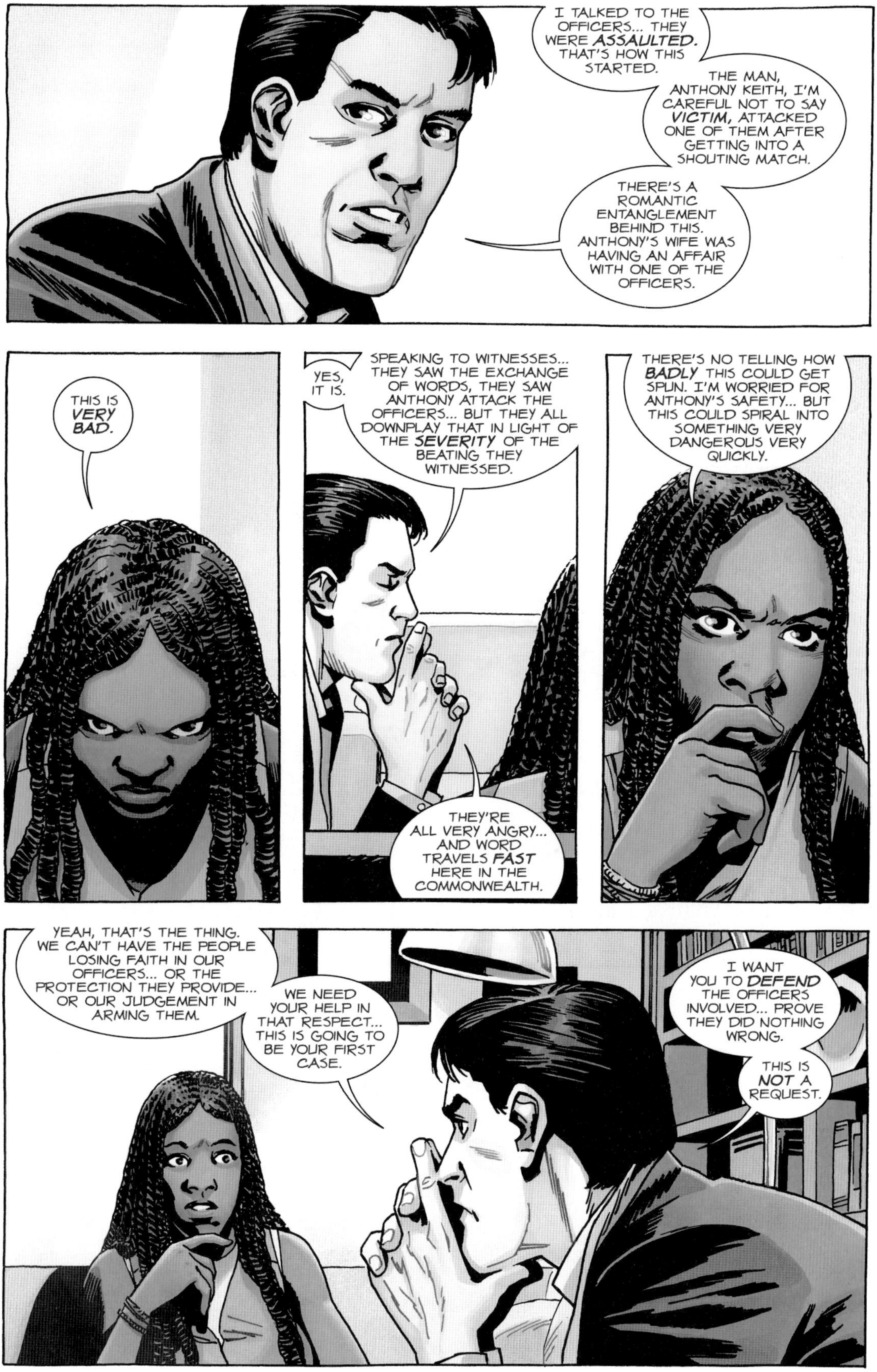
I TALKED TO THE OFFICERS... THEY WERE ASSAULTED. THAT'S HOW THIS STARTED.
THE MAN, ANTHONY KEITH, I'M CAREFUL NOT TO SAY VICTIM, ATTACKED ONE OF THEM AFTER GETTING INTO A SHOUTING MATCH.
THERE'S A ROMANTIC ENTANGLEMENT BEHIND THIS. ANTHONY'S WIFE WAS HAVING AN AFFAIR WITH ONE OF THE OFFICERS.
THIS IS VERY BAD.
YES, IT IS.
SPEAKING TO WITNESSES... THEY SAW THE EXCHANGE OF WORDS, THEY SAW ANTHONY ATTACK THE OFFICERS... BUT THEY ALL DOWNPLAY THAT IN LIGHT OF THE SEVERITY OF THE BEATING THEY WITNESSED.
THEY'RE ALL VERY ANGRY... AND WORD TRAVELS FAST HERE IN THE COMMONWEALTH.
THERE'S NO TELLING HOW BADLY THIS COULD GET SPUN. I'M WORRIED FOR ANTHONY'S SAFETY... BUT THIS COULD SPIRAL INTO SOMETHING VERY DANGEROUS VERY QUICKLY.
YEAH, THAT'S THE THING. WE CAN'T HAVE THE PEOPLE LOSING FAITH IN OUR OFFICERS... OR THE PROTECTION THEY PROVIDE... OR OUR JUDGEMENT IN ARMING THEM.
WE NEED YOUR HELP IN THAT RESPECT... THIS IS GOING TO BE YOUR FIRST CASE.
I WANT YOU TO DEFEND THE OFFICERS INVOLVED... PROVE THEY DID NOTHING WRONG.
THIS IS NOT A REQUEST.

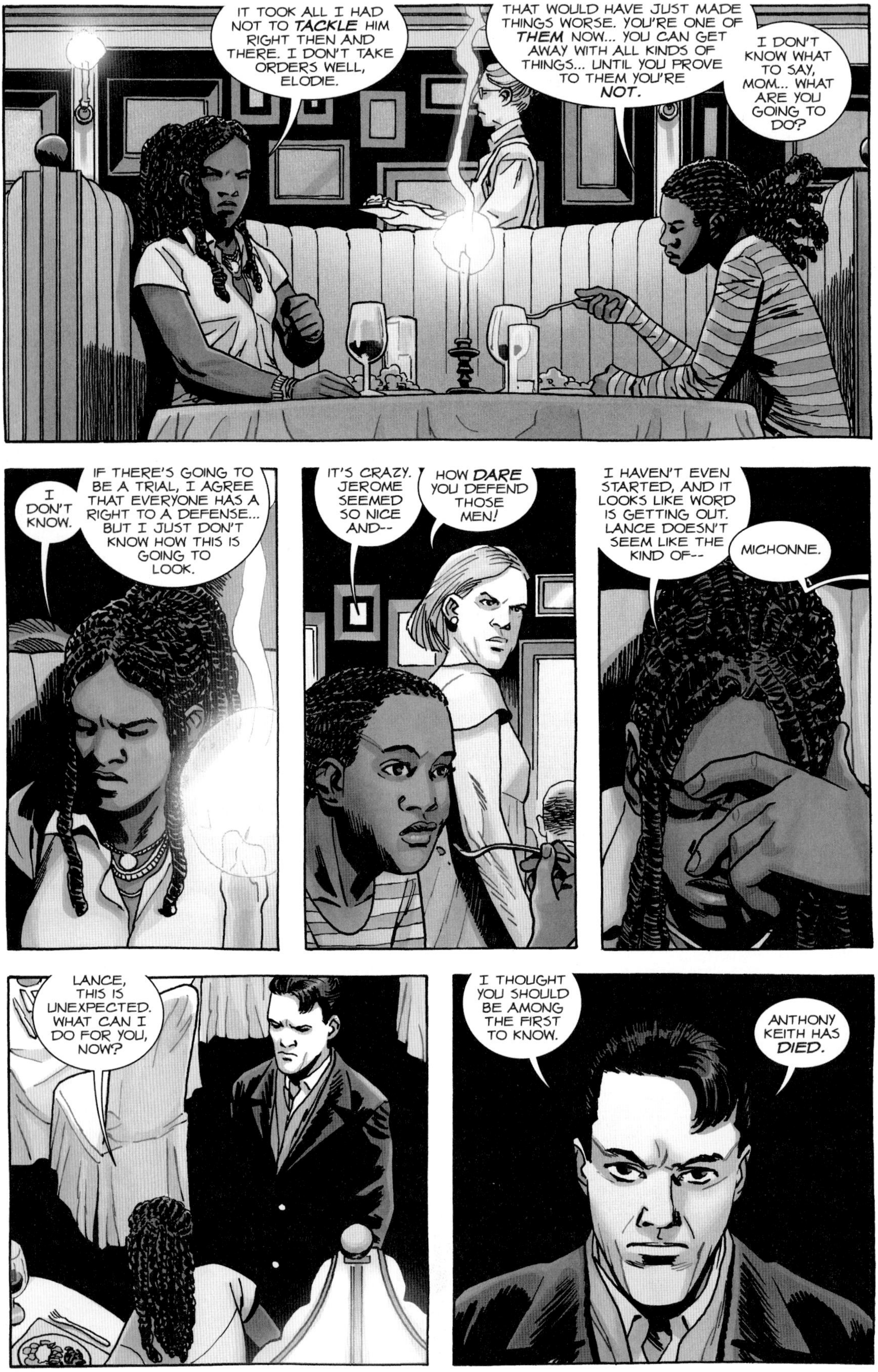
IT TOOK ALL I HAD NOT TO TACKLE HIM RIGHT THEN AND THERE. I DON'T TAKE ORDERS WELL, ELODIE.
THAT WOULD HAVE JUST MADE THINGS WORSE. YOU'RE ONE OF THEM NOW... YOU CAN GET AWAY WITH ALL KINDS OF THINGS... UNTIL YOU PROVE TO THEM YOU'RE NOT.
I DON'T KNOW WHAT TO SAY, MOM... WHAT ARE YOU GOING TO DO?
I DON'T KNOW.
IF THERE'S GOING TO BE A TRIAL, I AGREE THAT EVERYONE HAS A RIGHT TO A DEFENSE... BUT I JUST DON'T KNOW HOW THIS IS GOING TO LOOK.
IT'S CRAZY. JEROME SEEMED SO NICE AND--
HOW DARE YOU DEFEND THOSE MEN!
I HAVEN'T EVEN STARTED, AND IT LOOKS LIKE WORD IS GETTING OUT. LANCE DOESN'T SEEM LIKE THE KIND OF--
MICHONNE.
LANCE, THIS IS UNEXPECTED. WHAT CAN I DO FOR YOU, NOW?
I THOUGHT YOU SHOULD BE AMONG THE FIRST TO KNOW.
ANTHONY KEITH HAS DIED.

Signs: WRONG SIDE OF THE LAW · GUILTY · LEAVE MY MOTHER ALONE, YOU VULTURES! · SHE DIDN'T CAUSE THIS! · THE LAW MUST SERVE JUSTICE · DEFEND THE INNOCENT NOT THE GUILTY · OF THE LAW · THE LAW CAN BE BOUGHT

ASSHOLES!

YOU'RE JUST GOING TO MAKE THINGS WORSE.

I DON'T THINK THAT'S POSSIBLE.

IT'S GETTING REALLY BAD OUT THERE. EVEN MY FRIENDS ARE STARTING TO TALK ABOUT DOING SOMETHING... I'M WORRIED.

...

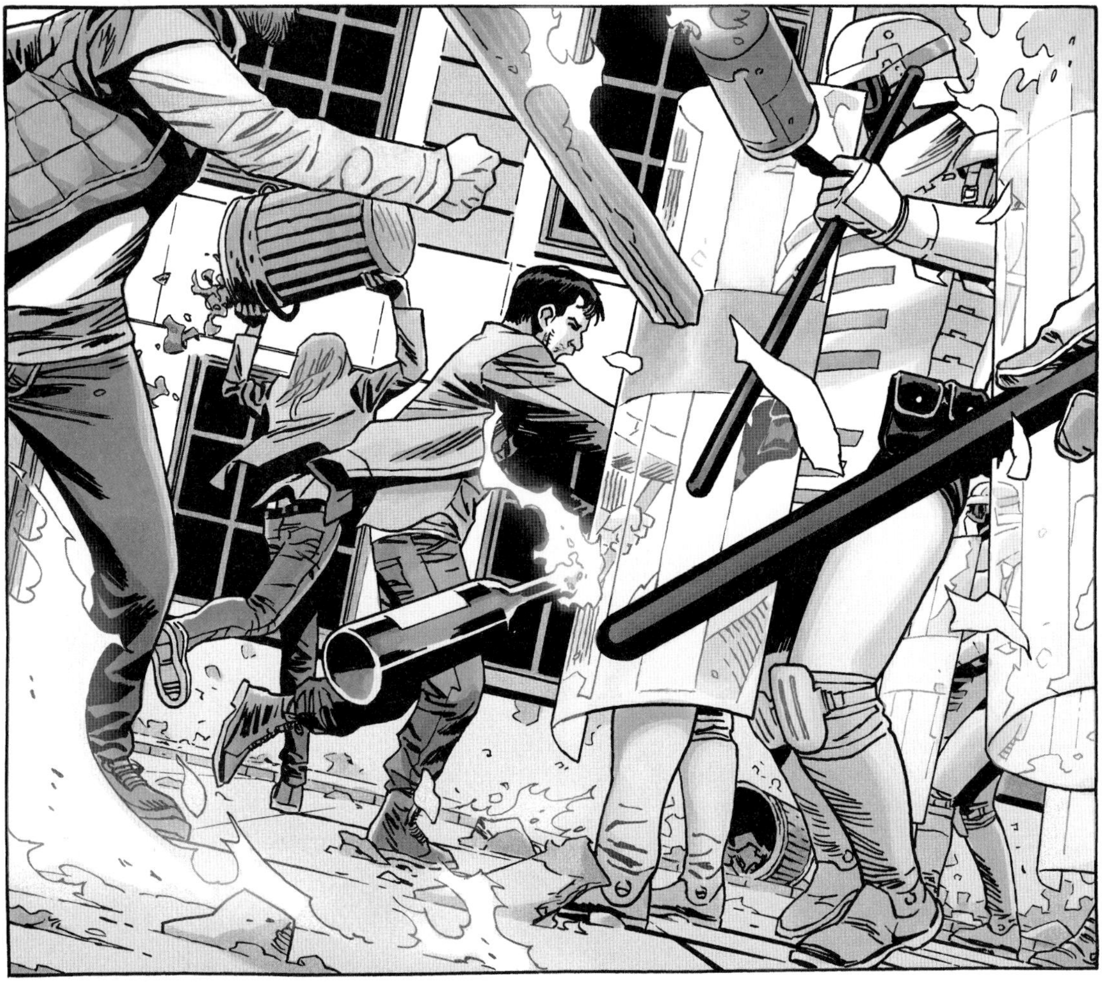

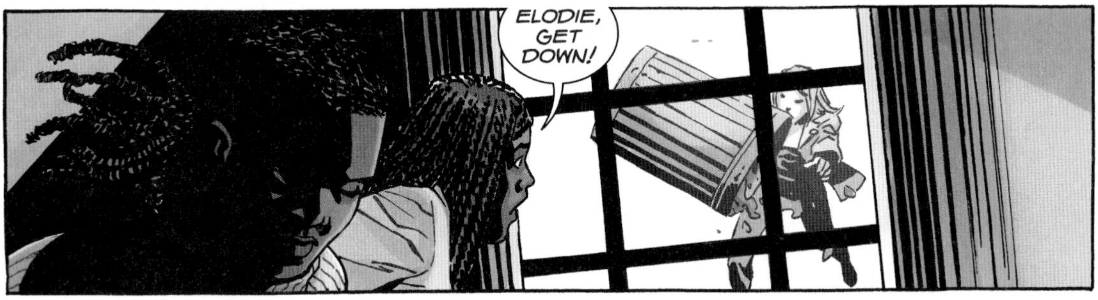
ELODIE, GET DOWN!

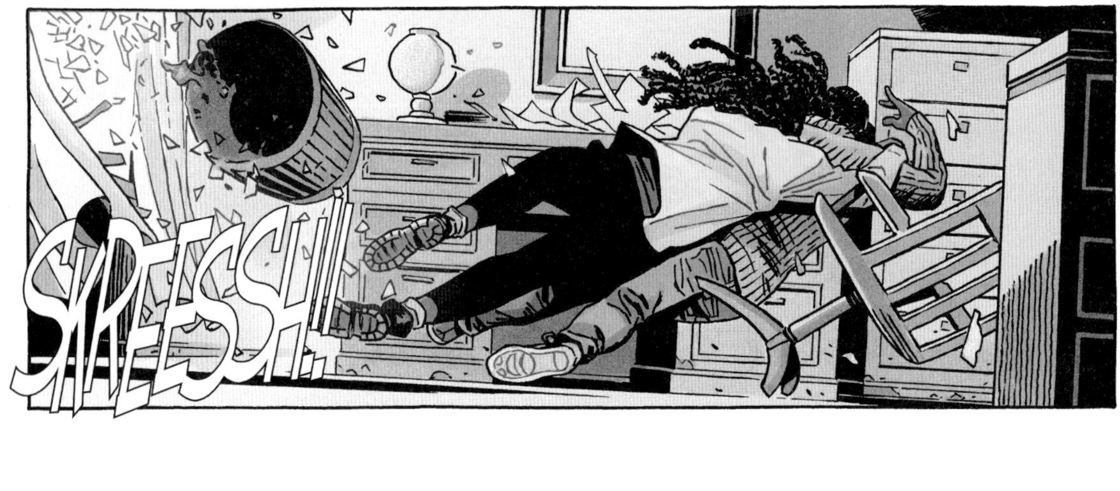
SKREESH!!

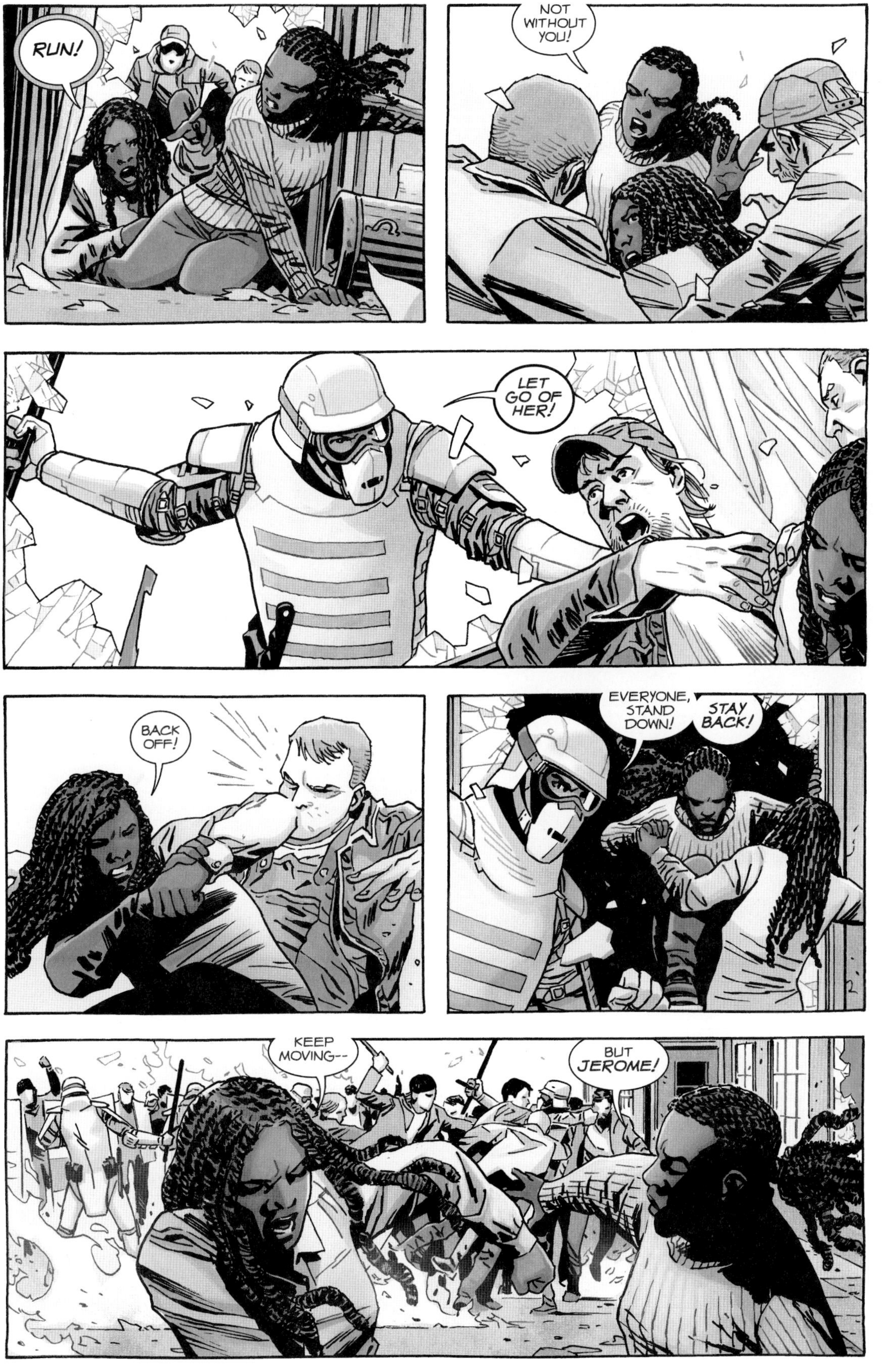
RUN!
NOT WITHOUT YOU!
LET GO OF HER!
BACK OFF!
EVERYONE, STAND DOWN!
STAY BACK!
KEEP MOVING--
BUT JEROME!

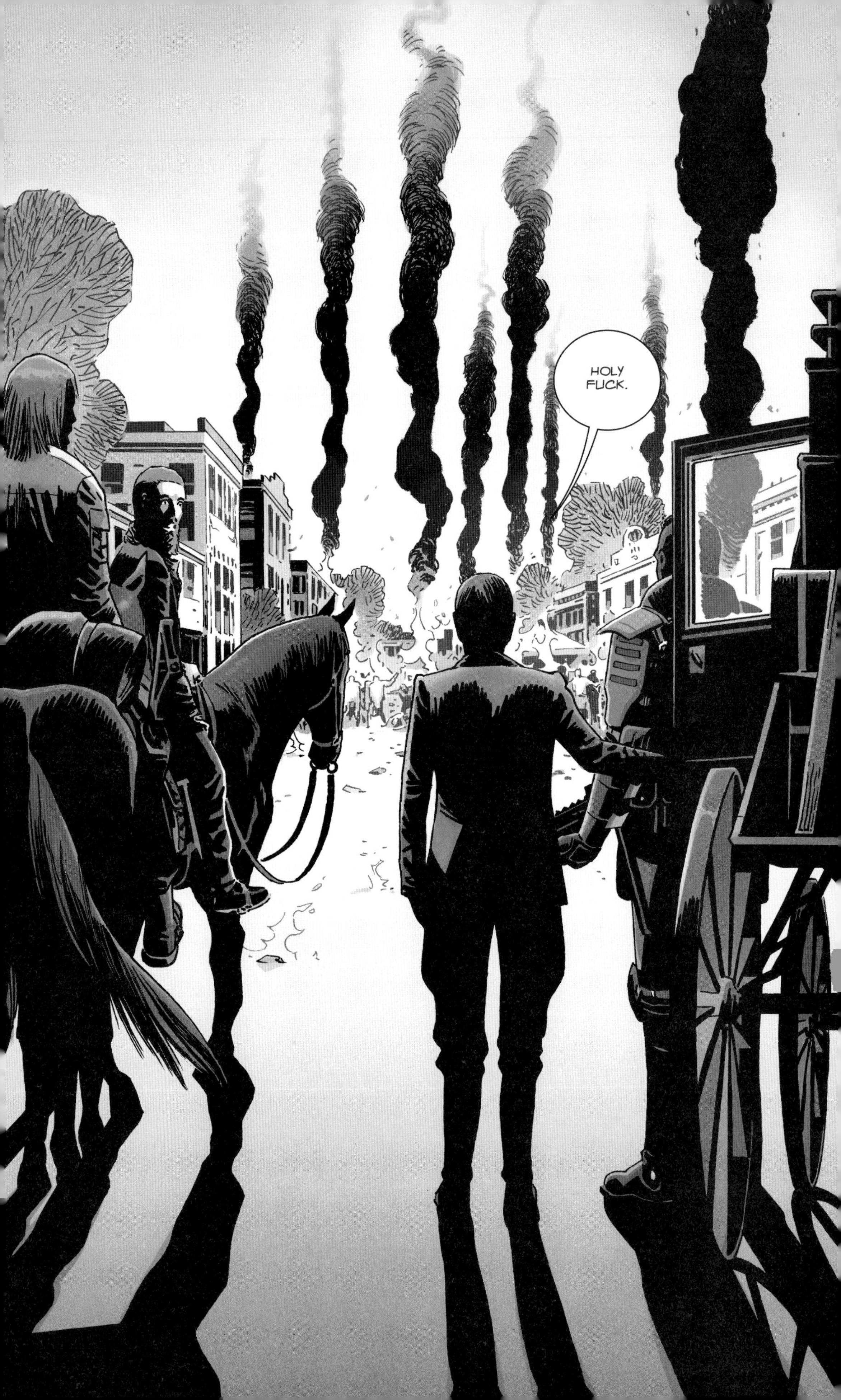
HOLY FUCK.

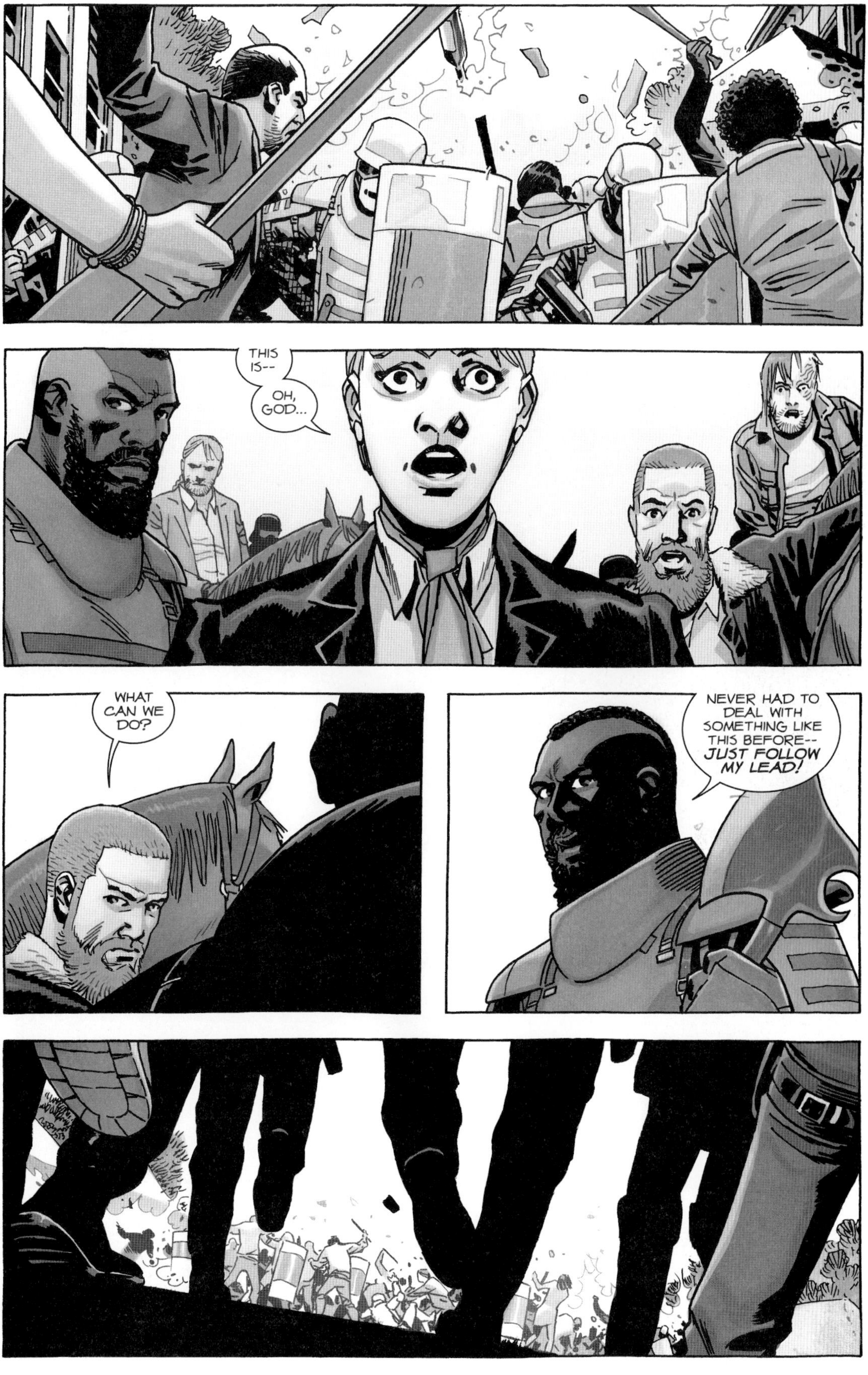
THIS IS--
OH, GOD...
WHAT CAN WE DO?
NEVER HAD TO DEAL WITH SOMETHING LIKE THIS BEFORE-- JUST FOLLOW MY LEAD!

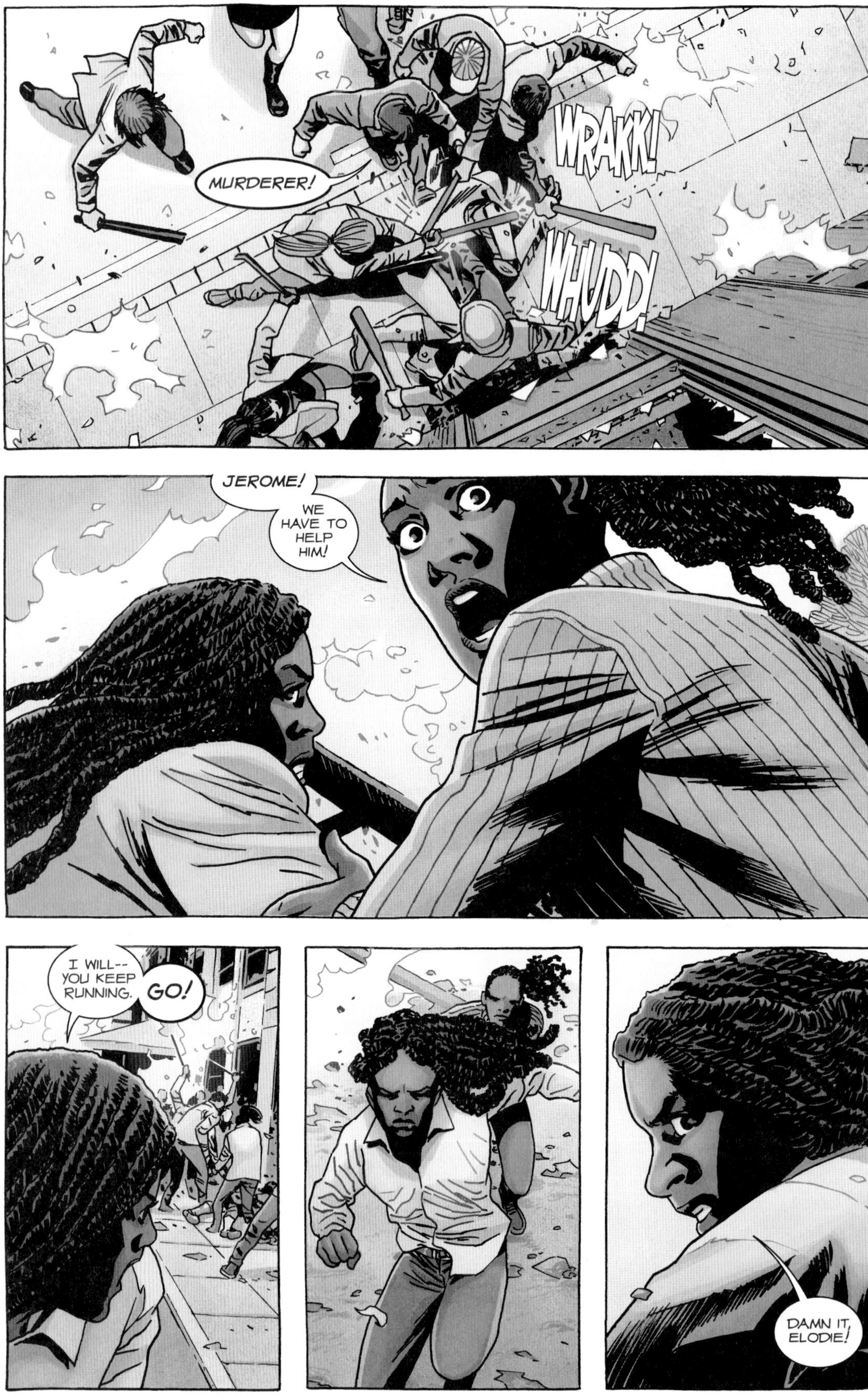

MURDERER!
WRAKK!
WHUDD!
JEROME!
WE HAVE TO HELP HIM!
I WILL-- YOU KEEP RUNNING.
GO!
DAMN IT, ELODIE!

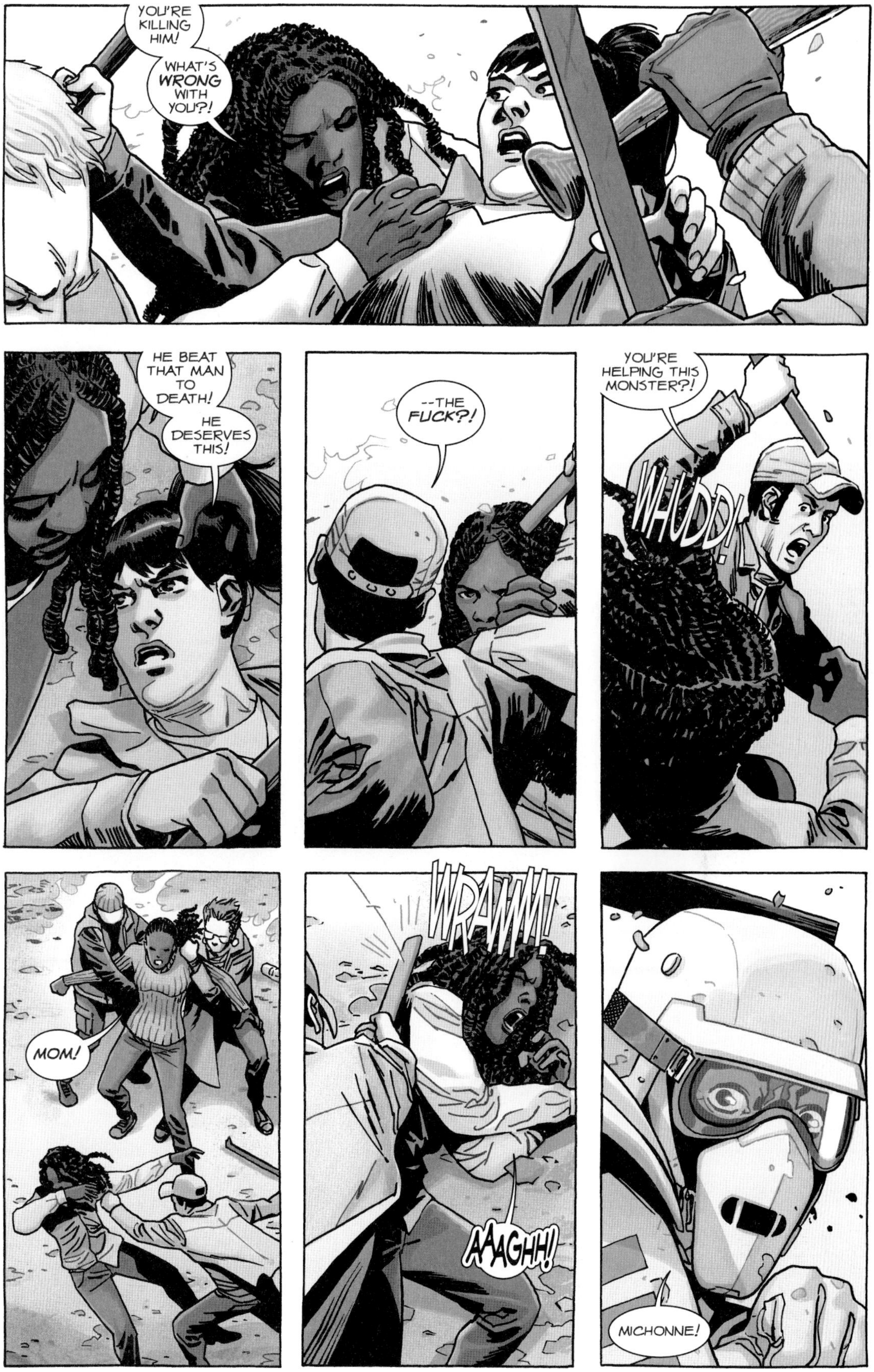
YOU'RE KILLING HIM!
WHAT'S WRONG WITH YOU?!
HE BEAT THAT MAN TO DEATH!
HE DESERVES THIS!
--THE FUCK?!
YOU'RE HELPING THIS MONSTER?!
WHUDD!
MOM!
WRAMM!
AAAGHH!
MICHONNE!

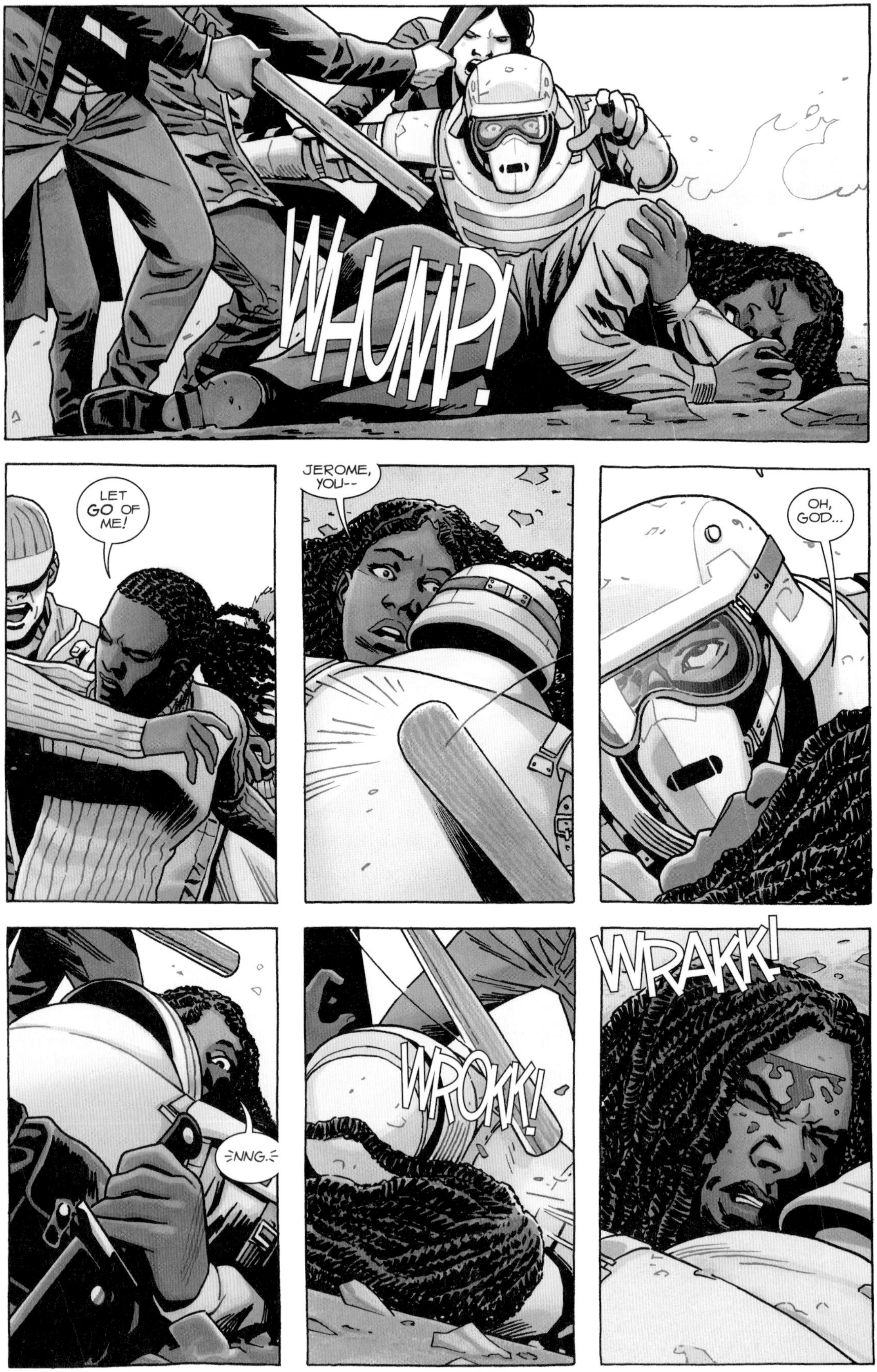
WHUMP!
LET GO OF ME!
JEROME, YOU--
OH, GOD...
NNG.
WROKK!
WRAKK!

THUNK!

GET INTO POSITION!

MICHONNE, MY GOD--

BRAKK! BRAKK! BRAKK! BRAKK! BRAKK! BRAKK! BRAKK! BRAKK! BRAKK! BRAKK! BRAKK! BRAKK! BRAKK! BRAKK! BRAKK!

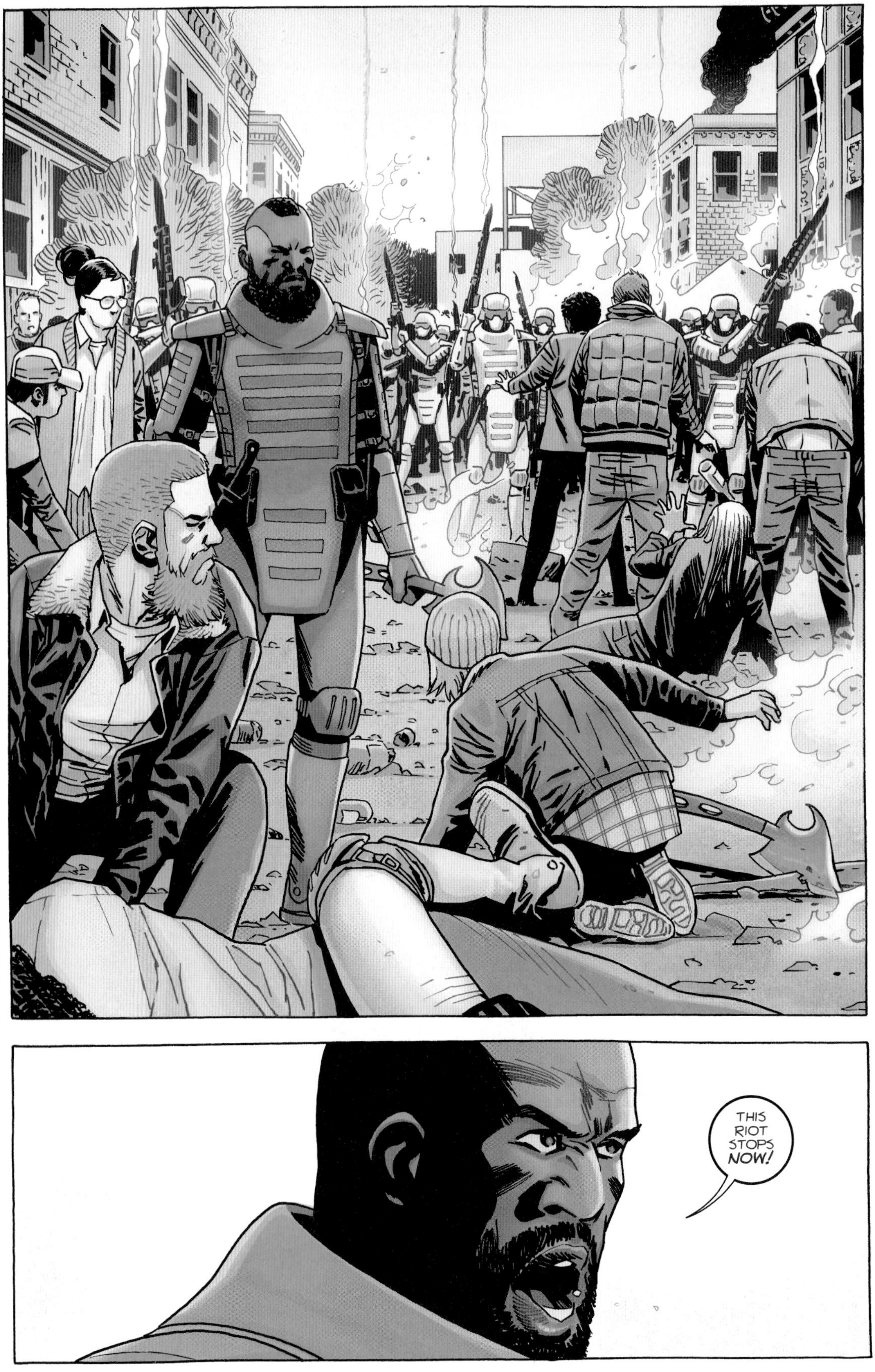
THIS RIOT STOPS NOW!

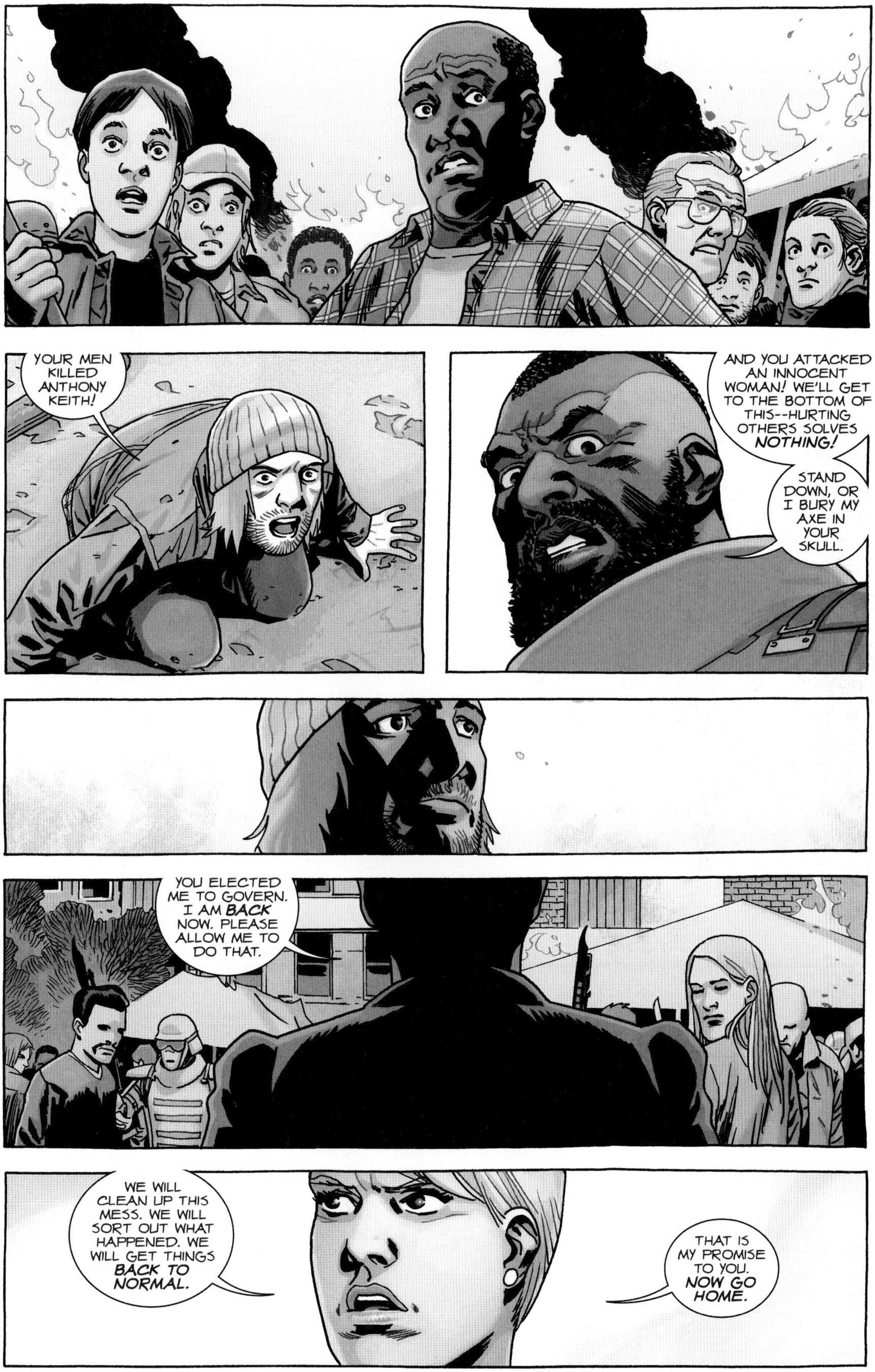
YOUR MEN KILLED ANTHONY KEITH!
AND YOU ATTACKED AN INNOCENT WOMAN! WE'LL GET TO THE BOTTOM OF THIS--HURTING OTHERS SOLVES NOTHING!
STAND DOWN, OR I BURY MY AXE IN YOUR SKULL.
YOU ELECTED ME TO GOVERN. I AM BACK NOW. PLEASE ALLOW ME TO DO THAT.
WE WILL CLEAN UP THIS MESS. WE WILL SORT OUT WHAT HAPPENED. WE WILL GET THINGS BACK TO NORMAL.
THAT IS MY PROMISE TO YOU. NOW GO HOME.

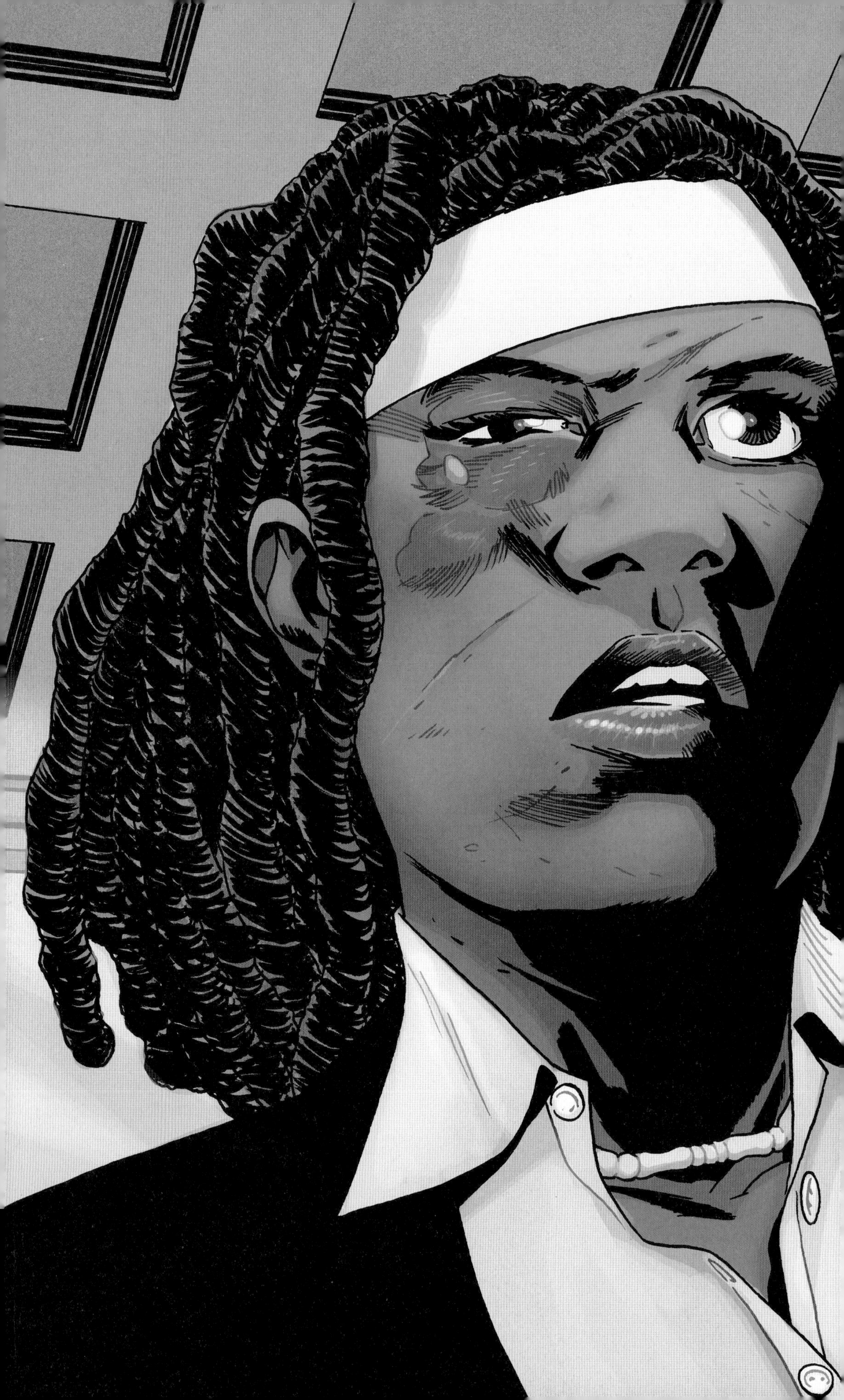

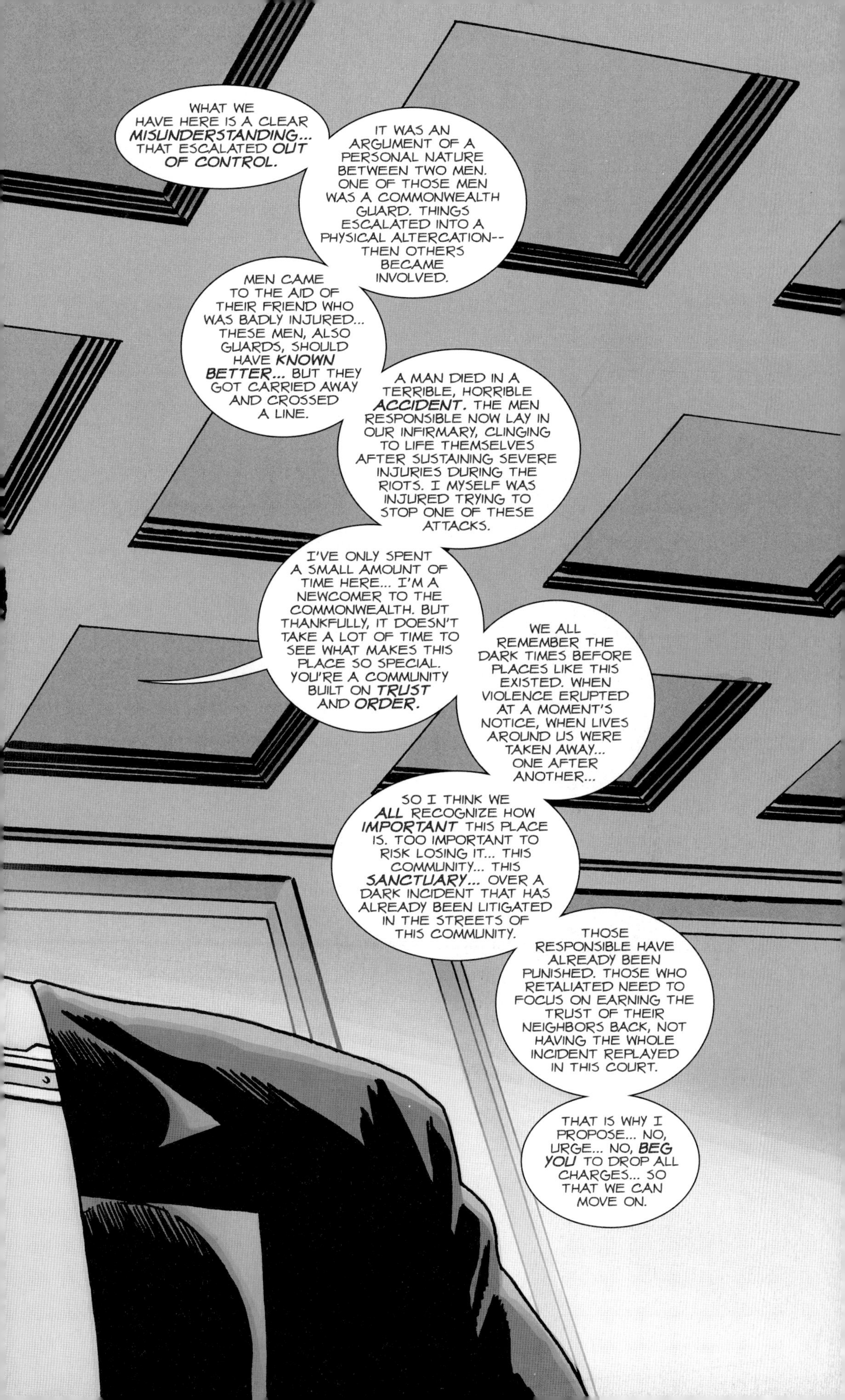
WHAT WE HAVE HERE IS A CLEAR MISUNDERSTANDING... THAT ESCALATED OUT OF CONTROL.
IT WAS AN ARGUMENT OF A PERSONAL NATURE BETWEEN TWO MEN. ONE OF THOSE MEN WAS A COMMONWEALTH GUARD. THINGS ESCALATED INTO A PHYSICAL ALTERCATION-- THEN OTHERS BECAME INVOLVED.
MEN CAME TO THE AID OF THEIR FRIEND WHO WAS BADLY INJURED... THESE MEN, ALSO GUARDS, SHOULD HAVE KNOWN BETTER... BUT THEY GOT CARRIED AWAY AND CROSSED A LINE.
A MAN DIED IN A TERRIBLE, HORRIBLE ACCIDENT. THE MEN RESPONSIBLE NOW LAY IN OUR INFIRMARY, CLINGING TO LIFE THEMSELVES AFTER SUSTAINING SEVERE INJURIES DURING THE RIOTS. I MYSELF WAS INJURED TRYING TO STOP ONE OF THESE ATTACKS.
I'VE ONLY SPENT A SMALL AMOUNT OF TIME HERE... I'M A NEWCOMER TO THE COMMONWEALTH. BUT THANKFULLY, IT DOESN'T TAKE A LOT OF TIME TO SEE WHAT MAKES THIS PLACE SO SPECIAL. YOU'RE A COMMUNITY BUILT ON TRUST AND ORDER.
WE ALL REMEMBER THE DARK TIMES BEFORE PLACES LIKE THIS EXISTED. WHEN VIOLENCE ERUPTED AT A MOMENT'S NOTICE, WHEN LIVES AROUND US WERE TAKEN AWAY... ONE AFTER ANOTHER...
SO I THINK WE ALL RECOGNIZE HOW IMPORTANT THIS PLACE IS. TOO IMPORTANT TO RISK LOSING IT... THIS COMMUNITY... THIS SANCTUARY... OVER A DARK INCIDENT THAT HAS ALREADY BEEN LITIGATED IN THE STREETS OF THIS COMMUNITY.
THOSE RESPONSIBLE HAVE ALREADY BEEN PUNISHED. THOSE WHO RETALIATED NEED TO FOCUS ON EARNING THE TRUST OF THEIR NEIGHBORS BACK, NOT HAVING THE WHOLE INCIDENT REPLAYED IN THIS COURT.
THAT IS WHY I PROPOSE... NO, URGE... NO, BEG YOU TO DROP ALL CHARGES... SO THAT WE CAN MOVE ON.

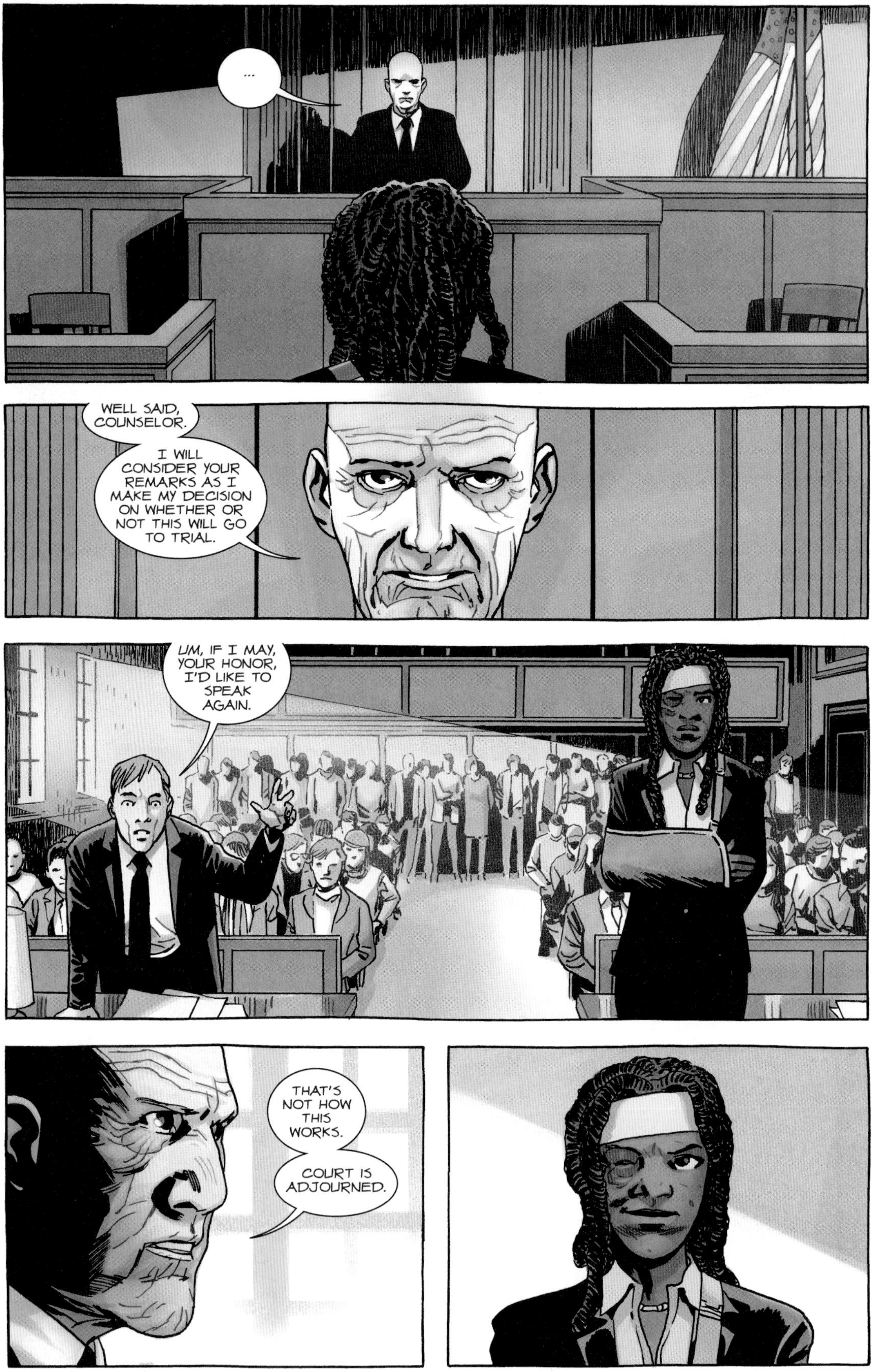
...
WELL SAID, COUNSELOR.
I WILL CONSIDER YOUR REMARKS AS I MAKE MY DECISION ON WHETHER OR NOT THIS WILL GO TO TRIAL.
UM, IF I MAY, YOUR HONOR, I'D LIKE TO SPEAK AGAIN.
THAT'S NOT HOW THIS WORKS.
COURT IS ADJOURNED.

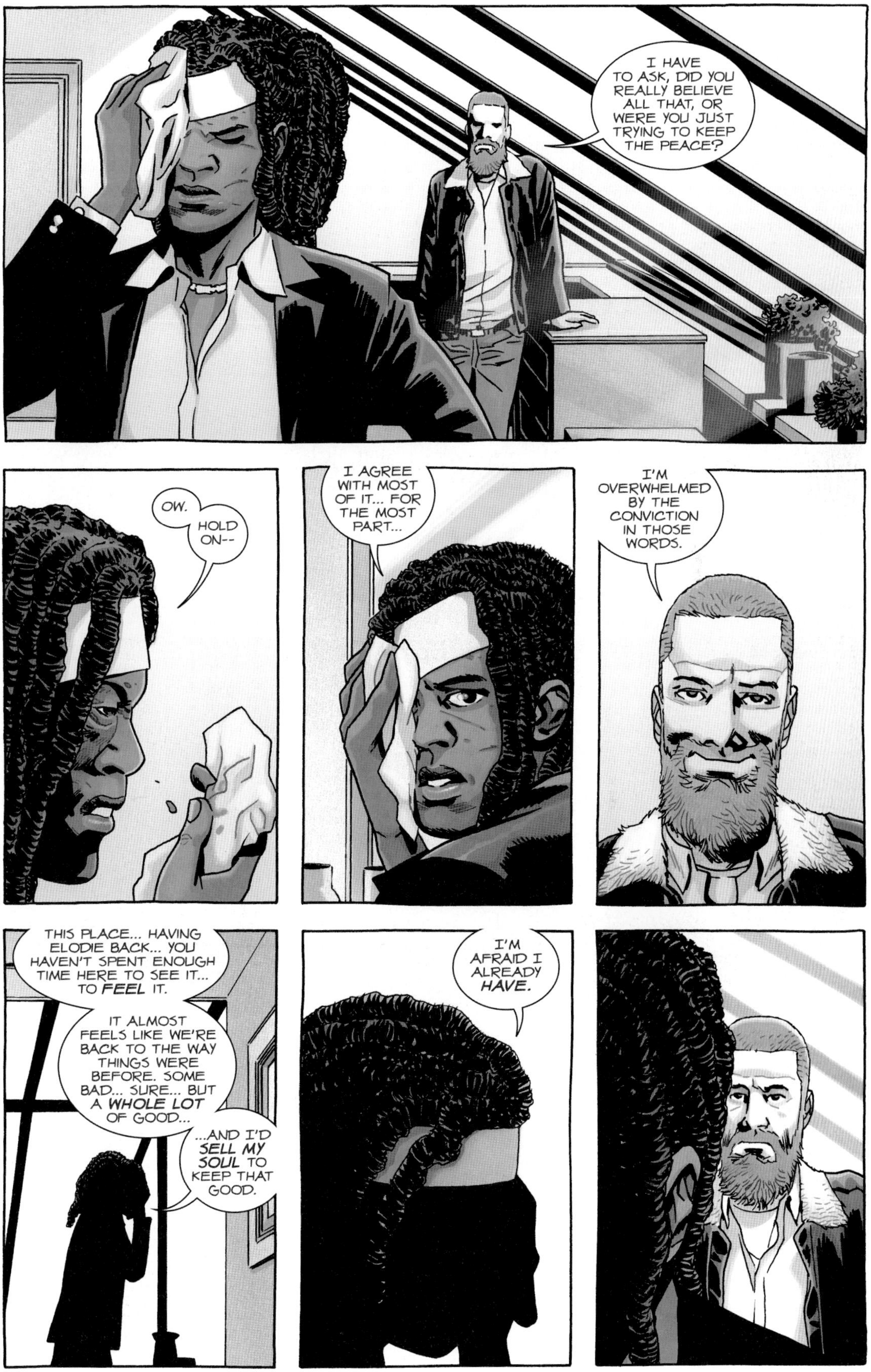
I HAVE TO ASK, DID YOU REALLY BELIEVE ALL THAT, OR WERE YOU JUST TRYING TO KEEP THE PEACE?
OW.
HOLD ON--
I AGREE WITH MOST OF IT... FOR THE MOST PART...
I'M OVERWHELMED BY THE CONVICTION IN THOSE WORDS.
THIS PLACE... HAVING ELODIE BACK... YOU HAVEN'T SPENT ENOUGH TIME HERE TO SEE IT... TO FEEL IT.
IT ALMOST FEELS LIKE WE'RE BACK TO THE WAY THINGS WERE BEFORE. SOME BAD... SURE... BUT A WHOLE LOT OF GOOD...
...AND I'D SELL MY SOUL TO KEEP THAT GOOD.
I'M AFRAID I ALREADY HAVE.

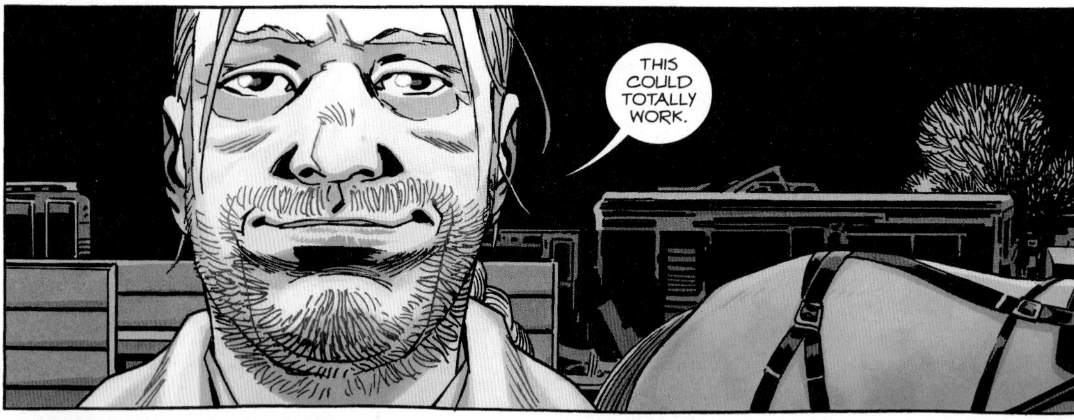
THIS COULD TOTALLY WORK.

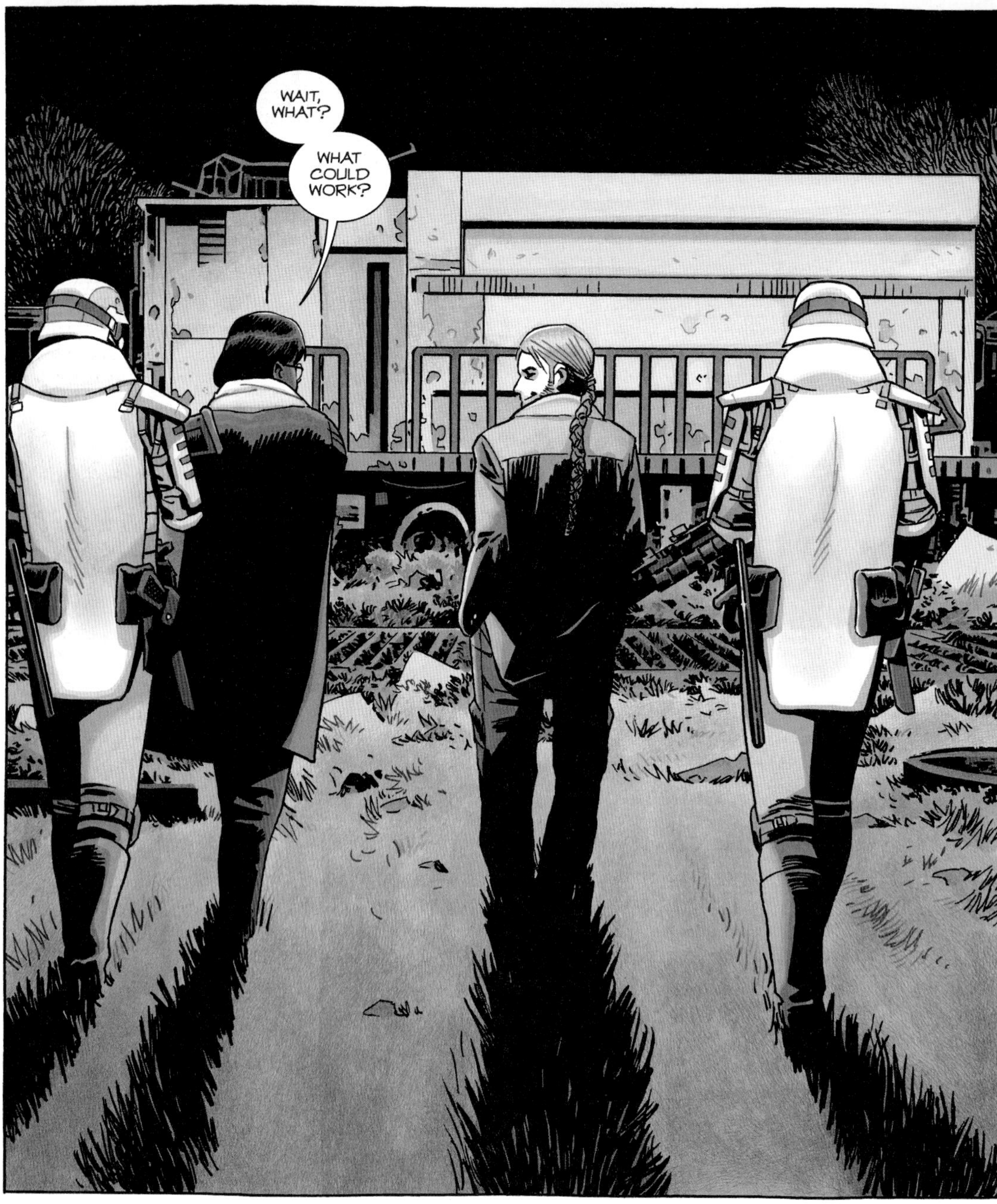
WAIT, WHAT?
WHAT COULD WORK?

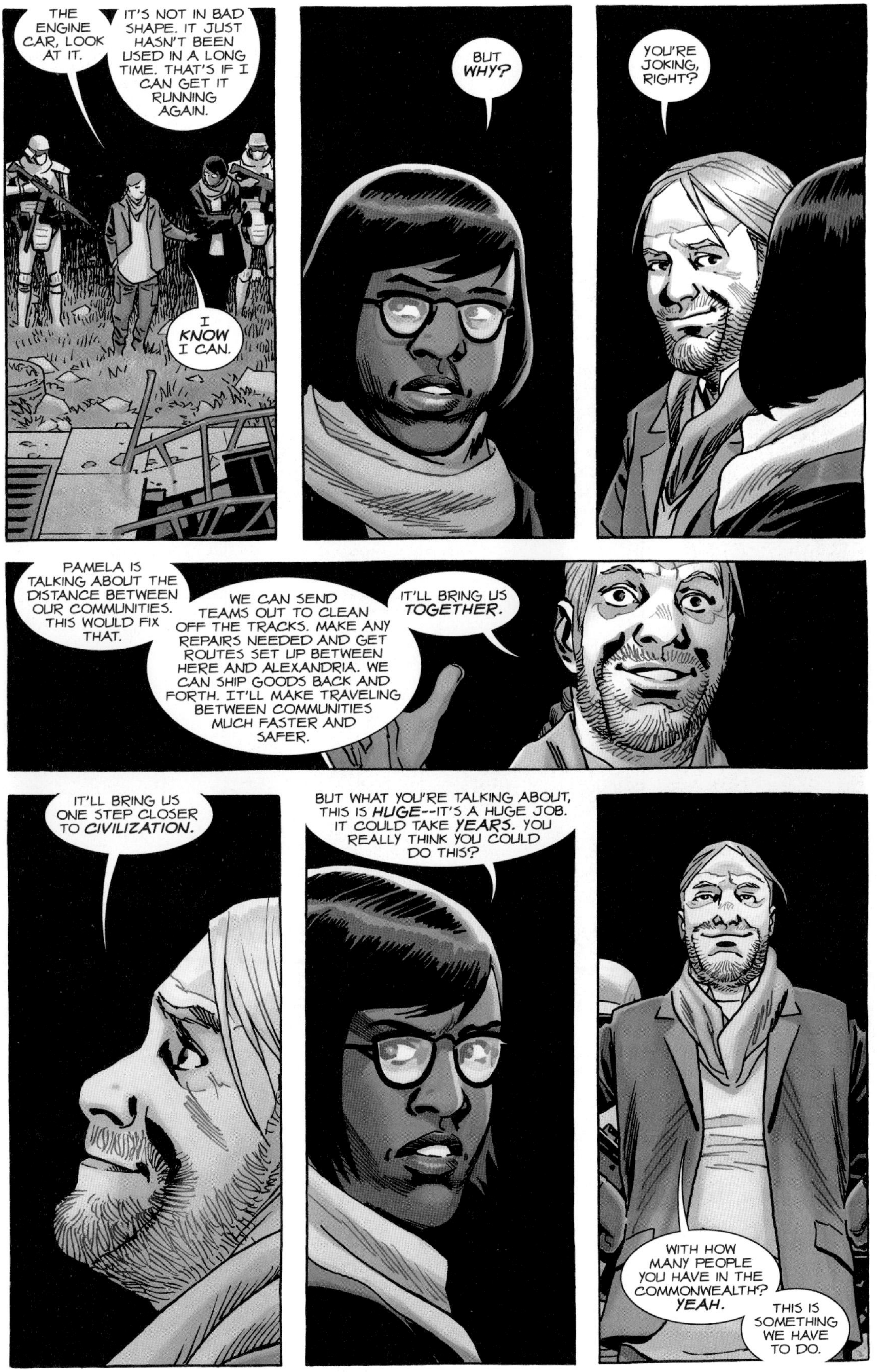
THE ENGINE CAR, LOOK AT IT.
IT'S NOT IN BAD SHAPE. IT JUST HASN'T BEEN USED IN A LONG TIME. THAT'S IF I CAN GET IT RUNNING AGAIN.
I *KNOW* I CAN.
BUT *WHY?*
YOU'RE JOKING, RIGHT?
PAMELA IS TALKING ABOUT THE DISTANCE BETWEEN OUR COMMUNITIES. THIS WOULD FIX THAT.
WE CAN SEND TEAMS OUT TO CLEAN OFF THE TRACKS. MAKE ANY REPAIRS NEEDED AND GET ROUTES SET UP BETWEEN HERE AND ALEXANDRIA. WE CAN SHIP GOODS BACK AND FORTH. IT'LL MAKE TRAVELING BETWEEN COMMUNITIES MUCH FASTER AND SAFER.
IT'LL BRING US *TOGETHER.*
IT'LL BRING US ONE STEP CLOSER TO *CIVILIZATION.*
BUT WHAT YOU'RE TALKING ABOUT, THIS IS *HUGE*--IT'S A HUGE JOB. IT COULD TAKE *YEARS.* YOU REALLY THINK YOU COULD DO THIS?
WITH HOW MANY PEOPLE YOU HAVE IN THE COMMONWEALTH? *YEAH.*
THIS IS SOMETHING WE HAVE TO DO.

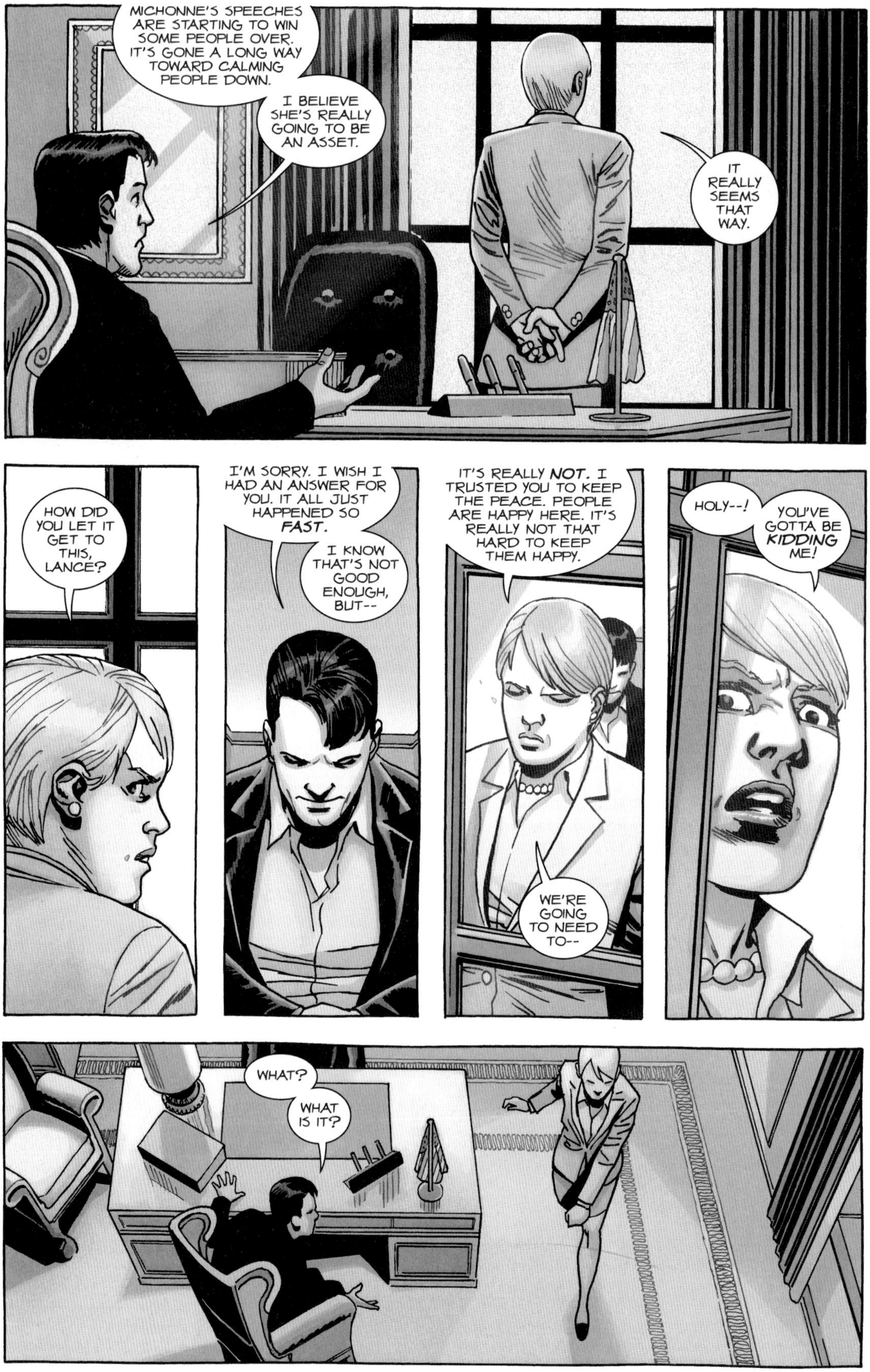
MICHONNE'S SPEECHES ARE STARTING TO WIN SOME PEOPLE OVER. IT'S GONE A LONG WAY TOWARD CALMING PEOPLE DOWN.
I BELIEVE SHE'S REALLY GOING TO BE AN ASSET.
IT REALLY SEEMS THAT WAY.
HOW DID YOU LET IT GET TO THIS, LANCE?
I'M SORRY. I WISH I HAD AN ANSWER FOR YOU. IT ALL JUST HAPPENED SO *FAST.*
I KNOW THAT'S NOT GOOD ENOUGH, BUT--
IT'S REALLY *NOT.* I TRUSTED YOU TO KEEP THE PEACE. PEOPLE ARE HAPPY HERE. IT'S REALLY NOT THAT HARD TO KEEP THEM HAPPY.
WE'RE GOING TO NEED TO--
HOLY--!
YOU'VE GOTTA BE *KIDDING* ME!
WHAT?
WHAT IS IT?

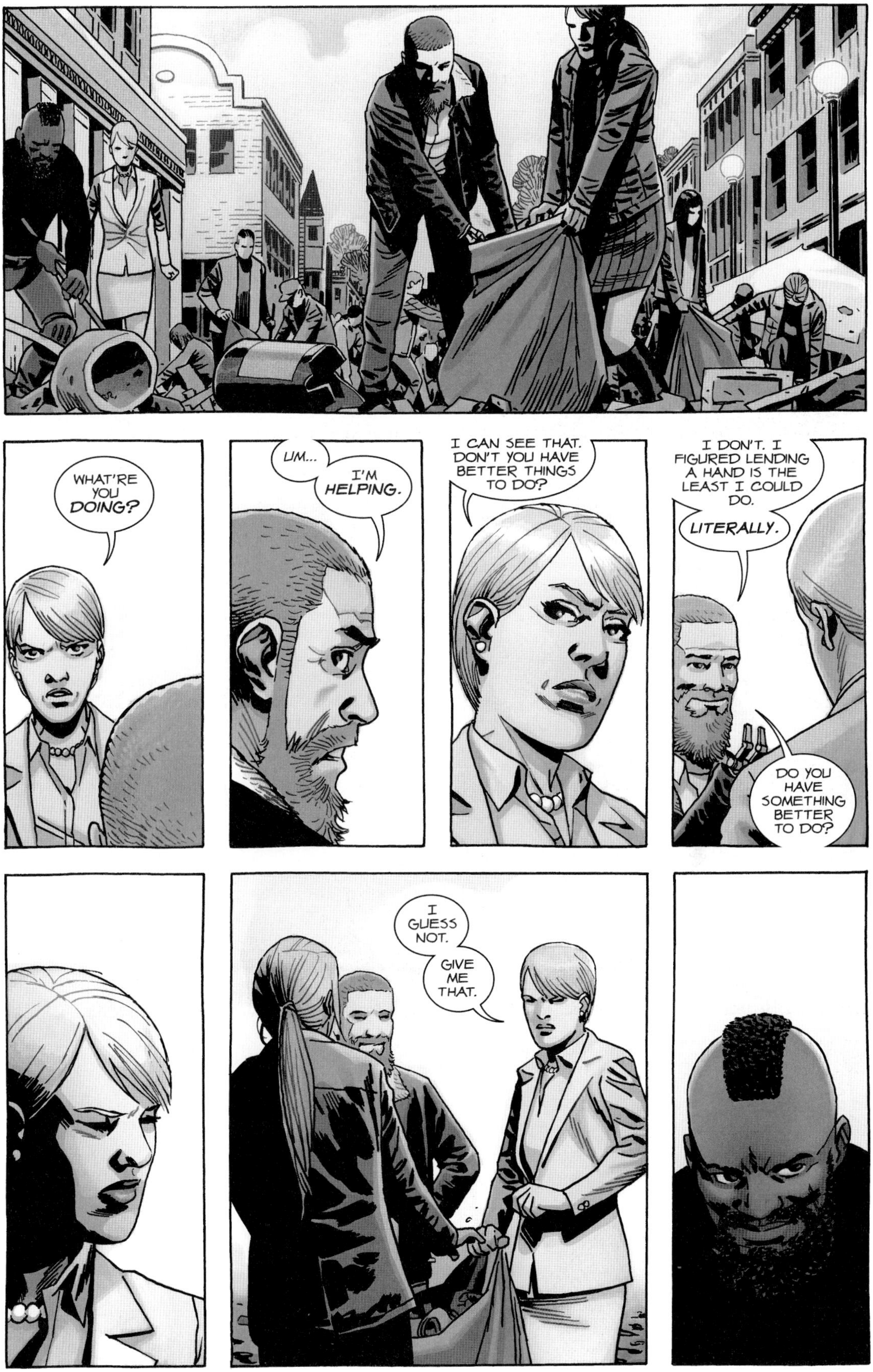

WHAT'RE YOU DOING?
UM...
I'M HELPING.
I CAN SEE THAT. DON'T YOU HAVE BETTER THINGS TO DO?
I DON'T. I FIGURED LENDING A HAND IS THE LEAST I COULD DO.
LITERALLY.
DO YOU HAVE SOMETHING BETTER TO DO?
I GUESS NOT.
GIVE ME THAT.

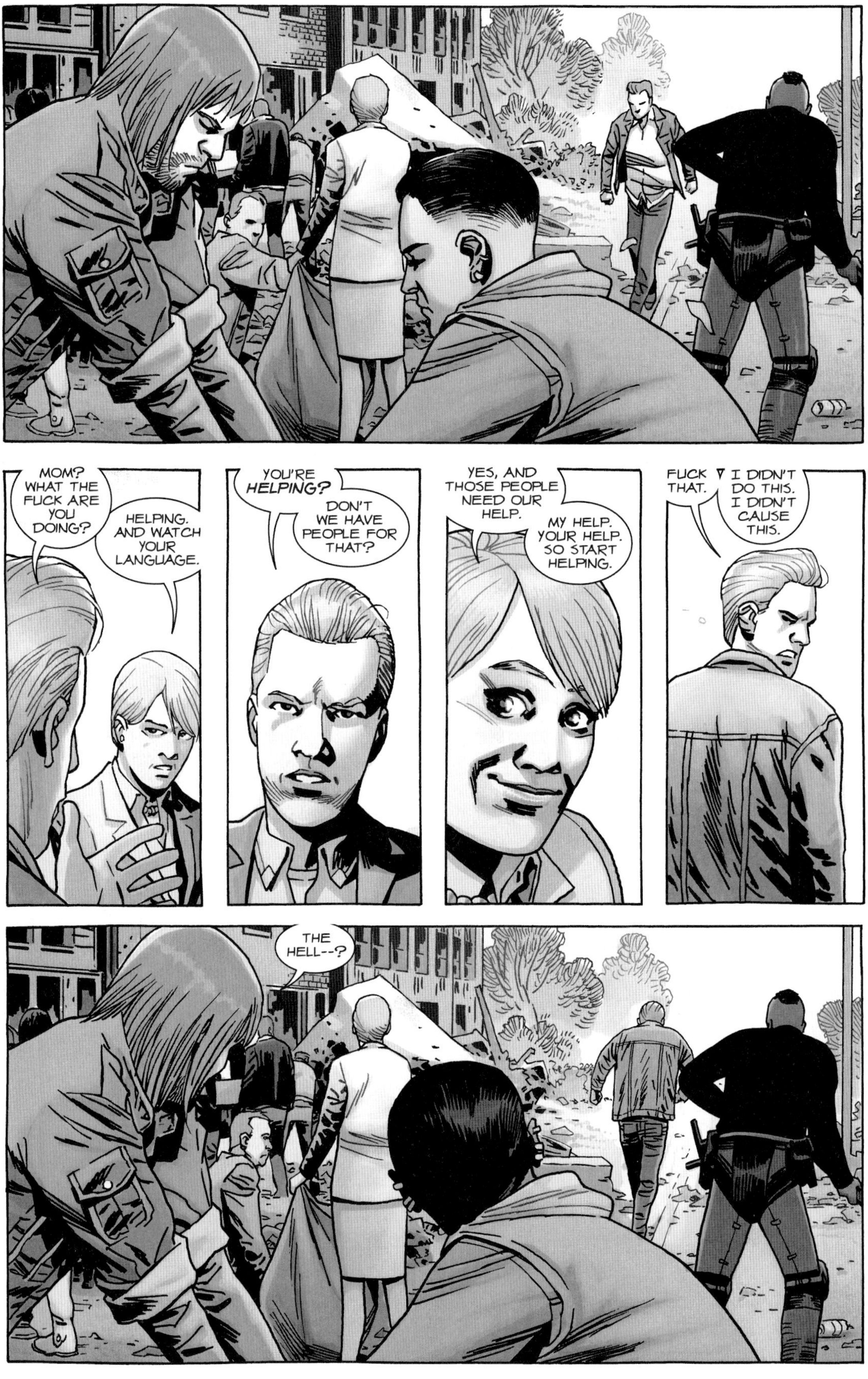
MOM? WHAT THE FUCK ARE YOU DOING?
HELPING. AND WATCH YOUR LANGUAGE.
YOU'RE *HELPING?*
DON'T WE HAVE PEOPLE FOR THAT?
YES, AND THOSE PEOPLE NEED OUR HELP.
MY HELP. YOUR HELP. SO START HELPING.
FUCK THAT.
I DIDN'T DO THIS. I DIDN'T CAUSE THIS.
THE HELL--?

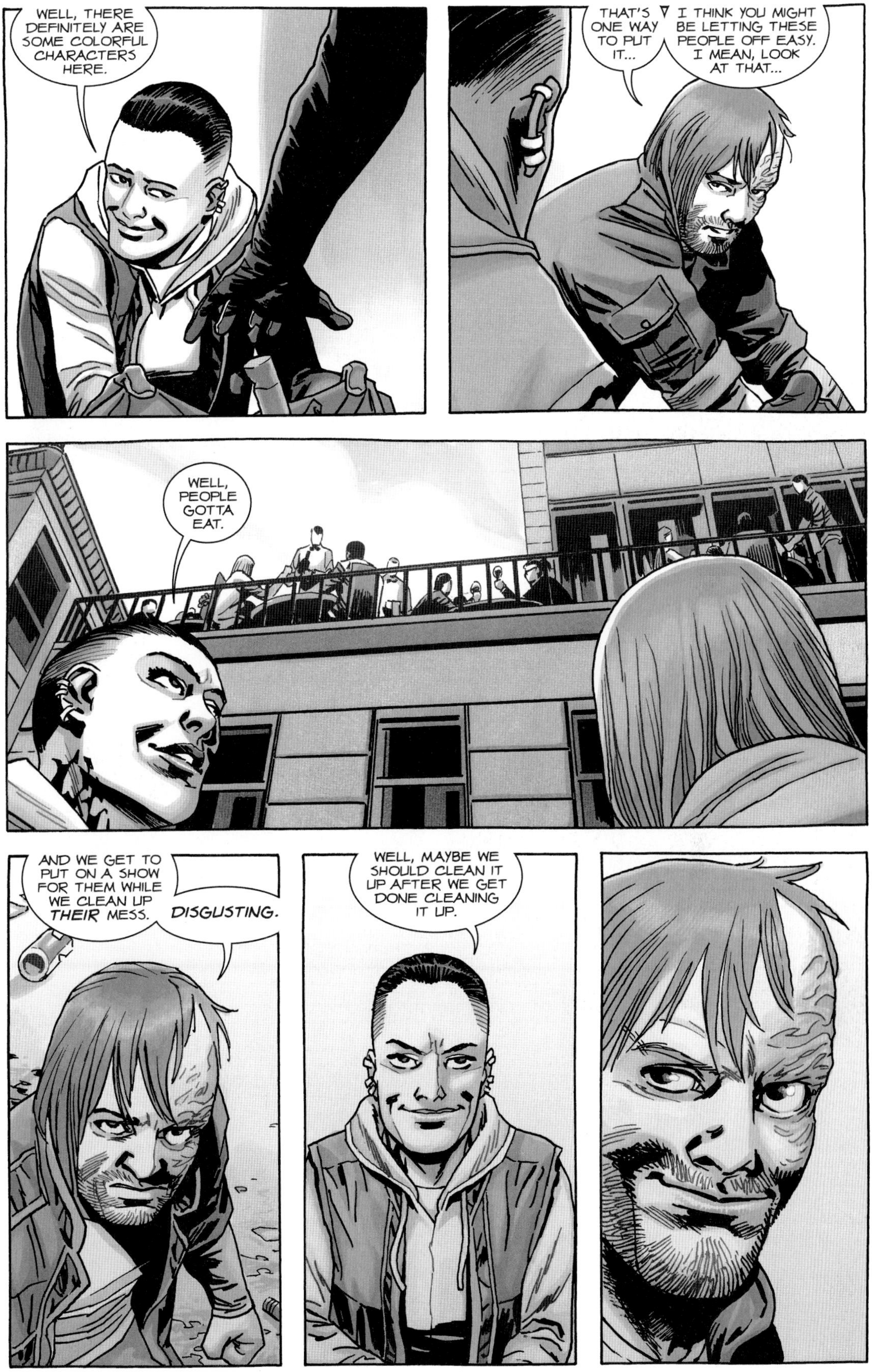
WELL, THERE DEFINITELY ARE SOME COLORFUL CHARACTERS HERE.
THAT'S ONE WAY TO PUT IT...
I THINK YOU MIGHT BE LETTING THESE PEOPLE OFF EASY. I MEAN, LOOK AT THAT...
WELL, PEOPLE GOTTA EAT.
AND WE GET TO PUT ON A SHOW FOR THEM WHILE WE CLEAN UP *THEIR* MESS.
DISGUSTING.
WELL, MAYBE WE SHOULD CLEAN IT UP AFTER WE GET DONE CLEANING IT UP.

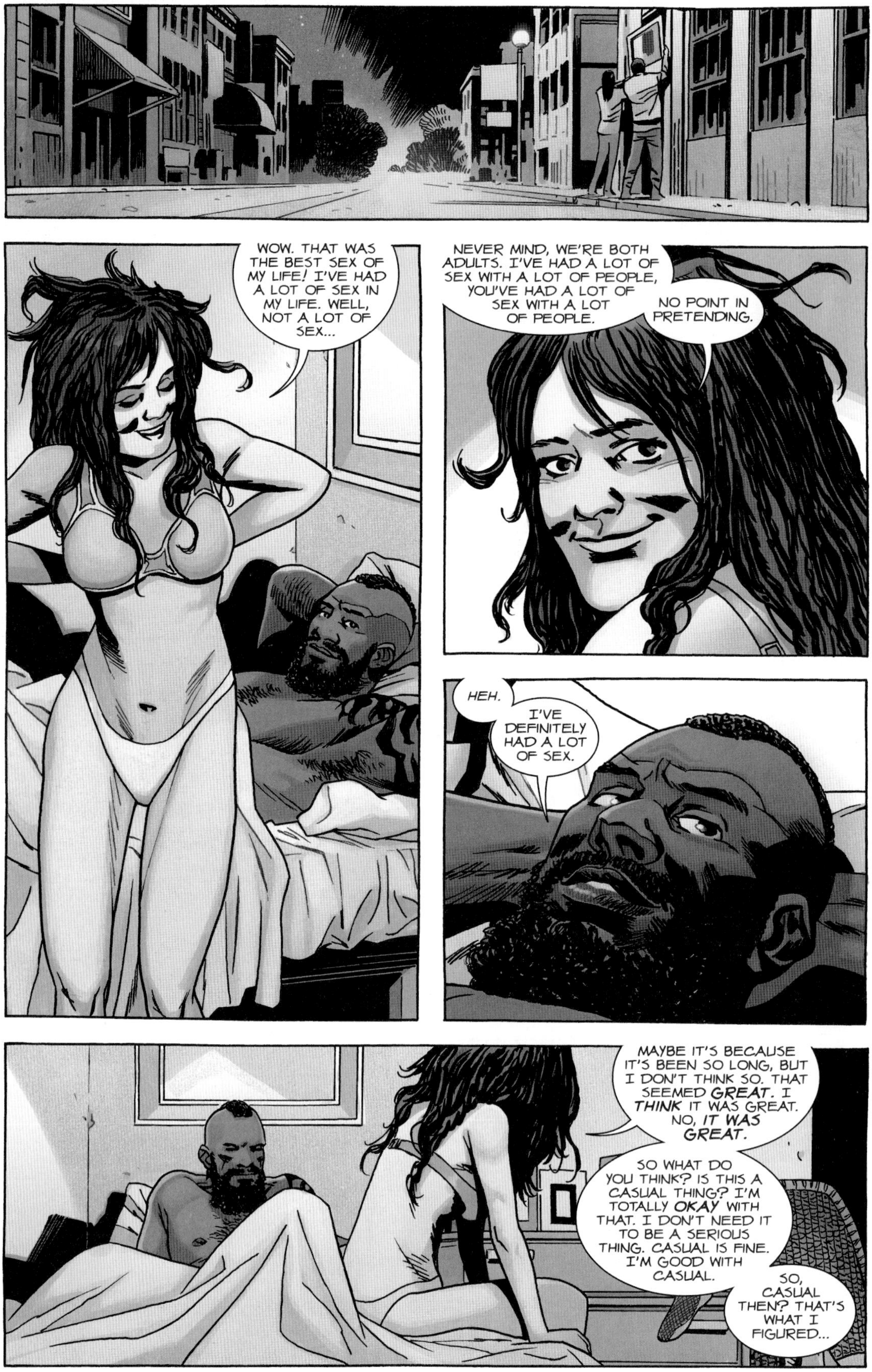

WOW. THAT WAS THE BEST SEX OF MY LIFE! I'VE HAD A LOT OF SEX IN MY LIFE. WELL, NOT A LOT OF SEX...
NEVER MIND, WE'RE BOTH ADULTS. I'VE HAD A LOT OF SEX WITH A LOT OF PEOPLE, YOU'VE HAD A LOT OF SEX WITH A LOT OF PEOPLE.
NO POINT IN PRETENDING.
HEH.
I'VE DEFINITELY HAD A LOT OF SEX.
MAYBE IT'S BECAUSE IT'S BEEN SO LONG, BUT I DON'T THINK SO. THAT SEEMED GREAT. I THINK IT WAS GREAT. NO, IT WAS GREAT.
SO WHAT DO YOU THINK? IS THIS A CASUAL THING? I'M TOTALLY OKAY WITH THAT. I DON'T NEED IT TO BE A SERIOUS THING. CASUAL IS FINE. I'M GOOD WITH CASUAL.
SO, CASUAL THEN? THAT'S WHAT I FIGURED...

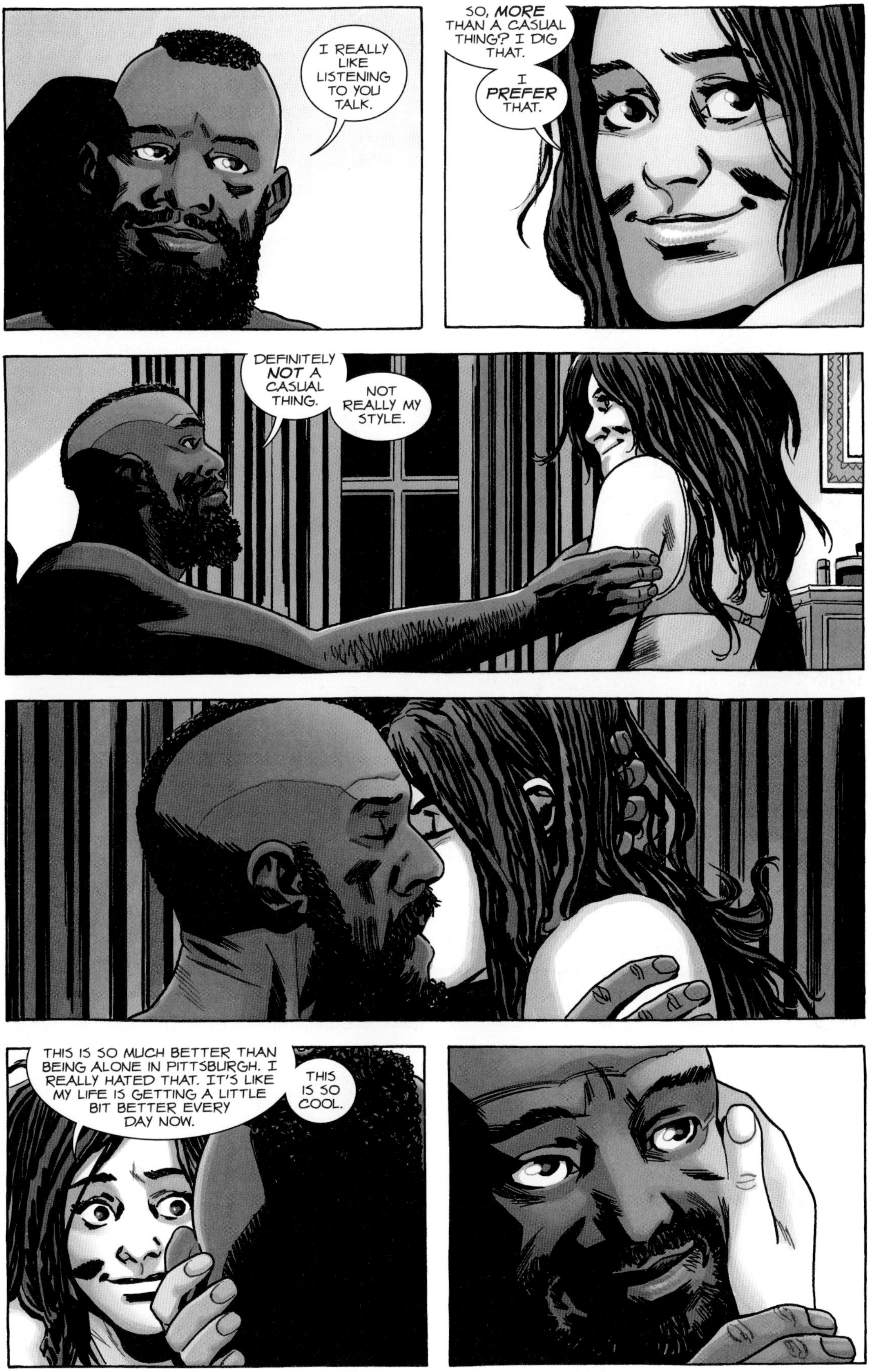
I REALLY LIKE LISTENING TO YOU TALK.
SO, MORE THAN A CASUAL THING? I DIG THAT.
I PREFER THAT.
DEFINITELY NOT A CASUAL THING.
NOT REALLY MY STYLE.
THIS IS SO MUCH BETTER THAN BEING ALONE IN PITTSBURGH. I REALLY HATED THAT. IT'S LIKE MY LIFE IS GETTING A LITTLE BIT BETTER EVERY DAY NOW.
THIS IS SO COOL.

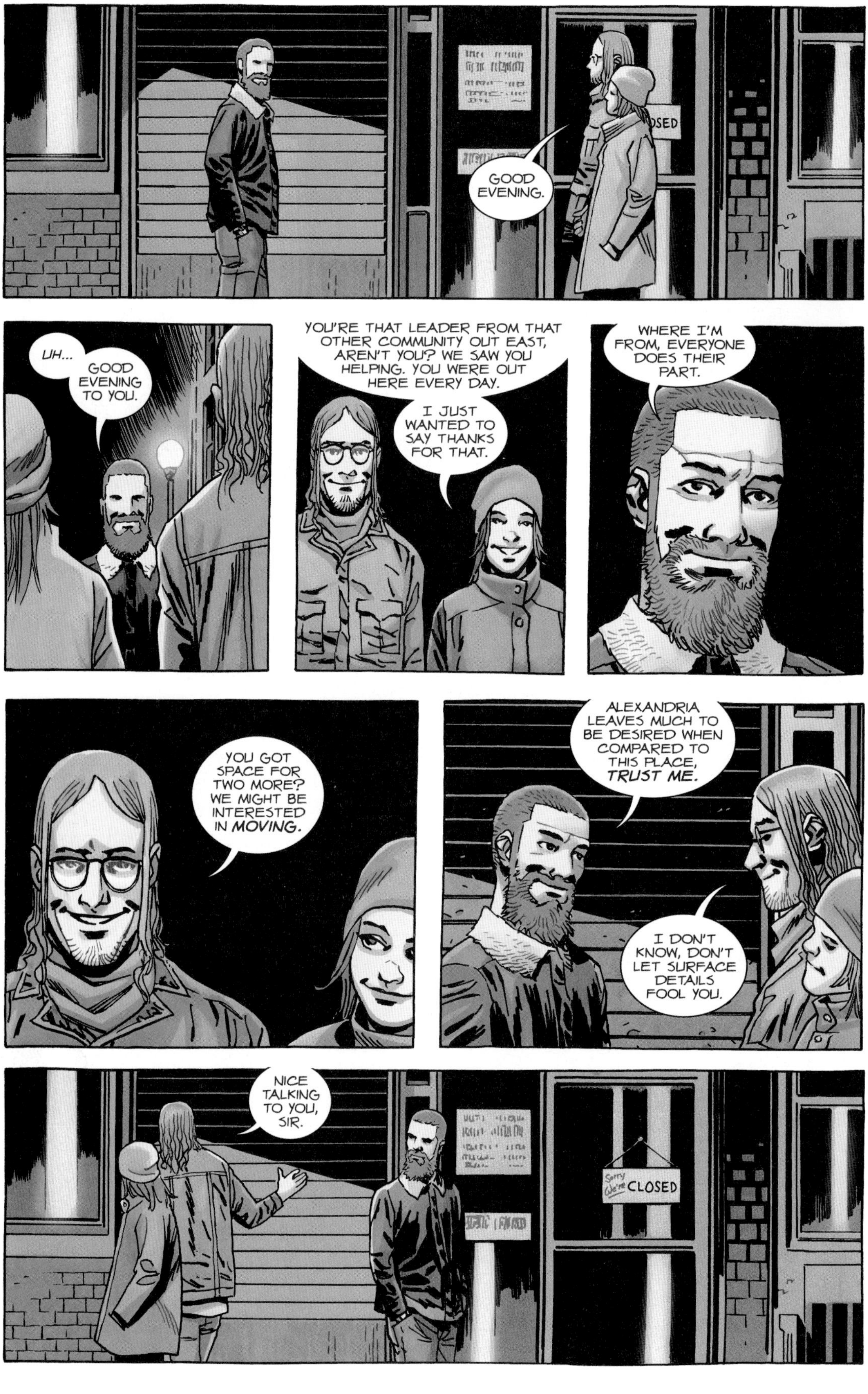
GOOD EVENING.
UH... GOOD EVENING TO YOU.
YOU'RE THAT LEADER FROM THAT OTHER COMMUNITY OUT EAST, AREN'T YOU? WE SAW YOU HELPING. YOU WERE OUT HERE EVERY DAY.
I JUST WANTED TO SAY THANKS FOR THAT.
WHERE I'M FROM, EVERYONE DOES THEIR PART.
YOU GOT SPACE FOR TWO MORE? WE MIGHT BE INTERESTED IN *MOVING*.
ALEXANDRIA LEAVES MUCH TO BE DESIRED WHEN COMPARED TO THIS PLACE, *TRUST ME*.
I DON'T KNOW, DON'T LET SURFACE DETAILS FOOL YOU.
NICE TALKING TO YOU, SIR.
Sorry We're CLOSED

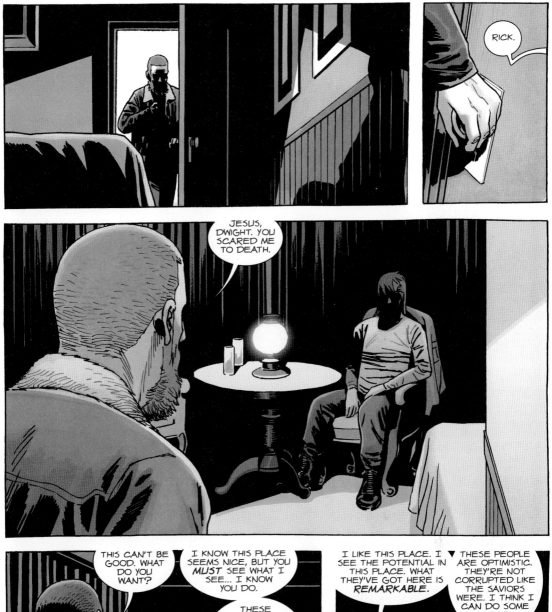

RICK.

JESUS, DWIGHT. YOU SCARED ME TO DEATH.

THIS CAN'T BE GOOD. WHAT DO YOU WANT?

I KNOW THIS PLACE SEEMS NICE, BUT YOU *MUST* SEE WHAT I SEE... I KNOW YOU DO.

THESE PEOPLE LIVE UNDERFOOT. THERE'S A BOOT ON THEIR NECKS, AND THEY *ALL* KNOW IT.

I LIKE THIS PLACE. I SEE THE POTENTIAL IN THIS PLACE. WHAT THEY'VE GOT HERE IS *REMARKABLE.*

THESE PEOPLE ARE OPTIMISTIC. THEY'RE NOT CORRUPTED LIKE THE SAVIORS WERE. I THINK I CAN DO SOME GOOD HERE.

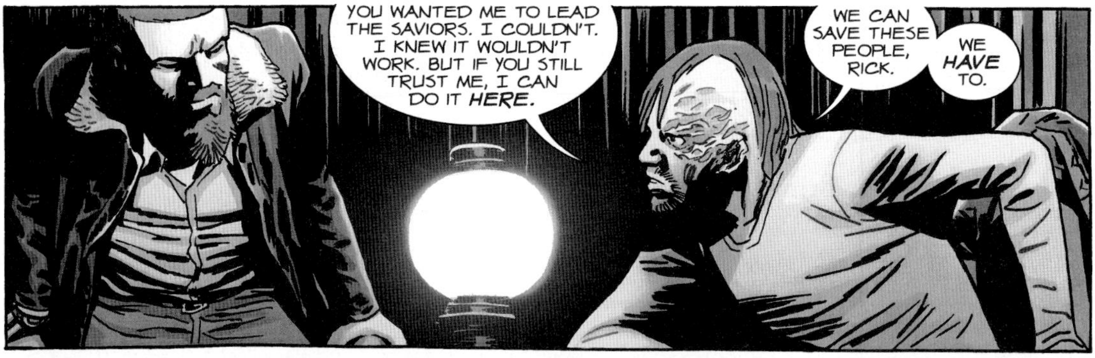
YOU WANTED ME TO LEAD THE SAVIORS. I COULDN'T. I KNEW IT WOULDN'T WORK. BUT IF YOU STILL TRUST ME, I CAN DO IT HERE.
WE CAN SAVE THESE PEOPLE, RICK.
WE HAVE TO.

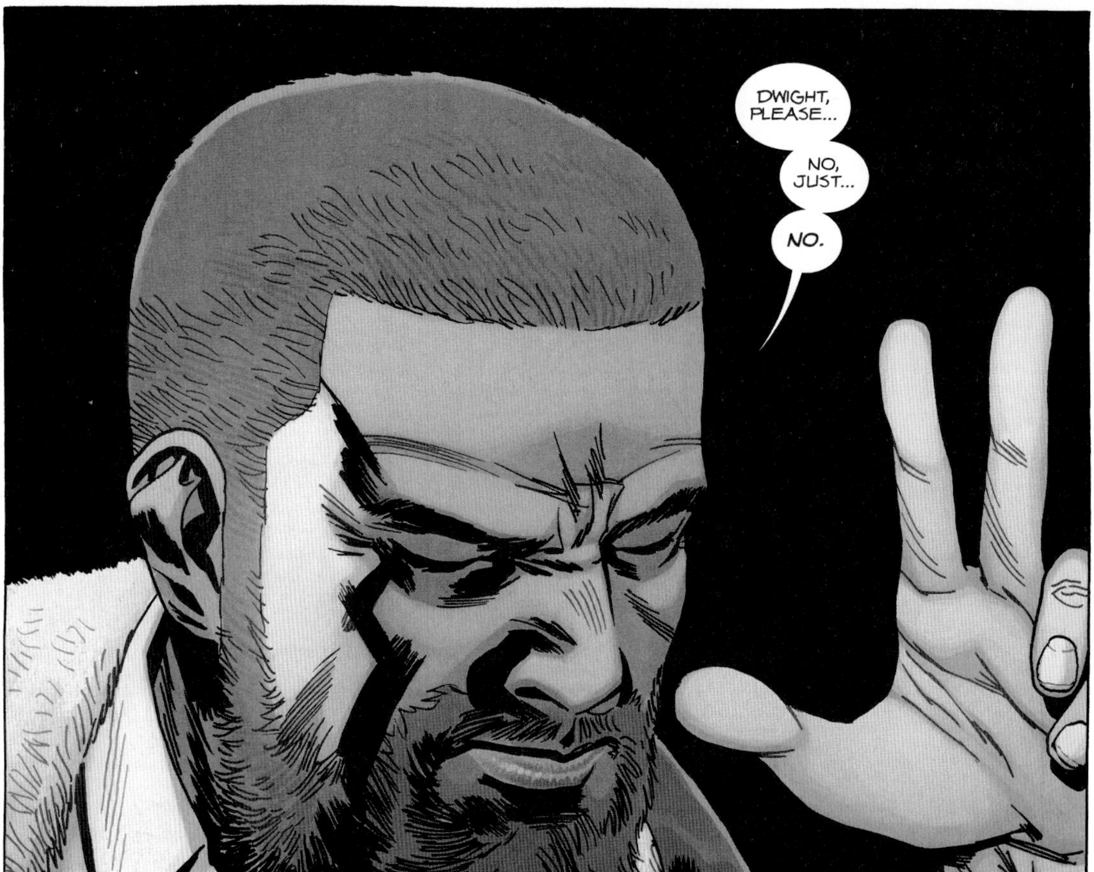
DWIGHT, PLEASE...
NO, JUST...
NO.

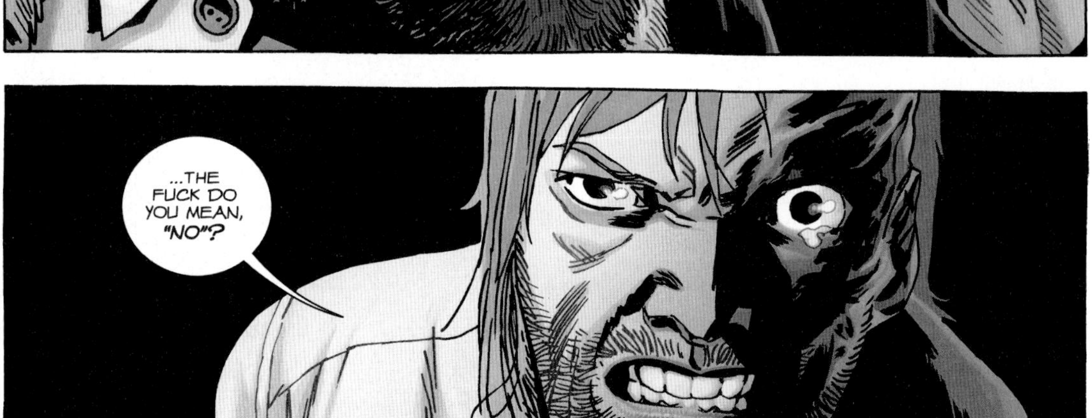
...THE FUCK DO YOU MEAN, "NO"?

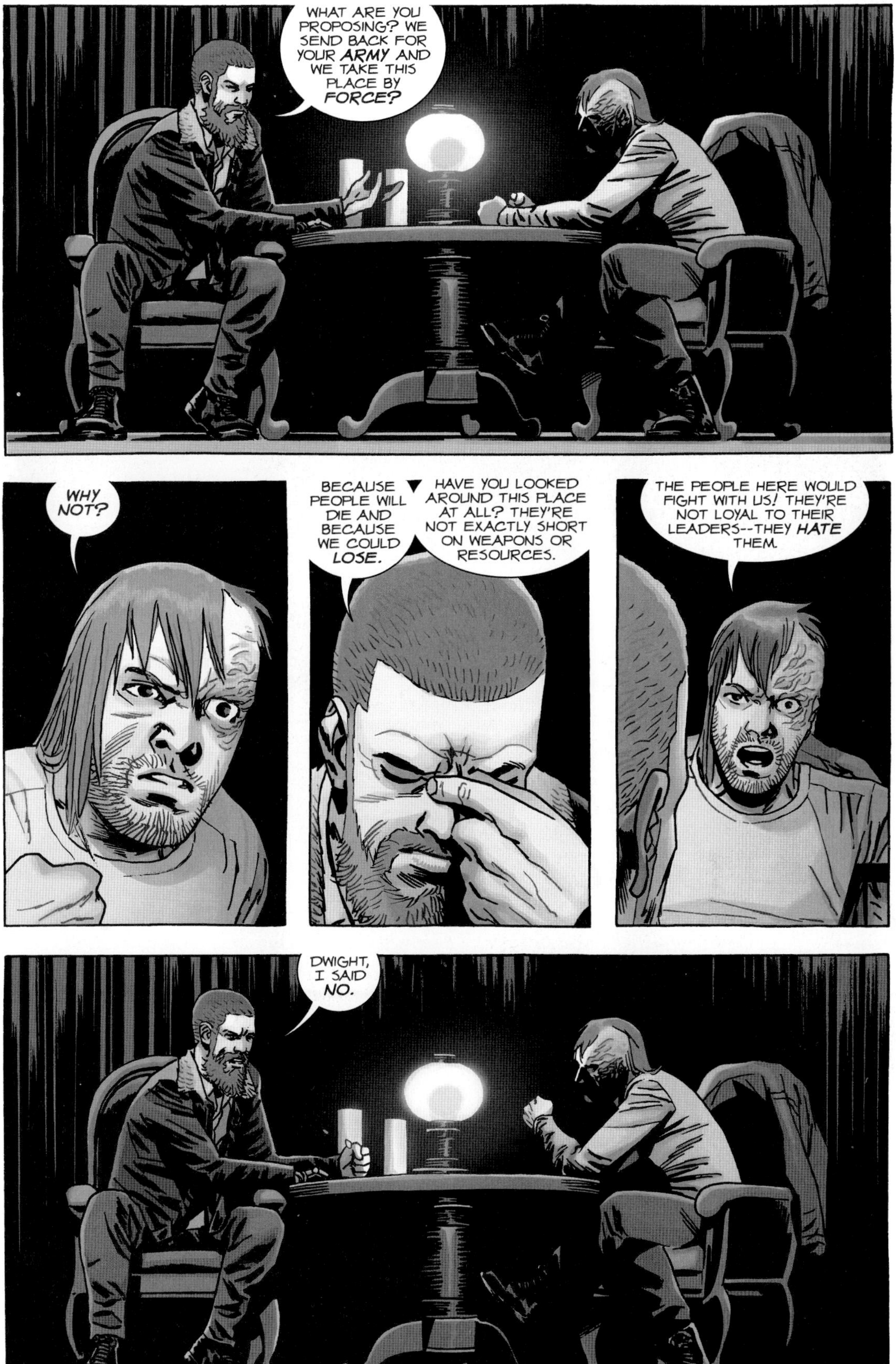
WHAT ARE YOU PROPOSING? WE SEND BACK FOR YOUR ARMY AND WE TAKE THIS PLACE BY FORCE?
WHY NOT?
BECAUSE PEOPLE WILL DIE AND BECAUSE WE COULD LOSE.
HAVE YOU LOOKED AROUND THIS PLACE AT ALL? THEY'RE NOT EXACTLY SHORT ON WEAPONS OR RESOURCES.
THE PEOPLE HERE WOULD FIGHT WITH US! THEY'RE NOT LOYAL TO THEIR LEADERS--THEY HATE THEM.
DWIGHT, I SAID NO.

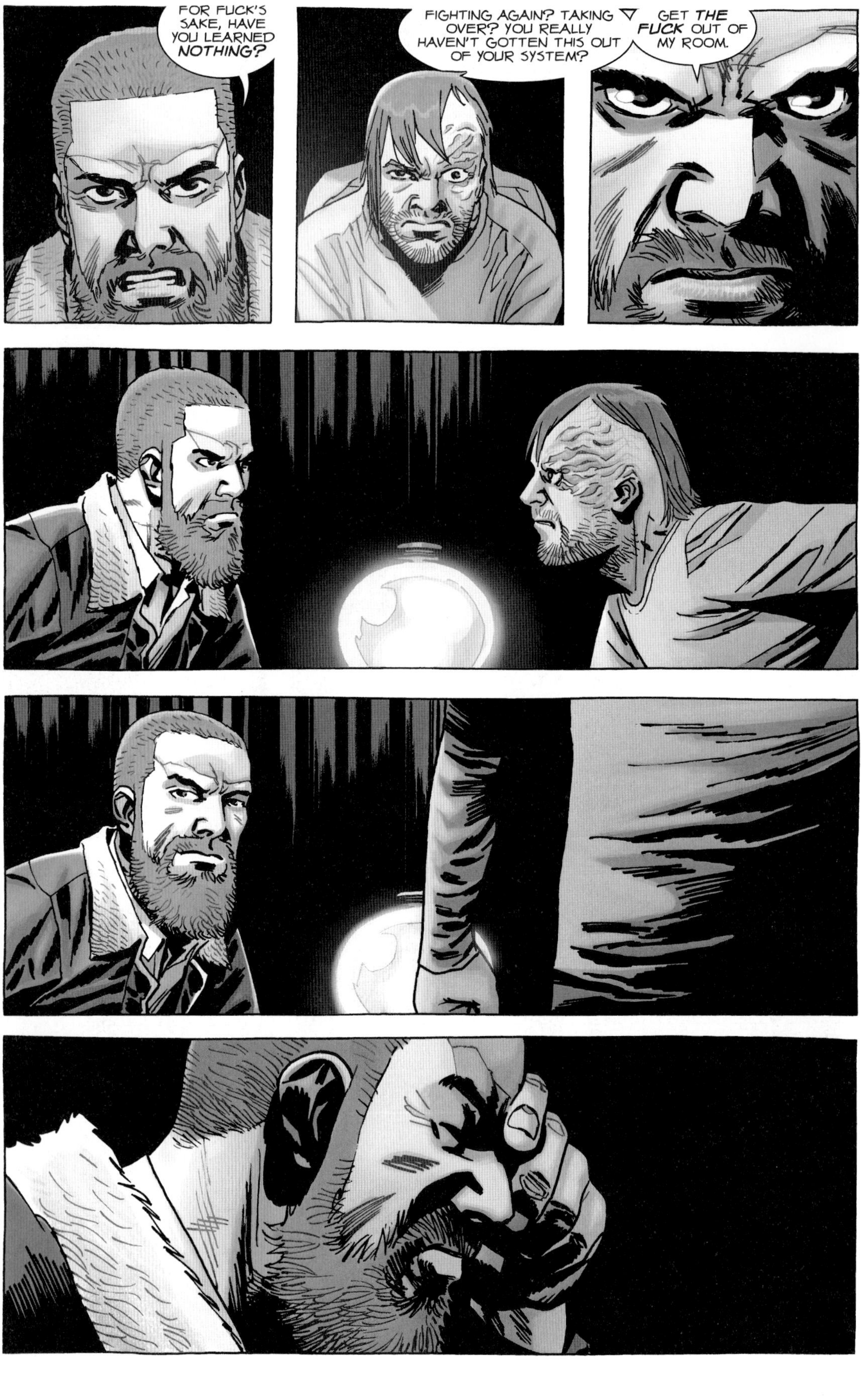

FOR FUCK'S SAKE, HAVE YOU LEARNED NOTHING?
FIGHTING AGAIN? TAKING OVER? YOU REALLY HAVEN'T GOTTEN THIS OUT OF YOUR SYSTEM?
GET THE FUCK OUT OF MY ROOM.

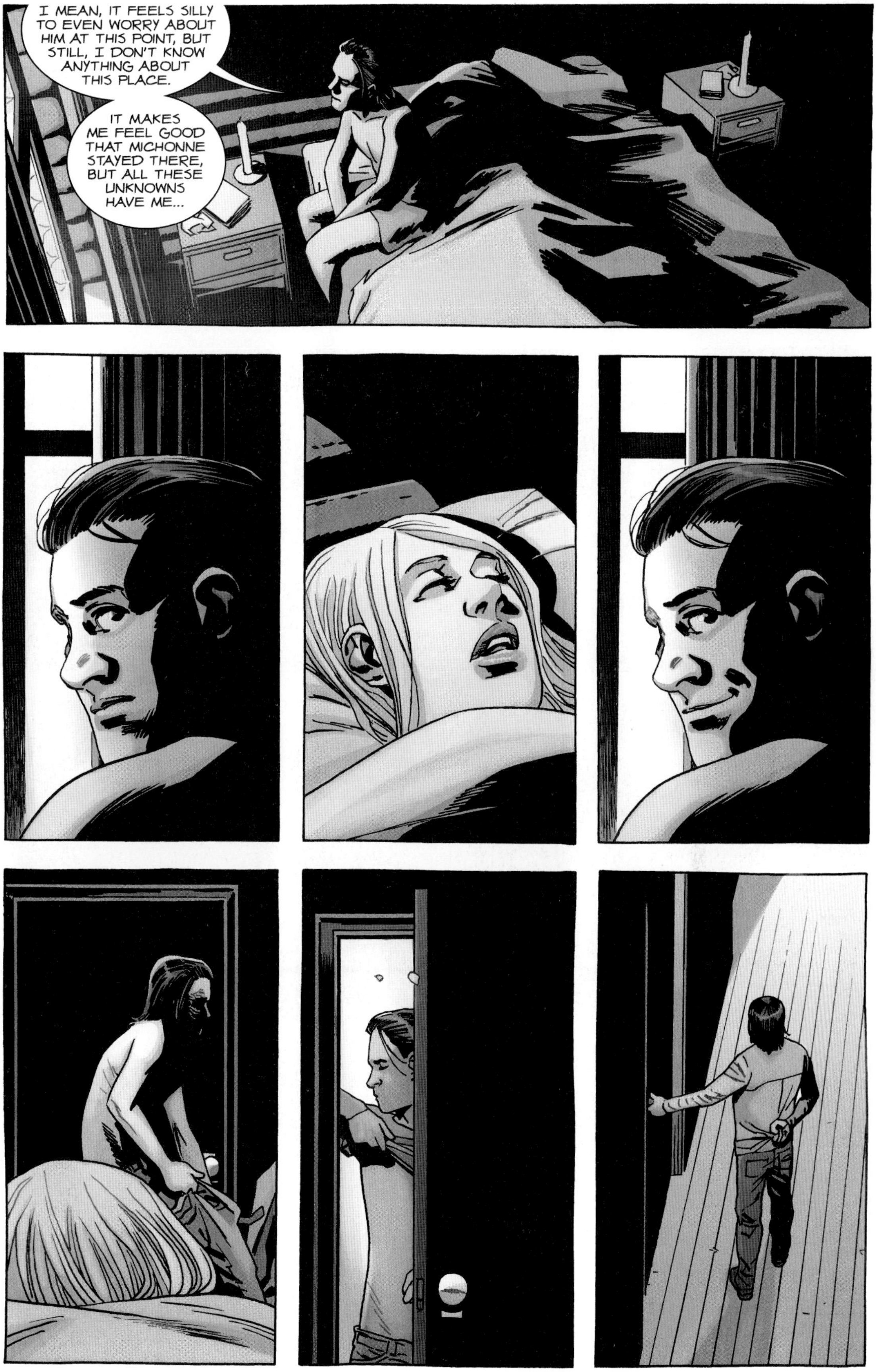

I MEAN, IT FEELS SILLY TO EVEN WORRY ABOUT HIM AT THIS POINT, BUT STILL, I DON'T KNOW ANYTHING ABOUT THIS PLACE.
IT MAKES ME FEEL GOOD THAT MICHONNE STAYED THERE, BUT ALL THESE UNKNOWNS HAVE ME...

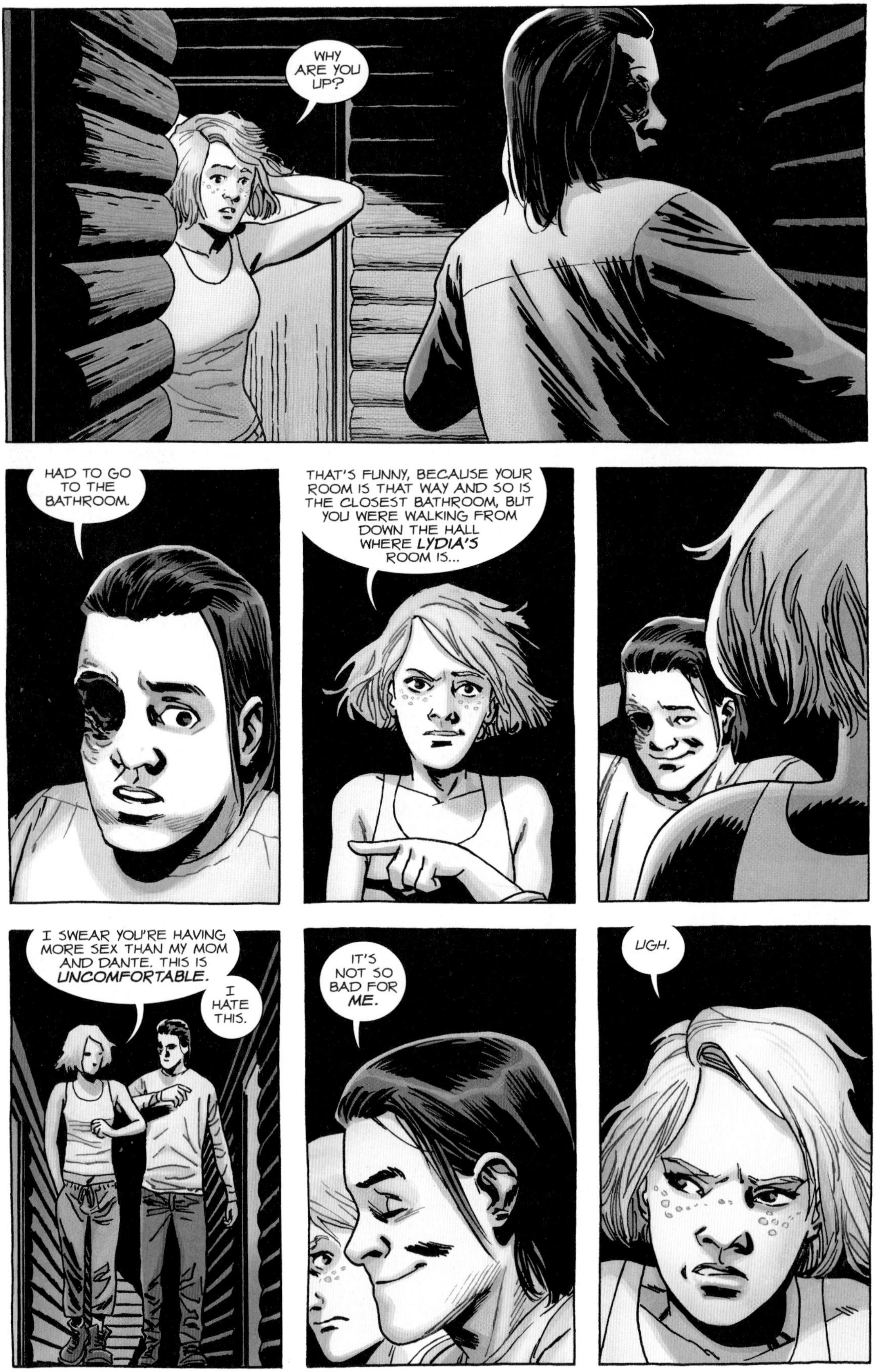

WHY ARE YOU UP?
HAD TO GO TO THE BATHROOM.
THAT'S FUNNY, BECAUSE YOUR ROOM IS THAT WAY AND SO IS THE CLOSEST BATHROOM, BUT YOU WERE WALKING FROM DOWN THE HALL WHERE LYDIA'S ROOM IS...
I SWEAR YOU'RE HAVING MORE SEX THAN MY MOM AND DANTE. THIS IS UNCOMFORTABLE.
I HATE THIS.
IT'S NOT SO BAD FOR ME.
UGH.

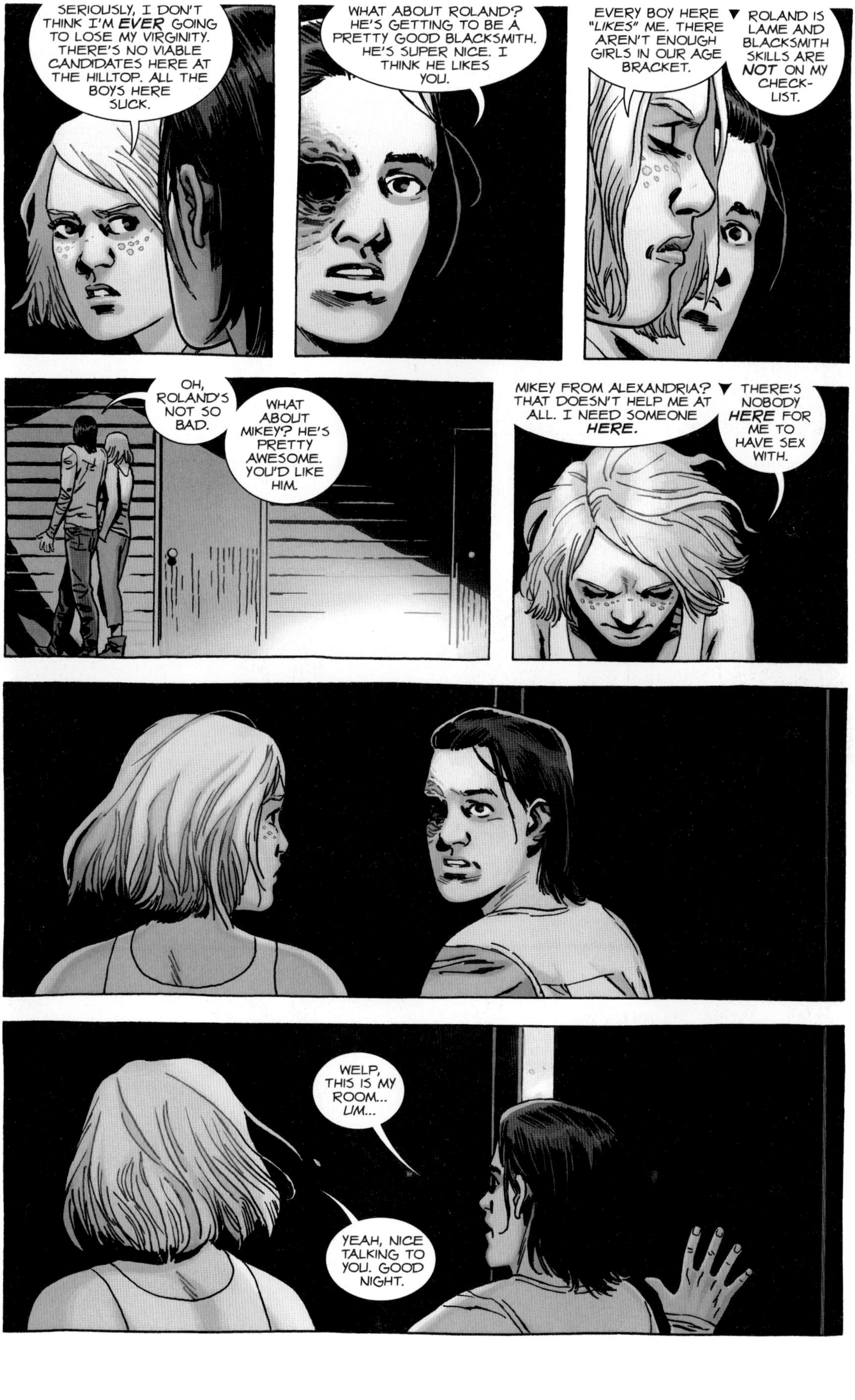
SERIOUSLY, I DON'T THINK I'M EVER GOING TO LOSE MY VIRGINITY. THERE'S NO VIABLE CANDIDATES HERE AT THE HILLTOP. ALL THE BOYS HERE SUCK.
WHAT ABOUT ROLAND? HE'S GETTING TO BE A PRETTY GOOD BLACKSMITH. HE'S SUPER NICE. I THINK HE LIKES YOU.
EVERY BOY HERE "LIKES" ME. THERE AREN'T ENOUGH GIRLS IN OUR AGE BRACKET.
ROLAND IS LAME AND BLACKSMITH SKILLS ARE NOT ON MY CHECK-LIST.
OH, ROLAND'S NOT SO BAD.
WHAT ABOUT MIKEY? HE'S PRETTY AWESOME. YOU'D LIKE HIM.
MIKEY FROM ALEXANDRIA? THAT DOESN'T HELP ME AT ALL. I NEED SOMEONE HERE.
THERE'S NOBODY HERE FOR ME TO HAVE SEX WITH.
WELP, THIS IS MY ROOM... UM...
YEAH, NICE TALKING TO YOU. GOOD NIGHT.

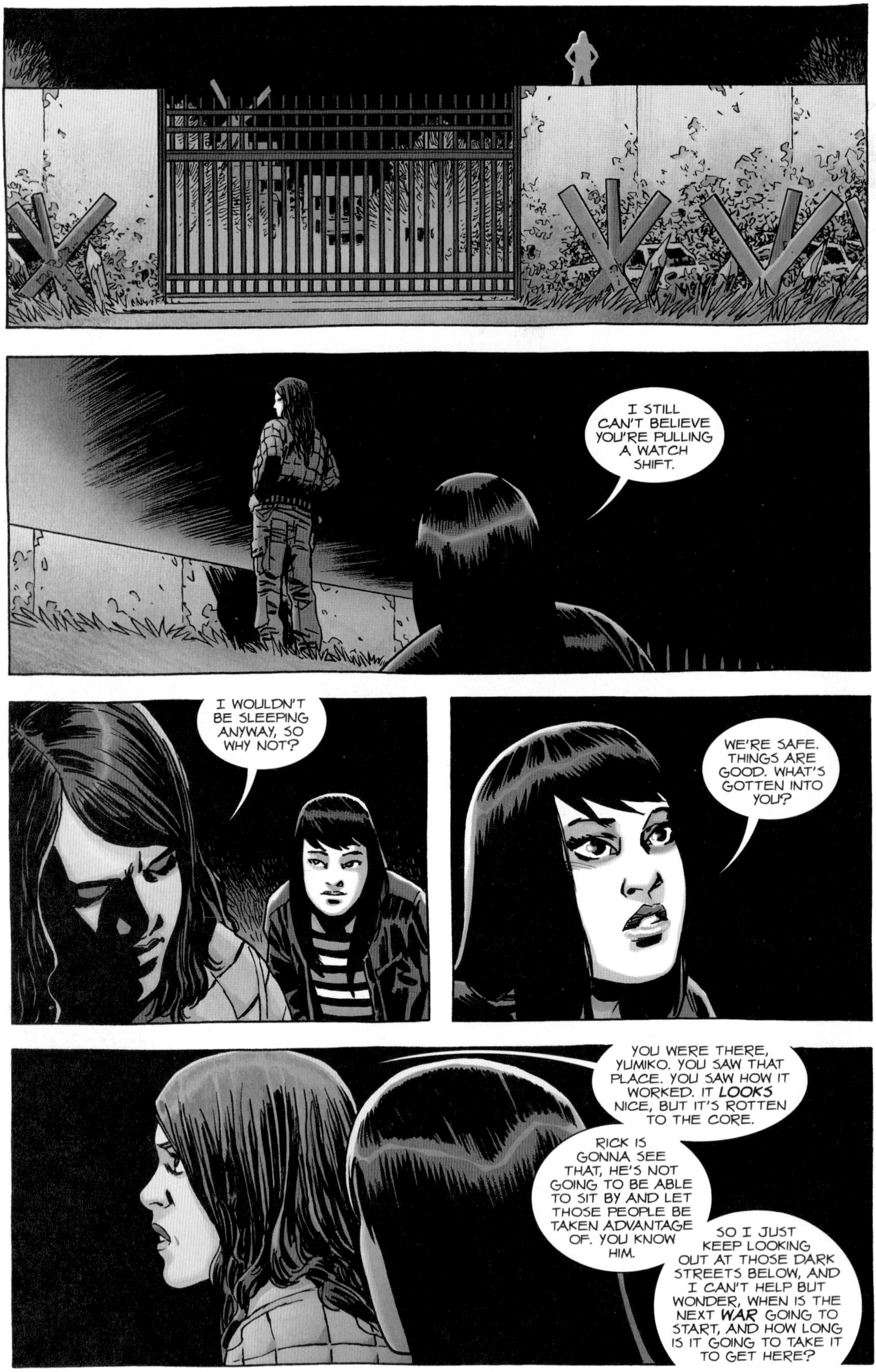
I STILL CAN'T BELIEVE YOU'RE PULLING A WATCH SHIFT.
I WOULDN'T BE SLEEPING ANYWAY, SO WHY NOT?
WE'RE SAFE. THINGS ARE GOOD. WHAT'S GOTTEN INTO YOU?
YOU WERE THERE, YUMIKO. YOU SAW THAT PLACE. YOU SAW HOW IT WORKED. IT *LOOKS* NICE, BUT IT'S ROTTEN TO THE CORE.
RICK IS GONNA SEE THAT, HE'S NOT GOING TO BE ABLE TO SIT BY AND LET THOSE PEOPLE BE TAKEN ADVANTAGE OF. YOU KNOW HIM.
SO I JUST KEEP LOOKING OUT AT THOSE DARK STREETS BELOW, AND I CAN'T HELP BUT WONDER, WHEN IS THE NEXT *WAR* GOING TO START, AND HOW LONG IS IT GOING TO TAKE IT TO GET HERE?

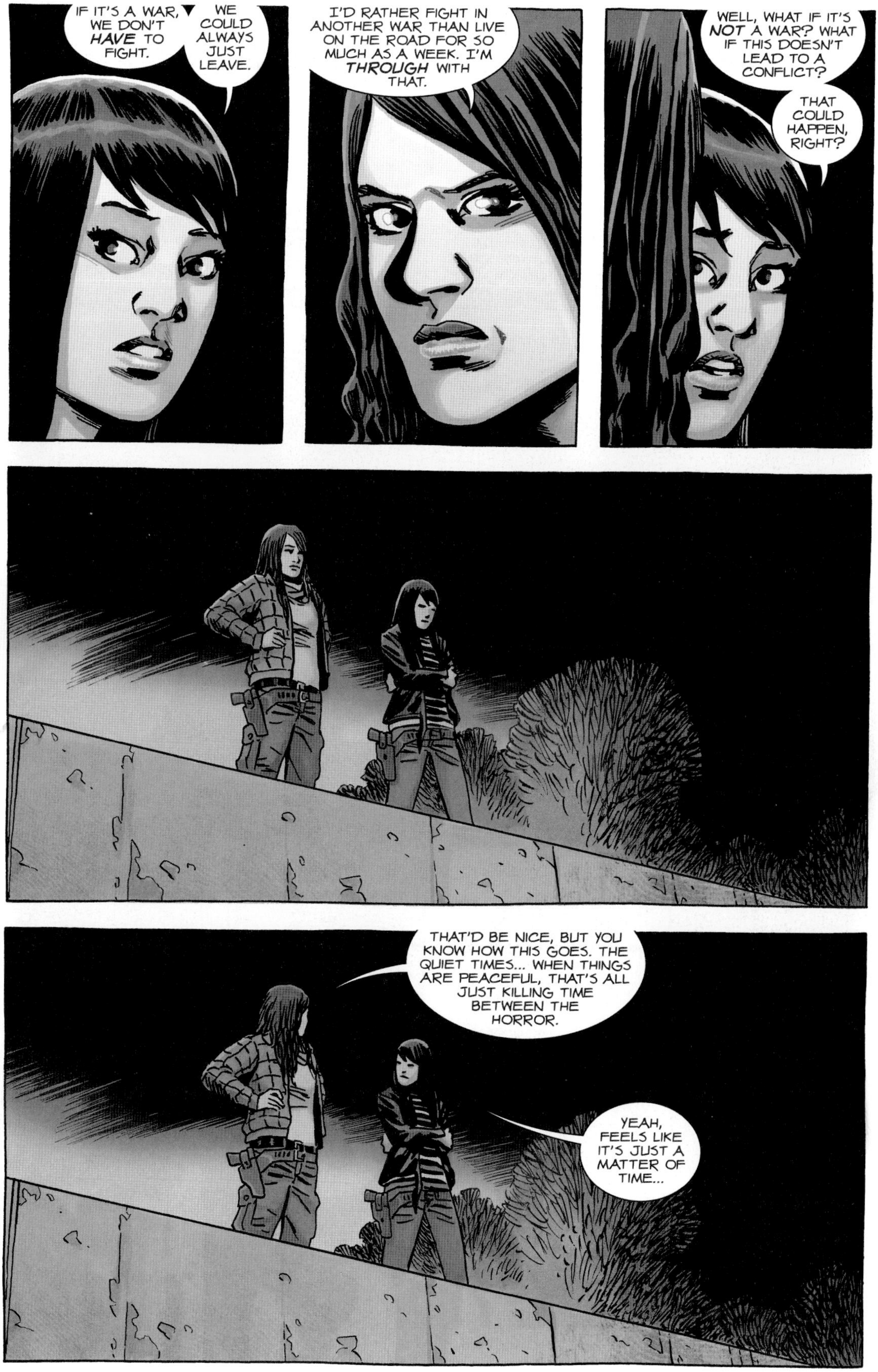
IF IT'S A WAR, WE DON'T HAVE TO FIGHT.
WE COULD ALWAYS JUST LEAVE.
I'D RATHER FIGHT IN ANOTHER WAR THAN LIVE ON THE ROAD FOR SO MUCH AS A WEEK. I'M THROUGH WITH THAT.
WELL, WHAT IF IT'S NOT A WAR? WHAT IF THIS DOESN'T LEAD TO A CONFLICT?
THAT COULD HAPPEN, RIGHT?
THAT'D BE NICE, BUT YOU KNOW HOW THIS GOES. THE QUIET TIMES... WHEN THINGS ARE PEACEFUL, THAT'S ALL JUST KILLING TIME BETWEEN THE HORROR.
YEAH, FEELS LIKE IT'S JUST A MATTER OF TIME...

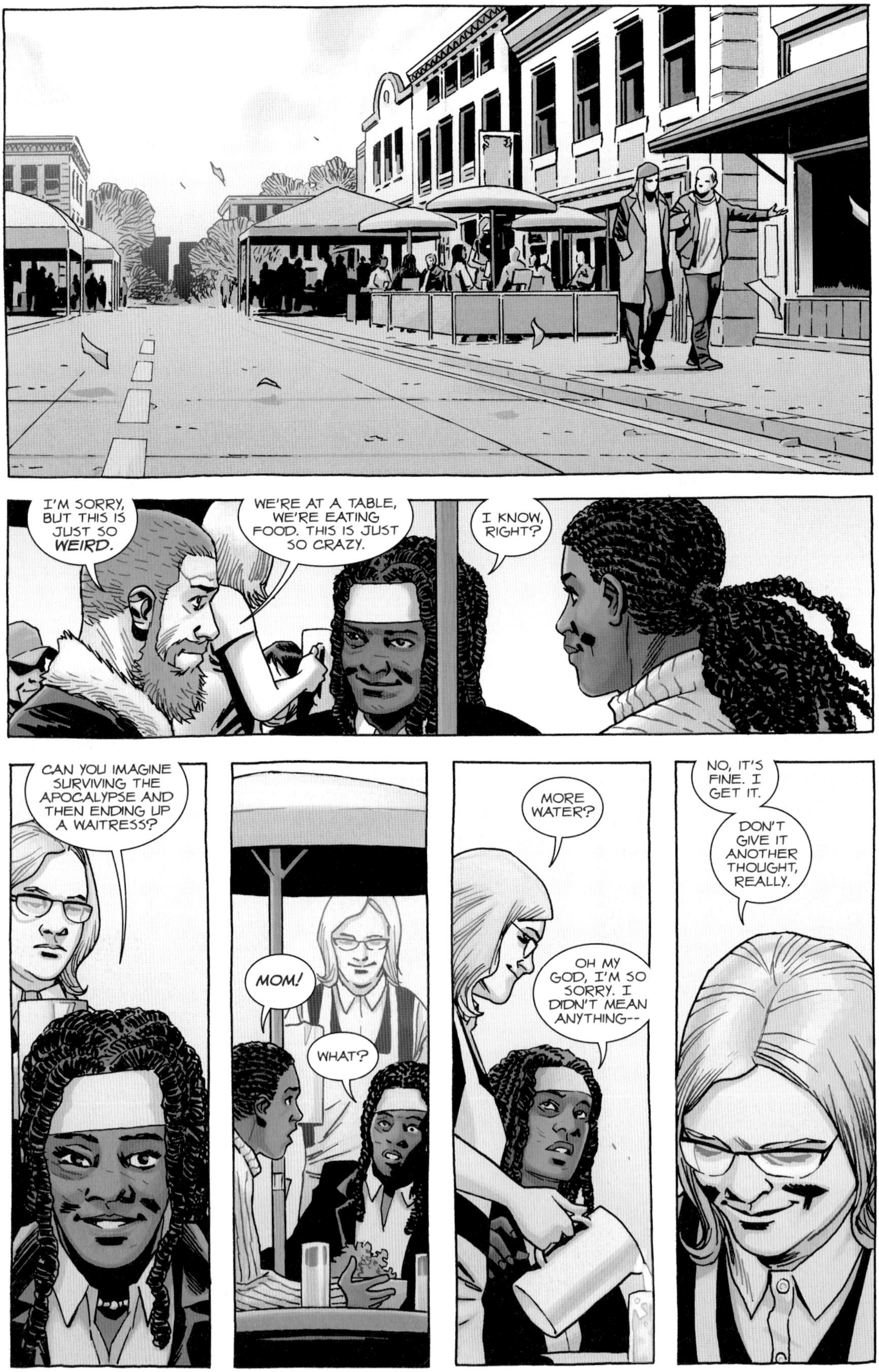
I'M SORRY, BUT THIS IS JUST SO WEIRD.
WE'RE AT A TABLE, WE'RE EATING FOOD. THIS IS JUST SO CRAZY.
I KNOW, RIGHT?
CAN YOU IMAGINE SURVIVING THE APOCALYPSE AND THEN ENDING UP A WAITRESS?
MOM!
WHAT?
MORE WATER?
OH MY GOD, I'M SO SORRY. I DIDN'T MEAN ANYTHING--
NO, IT'S FINE. I GET IT.
DON'T GIVE IT ANOTHER THOUGHT, REALLY.

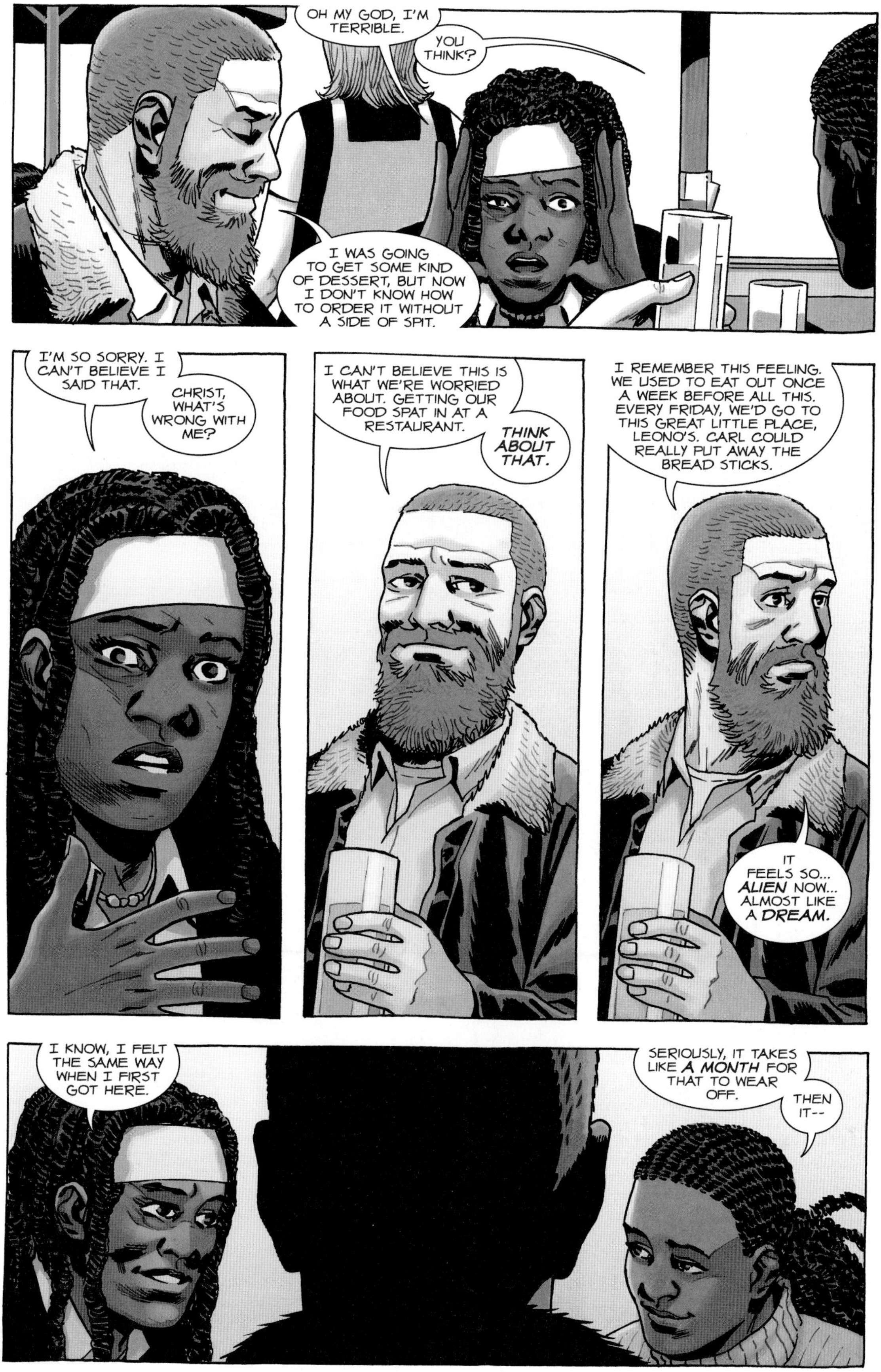
OH MY GOD, I'M TERRIBLE.
YOU THINK?
I WAS GOING TO GET SOME KIND OF DESSERT, BUT NOW I DON'T KNOW HOW TO ORDER IT WITHOUT A SIDE OF SPIT.
I'M SO SORRY. I CAN'T BELIEVE I SAID THAT.
CHRIST, WHAT'S WRONG WITH ME?
I CAN'T BELIEVE THIS IS WHAT WE'RE WORRIED ABOUT. GETTING OUR FOOD SPAT IN AT A RESTAURANT.
THINK ABOUT THAT.
I REMEMBER THIS FEELING. WE USED TO EAT OUT ONCE A WEEK BEFORE ALL THIS. EVERY FRIDAY, WE'D GO TO THIS GREAT LITTLE PLACE, LEONO'S. CARL COULD REALLY PUT AWAY THE BREAD STICKS.
IT FEELS SO... ALIEN NOW... ALMOST LIKE A DREAM.
I KNOW, I FELT THE SAME WAY WHEN I FIRST GOT HERE.
SERIOUSLY, IT TAKES LIKE A MONTH FOR THAT TO WEAR OFF.
THEN IT--

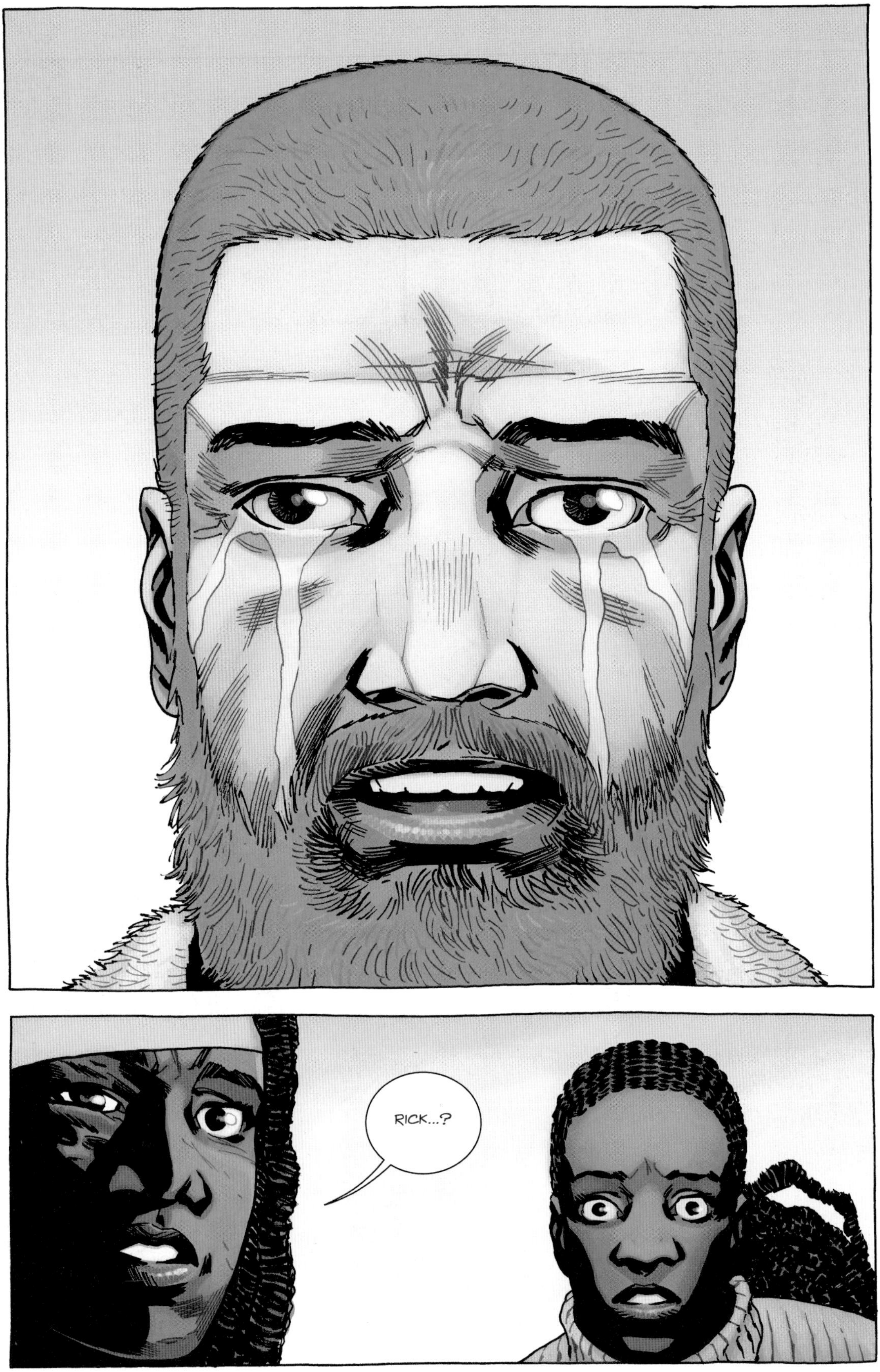
RICK...?

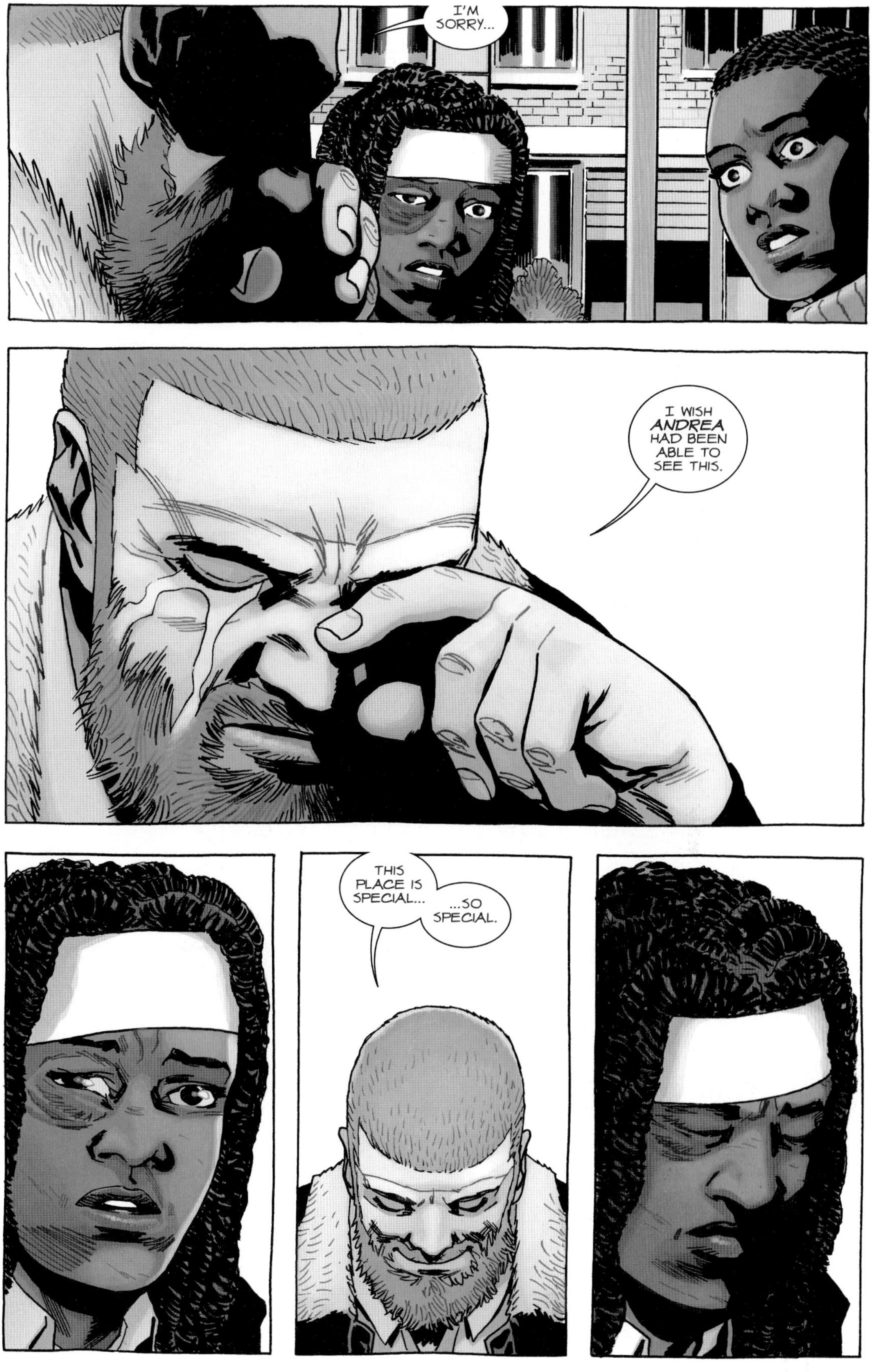
I'M SORRY...
I WISH ANDREA HAD BEEN ABLE TO SEE THIS.
THIS PLACE IS SPECIAL...
...SO SPECIAL.

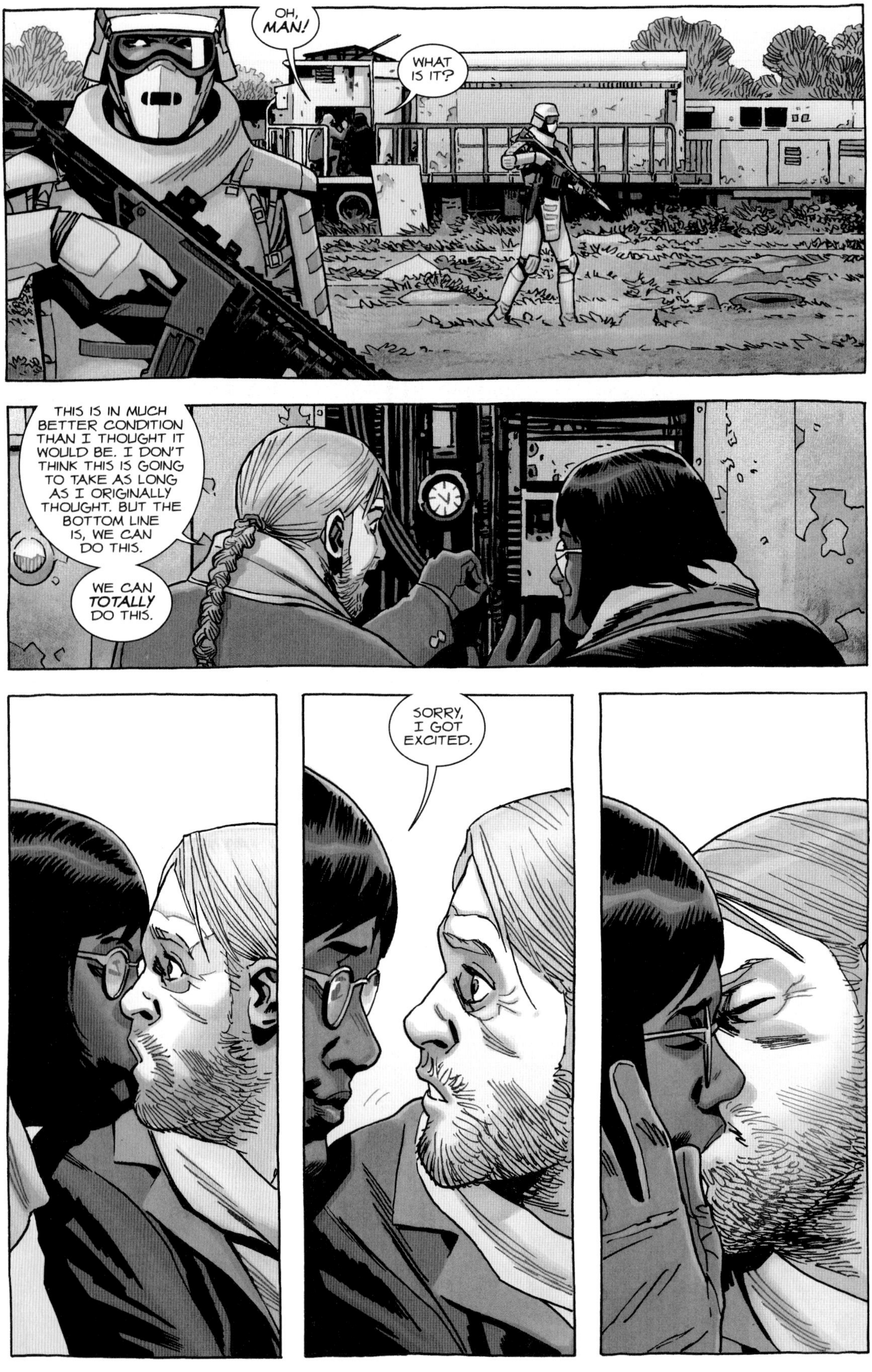
OH, *MAN!*
WHAT IS IT?
THIS IS IN MUCH BETTER CONDITION THAN I THOUGHT IT WOULD BE. I DON'T THINK THIS IS GOING TO TAKE AS LONG AS I ORIGINALLY THOUGHT. BUT THE BOTTOM LINE IS, WE CAN DO THIS.
WE CAN *TOTALLY* DO THIS.
SORRY, I GOT EXCITED.

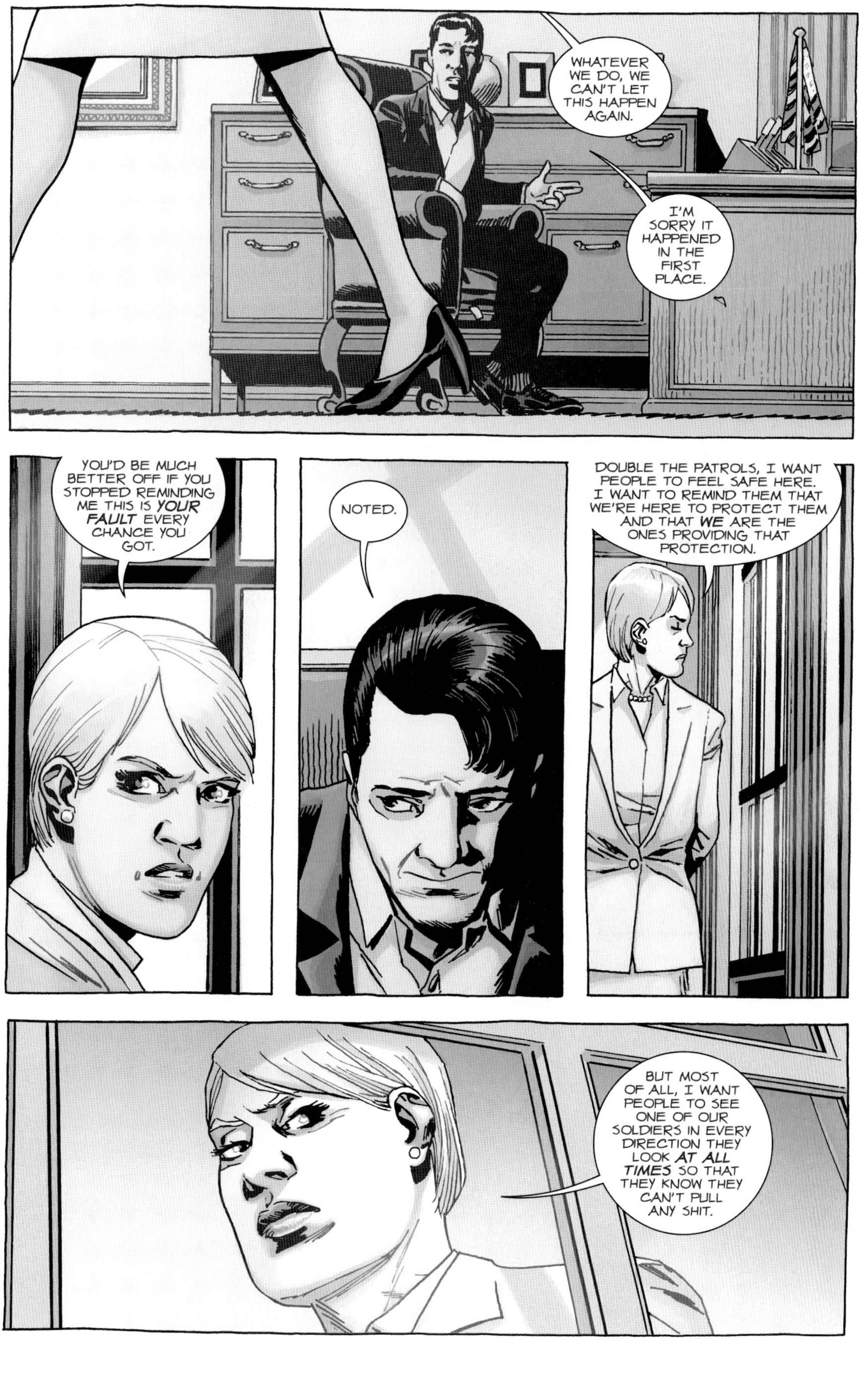

WHATEVER WE DO, WE CAN'T LET THIS HAPPEN AGAIN.
I'M SORRY IT HAPPENED IN THE FIRST PLACE.
YOU'D BE MUCH BETTER OFF IF YOU STOPPED REMINDING ME THIS IS *YOUR FAULT* EVERY CHANCE YOU GOT.
NOTED.
DOUBLE THE PATROLS, I WANT PEOPLE TO FEEL SAFE HERE. I WANT TO REMIND THEM THAT WE'RE HERE TO PROTECT THEM AND THAT *WE* ARE THE ONES PROVIDING THAT PROTECTION.
BUT MOST OF ALL, I WANT PEOPLE TO SEE ONE OF OUR SOLDIERS IN EVERY DIRECTION THEY LOOK *AT ALL TIMES* SO THAT THEY KNOW THEY CAN'T PULL ANY SHIT.

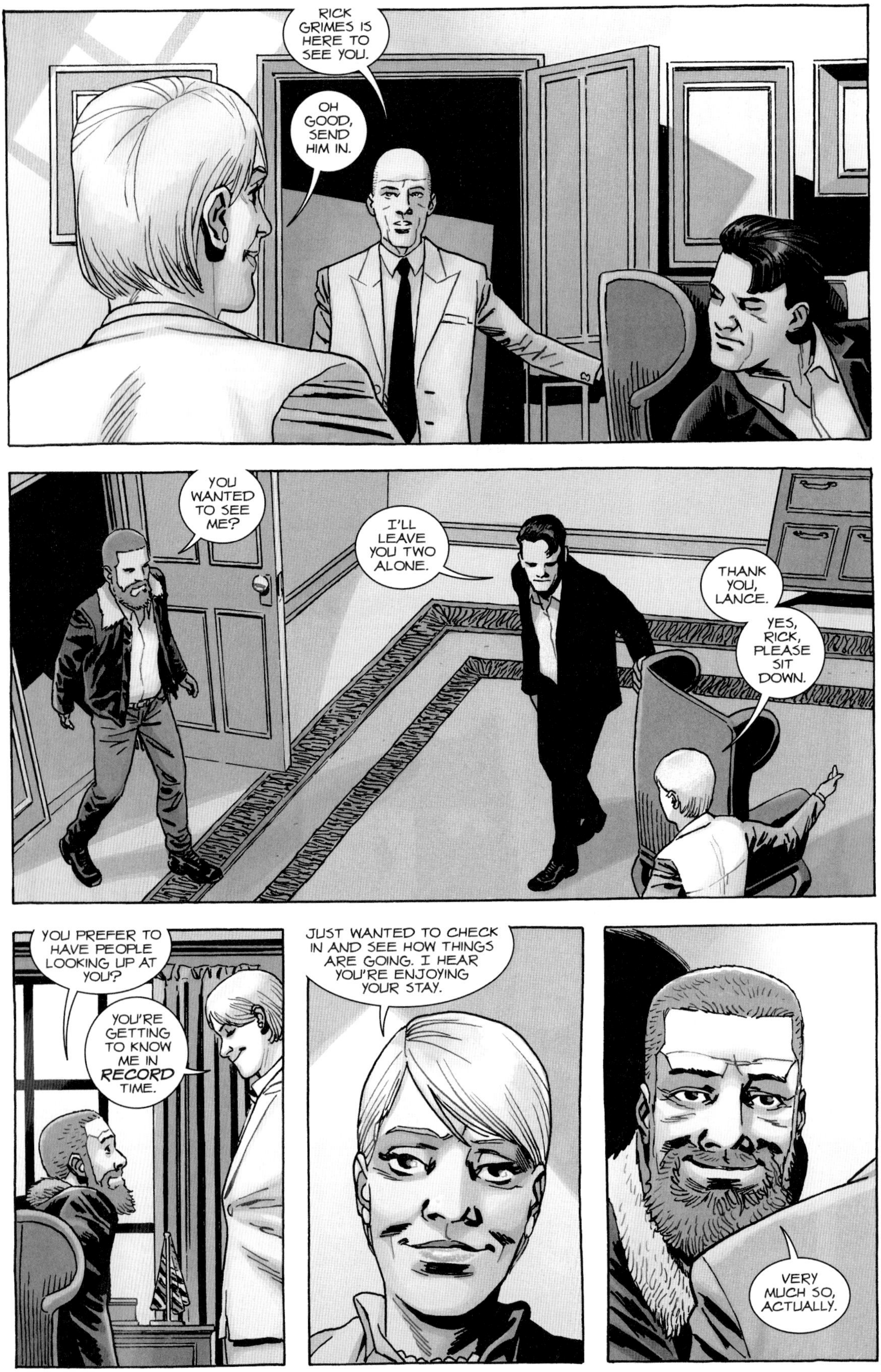
RICK GRIMES IS HERE TO SEE YOU.
OH GOOD, SEND HIM IN.
YOU WANTED TO SEE ME?
I'LL LEAVE YOU TWO ALONE.
THANK YOU, LANCE.
YES, RICK, PLEASE SIT DOWN.
YOU PREFER TO HAVE PEOPLE LOOKING UP AT YOU?
YOU'RE GETTING TO KNOW ME IN RECORD TIME.
JUST WANTED TO CHECK IN AND SEE HOW THINGS ARE GOING. I HEAR YOU'RE ENJOYING YOUR STAY.
VERY MUCH SO, ACTUALLY.

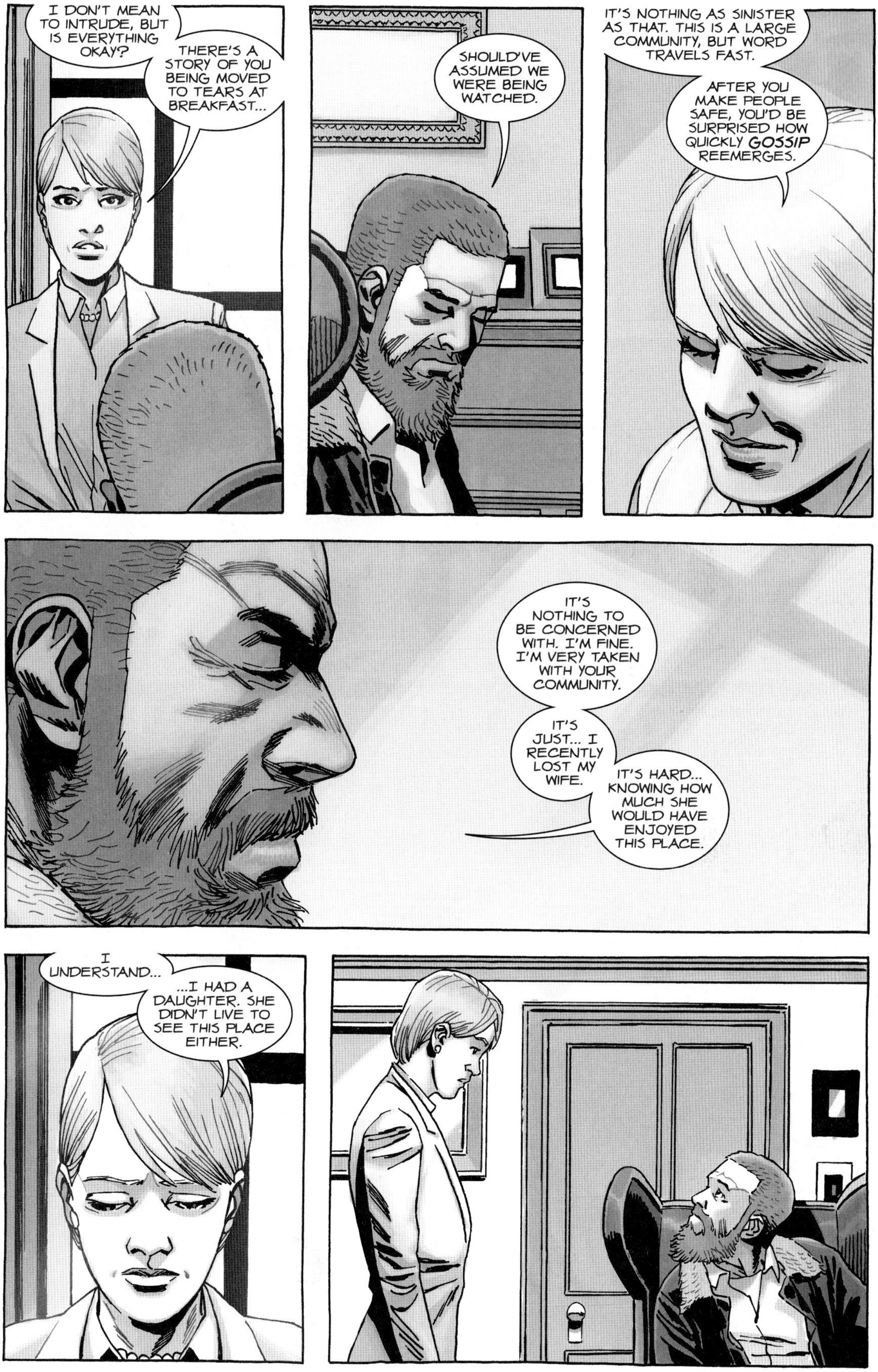
I DON'T MEAN TO INTRUDE, BUT IS EVERYTHING OKAY?
THERE'S A STORY OF YOU BEING MOVED TO TEARS AT BREAKFAST...
SHOULD'VE ASSUMED WE WERE BEING WATCHED.
IT'S NOTHING AS SINISTER AS THAT. THIS IS A LARGE COMMUNITY, BUT WORD TRAVELS FAST.
AFTER YOU MAKE PEOPLE SAFE, YOU'D BE SURPRISED HOW QUICKLY GOSSIP REEMERGES.
IT'S NOTHING TO BE CONCERNED WITH. I'M FINE. I'M VERY TAKEN WITH YOUR COMMUNITY.
IT'S JUST... I RECENTLY LOST MY WIFE.
IT'S HARD... KNOWING HOW MUCH SHE WOULD HAVE ENJOYED THIS PLACE.
I UNDERSTAND...
...I HAD A DAUGHTER. SHE DIDN'T LIVE TO SEE THIS PLACE EITHER.

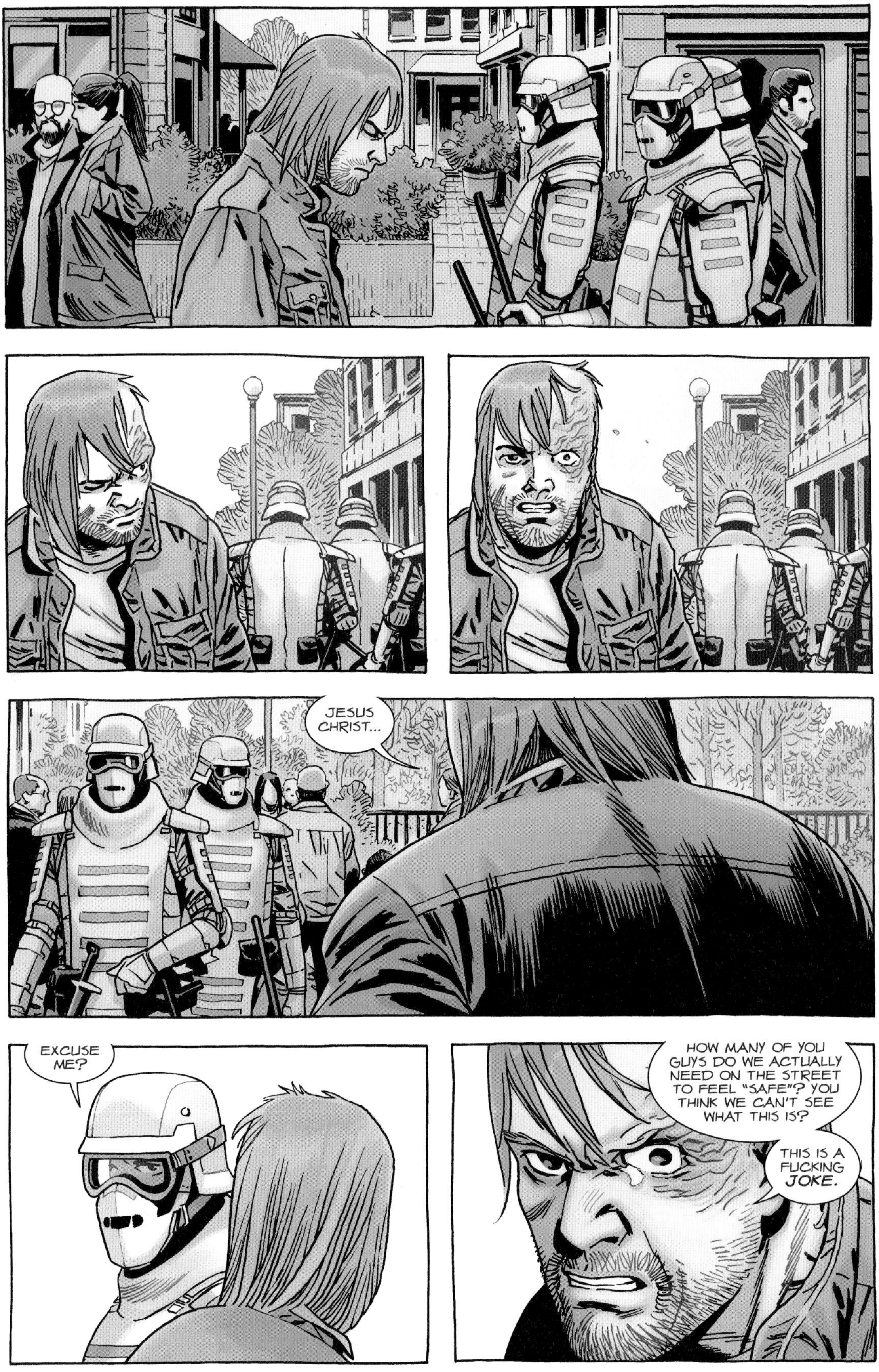
JESUS CHRIST...
EXCUSE ME?
HOW MANY OF YOU GUYS DO WE ACTUALLY NEED ON THE STREET TO FEEL "SAFE"? YOU THINK WE CAN'T SEE WHAT THIS IS?
THIS IS A FUCKING JOKE.

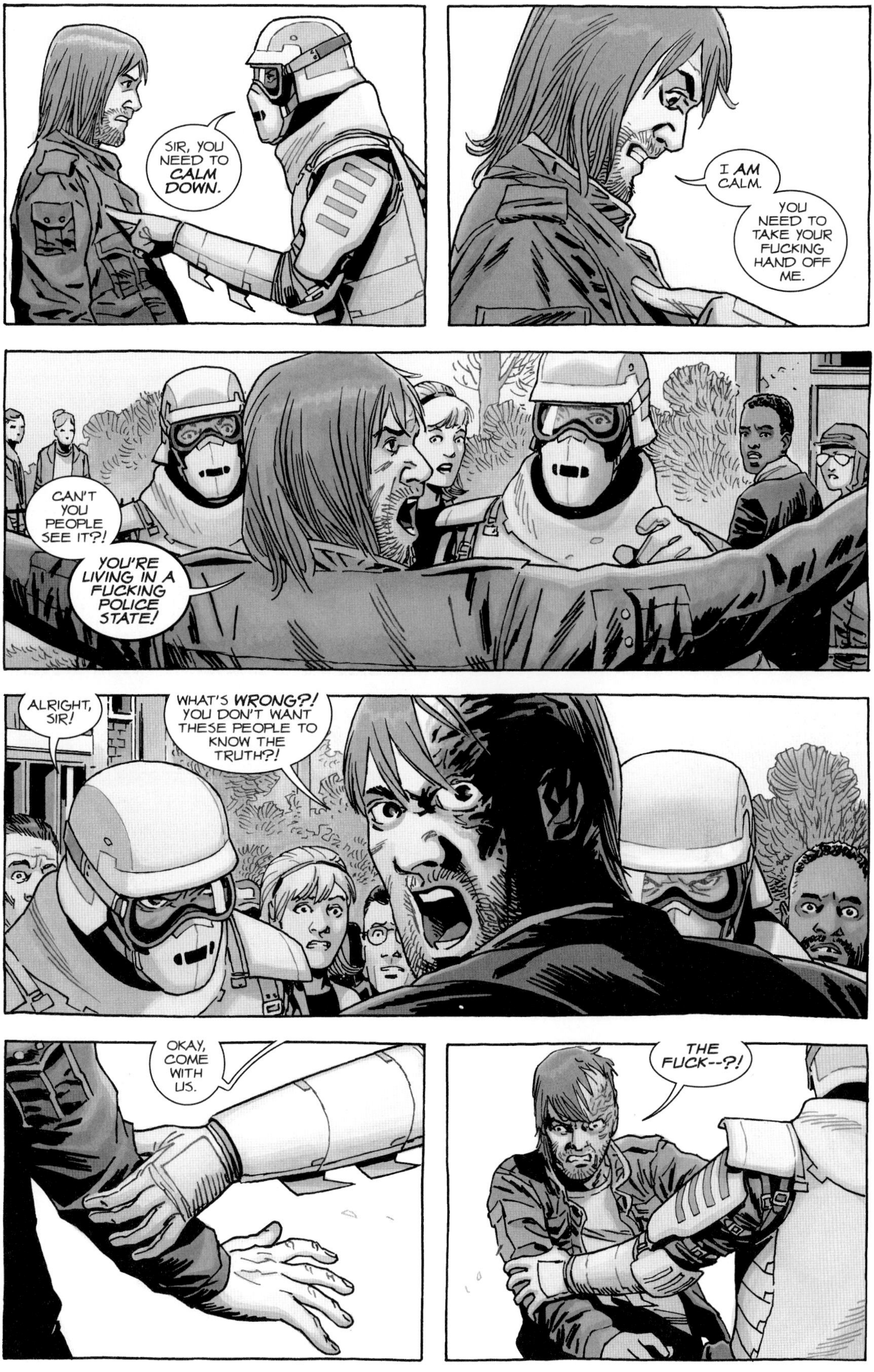

SIR, YOU NEED TO *CALM DOWN.*
I *AM* CALM.
YOU NEED TO TAKE YOUR FUCKING HAND OFF ME.
CAN'T YOU PEOPLE SEE IT?!
YOU'RE LIVING IN A FUCKING POLICE STATE!
ALRIGHT, SIR!
WHAT'S *WRONG?!* YOU DON'T WANT THESE PEOPLE TO KNOW THE TRUTH?!
OKAY, COME WITH US.
THE FUCK--?!

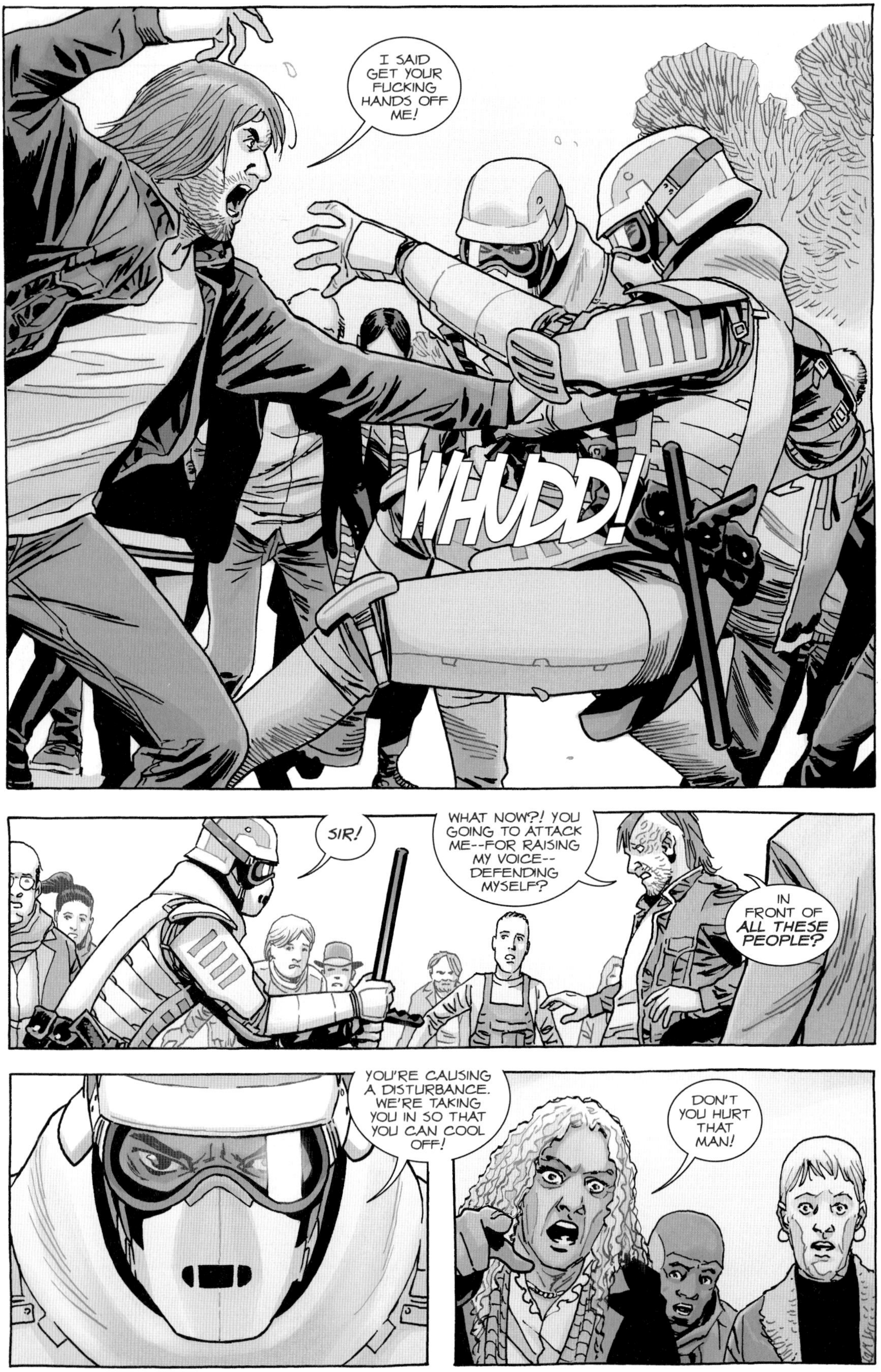

I SAID GET YOUR FUCKING HANDS OFF ME!
WHUDD!
SIR!
WHAT NOW?! YOU GOING TO ATTACK ME--FOR RAISING MY VOICE-- DEFENDING MYSELF?
IN FRONT OF ALL THESE PEOPLE?
YOU'RE CAUSING A DISTURBANCE. WE'RE TAKING YOU IN SO THAT YOU CAN COOL OFF!
DON'T YOU HURT THAT MAN!

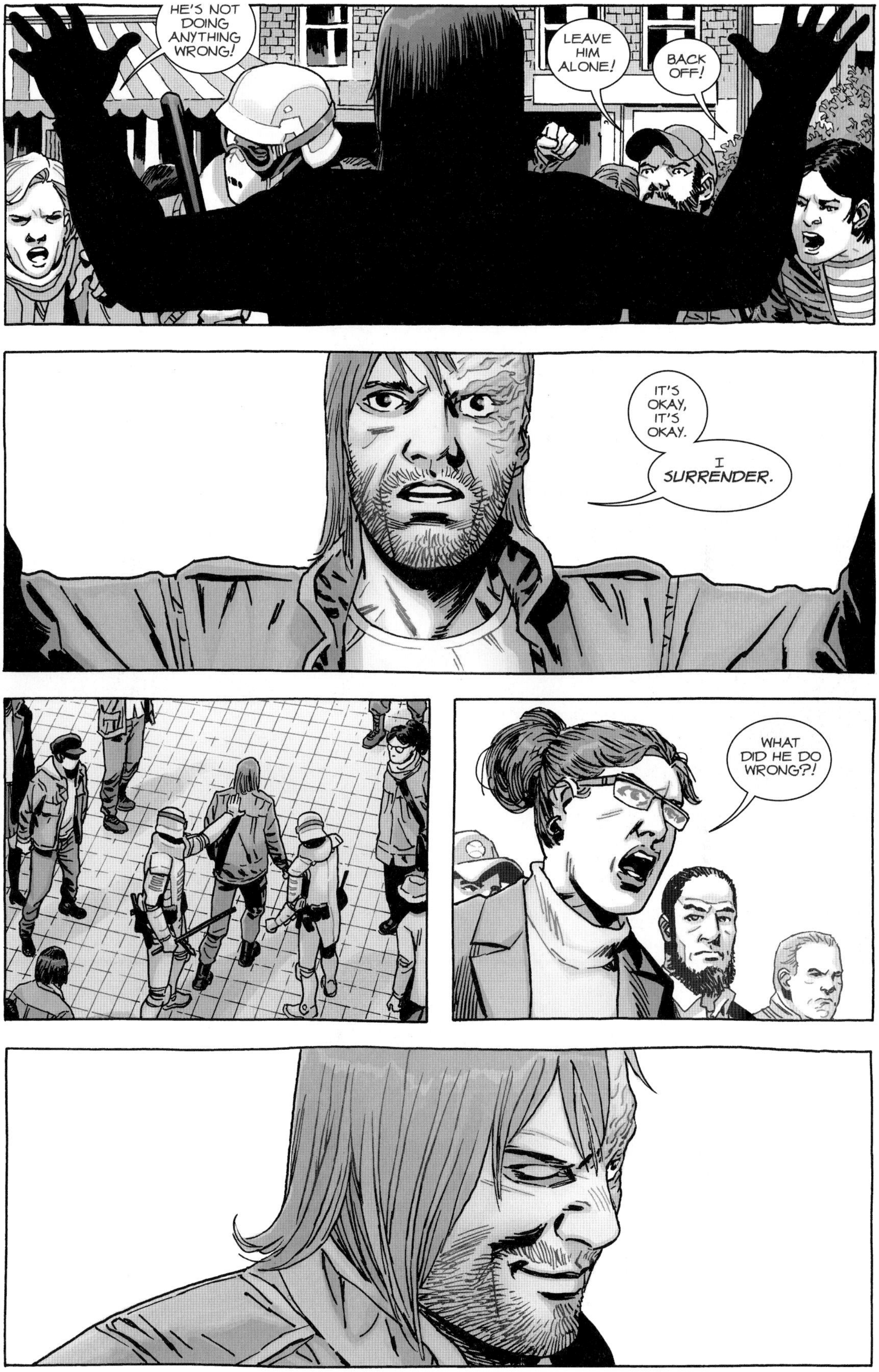
HE'S NOT DOING ANYTHING WRONG!
LEAVE HIM ALONE!
BACK OFF!
IT'S OKAY, IT'S OKAY.
I SURRENDER.
WHAT DID HE DO WRONG?!

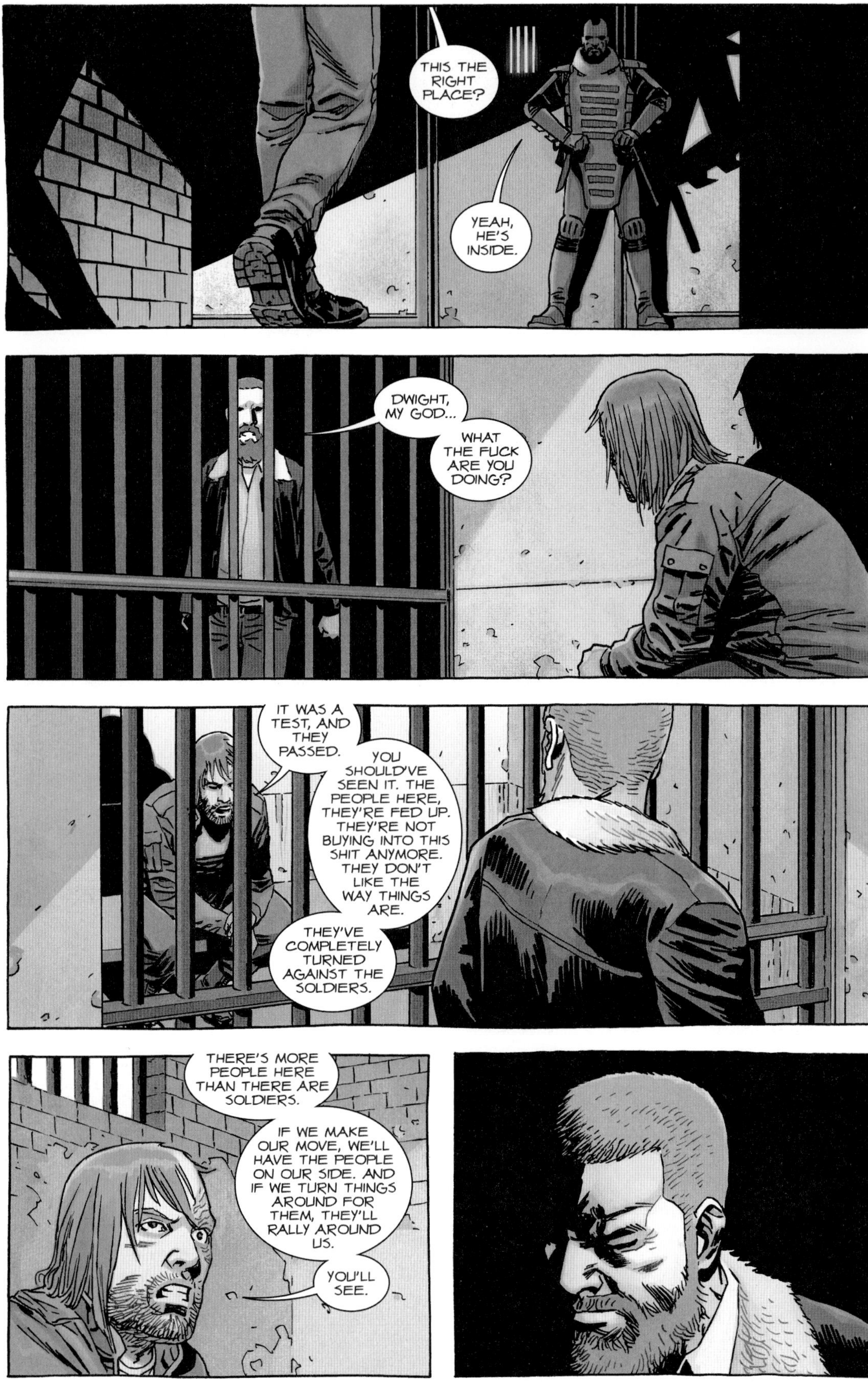
THIS THE RIGHT PLACE?
YEAH, HE'S INSIDE.
DWIGHT, MY GOD...
WHAT THE FUCK ARE YOU DOING?
IT WAS A TEST, AND THEY PASSED.
YOU SHOULD'VE SEEN IT. THE PEOPLE HERE, THEY'RE FED UP. THEY'RE NOT BUYING INTO THIS SHIT ANYMORE. THEY DON'T LIKE THE WAY THINGS ARE.
THEY'VE COMPLETELY TURNED AGAINST THE SOLDIERS.
THERE'S MORE PEOPLE HERE THAN THERE ARE SOLDIERS.
IF WE MAKE OUR MOVE, WE'LL HAVE THE PEOPLE ON OUR SIDE. AND IF WE TURN THINGS AROUND FOR THEM, THEY'LL RALLY AROUND US.
YOU'LL SEE.

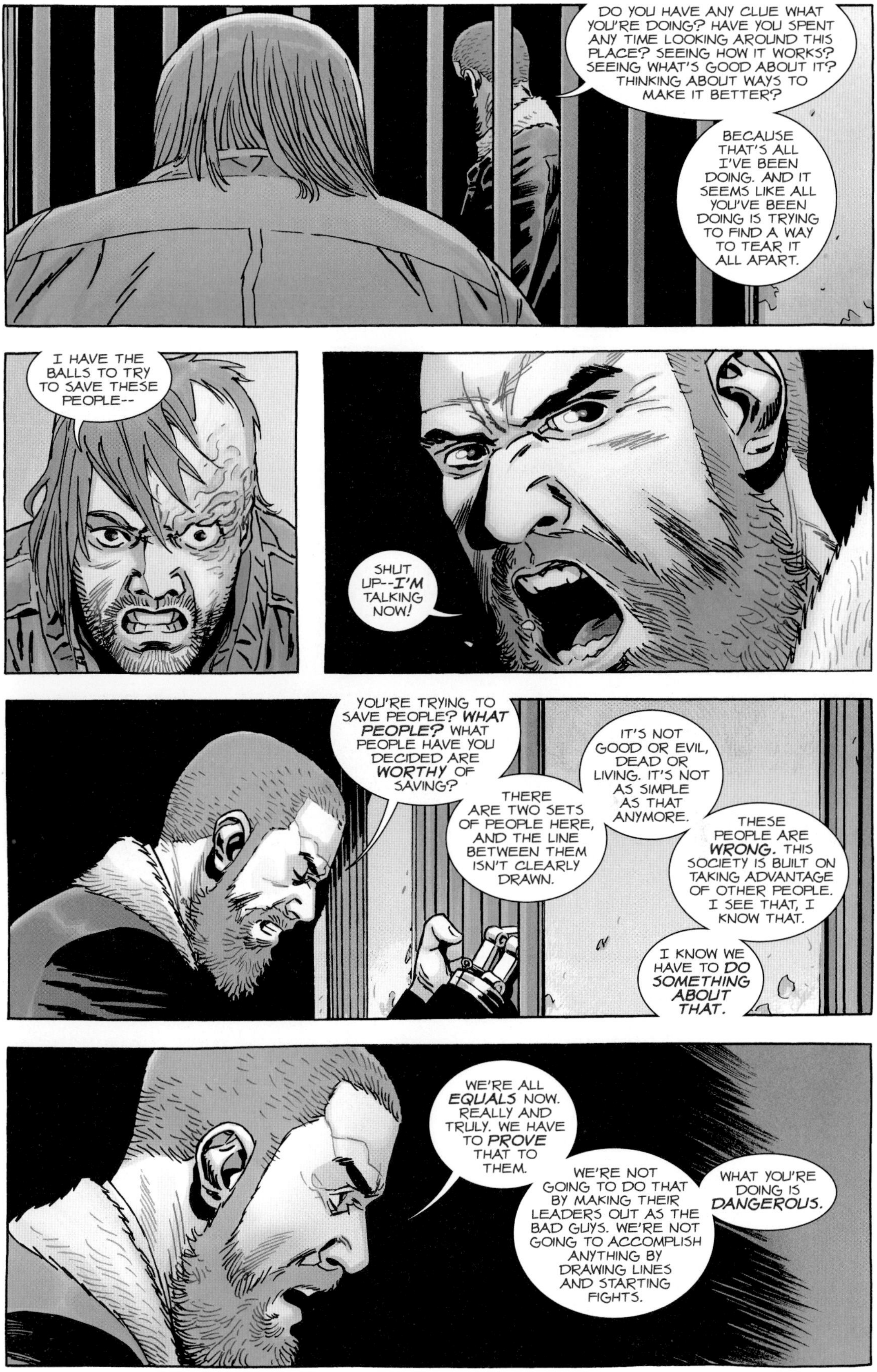
DO YOU HAVE ANY CLUE WHAT YOU'RE DOING? HAVE YOU SPENT ANY TIME LOOKING AROUND THIS PLACE? SEEING HOW IT WORKS? SEEING WHAT'S GOOD ABOUT IT? THINKING ABOUT WAYS TO MAKE IT BETTER?
BECAUSE THAT'S ALL I'VE BEEN DOING. AND IT SEEMS LIKE ALL YOU'VE BEEN DOING IS TRYING TO FIND A WAY TO TEAR IT ALL APART.
I HAVE THE BALLS TO TRY TO SAVE THESE PEOPLE--
SHUT UP--*I'M* TALKING NOW!
YOU'RE TRYING TO SAVE PEOPLE? *WHAT PEOPLE?* WHAT PEOPLE HAVE YOU DECIDED ARE *WORTHY* OF SAVING?
THERE ARE TWO SETS OF PEOPLE HERE, AND THE LINE BETWEEN THEM ISN'T CLEARLY DRAWN.
IT'S NOT GOOD OR EVIL, DEAD OR LIVING. IT'S NOT AS SIMPLE AS THAT ANYMORE.
THESE PEOPLE ARE *WRONG.* THIS SOCIETY IS BUILT ON TAKING ADVANTAGE OF OTHER PEOPLE. I SEE THAT, I KNOW THAT.
I KNOW WE HAVE TO *DO SOMETHING ABOUT THAT.*
WE'RE ALL *EQUALS* NOW. REALLY AND TRULY. WE HAVE TO *PROVE* THAT TO THEM.
WE'RE NOT GOING TO DO THAT BY MAKING THEIR LEADERS OUT AS THE BAD GUYS. WE'RE NOT GOING TO ACCOMPLISH ANYTHING BY DRAWING LINES AND STARTING FIGHTS.
WHAT YOU'RE DOING IS *DANGEROUS.*

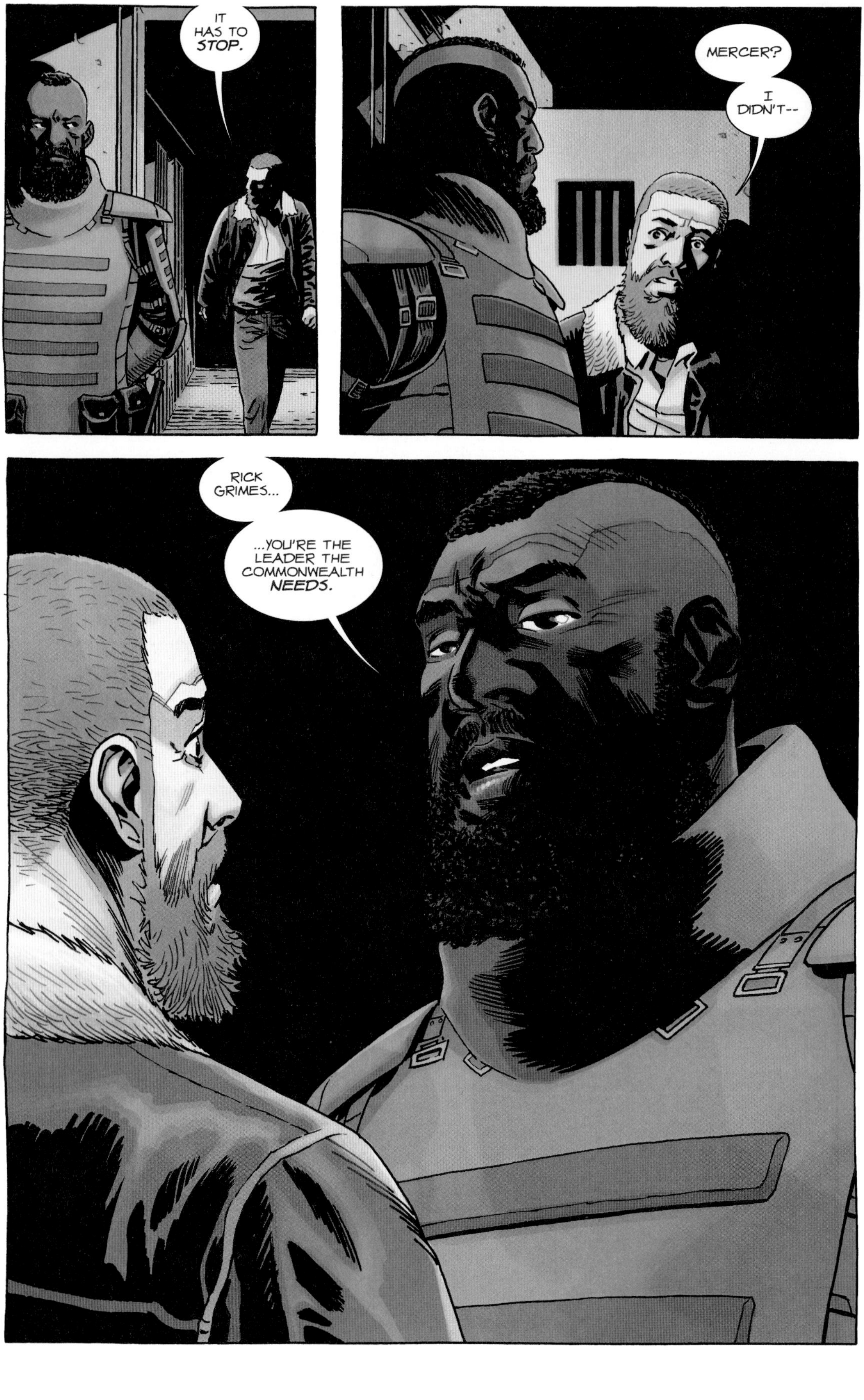
IT HAS TO *STOP.*
MERCER?
I DIDN'T--
RICK GRIMES...
...YOU'RE THE LEADER THE COMMONWEALTH *NEEDS.*

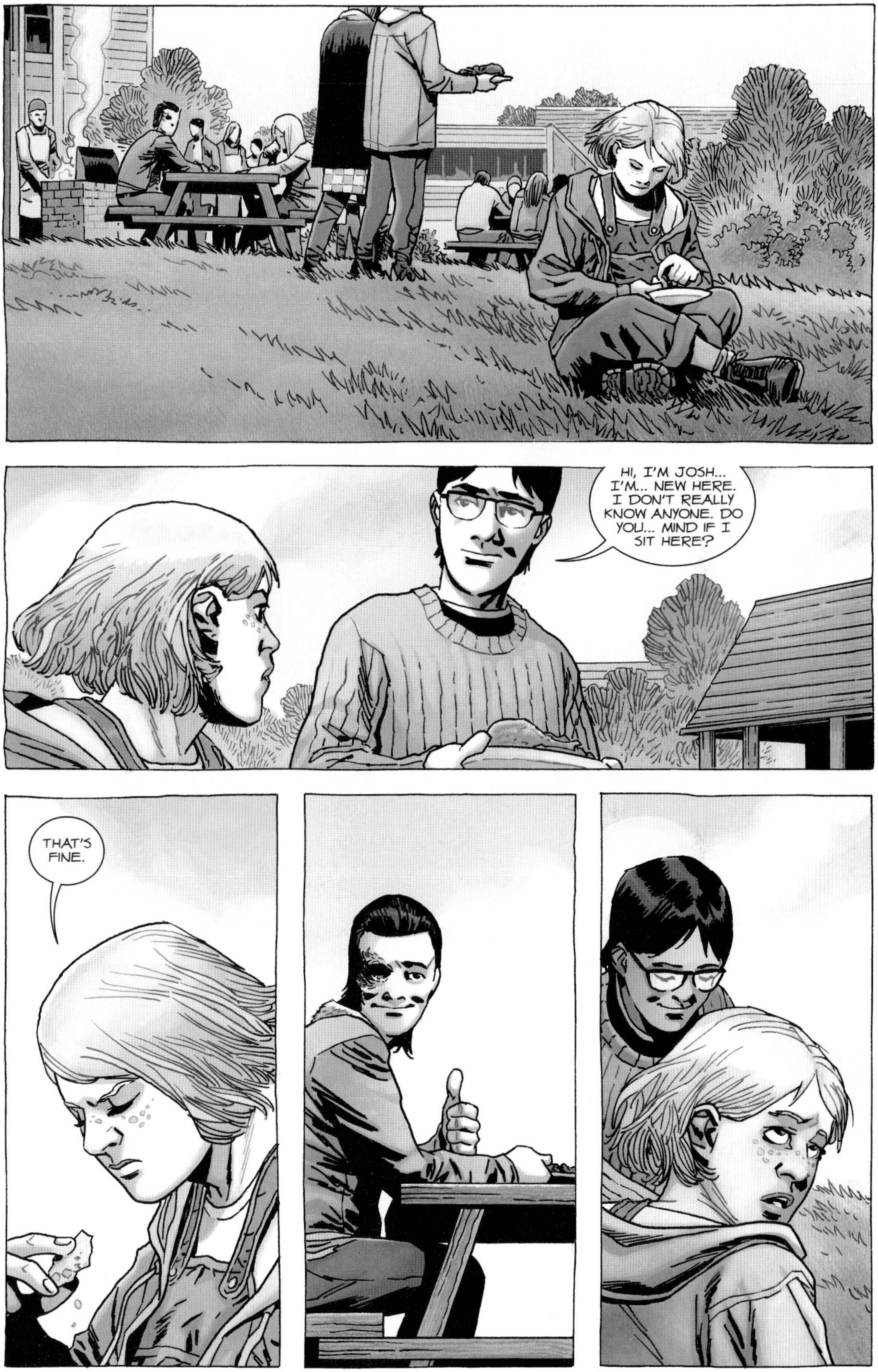
HI, I'M JOSH... I'M... NEW HERE. I DON'T REALLY KNOW ANYONE. DO YOU... MIND IF I SIT HERE?
THAT'S FINE.

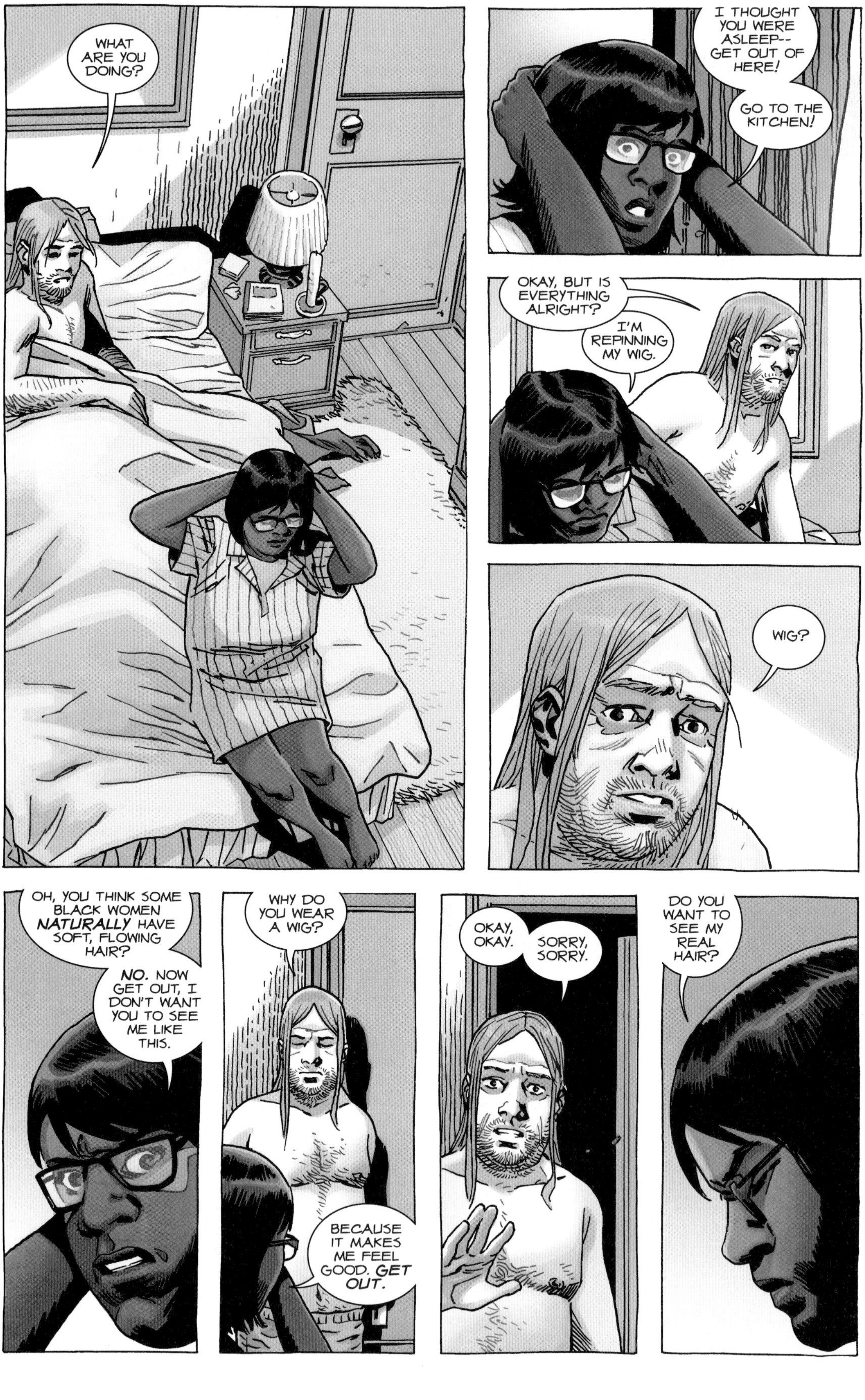
WHAT ARE YOU DOING?
I THOUGHT YOU WERE ASLEEP-- GET OUT OF HERE!
GO TO THE KITCHEN!
OKAY, BUT IS EVERYTHING ALRIGHT?
I'M REPINNING MY WIG.
WIG?
OH, YOU THINK SOME BLACK WOMEN NATURALLY HAVE SOFT, FLOWING HAIR?
NO. NOW GET OUT, I DON'T WANT YOU TO SEE ME LIKE THIS.
WHY DO YOU WEAR A WIG?
BECAUSE IT MAKES ME FEEL GOOD. GET OUT.
OKAY, OKAY.
SORRY, SORRY.
DO YOU WANT TO SEE MY REAL HAIR?

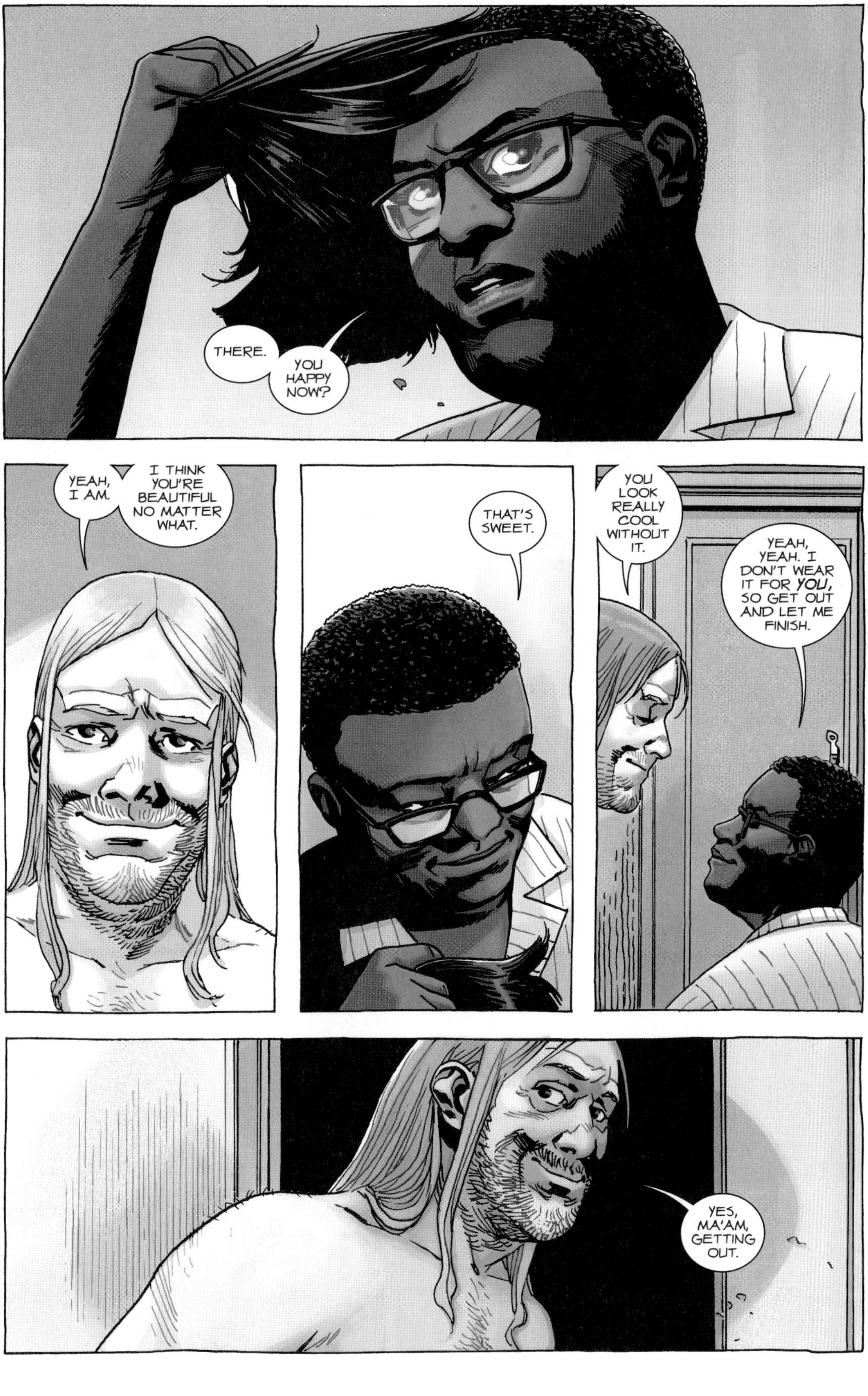
THERE.
YOU HAPPY NOW?
YEAH, I AM.
I THINK YOU'RE BEAUTIFUL NO MATTER WHAT.
THAT'S SWEET.
YOU LOOK REALLY COOL WITHOUT IT.
YEAH, YEAH. I DON'T WEAR IT FOR *YOU*, SO GET OUT AND LET ME FINISH.
YES, MA'AM, GETTING OUT.

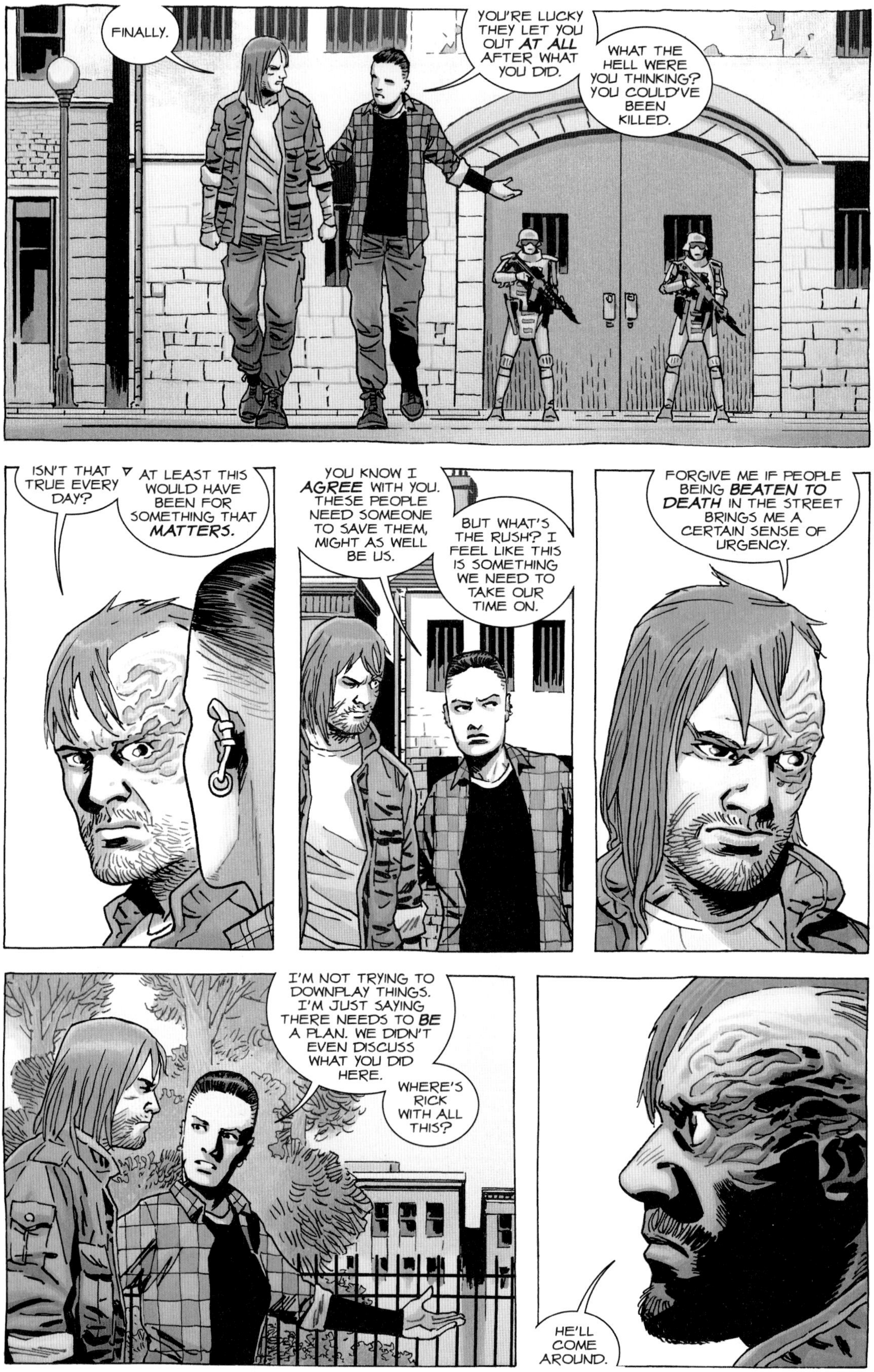
FINALLY.
YOU'RE LUCKY THEY LET YOU OUT AT ALL AFTER WHAT YOU DID.
WHAT THE HELL WERE YOU THINKING? YOU COULD'VE BEEN KILLED.
ISN'T THAT TRUE EVERY DAY?
AT LEAST THIS WOULD HAVE BEEN FOR SOMETHING THAT MATTERS.
YOU KNOW I AGREE WITH YOU. THESE PEOPLE NEED SOMEONE TO SAVE THEM, MIGHT AS WELL BE US.
BUT WHAT'S THE RUSH? I FEEL LIKE THIS IS SOMETHING WE NEED TO TAKE OUR TIME ON.
FORGIVE ME IF PEOPLE BEING BEATEN TO DEATH IN THE STREET BRINGS ME A CERTAIN SENSE OF URGENCY.
I'M NOT TRYING TO DOWNPLAY THINGS. I'M JUST SAYING THERE NEEDS TO BE A PLAN. WE DIDN'T EVEN DISCUSS WHAT YOU DID HERE.
WHERE'S RICK WITH ALL THIS?
HE'LL COME AROUND.

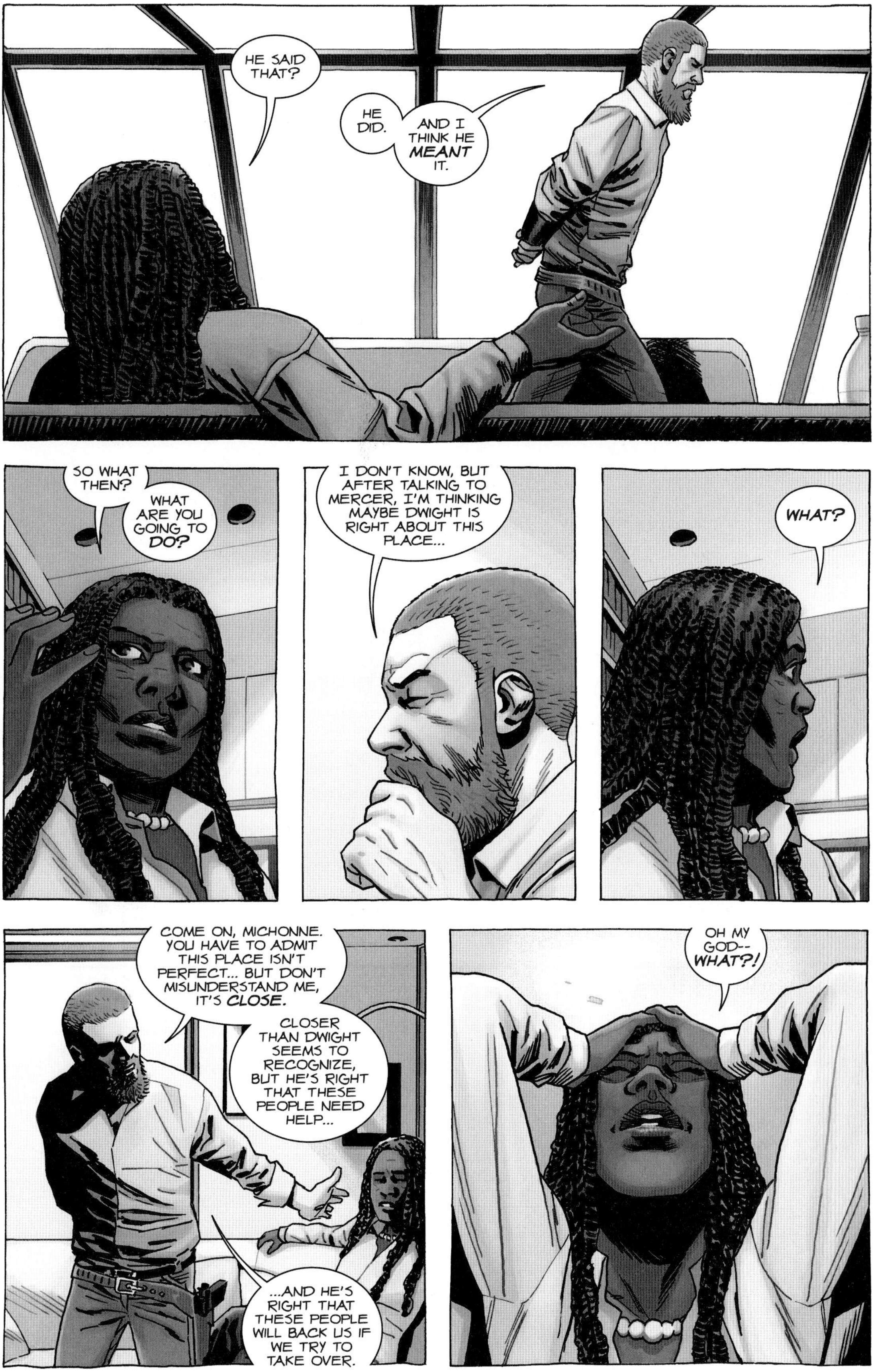
HE SAID THAT?
HE DID.
AND I THINK HE MEANT IT.
SO WHAT THEN?
WHAT ARE YOU GOING TO DO?
I DON'T KNOW, BUT AFTER TALKING TO MERCER, I'M THINKING MAYBE DWIGHT IS RIGHT ABOUT THIS PLACE...
WHAT?
COME ON, MICHONNE. YOU HAVE TO ADMIT THIS PLACE ISN'T PERFECT... BUT DON'T MISUNDERSTAND ME, IT'S CLOSE.
CLOSER THAN DWIGHT SEEMS TO RECOGNIZE, BUT HE'S RIGHT THAT THESE PEOPLE NEED HELP...
...AND HE'S RIGHT THAT THESE PEOPLE WILL BACK US IF WE TRY TO TAKE OVER.
OH MY GOD-- WHAT?!

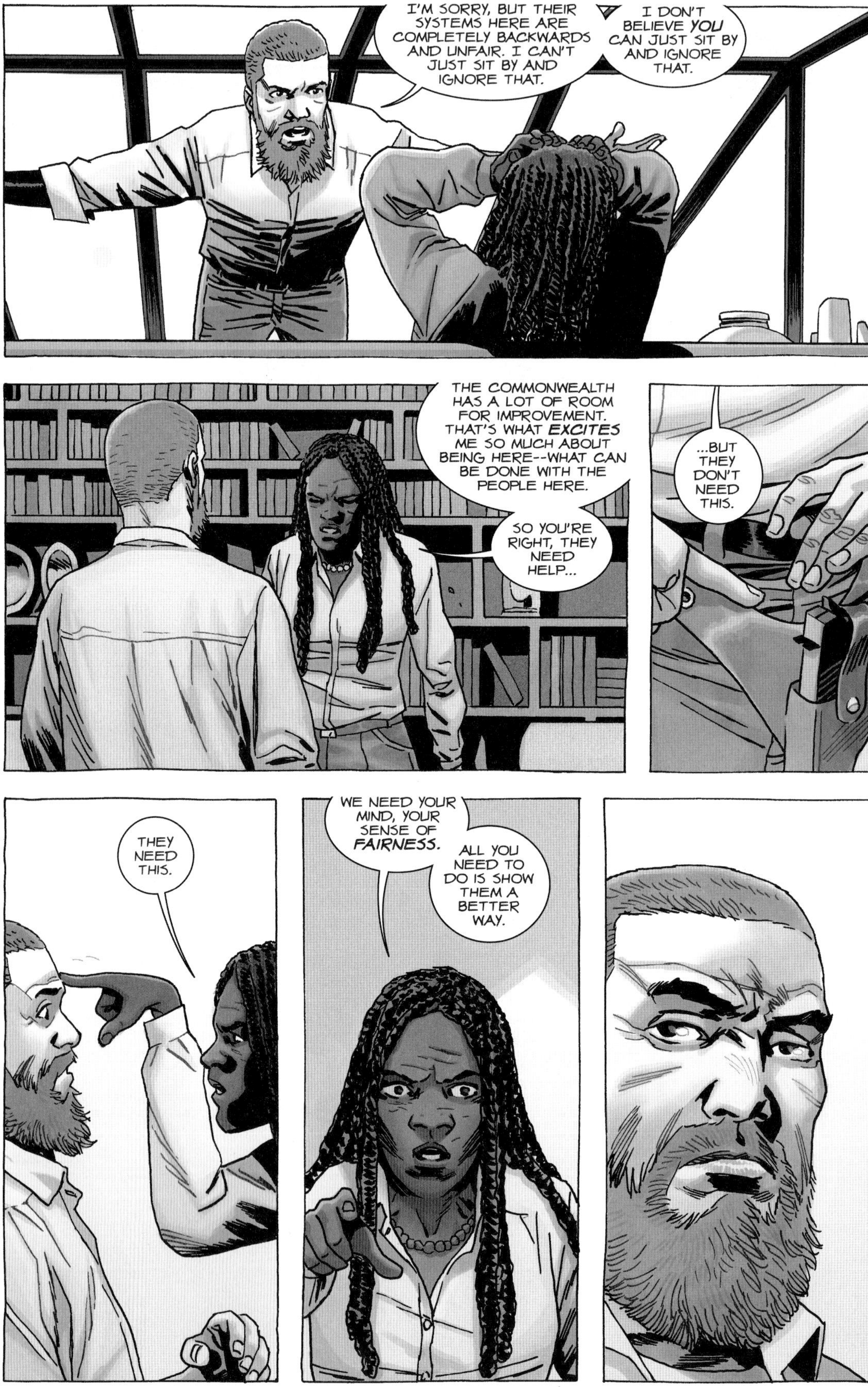
I'M SORRY, BUT THEIR SYSTEMS HERE ARE COMPLETELY BACKWARDS AND UNFAIR. I CAN'T JUST SIT BY AND IGNORE THAT.
I DON'T BELIEVE *YOU* CAN JUST SIT BY AND IGNORE THAT.
THE COMMONWEALTH HAS A LOT OF ROOM FOR IMPROVEMENT. THAT'S WHAT *EXCITES* ME SO MUCH ABOUT BEING HERE--WHAT CAN BE DONE WITH THE PEOPLE HERE.
SO YOU'RE RIGHT, THEY NEED HELP...
...BUT THEY DON'T NEED THIS.
THEY NEED THIS.
WE NEED YOUR MIND, YOUR SENSE OF *FAIRNESS.*
ALL YOU NEED TO DO IS SHOW THEM A BETTER WAY.

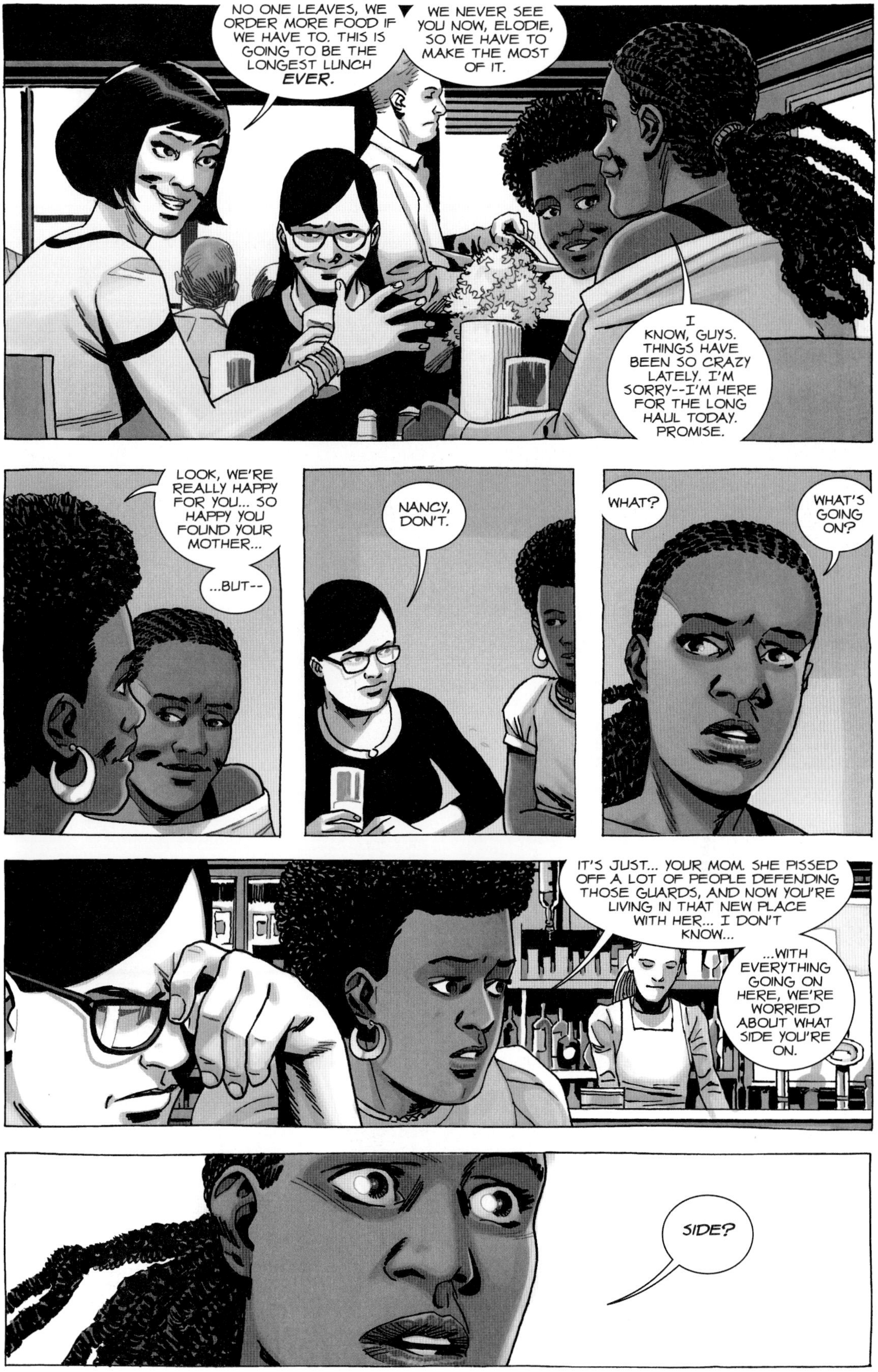
NO ONE LEAVES, WE ORDER MORE FOOD IF WE HAVE TO. THIS IS GOING TO BE THE LONGEST LUNCH *EVER*.
WE NEVER SEE YOU NOW, ELODIE, SO WE HAVE TO MAKE THE MOST OF IT.
I KNOW, GUYS. THINGS HAVE BEEN SO CRAZY LATELY. I'M SORRY--I'M HERE FOR THE LONG HAUL TODAY. PROMISE.
LOOK, WE'RE REALLY HAPPY FOR YOU... SO HAPPY YOU FOUND YOUR MOTHER...
...BUT--
NANCY, DON'T.
WHAT?
WHAT'S GOING ON?
IT'S JUST... YOUR MOM. SHE PISSED OFF A LOT OF PEOPLE DEFENDING THOSE GUARDS, AND NOW YOU'RE LIVING IN THAT NEW PLACE WITH HER... I DON'T KNOW...
...WITH EVERYTHING GOING ON HERE, WE'RE WORRIED ABOUT WHAT SIDE YOU'RE ON.
SIDE?

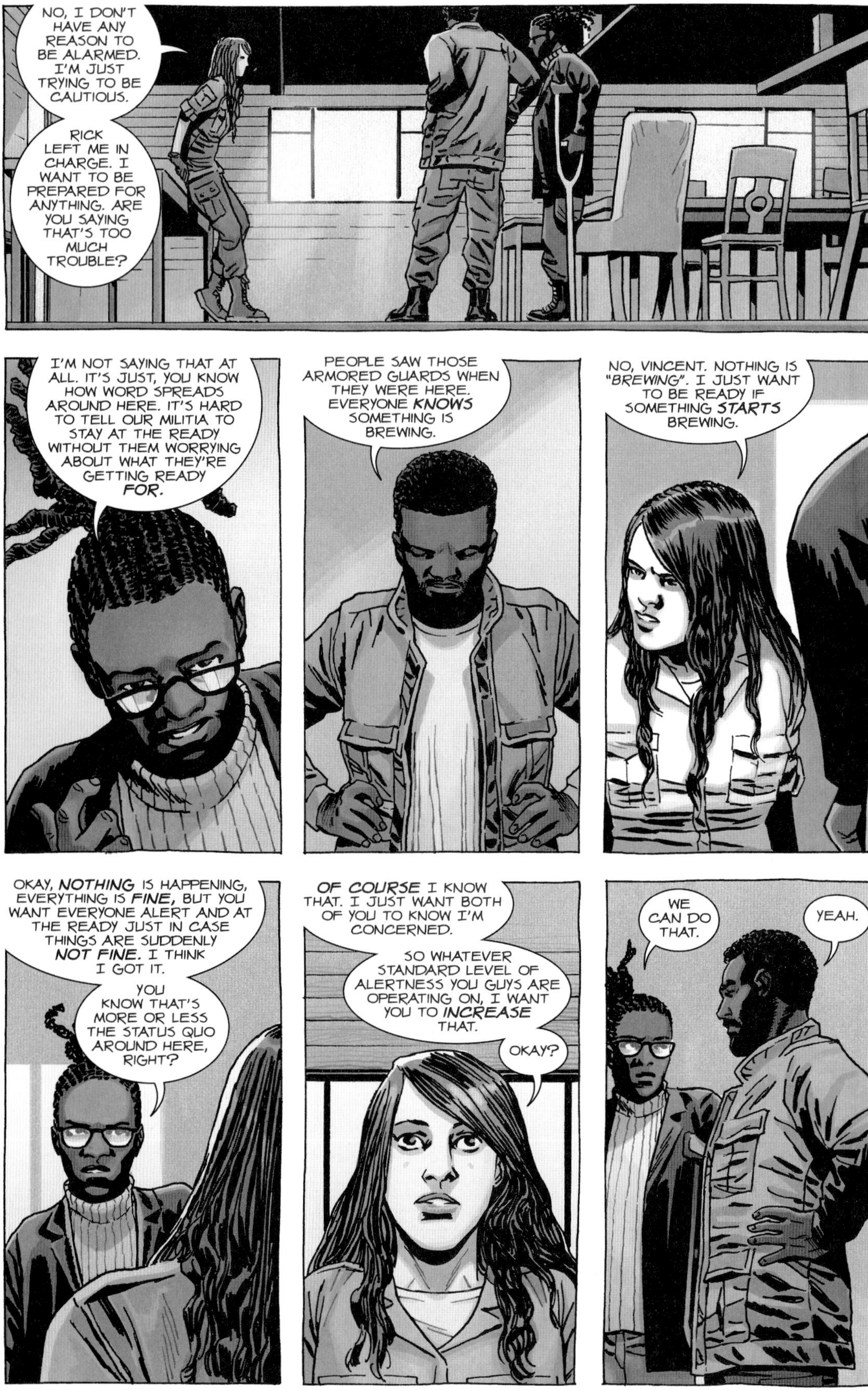
NO, I DON'T HAVE ANY REASON TO BE ALARMED. I'M JUST TRYING TO BE CAUTIOUS.
RICK LEFT ME IN CHARGE. I WANT TO BE PREPARED FOR ANYTHING. ARE YOU SAYING THAT'S TOO MUCH TROUBLE?
I'M NOT SAYING THAT AT ALL. IT'S JUST, YOU KNOW HOW WORD SPREADS AROUND HERE. IT'S HARD TO TELL OUR MILITIA TO STAY AT THE READY WITHOUT THEM WORRYING ABOUT WHAT THEY'RE GETTING READY ***FOR.***
PEOPLE SAW THOSE ARMORED GUARDS WHEN THEY WERE HERE. EVERYONE ***KNOWS*** SOMETHING IS BREWING.
NO, VINCENT. NOTHING IS *"BREWING"*. I JUST WANT TO BE READY IF SOMETHING ***STARTS*** BREWING.
OKAY, ***NOTHING*** IS HAPPENING, EVERYTHING IS ***FINE,*** BUT YOU WANT EVERYONE ALERT AND AT THE READY JUST IN CASE THINGS ARE SUDDENLY ***NOT FINE.*** I THINK I GOT IT.
YOU KNOW THAT'S MORE OR LESS THE STATUS QUO AROUND HERE, RIGHT?
OF COURSE I KNOW THAT. I JUST WANT BOTH OF YOU TO KNOW I'M CONCERNED.
SO WHATEVER STANDARD LEVEL OF ALERTNESS YOU GUYS ARE OPERATING ON, I WANT YOU TO ***INCREASE*** THAT.
OKAY?
WE CAN DO THAT.
YEAH.

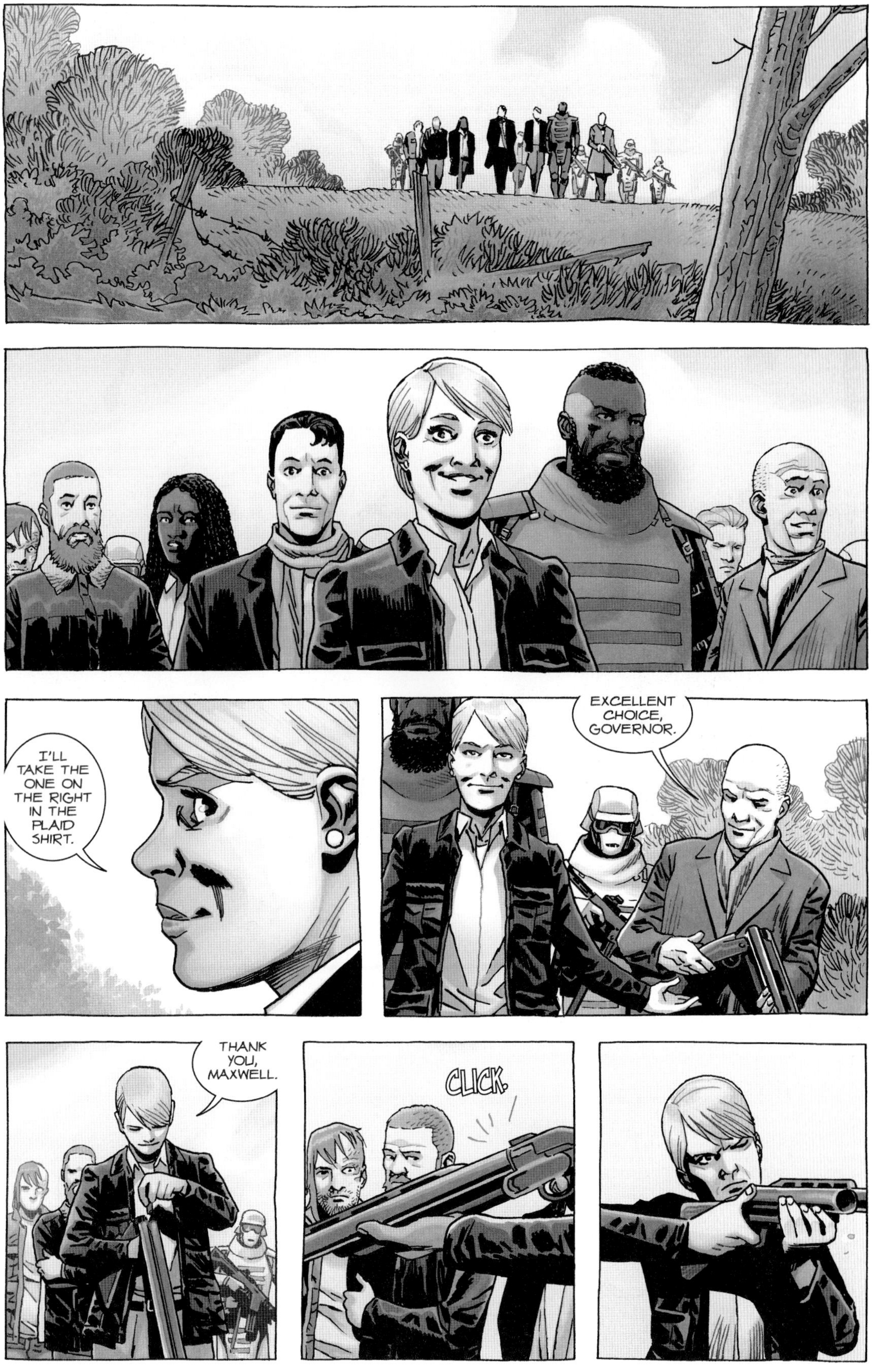
I'LL TAKE THE ONE ON THE RIGHT IN THE PLAID SHIRT.
EXCELLENT CHOICE, GOVERNOR.
THANK YOU, MAXWELL.
CLICK.

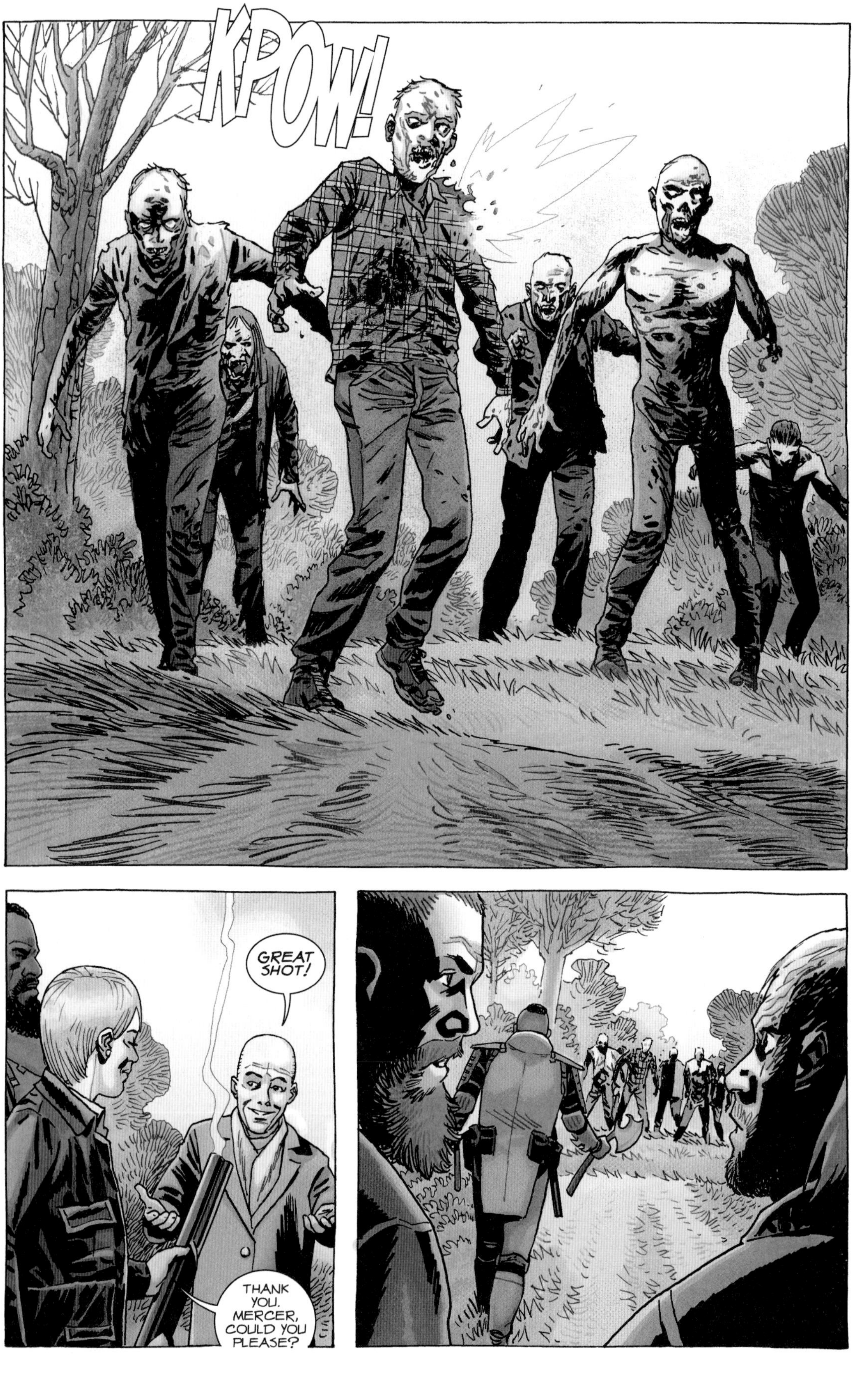
KPOW!
GREAT SHOT!
THANK YOU. MERCER, COULD YOU PLEASE?

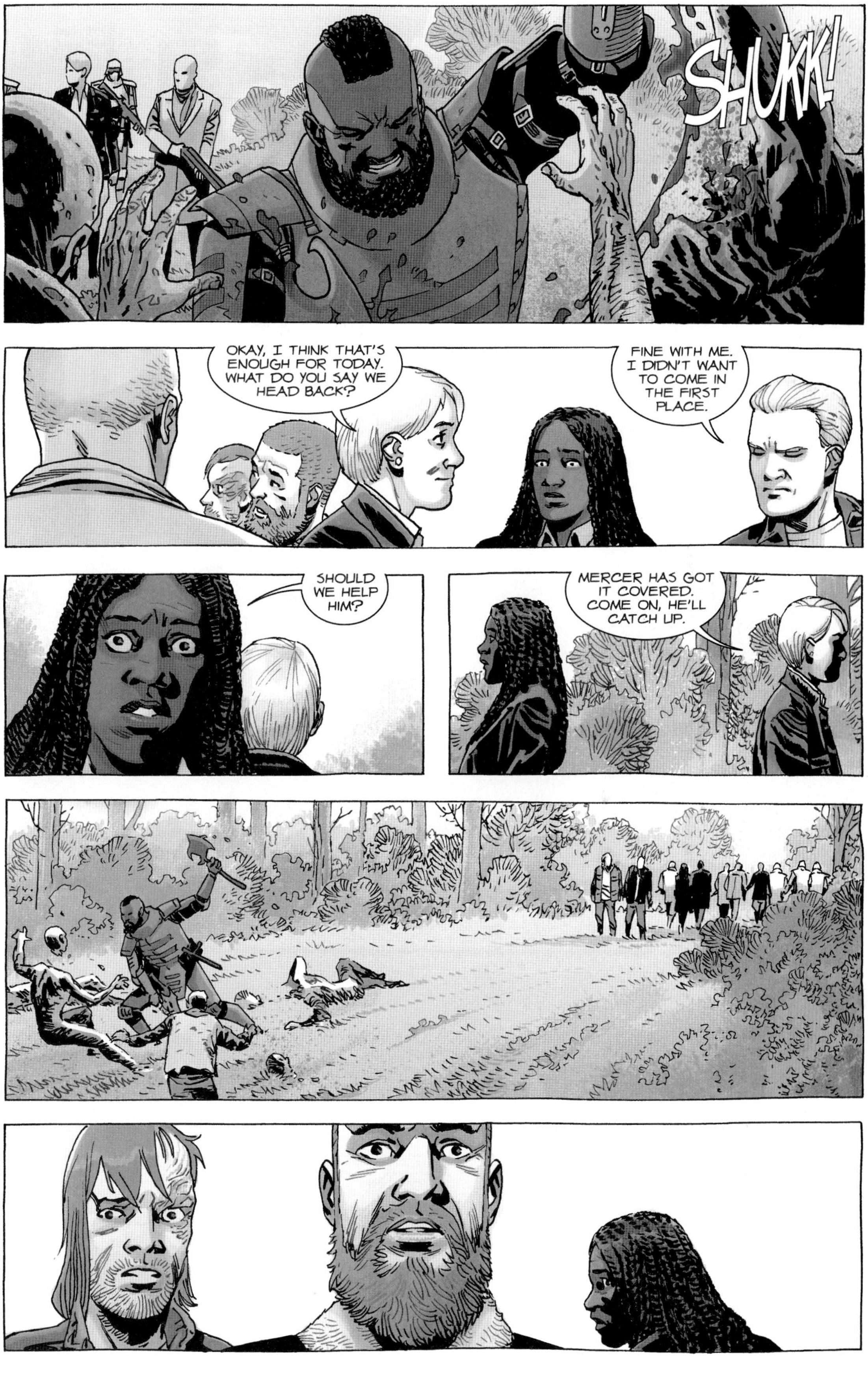
SHUKK!
OKAY, I THINK THAT'S ENOUGH FOR TODAY. WHAT DO YOU SAY WE HEAD BACK?
FINE WITH ME. I DIDN'T WANT TO COME IN THE FIRST PLACE.
SHOULD WE HELP HIM?
MERCER HAS GOT IT COVERED. COME ON, HE'LL CATCH UP.

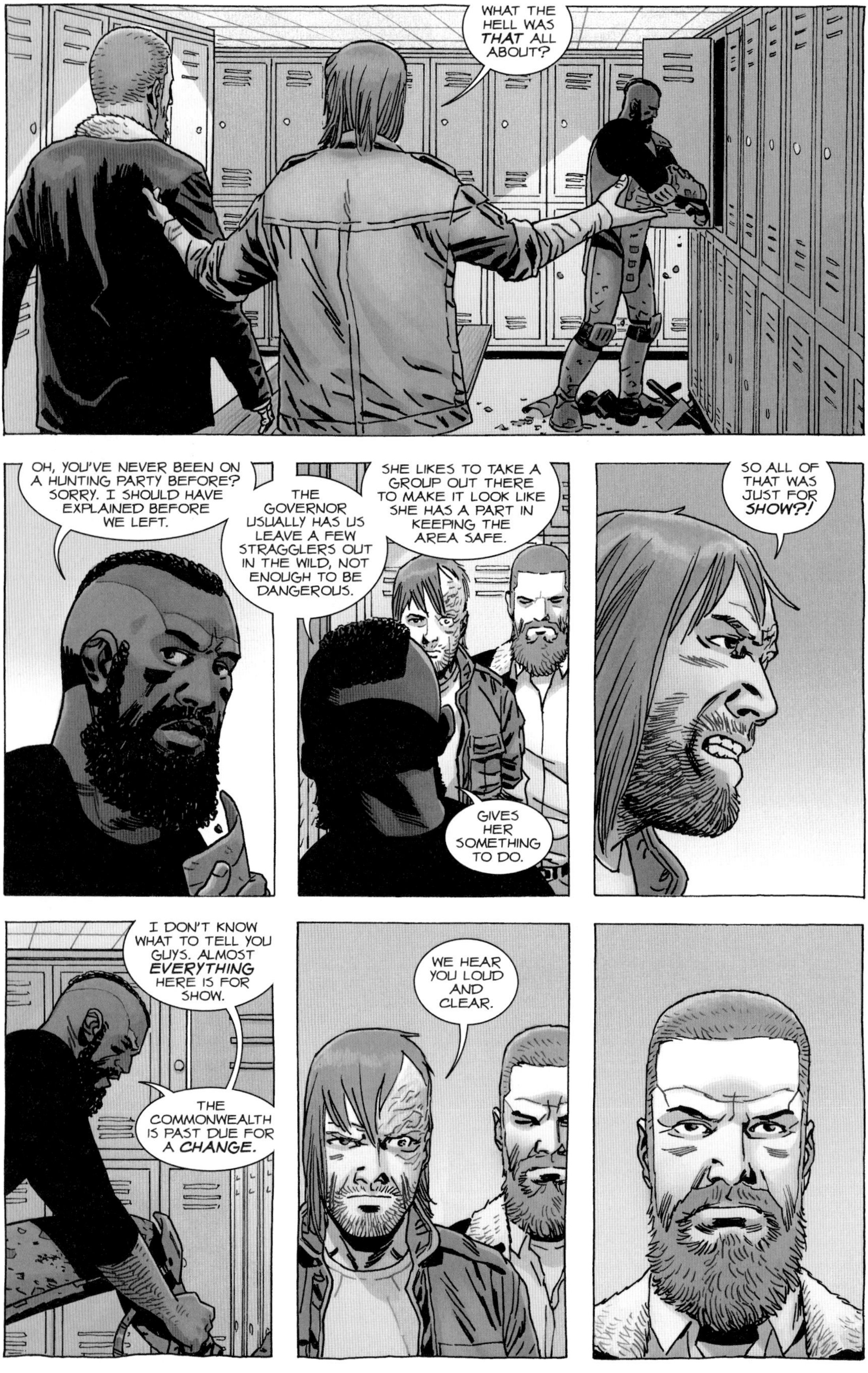
WHAT THE HELL WAS THAT ALL ABOUT?
OH, YOU'VE NEVER BEEN ON A HUNTING PARTY BEFORE? SORRY. I SHOULD HAVE EXPLAINED BEFORE WE LEFT.
THE GOVERNOR USUALLY HAS US LEAVE A FEW STRAGGLERS OUT IN THE WILD, NOT ENOUGH TO BE DANGEROUS.
SHE LIKES TO TAKE A GROUP OUT THERE TO MAKE IT LOOK LIKE SHE HAS A PART IN KEEPING THE AREA SAFE.
GIVES HER SOMETHING TO DO.
SO ALL OF THAT WAS JUST FOR SHOW?!
I DON'T KNOW WHAT TO TELL YOU GUYS. ALMOST EVERYTHING HERE IS FOR SHOW.
THE COMMONWEALTH IS PAST DUE FOR A CHANGE.
WE HEAR YOU LOUD AND CLEAR.

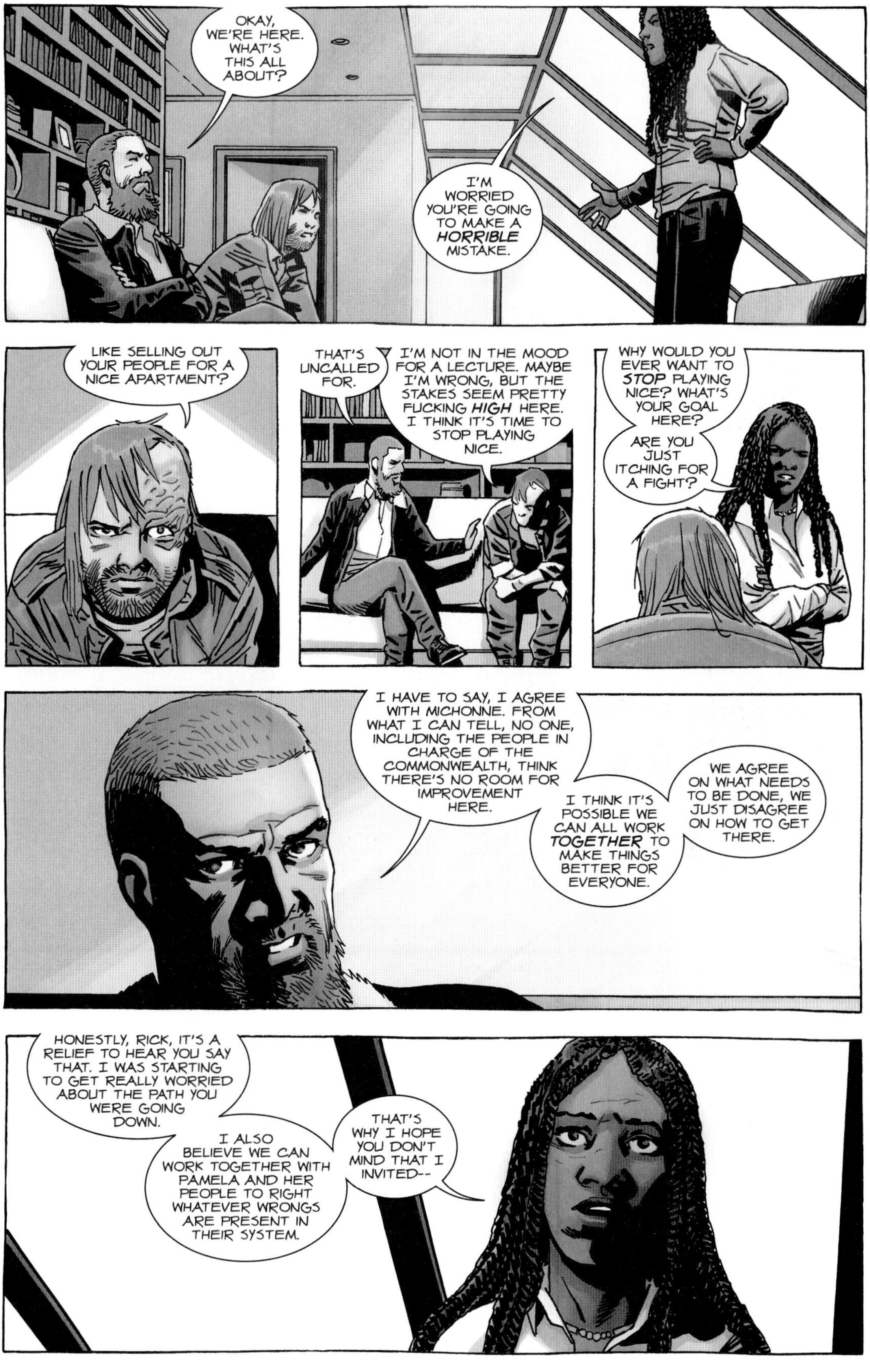

OKAY, WE'RE HERE. WHAT'S THIS ALL ABOUT?
I'M WORRIED YOU'RE GOING TO MAKE A HORRIBLE MISTAKE.
LIKE SELLING OUT YOUR PEOPLE FOR A NICE APARTMENT?
THAT'S UNCALLED FOR.
I'M NOT IN THE MOOD FOR A LECTURE. MAYBE I'M WRONG, BUT THE STAKES SEEM PRETTY FUCKING HIGH HERE. I THINK IT'S TIME TO STOP PLAYING NICE.
WHY WOULD YOU EVER WANT TO STOP PLAYING NICE? WHAT'S YOUR GOAL HERE?
ARE YOU JUST ITCHING FOR A FIGHT?
I HAVE TO SAY, I AGREE WITH MICHONNE. FROM WHAT I CAN TELL, NO ONE, INCLUDING THE PEOPLE IN CHARGE OF THE COMMONWEALTH, THINK THERE'S NO ROOM FOR IMPROVEMENT HERE.
I THINK IT'S POSSIBLE WE CAN ALL WORK TOGETHER TO MAKE THINGS BETTER FOR EVERYONE.
WE AGREE ON WHAT NEEDS TO BE DONE, WE JUST DISAGREE ON HOW TO GET THERE.
HONESTLY, RICK, IT'S A RELIEF TO HEAR YOU SAY THAT. I WAS STARTING TO GET REALLY WORRIED ABOUT THE PATH YOU WERE GOING DOWN.
I ALSO BELIEVE WE CAN WORK TOGETHER WITH PAMELA AND HER PEOPLE TO RIGHT WHATEVER WRONGS ARE PRESENT IN THEIR SYSTEM.
THAT'S WHY I HOPE YOU DON'T MIND THAT I INVITED--

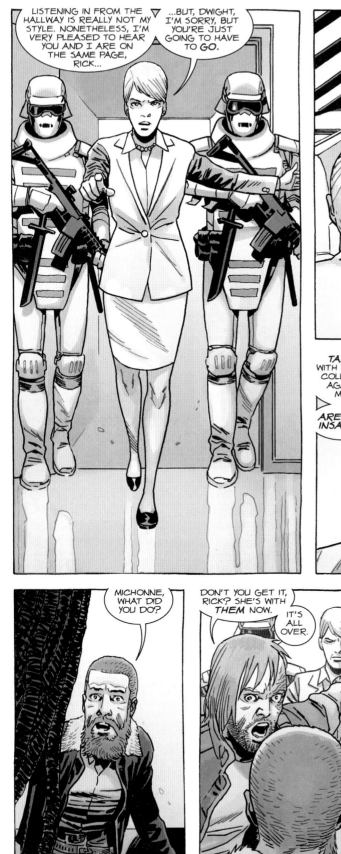

LISTENING IN FROM THE HALLWAY IS REALLY NOT MY STYLE. NONETHELESS, I'M VERY PLEASED TO HEAR YOU AND I ARE ON THE SAME PAGE, RICK...

...BUT, DWIGHT, I'M SORRY, BUT YOU'RE JUST GOING TO HAVE TO GO.

WHAT ARE YOU DOING? IT WAS JUST SUPPOSED TO BE YOU. WHY DID YOU BRING THEM?!

YOU AGREED TO COME HERE TO TALK!

TALK?! WITH PEOPLE COLLUDING AGAINST ME?!

ARE YOU INSANE?

MICHONNE, WHAT DID YOU DO?

DON'T YOU GET IT, RICK? SHE'S WITH *THEM* NOW.

IT'S ALL OVER.

I'M ON THE SIDE OF WHOEVER WANTS TO WORK THIS OUT *PEACEFULLY.*

I BROUGHT YOU ALL HERE SO THAT WE COULD *TALK.* WE ALL NEED TO CALM DOWN AND JUST DO THAT.

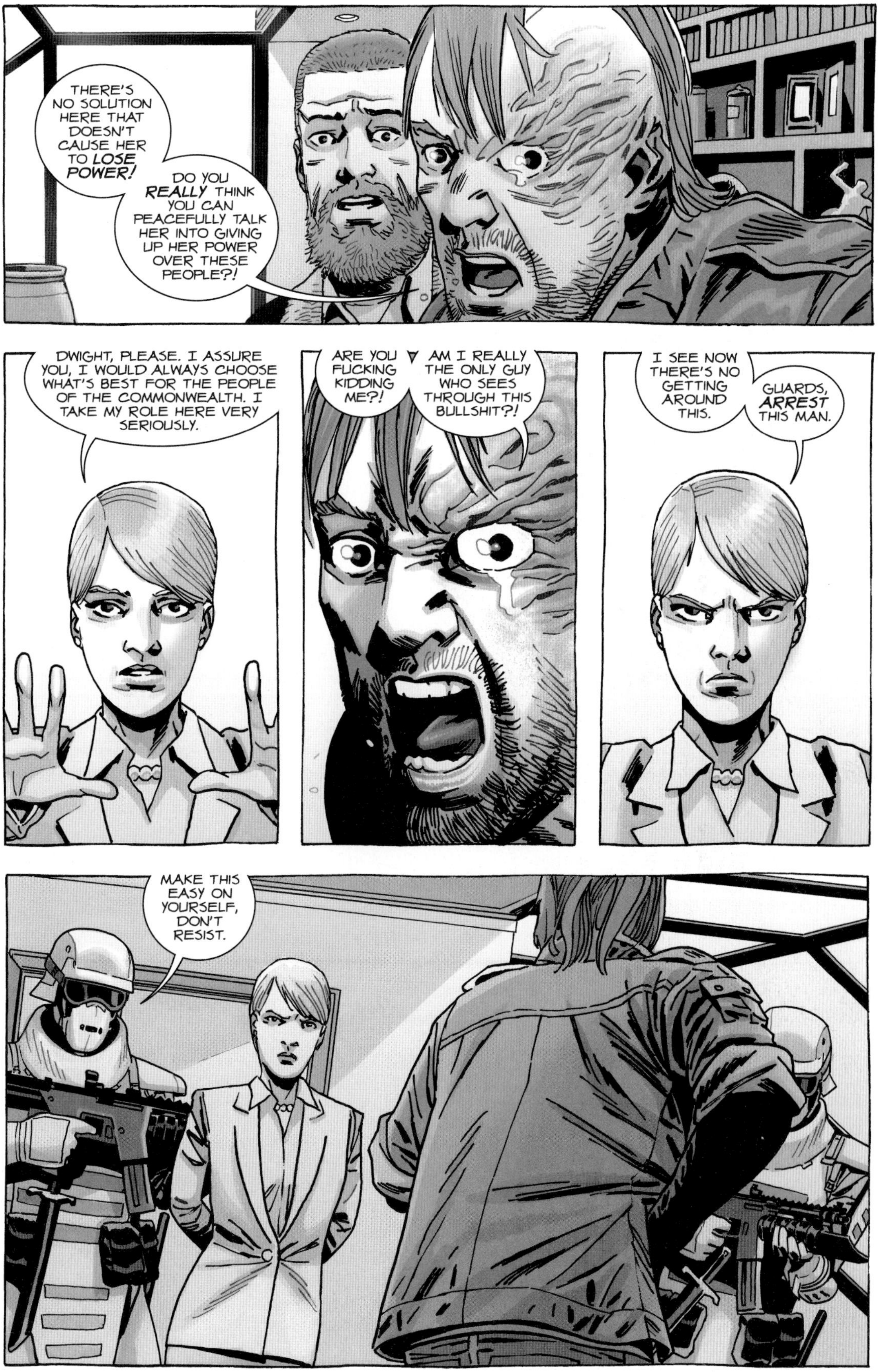
THERE'S NO SOLUTION HERE THAT DOESN'T CAUSE HER TO LOSE POWER!
DO YOU REALLY THINK YOU CAN PEACEFULLY TALK HER INTO GIVING UP HER POWER OVER THESE PEOPLE?!
DWIGHT, PLEASE. I ASSURE YOU, I WOULD ALWAYS CHOOSE WHAT'S BEST FOR THE PEOPLE OF THE COMMONWEALTH. I TAKE MY ROLE HERE VERY SERIOUSLY.
ARE YOU FUCKING KIDDING ME?!
AM I REALLY THE ONLY GUY WHO SEES THROUGH THIS BULLSHIT?!
I SEE NOW THERE'S NO GETTING AROUND THIS.
GUARDS, ARREST THIS MAN.
MAKE THIS EASY ON YOURSELF, DON'T RESIST.

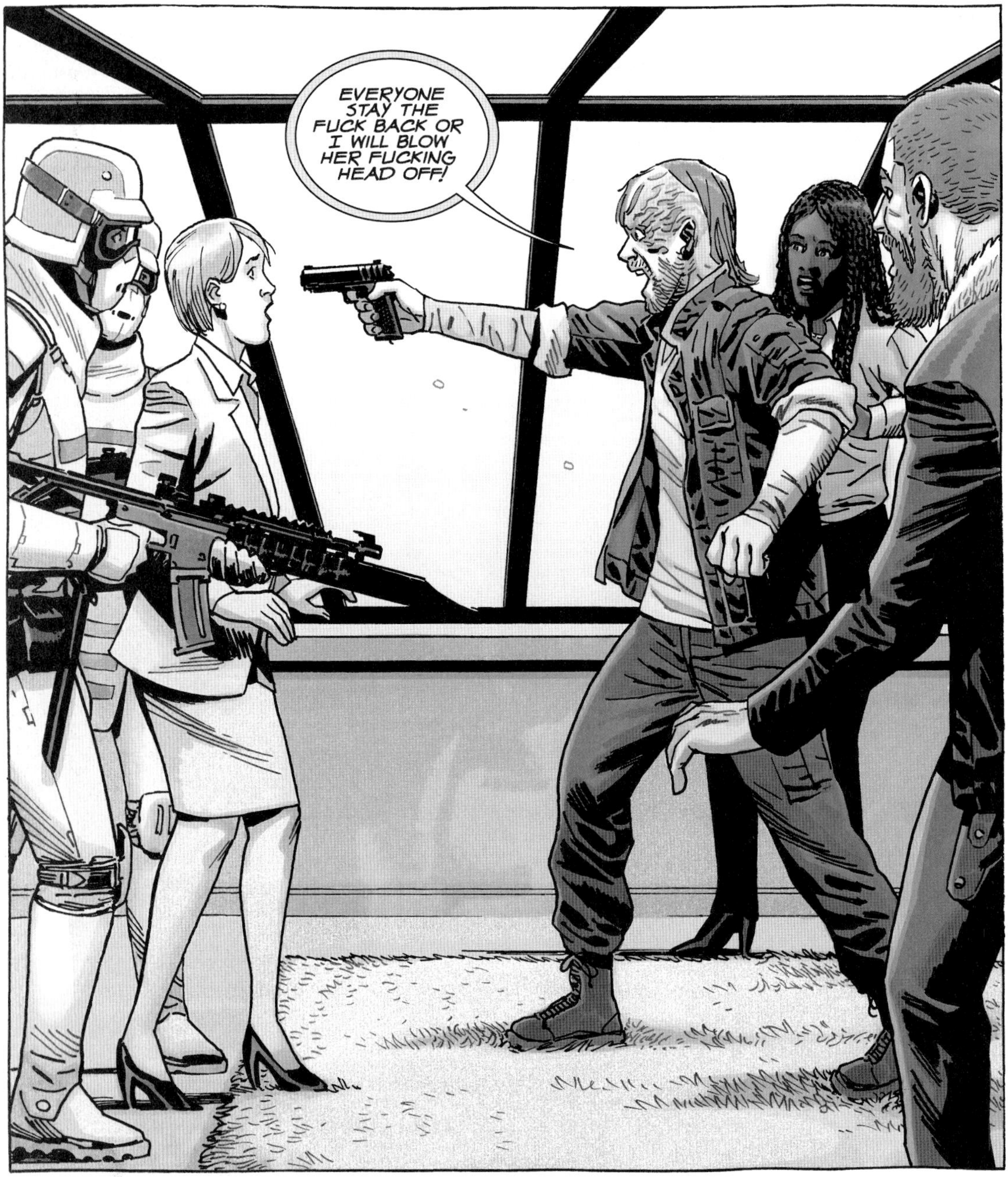
EVERYONE STAY THE FUCK BACK OR I WILL BLOW HER FUCKING HEAD OFF!

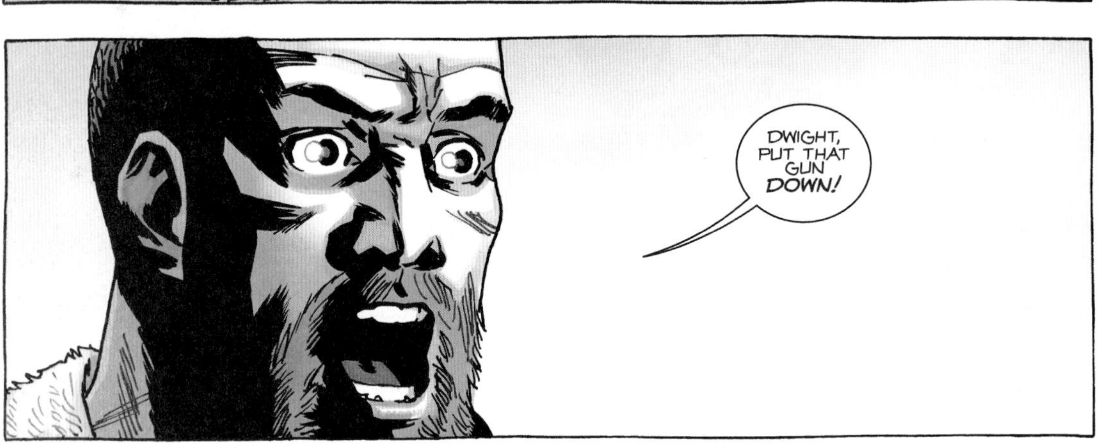
DWIGHT, PUT THAT GUN DOWN!

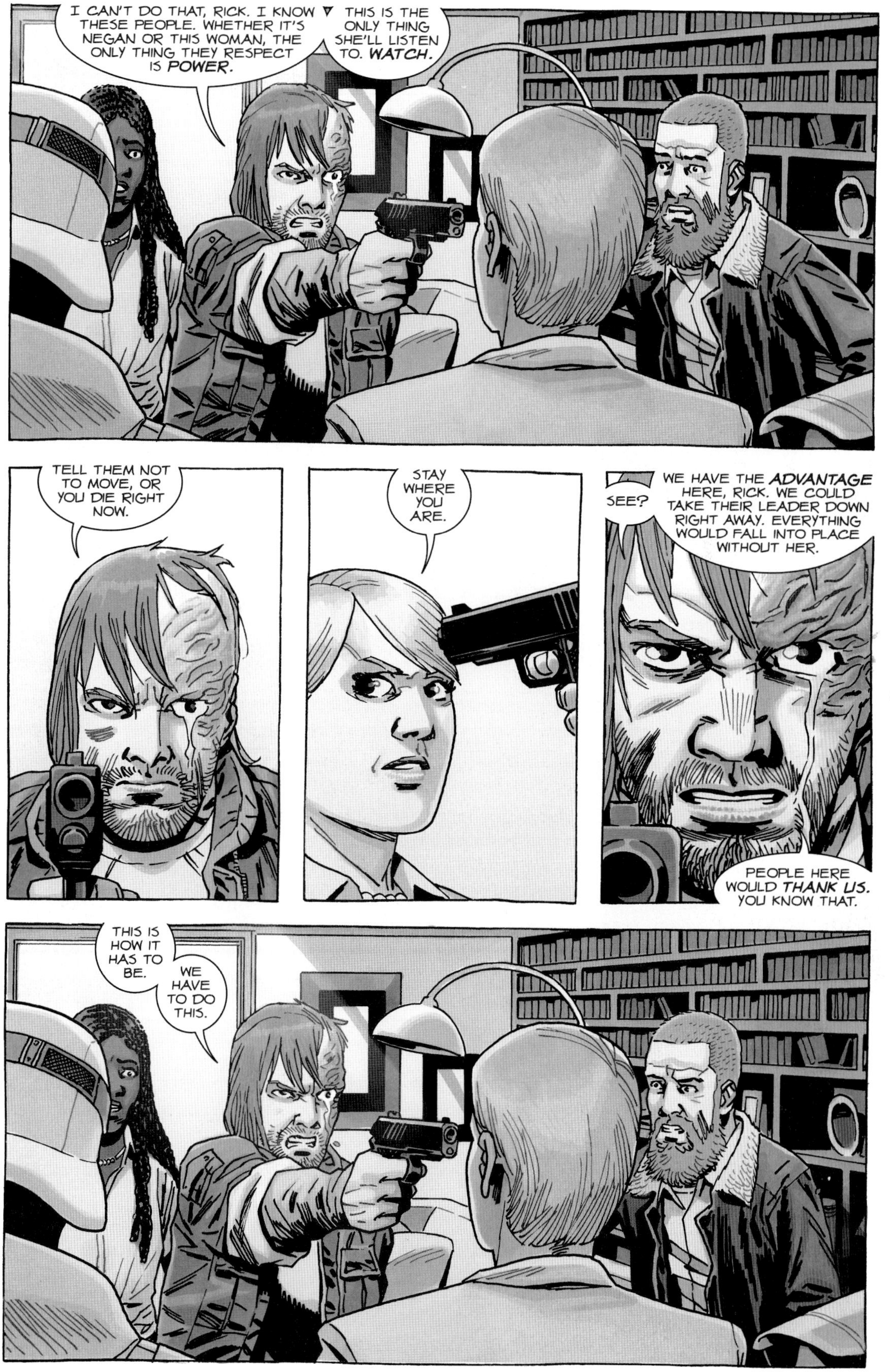
I CAN'T DO THAT, RICK. I KNOW THESE PEOPLE. WHETHER IT'S NEGAN OR THIS WOMAN, THE ONLY THING THEY RESPECT IS POWER.
THIS IS THE ONLY THING SHE'LL LISTEN TO. WATCH.
TELL THEM NOT TO MOVE, OR YOU DIE RIGHT NOW.
STAY WHERE YOU ARE.
SEE?
WE HAVE THE ADVANTAGE HERE, RICK. WE COULD TAKE THEIR LEADER DOWN RIGHT AWAY. EVERYTHING WOULD FALL INTO PLACE WITHOUT HER.
PEOPLE HERE WOULD THANK US. YOU KNOW THAT.
THIS IS HOW IT HAS TO BE.
WE HAVE TO DO THIS.

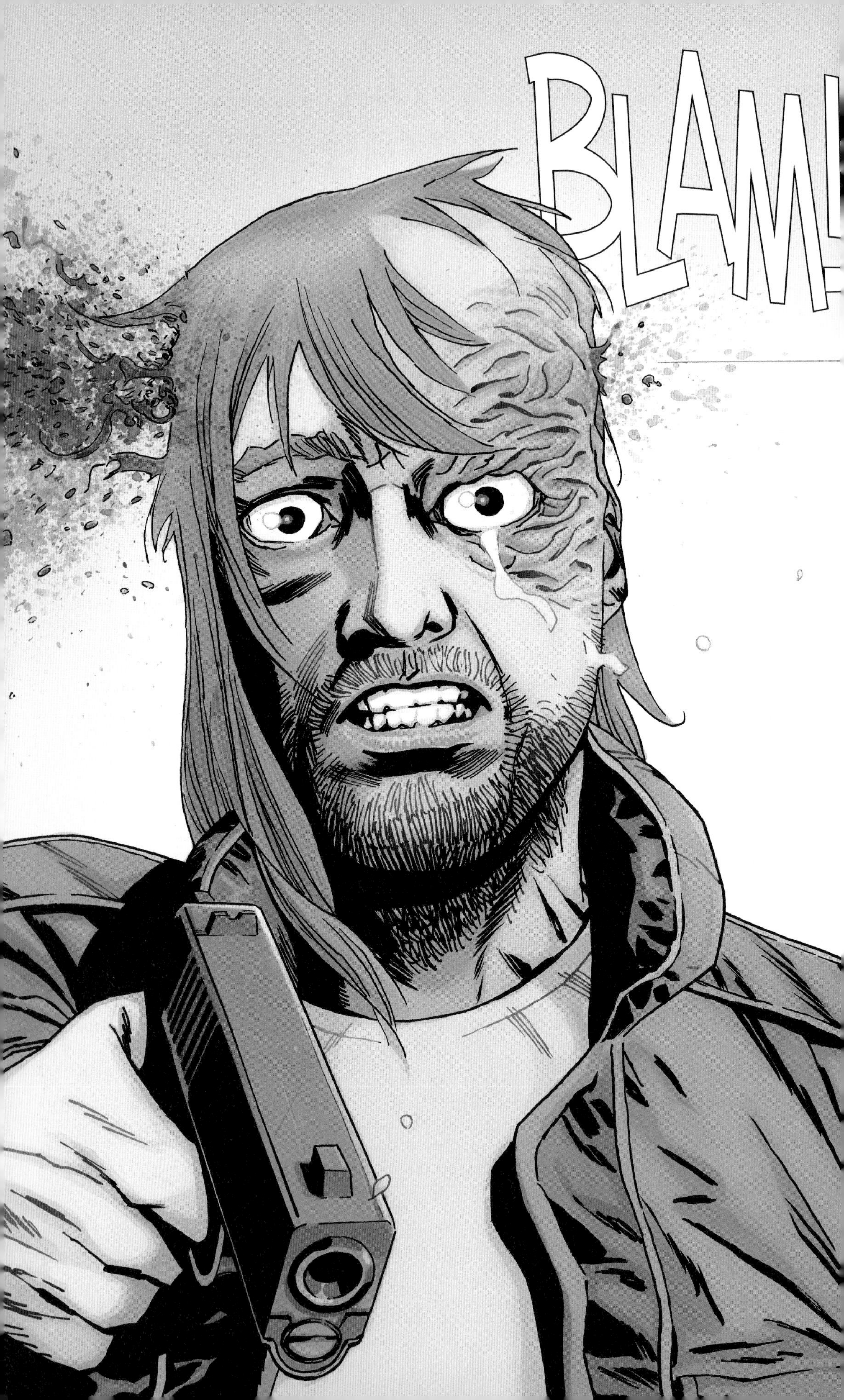
BLAM!

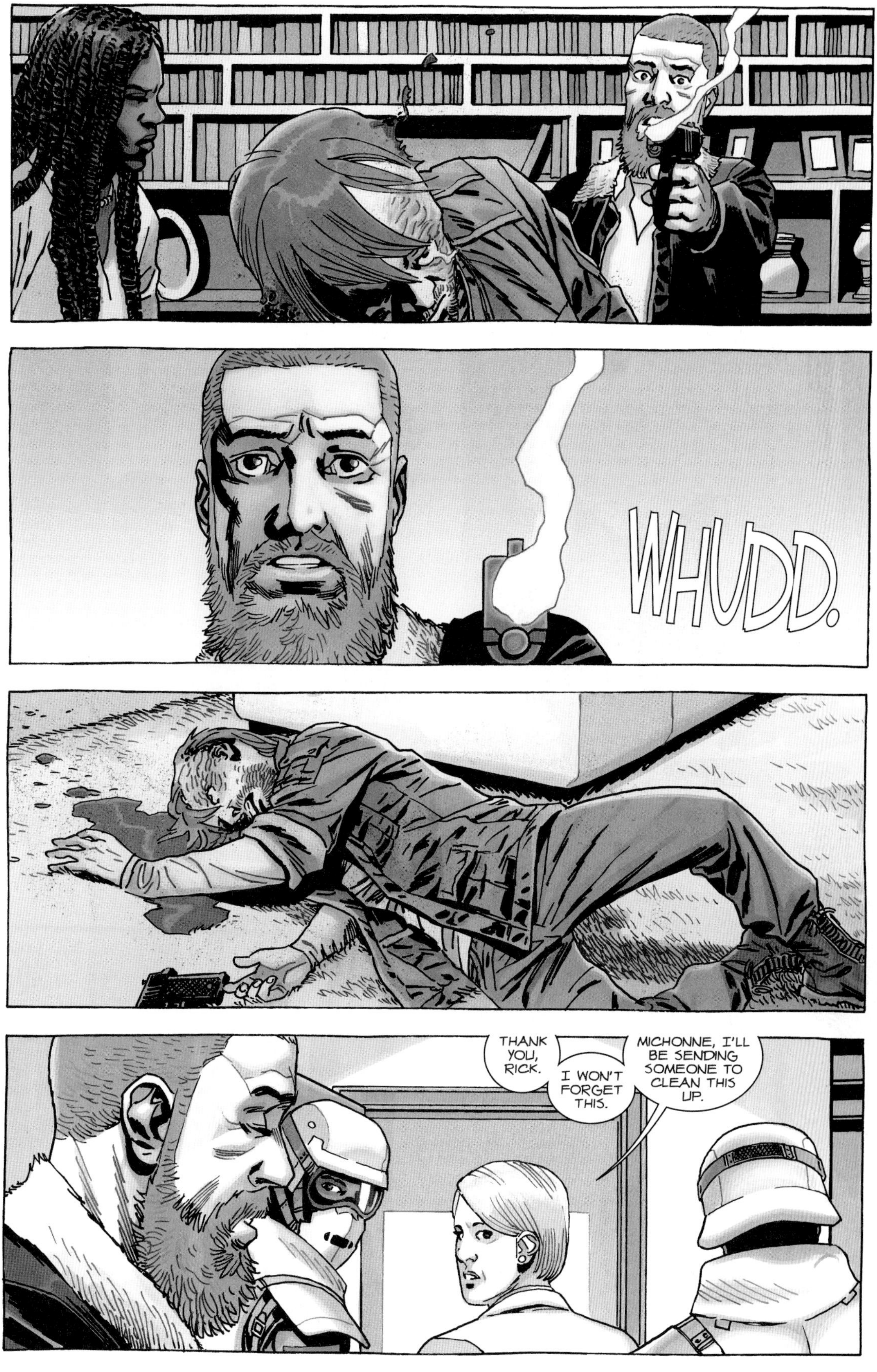
WHUDD.
THANK YOU, RICK.
I WON'T FORGET THIS.
MICHONNE, I'LL BE SENDING SOMEONE TO CLEAN THIS UP.

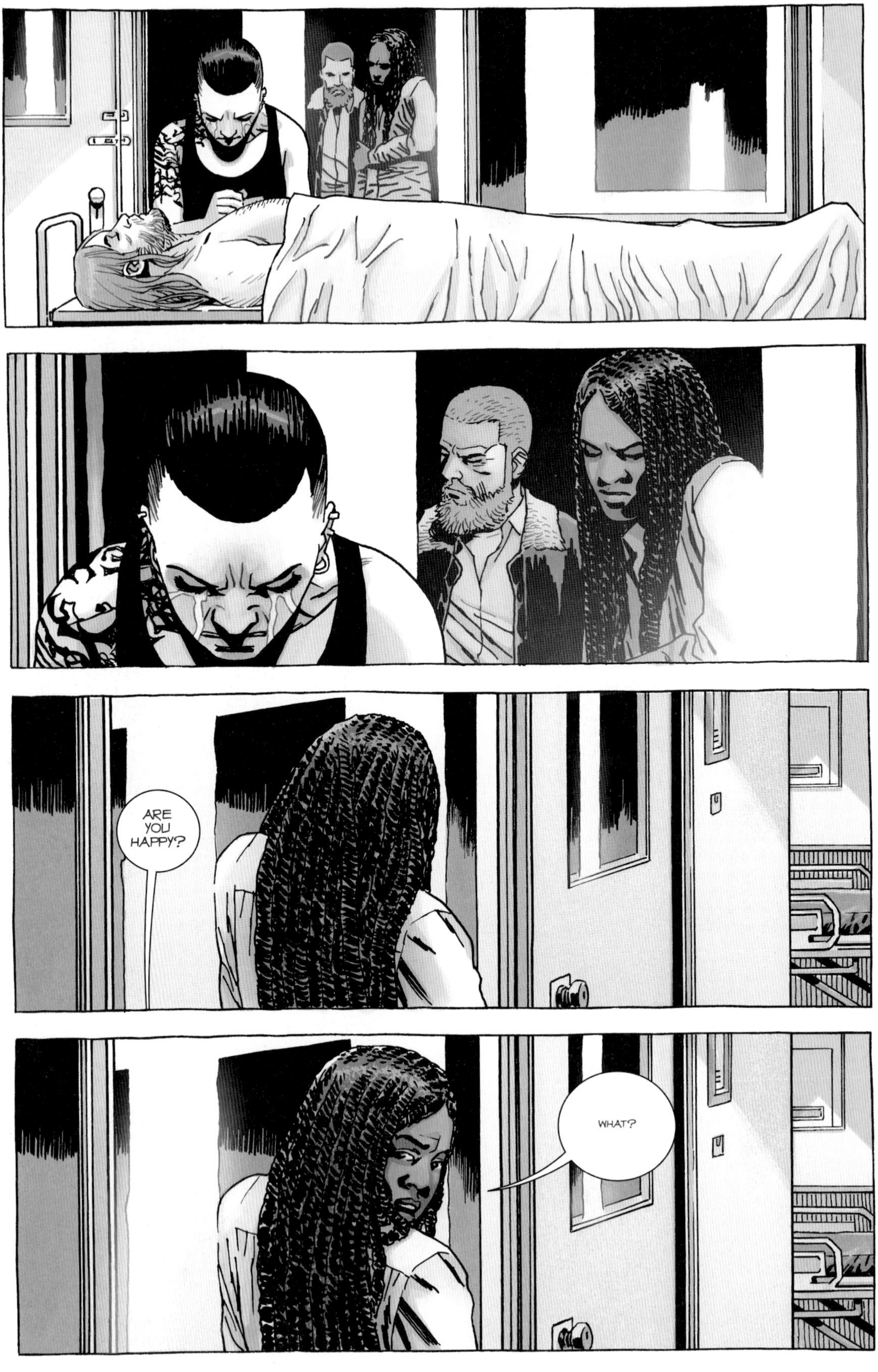
ARE YOU HAPPY?
WHAT?

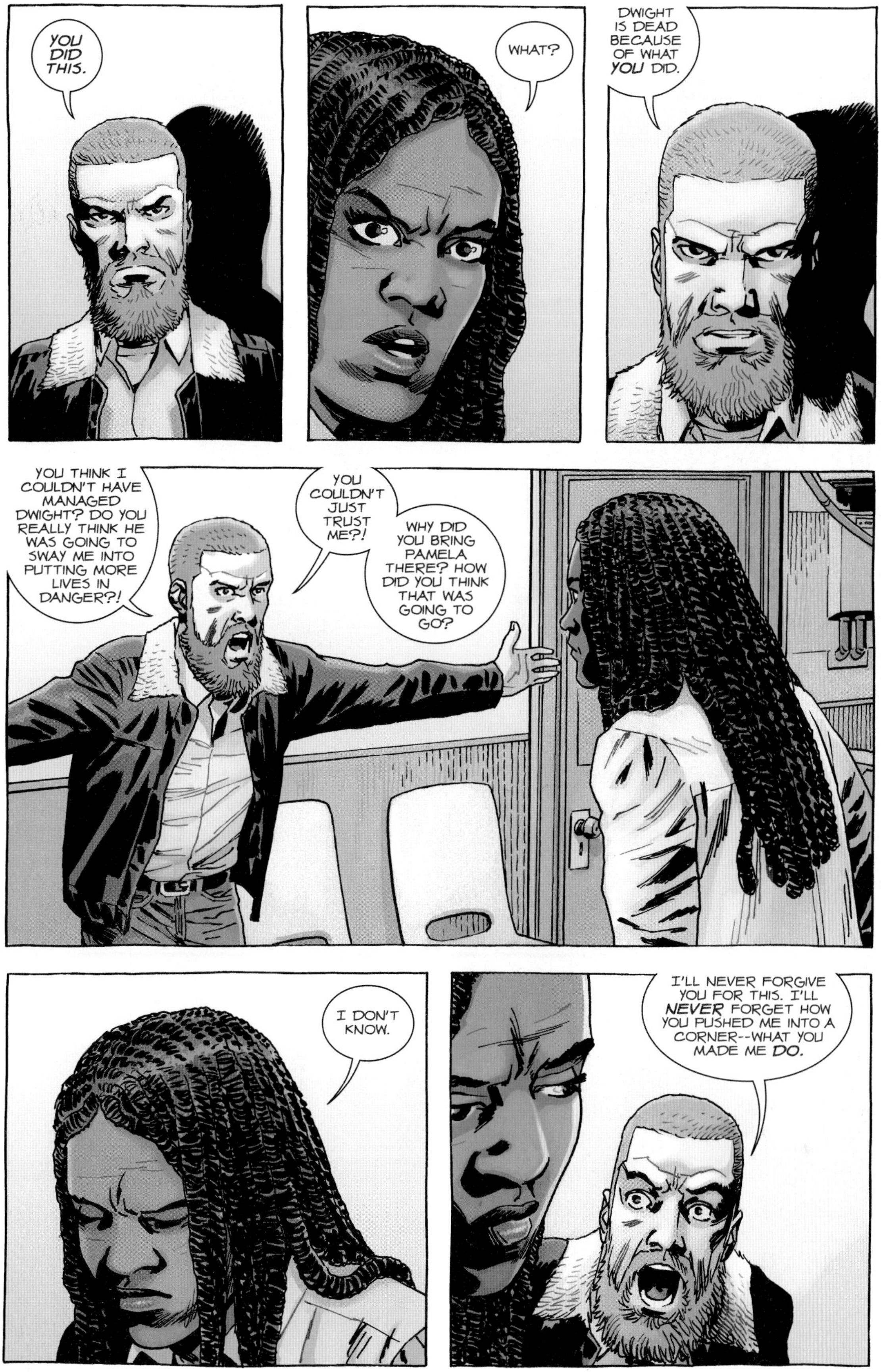
YOU DID THIS.
WHAT?
DWIGHT IS DEAD BECAUSE OF WHAT YOU DID.
YOU THINK I COULDN'T HAVE MANAGED DWIGHT? DO YOU REALLY THINK HE WAS GOING TO SWAY ME INTO PUTTING MORE LIVES IN DANGER?!
YOU COULDN'T JUST TRUST ME?!
WHY DID YOU BRING PAMELA THERE? HOW DID YOU THINK THAT WAS GOING TO GO?
I DON'T KNOW.
I'LL NEVER FORGIVE YOU FOR THIS. I'LL NEVER FORGET HOW YOU PUSHED ME INTO A CORNER--WHAT YOU MADE ME DO.

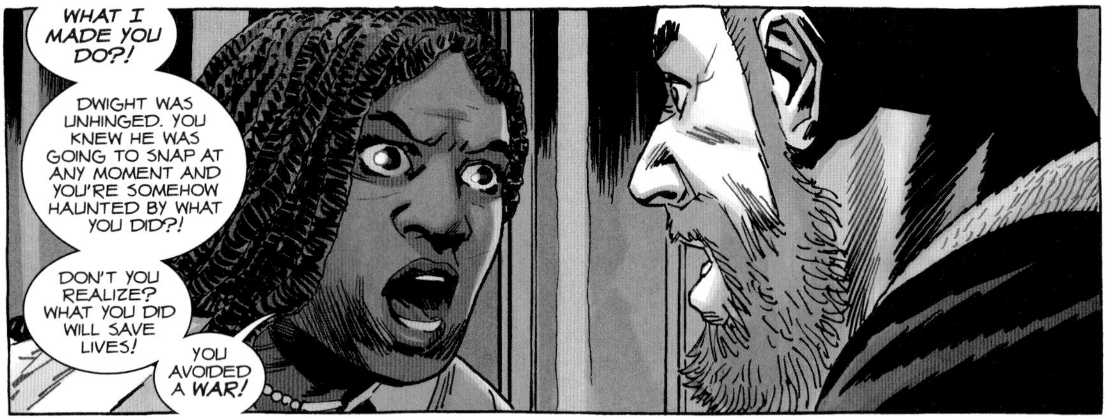
WHAT I MADE YOU DO?!
DWIGHT WAS UNHINGED. YOU KNEW HE WAS GOING TO SNAP AT ANY MOMENT AND YOU'RE SOMEHOW HAUNTED BY WHAT YOU DID?!
DON'T YOU REALIZE? WHAT YOU DID WILL SAVE LIVES!
YOU AVOIDED A WAR!

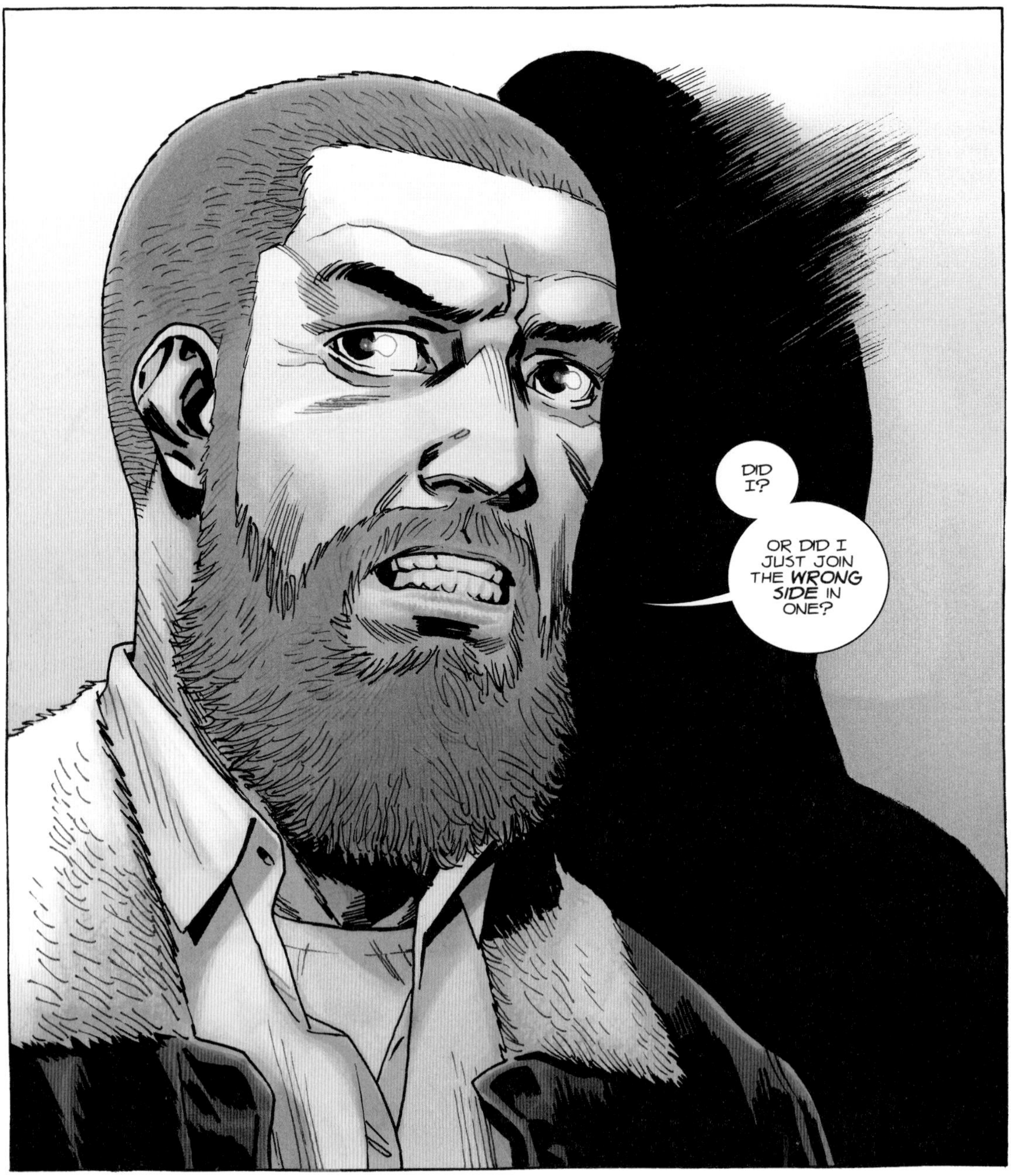
DID I?
OR DID I JUST JOIN THE WRONG SIDE IN ONE?

TO BE CONTINUED...

FOR MORE OF THE WALKING DEAD

TRADEPAPERBACKS

ROBERT KIRKMAN TONY MOORE
THE WALKING DEAD
VOLUME 1
DAYS GONE BYE

VOL. 1: DAYS GONE BYE TP
ISBN: 978-1-58240-672-5
$14.99
VOL. 2: MILES BEHIND US TP
ISBN: 978-1-58240-775-3
$14.99
VOL. 3: SAFETY BEHIND BARS TP
ISBN: 978-1-58240-805-7
$14.99
VOL. 4: THE HEART'S DESIRE TP
ISBN: 978-1-58240-530-8
$14.99
VOL. 5: THE BEST DEFENSE TP
ISBN: 978-1-58240-612-1
$14.99
VOL. 6: THIS SORROWFUL LIFE TP
ISBN: 978-1-58240-684-8
$14.99
VOL. 7: THE CALM BEFORE TP
ISBN: 978-1-58240-828-6
$14.99
VOL. 8: MADE TO SUFFER TP
ISBN: 978-1-58240-883-5
$14.99
VOL. 9: HERE WE REMAIN TP
ISBN: 978-1-60706-022-2
$14.99
VOL. 10: WHAT WE BECOME TP
ISBN: 978-1-60706-075-8
$14.99
VOL. 11: FEAR THE HUNTERS TP
ISBN: 978-1-60706-181-6
$14.99
VOL. 12: LIFE AMONG THEM TP
ISBN: 978-1-60706-254-7
$14.99
VOL. 13: TOO FAR GONE TP
ISBN: 978-1-60706-329-2
$14.99
VOL. 14: NO WAY OUT TP
ISBN: 978-1-60706-392-6
$14.99
VOL. 15: WE FIND OURSELVES TP
ISBN: 978-1-60706-440-4
$14.99
VOL. 16: A LARGER WORLD TP
ISBN: 978-1-60706-559-3
$14.99
VOL. 17: SOMETHING TO FEAR TP
ISBN: 978-1-60706-615-6
$14.99
VOL. 18: WHAT COMES AFTER TP
ISBN: 978-1-60706-687-3
$14.99
VOL. 19: MARCH TO WAR TP
ISBN: 978-1-60706-818-1
$14.99
VOL. 20: ALL OUT WAR PART ONE TP
ISBN: 978-1-60706-882-2
$14.99
VOL. 21: ALL OUT WAR PART TWO TP
ISBN: 978-1-63215-030-1
$14.99
VOL. 22: A NEW BEGINNING TP
ISBN: 978-1-63215-041-7
$14.99
VOL. 23: WHISPERS INTO SCREAMS TP
ISBN: 978-1-63215-258-9
$14.99
VOL. 24: LIFE AND DEATH TP
ISBN: 978-1-63215-402-6
$14.99
VOL. 25: NO TURNING BACK TP
ISBN: 978-1-63215-612-9
$14.99
VOL. 26: CALL TO ARMS TP
ISBN: 978-1-63215-917-5
$14.99
VOL. 27: THE WHISPERER WAR TP
ISBN: 978-1-5343-0052-1
$14.99
VOL. 28: A CERTAIN DOOM TP
ISBN: 978-1-5343-0244-0
$16.99
VOL. 29: LINES WE CROSS TP
ISBN: 978-1-5343-0497-0
$16.99
VOL. 30: NEW WORLD ORDER TP
ISBN: 978-1-5343-0497-0
$16.99
VOL. 31: THE ROTTEN CORE TP
ISBN: 978-1-5343-1052-0
$16.99
VOL. 1: SPANISH EDITION TP
ISBN: 978-1-60706-797-9
$14.99
VOL. 2: SPANISH EDITION TP
ISBN: 978-1-60706-845-7
$14.99
VOL. 3: SPANISH EDITION TP
ISBN: 978-1-60706-883-9
$14.99
VOL. 4: SPANISH EDITION TP
ISBN: 978-1-63215-035-6
$14.99

HARDCOVERS

THE WALKING
DEAD
BOOK ONE
a continuing story of survival horror.

BOOK ONE HC
ISBN: 978-1-58240-619-0
$34.99
BOOK TWO HC
ISBN: 978-1-58240-698-5
$34.99
BOOK THREE HC
ISBN: 978-1-58240-825-5
$34.99
BOOK FOUR HC
ISBN: 978-1-60706-000-0
$34.99
BOOK FIVE HC
ISBN: 978-1-60706-171-7
$34.99
BOOK SIX HC
ISBN: 978-1-60706-327-8
$34.99
BOOK SEVEN HC
ISBN: 978-1-60706-439-8
$34.99
BOOK EIGHT HC
ISBN: 978-1-60706-593-7
$34.99
BOOK NINE HC
ISBN: 978-1-60706-798-6
$34.99
BOOK TEN HC
ISBN: 978-1-63215-034-9
$34.99
BOOK ELEVEN HC
ISBN: 978-1-63215-271-8
$34.99
BOOK TWELVE HC
ISBN: 978-1-63215-451-4
$34.99
BOOK THIRTEEN HC
ISBN: 978-1-63215-916-8
$34.99
BOOK FOURTEEN HC
ISBN: 978-1-5343-0329-4
$34.99
BOOK FIFTEEN HC
ISBN: 978-1-5343-0850-3
$34.99

COMPENDIUMS

THE WALKING DEAD
COMPENDIUM ONE

COMPENDIUM TP, VOL. 1
ISBN: 978-1-60706-076-5
$59.99
COMPENDIUM TP, VOL. 2
ISBN: 978-1-60706-596-8
$59.99
COMPENDIUM TP, VOL. 3
ISBN: 978-1-63215-456-9
$59.99

SPECIALTY BOOKS

THE WALKING
DEAD
THE COVERS

THE WALKING DEAD: THE COVERS, VOL. 1 HC
ISBN: 978-1-60706-002-4
$24.99
THE WALKING DEAD: ALL OUT WAR HC
ISBN: 978-1-63215-038-7
$34.99
THE WALKING DEAD COLORING BOOK
ISBN: 978-1-63215-774-4
$14.99
THE WALKING DEAD RICK GRIMES COLORING BOOK
ISBN: 978-1-5343-0003-3
$14.99

OMNIBUS

THE WALKING
DEAD

OMNIBUS, VOL. 1
ISBN: 978-1-60706-503-6
$100.00
OMNIBUS, VOL. 2
ISBN: 978-1-60706-515-9
$100.00
OMNIBUS, VOL. 3
ISBN: 978-1-60706-330-8
$100.00
OMNIBUS, VOL. 4
ISBN: 978-1-60706-616-3
$100.00
OMNIBUS, VOL. 5
ISBN: 978-1-63215-042-4
$100.00
OMNIBUS, VOL. 6
ISBN: 978-1-63215-521-4
$100.00
OMNIBUS, VOL. 7
ISBN: 978-1-5343-0335-5
$100.00

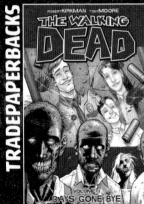